THE
PEARL
PAGODA

A NOVEL

SUSANNAH BROOME

SIMON AND SCHUSTER
NEW YORK

34654

1 2 3 4 5 6 7 8 9 10

Library of Congress Cataloging in Publication Data

Broome, Susannah.
  The Pearl Pagoda.

  I. Title.
PZ4.B8734Pe 1980 [PR6052.R5828] 823'.914 80-15143
ISBN 0-671-25535-5

PART ONE

MACAO

CHAPTER I

SOMETIMES when I walk in the Great Park at Hawkestone where the cattle graze peacefully under the trees, and, looking back over my shoulder, see the house on the knoll above the lake, its long façade golden in the sunlight, I find it hard to believe I ever lived anywhere else.

Then I cross the bridge and take the winding path that leads through the dell and suddenly, surprisingly, there before me is the Pearl Pagoda. Its curving roof rises in tiers above the dense foliage of shrub and tree and the latticework shines silvery against the green, and as I gaze at it I seem to see the other pagoda I knew once in faraway China. I remember the strange and terrible things that happened to me. But that was long, long ago.

We had left The Downs on the last day of December. Earlier on snow had fallen, and through the winter dusk I could see the ivory gleam of it still lying on mast and bulwark. Above my head the great sails of the *Lotus Wind* creaked and strained in the wind as, with The Lizard left behind us, the ship met the full force of the Atlantic. Clutching the new warm plaid cloak that kind Mrs. Williams had given me as a parting present, I watched the dark of the sea fade into the dark of the sky. Although the ocean was roughening with every moment that passed, I was reluctant to go below and went on staring across the limitless waves as if by so doing I might catch a last glimpse of England. Or rather, of Wales, from whence I had come.

Wales and the Black Mountains and, most of all, Hafod Trefeiddan, where my grandfather's sheep farm had been. *Hafod* means high pasture and the farm had been high up in the Grwyne Fawr, wild and beautiful, sometimes lonely, yet always—*home.*

It had been my home since a child, for when I was nine years old both my parents died during the same week of a typhus fever. We were living in Brecon at the time, my English father, who was a schoolmaster, teaching English to Welsh pupils. After my parents' death I was taken to live with my maternal Welsh grandparents on their farm near Partrishow.

And now I had no home. It had gone with my grandfather's death.

I bowed my head to the ship's rail, my eyes stinging with something more than the salt spray, for I was overcome with longing for Hafod Trefeiddan, remembering its thick stone walls and crooked slate roof, and within, the red tiled floors and rough whitewash and the old black settle beside the inglenook, and Bedwin, grandfather's collie dog, lying on the homemade rag rug in front of the fire.

I thought of my grandfather, gray and grizzled and not overly tall, a man of great warmth and kindliness; and I thought of my little grandmother, ever smiling, her eyes as blue as harebells and her mouth as soft and upturned as a child's, even into her seventies, when she died. I was eighteen at the time, now I was twenty-six. The years had whipped away in caring for my grandfather and working on the farm, and I had been contented enough.

Now, for more than three months, this ship was to be my home. Until we reached Macao, where, within the week, I would be married.

I lifted my head. This was no time in which to regret the past. I was going half across the world to marry the man I loved, and though I was naturally apprehensive at the thought of the strange and different life that lay ahead of me, I knew that I should be happy and secure with Arthur. We had known each other for only the few months of golden summer when he had returned from China to the Black Mountains, but for two years he had written long and frequent letters to me. When, after my grandfather's death, Arthur asked me to marry him, I hesitated only a little before I accepted his proposal. I knew from his letters that he was as lonely as myself, and I hoped, from what he had told me, that I might be of help to him in teaching the Chinese children and doing simple nursing. There was a dispensary attached to the Mission and there I might be of use.

A hurtle of spray over the ship's rail all but drenched me and I started back, my footing unsteady in the increased rolling of the *Lotus Wind*. I could stay no longer on deck but must go below, and holding my cloak about me, I turned and picked my way carefully down the brass embossed steps of the companionway. It was the first time in my life I had been on board ship and the surprising thing was that I should have found my sea legs so quickly. I had been secretly dreading the thought of the long voyage, but to my relief and thankfulness, I discovered, after an initial feeling of uneasiness, that I was seemingly a good sailor.

Which was as well, for poor Mrs. Meade, under whose auspices I was traveling, had lain prostrate in her cabin these past three days. Her eighteen-year-old daughter, Sylvia, was in little better straits, but as we were sharing a cabin I was able to assist her, as well as help Mrs. Meade when she needed me.

On one side of the passageway leading to the saloon were the two cabins that had been allotted to the passengers. I opened the first door on the left and went quietly in. It was small and confined; there was little room for more than two wooden-sided bunks placed one above another, a dressing chest and a small washing arrangement. Some attempt had been made for extra comfort in the shape of a handsome rug spread over the wooden floor and a scattering of cushions and a fur rug thrown across the leather couchette that ran along the short side of the cabin.

Sylvia was asleep. In the light from the lantern hanging above the bunks I saw her face on the pillow, a pale oval framed in curling golden hair, her heavy eyelids, with their fringe of dark lashes, closed. I thought her a most beautiful girl. The more so perhaps because of my own plainness. If I looked in the shadowy mirror I knew what I should see. Straight black hair worn in a chignon and straight black brows above dark-hazel eyes, a mouth too wide and full for my small features and snub nose. A cat's face. A clown's face, I thought ruefully as I hung my sea-dampened cloak on one of the hooks.

I washed my hands quietly in the corner basin and smoothing my hair into a semblance of tidiness tiptoed out of the cabin and, after tapping on the door, entered the one next to it. Here, in a slightly larger space, were two bed bunks, side by side, and the same limited dressing facilities, but a more luxurious effect had been obtained with the addition of rugs and a cane chair with cushions and a gilt-framed mirror, which contrasted with the spotted one we had. There were books and some silver-framed photographs on a small polished table. The lamp above the dressing chest was lit and Mrs. Meade was awake. She sighed plaintively as I went to stand beside the bed.

"Oh, dear Miss Jones, is it you? I have been trying to sleep, but my head throbs so and when I tried to sit up a little while ago I became so dreadfully giddy I had to lie down again."

I could not help but feel sorry for her, lying there, her kind, jolly face fallen into woebegone lines and her treble chins, for she was very stout, quivering like jelly as she turned her head restlessly upon the pillow.

I said diffidently, being still a little in awe of her, as I was of Mr. Meade, despite their kindness to me, "Shall I get you some more hartshorn? Or a little aromatic vinegar? It may give you comfort."

She put out a plump hand, covered in glittering rings, to touch mine.

"I don't know what we should have done without you, Miss Jones, especially with my poor Sylvia being indisposed too. It is this weather, you see. I have never sailed in midwinter before."

"Mr. Meade tells me we shall run into smoother seas in a

few days' time. When we get to—is it Madeira? Then you will be able to go on deck again."

She shook her head mournfully.

"Let us hope so. I wish we had not come on a clipper. Something slower and more comfortable would have suited me better, as on our last voyage. But Mr. Meade is well acquainted with Captain Hawkes and nothing would please him but that we should sail to Macao on his ship. My husband is an excellent sailor himself and he cannot understand how other people can suffer from this wretched *mal de mer*." She hesitated and then added confidentially, "I am truly thankful that you are traveling with us, Miss Jones, for I should have felt a great burden to Mr. Meade otherwise. Kind though he is, he abhors to remain in the cabin, except to sleep. And though the steward is efficient enough it is not the same to be looked after by a seaman."

"I am only too glad to be of use," I said, "in return for your kindness to me."

"My dear, it is a small thing to take you under our wing on this voyage to Macao. And you are company for Sylvia too." Then she added slowly, "And older and more sensible."

"You have three daughters, I believe?"

"Yes. Two are married—my second daughter only last September. I came home in spring to make arrangements for the wedding and Mr. Meade returned to England later on." She frowned. "Sylvia has been living these past two years with her elder sister, who has three children. It was not a very satisfactory arrangement and so we are taking her out to Macao with us." She shook her head. "She did not want to come."

"I am sorry. I understand Macao is a strange and fascinating place."

"I hope you will find it so." She sighed and frowned, as if the effort of talking had increased her headache.

I said quickly, "I will leave you to rest again, Mrs. Meade. Is there anything I can procure for you—any food I can bring you at suppertime?"

She closed her eyes.

"Thank you, but there is nothing. Certainly nothing to

eat. I could not take the gruel they sent in to me earlier. But I appreciate your thoughtfulness, Miss Jones."

I went quietly out of the cabin and across the passageway into the saloon. The sea must have roughened even more for the timbers creaked and groaned above my head and when I pushed open the door a sudden lurch of the ship sent me plunging forward so that I had to catch hold of the edge of the dining table to steady myself. Mr. Meade, who had been seated reading, threw down his book onto the padded leather couch and sprang to his feet.

"Miss Jones—are you all right?"

I slipped down onto the mahogany bench placed alongside the dining table.

"Thank you, yes. It was the rolling of the ship which caught me unawares."

Mr. Meade, who was tall and heavily built, with gray side-whiskers framing plum-colored cheeks, shook his head as he stared down at me.

"You must take care, Miss Jones. The sea is an uncertain element and no liberties may be taken with it. You have been on deck I perceive."

My hand went in a guilty movement to my black locks made limp by the sea mist.

"Yes. For a breath of air before supper."

"Ah. Well, bear in mind my words and take no risks." He turned to pick up his book. "I will go and see how my poor wife fares."

"I have been in to her. I think she is resting and does not wish for any supper."

He frowned as he sat down again.

"She would be better to attempt some gruel. Or a little boiled rice, as would Sylvia."

"Miss Meade was sleeping when I went into the cabin."

He pursed his lips. He had a choleric look and I could imagine that he would quickly lose his temper.

"It seems we shall be dining _à deux_ again, Miss Jones, unless Mr. Benson or Mr. Travers joins us."

Mr. Benson and Mr. Travers were the first and second

mates, respectively. I noticed that Mr. Meade made no mention of Captain Hawkes, who had so far not put in an appearance at meals but remained a distant figure of command.

The steward came in and laid the table for three so I hoped that Mr. Benson, who was genial and informative, would be joining us rather than Mr. Travers, who was preoccupied and melancholy, appearing to find all conversation a trial.

The dining table, made of rich shining mahogany, was large enough to seat twelve. The saloon itself, paneled in teak and bird's-eye maple, was remarkably comfortable. At one end of the saloon a small fire grate, which backed on to the pantry on the other side of the partition, gave out a warming glow. The shining brass lamp hanging overhead was lit and its golden gleam shone a reflection onto the squares of skylight set in the raised deck above. The movement of the ship caused the lamp to sway in an alarming manner and I was staring nervously up at it when the door opened and the figure of Captain Hawkes appeared on the threshold.

I had not seen him at such close quarters before and I was startled by his height and the breadth of shoulder that seemed to fill the entire aperture so that he had to stand with head bent forward to avoid the framework. This stance, in addition to frowning brows above deep-set eyes, gave him an almost menacing look. Although his shoulders were wide, he had a whipcoard leanness, an air of muscular toughness undisguised by the coat of fine blue cloth he wore, its cuffs and lapels trimmed with black velvet, a row of gilt buttons across his broad chest.

He came forward, straightening up as he did so, and with a stiff nod and the briefest "Good evening" in my direction turned to Mr. Meade and shook hands with him.

"Good evening, sir. I thought of joining you for supper but I see you are not alone as I had supposed." He moved to the chair at the head of the table. "Please be seated."

Mr. Meade sat down, beaming all over his usually solemn face.

"Good evening. This is a pleasure, Captain. We have seen

little of you so far. But there, the exigencies of your duties absorb your time and energies to the full I am sure." He gestured to where I sat on the bench across the table from him. "You have met Miss Jones, I think."

Captain Hawkes turned to look at me. If I had been of timid disposition his hard appraising glance would have frightened me. As it was I felt a tremor of alarm go through me, which I quickly suppressed.

"Miss Jones and I are so far unacquainted," he said in a deep abrupt-sounding voice. He inclined his head in a jerk of acknowledgment. "Ma'am."

"Good evening, sir."

Mr. Meade leaned forward to say, "Although Miss Jones has never been to sea before she is fortunate enough to be a good sailor and so we have kept each other company while Mrs. Meade and my daughter remain perforce in their cabins."

One eyebrow lifted above the narrow measuring stare, the firm mouth curled skeptically.

"Indeed? Do you travel all the way to Macao with us, Miss Jones?"

Something in the tone of his voice irked me so that I answered stiffly, "Yes. I am to be married there upon arrival. My fiancé is attached to the Methodist Mission in Macao."

He frowned with so dark an opprobrium that I was momentarily startled.

"You are a *missionary* then?" He made the word sound as if it were a criminal appellation.

"No. That is my fiancé's vocation."

"I see." He gave me a quick, hard glance, and I saw that his eyes were a dark steely blue. His skin was smoothly tanned, a thin mustache edged his upper lip, his resolute chin, beneath a full bottom lip, was clean-shaven and showed a cleft fringed by brown beard. He would have been handsome, but his good looks were marred by the sternness of his expression, a boniness of features, as if every trace of softness had been pared from them.

His cold glance dismissed me. From then on he addressed few remarks in my direction but confined his conversation for the most part to Mr. Meade, and by the end of the meal I was thankful to make my excuses and leave the saloon.

On my return to the cabin I found Sylvia awake and somewhat alarmed by the increased rolling of the ship, and when a pair of slippers slithered, as if propelled by unseen hands, across the floor, she gave a gasp.

"Oh, dear. The sea is becoming rougher every minute, I am sure. How can you stand there, Miss Jones, so quiet and unmoved? Don't tell me that you feel no discomfort whatsoever and have eaten your supper."

"I have managed to eat my supper certainly, but if I have any feeling of discomfort it is not on account of the sea but because Captain Hawkes shared the meal with your father and me."

She pulled herself up on one elbow to stare at me. She had the irresistible combination of velvety brown eyes with rich golden hair, but over her loveliness lay a shadow of wistfulness that seemed hard to account for. It seemed to me that Sylvia was blessed with everything a girl could wish for. Beauty, wealth, and, above all, loving parents, as well as affectionate sisters.

Now she exclaimed, "*Captain Hawkes!* But should that not have been a stimulating experience? He looks a most interesting man. Mama told me he is very well connected and was formerly an officer in the Navy. I believe he served in some sea battle with distinction and courage."

"In that case it is regrettable that his manners do not match his bravery, for he was not very polite when he discovered he had to eat his supper with a lone female, unlike your father, who is always most courteous."

Sylvia laid her golden head back on the pillow and closed her eyes.

"I do not care about the captain's manners. I do not care for anything concerning this voyage to Macao." She sighed heavily. "I wish that I had never come."

I took a step nearer the bunk.

"Do you feel as ill as that? If only you would take a little something to eat—some bouillon or some gruel."

Sylvia shook her head without opening her eyes.

"It is worse than seasickness. Much worse." She laid a delicate hand upon her bosom. "It is the pain I have here because Mama insisted that I accompany her and Papa in the *Lotus Wind* instead of remaining in England." She opened her eyes suddenly to stare up at me. "It is because I have had to leave—" She paused and added almost in a whisper, "I formed an—an attachment of which Mama, but most particularly Papa, does not approve." The soft brown eyes were luminous with tears. "He is poor, you see. A tutor to my eldest sister's children." Her voice trembled as she said, "If I had not come away now he would have been dismissed from his position."

I put a hand out and touched the one lying on the coverlet.

"I am so sorry, Miss Meade. I had no idea. I thought—you are so young, I thought you were heart-free."

She shook her head.

"I have been in love with Henry this past year. And now we are separated. Perhaps forever. Oh, I cannot bear it."

I did not know how best to console her.

"Do not say that. When you return to England you may see him again. Is there no chance for him to improve his position in life during your absence?"

"I do not know. He is the youngest son of eight children. His father is a clergyman in Dorset, but his living is a poor one. Henry is clever and well informed but he has had little opportunity to further himself. I do not care about that. I could be happy enough as the wife of a schoolmaster, which is what he talked of becoming. It is my father who is so against him, and simply because Henry is not rich and successful like my sisters' husbands. Beatrice has been married these past seven years to a wealthy merchant, like my father, and Caroline, my older sister, was married last September to a well-known London specialist. My parents came home for the wedding, and when they discovered that while I was staying with Beatrice I—Henry and I had fallen in love with each other, they forbade us to meet again and were determined that I should return with them to Macao." Her fingers tightened around my own. "Oh, Miss Jones, how fortunate you are. To be on your way to marry the man you love. I envy you with all my heart."

"I wish it could be the same for you. Please do not despair. All may yet come right."

"You do not understand. I have been brought here not solely to be parted from Henry but in the hopes I shall find a rich husband among the Canton merchants."

I stared at her.

"But—your mother? She would not wish that for you if you love another man. She is so kind—so devoted a parent."

"She is a more devoted wife. It is my father who is ambitious for me—for all of us." A tear trickled down her soft pink cheek. "He will never agree to my marrying Henry. I know that. What is to become of me? I feel my heart will break."

I clasped her hand in mine.

"Oh, Sylvia—Miss Meade, I am so very sorry. I do not know what to say to comfort you."

"Please call me Sylvia and I will call you Megan. We must be friends—I have no one else with whom I can talk. You understand how I feel, for you are in love with Mr. Crosby."

"Yes." I wondered if I were in Sylvia's place if I should be as despairing. I could not imagine myself being in so emotional a state, but perhaps that was because I was less demonstrative by nature, and although Arthur and I were deeply attached to each other, our affections had been expressed only in the letters written long after he had left England.

For a long time Sylvia and I talked together and I learned a great deal about Henry Rochford, who sounded like a clever and charming young man. At last Sylvia fell asleep and as I pulled the coverlet over her bare arms and shoulders I thought she looked as beautiful as an angel lying there in her embroidered lawn nightdress with her golden hair spread about the pillow. I hoped very much that one day she would be reunited with her Henry and, as in fairy tales, live happily ever after. But I was not sure how strong the influence of her parents would prove.

Two days later we ran into warmer weather and calmer

seas, and on the eighth day out from leaving The Downs, we arrived at Madeira.

Madeira. A green, green island rising sheer out of a blue, blue sea. I wished that we could have disembarked there but it was not to be. Captain Hawkes was rowed away in the jolly boat and remained ashore for a few hours while we had to content ourselves with leaning over the bulwarks, watching the traffic of small boats bringing fresh greens and fresh water to be taken abroad.

It was a colorful scene for the sun was warm and the breeze almost balmy after the storms of a few days ago. On the sparkling sea danced gaily painted craft manned by brown-skinned, dark-eyed men who waved and smiled at us, calling out greetings in Portuguese. Some of the boats rowed along-side to present their wares, their occupants holding up for our inspection beautifully embroidered linen cloths, table runners and work bags, as well as a good deal of basketwork.

Mrs. Meade and Sylvia besought Mr. Meade to throw down money sufficient to make a purchase or two, and although he protested that this would only increase the clamorous demand of the vendors, he eventually acceded to their request and a transaction was made with one of the men.

My means were far too straitened to make any similar purchase, and to save embarrassment I moved away along the deck to watch the spectacle from another vantage point. I would have liked to have bought one of the tablecloths or even a few handkerchiefs, but I dared not squander even a small amount on the least unnecessary thing.

The realization of this made me aware again of my own poverty. During the last years of my grandfather's life, when he was old and frail, Trefeiddan had, despite my own strug-gling, efforts, fallen into sad decline. Never a rich farm—for what hill farm in Wales can be that?—a series of misfortunes, including a particularly bitter winter in which sheep losses were heavy, followed by a summer when disease decimated the flock, drove us to the edge of existence. And then, before we were given time in which to recover, my grandfather died of a seizure.

I was deeply distressed. We had been very close, especially in the years since my grandmother had died. Now on top of the grief I suffered came the knowledge that even if I had been able to run the farm single-handed, debts and circumstances had virtually destroyed it. With the help and advice of Mr. Williams, our minister, I sold the remnants of the stock and the house and some of the furniture. The lease of the land was transferred to another farmer who lived with his family farther down the valley. I planned to bank the small nest egg and obtain a post as governess or companion, again through the help of Mr. Williams. And then, surprisingly, came the letter from Arthur Crosby with his proposal of marriage.

Although, as I have said, we had not met for two years, I remembered Arthur clearly, and as I gazed across the glittering waves I saw not the mountains of Funchal but Arthur's face and figure. I think I had fallen a little in love with him at first sight, for he was tall and good-looking, with curly chestnut hair and warm hazel eyes, and he had a smile of such radiance that one was drawn immediately to him. Added to these physical attributes were the fire and zeal of the evangelist, so that the first time I heard him preach I was carried away by the force of his personality.

My grandfather had been a follower of John Wesley and he had often told me how, as a child of six, he was taken by his parents to join the throngs at the crossroads who stood to see the great man pass, holding their children in their arms for blessing. My grandfather never forgot the occasion or the veneration in which John Wesley was held and how the people waved and cheered and prayed as the tall black-clad figure walked by them on his way from the Black Mountains to Dolgelley.

Arthur had come over the mountains in the same way, tramping the rough roads from valley to valley, preaching wherever he went on the future of the Mission Church in China. I was not an evangelist myself, but when Arthur wrote and asked me to marry him I knew that, in addition to loving him, I could be of use to him in his work.

In my mood of introspection I was not aware of the return of the jolly boat until the sound of voices and a clanking noise brought me to with a jerk. I looked over the side of the ship and was startled to see the figure of Captain Hawkes scrambling up the rope ladder only a few feet from where I stood. As he swung his long legs over the side he met my glance and after a moment's frowning hesitation paused and turned to me.

"Good morning, Miss Jones. You are observing the scenery?"

"Good morning. Yes—it is beautiful, so rich and green. I am only sorry we are not permitted to go ashore here."

The wide shoulders lifted and fell in a shrug. In the sunlight his eyes shone a deep, dark sapphire blue.

"There is little leisure for such junketings. If you sail on a clipper ship you sail against time."

"I thought that was only on the tea run, Captain. Isn't it on the voyage home that you try to make all speed possible?"

"For someone who has never been to sea before you seem strangely knowledgeable on maritime matters. But allow me to decide when and where we put into port."

"I am not disputing your authority, sir, only voicing my regrets."

He gave me a hard, uncompromising stare and then, with a jerk of his head and a curt "Ma'am," strode away.

I watched him go, thinking what a disagreeable man he was. He paused by the forward deckhouse to speak to the ship's carpenter. There was authority in every line of his lithe frame. I thought him a man whom people would fear rather than like and yet I was surprised to see the carpenter look up at him and grin, touching his cap with a forefinger. When the captain had passed on, the man began to whistle softly in a fashion to make me suppose that Captain Hawkes was possibly more agreeable to his crew than to his passengers.

As THE DAYS passed I came under the spell of life aboard ship. It was a new experience for me and every day seemed to bring a fresh interest. The weather grew imperceptibly warmer, and often Mrs. Meade, Sylvia and I sat on the poop deck, sewing or reading or talking together. One morning we arrived at St. Helena, that island forever linked with the name of Napoleon, the very thought of him causing us to shudder in recollection of his tyranny. At St. Helena we took on a supply of fresh vegetables and fresh water and not long after this we crossed the equator with due ceremony and entertainment for the passengers.

Sometimes Mrs. Meade spoke to me of Macao, which, I had already learned from Arthur, was a colony held by the Portuguese under tolerance from the Chinese since 1557. With the opening of the great "hongs," the word meaning a commercial establishment or warehouse, along the waterfront at Canton City, many of the beautiful old villas that had been built in Macao by the Portuguese were rented by foreign merchants, who were not permitted to live with their wives and children in Canton. In consequence, when the tea sales were over, the merchants, of different nationalities, came back to live in Macao with their families before returning once again to Canton to carry on the trade that existed between China and the outside world. It seemed an uncomfortable arrangement, and Mrs. Meade sighed and lamented that her husband was perforce separated so much from her.

"But what is one to do, my dear? At least we are together

from time to time during the year, whereas if I remained in England we should not meet once in a twelvemonth. It is the custom here and we abide by it, although Mr. Meade and his colleagues are working all the time for reform and more liberal treatment from the Chinese."

I suppose that this was the price the merchants must pay for the acquisition of the immense wealth that I had heard they were able to amass. Much of it, Arthur had told me, was gained through the vile opium traffic, to which the Chinese authorities were understandably so bitterly opposed. They called opium "foreign mud" and the trade was forbidden by imperial edict as well as by the Canton authorities, yet it still persisted, and opium smuggling had become a highly profitable business.

Mrs. Meade was too discreet to make comment upon all this, for the East India Company, with which Mr. Meade worked, had absolved itself of formal responsibility for the illegal trade, while continuing to maintain friendly relations with the traders. So she said little and in all truth I do not suppose she often thought about it, for though she was such a kindly person she was not the type to concern herself with the larger issues of life.

One day I walked to the bow of the ship where, under the lamp room, were kept some livestock. There was a goat and some sheep and a coop of hens. There was also a large pig. I was unhappy about the pig and tried not to think of eating roast pork or boiled ham. Mr. Meade had explained to me that a provident captain did his best to see that the crew had fresh food and meat whenever possible. It appeared also that Captain Hawkes followed the principle of the famous Captain Cook and insisted on serving sauerkraut to the men as a preventive for scurvy.

This particular morning I gave the pig a scratch upon its broad back with a stick and listened to its grunts of appreciation, and I addressed the goat, which stared impassively at me out of glassy yellow eyes. As I walked back past the forward deckhouse I heard someone singing and to my astonishment discovered that a deep and not unmelodious man's voice was singing in Welsh. The song was "*Myfanwy.*" I stopped abruptly in my tracks and a wave of emotion came over me as I listened to the Welsh love song.

The song ended and on an impulse I put my head around the door of the galley and said in Welsh, "Good morning. I enjoyed your singing."

The man at the black stove swung around. He was short and stout, with grizzled gray hair under a red woolen cap. His watery blue eyes widened; he put down the pan in his hand with a clatter and said, in answering Welsh, "Good morning, missy. Here is a surprise, indeed, to be spoken to me in my own tongue. What part would you be coming from, may I ask?"

I smiled warmly at him. He was such a kindly-looking little man.

"I am from Trefeiddan, near Partrishow."

"Ah, from the Black Mountains, is it?" He shook his head wistfully. "I know they well for I had an auntie lived up there on one of the farms. It is from Llandovery I come myself, the finest sheep market in Wales, do you know?"

"Yes. My grandfather used often to take his flocks there, for he was a sheep farmer."

"Well now, there's strange." He beamed at me. "It seems we have been all but neighbors." The smile faded. "But how is it that you are so far away from your home, young missy, and sailing to a foreign land."

I told him something of my circumstances, that I was going to Macao to be married.

"So long as it is to good young Welshman you are to be wed, you will come to no harm," he declared.

I was about to answer him when I saw the expression on his face change. He frowned and, turning back to the stove, said hurriedly, "I must be getting on with my work. Good morning, miss."

The way his glance went past me caused me to look around and I saw the tall figure of Captain Hawkes standing a few paces behind me.

I said, still in Welsh, "Good morning," and turned away from the galley to confront the captain's black frown.

Without speaking he gestured for me to walk ahead, and

only when we were out of sight and earshot of the galley did he pause to say in a cold-sounding voice, "I should prefer that you do not fraternize with members of the crew."

I was so taken aback that I could only stare at him. Then I found the words to stammer a protest.

"Fr— Fraternize? I heard the man singing in Welsh and I said good morning to him and we—we spoke a few words together in our mutual language." I added quickly, with emphasis upon the pronoun, "Please do not reprimand *him*. It was entirely my fault, for speaking to him in the first place."

"I do not doubt that. It is a female trait to gossip. You are not used to the discipline of life aboard ship, Miss Jones. The man has his duties to fulfill and these do not include wasting time in small talk with the passengers. Be so good as to remember that in future." He gave me a brief salute and turned away, leaving me to go below.

In my indignation I nearly fell down the companionway, and I was relieved that Sylvia was not in the cabin when I reached it. I would surely have burst into a tirade of resentment and Sylvia would have been astonished, for she regarded Captain Hawkes as an admirable if somewhat aloof character.

Perhaps he was. Perhaps with Mr. and Mrs. Meade and Sylvia he was polite and agreeable enough. With me, for some reason, he bore a latent animosity and I could not imagine why.

Soon after this incident the weather began to change as we turned toward South Africa and the Cape of Good Hope. Squalls became increasingly frequent and the sea unpleasantly choppy. The blue skies vanished under a pall of gray cloud and soon the *Lotus Wind* was rolling and plunging through massive seas.

Mrs. Meade took to her bunk first, followed by Sylvia. This time they suffered more than queasiness and loss of appetite. They were both so desperately ill that I became truly anxious for them. To add to their difficulties, Mr. Meade was seasick too, though he kept manfully on his feet, retiring at sudden intervals to re-emerge drawn and green visaged.

I felt far from easy myself, but I struggled to the saloon

for the little food I could eat. I knew that if I stayed with Sylvia in the disagreeable stuffiness of the cabin I would surely be ill.

With every hour that passed, the sea seemed to become rougher and the ship's pitch and roll became even more pronounced. It was difficult to keep upright and several times I was flung the length of the cabin or across the saloon, where I now sat in solitary state, Captain Hawkes and the first and second mates having absented themselves.

I was made very apprehensive by the noises around me. The ship's timbers groaned as the vessel pitched and tossed in terrifying fashion. At intervals would come the thump of the waves against her sides, and the rattle of spray fell onto the skylight above my head with a sound as sharp as hail. Occasionally a lull came, but scarcely had I drawn a trembling breath of relief than the noise started up afresh and the terrible lurching of the ship would be resumed.

I went to the Meadeses' cabin, where Mr. Meade was now stretched on his bunk with his wife lying alongside him in hers. They were like two recumbent corpses and if I had not been so sorry for them and anxious for my own well-being I would have smiled. I did what I could for Mrs. Meade and went back to Sylvia, who was still retching at intervals. I dampened her forehead with a cloth soaked in aromatic vinegar and reassured her as best I could. By the time I had finished my ministrations it was all I could do to retain control of my own churning stomach. Longing desperately for some air and an escape from the fetid atmosphere, I seized my cloak and somehow, on hands and knees, clambered up the steps of the companionway. The opening was closed and for a moment I thought it was fastened down, but when I pushed at it, it fell back and I struggled onto the deck. As I did so a tremendous gust of wind caught me up in one wild and unexpected sweep so that I was carried across the deck without volition.

It was as if a giant's hand had reached down and seized me in its grasp and then flung me away in derision. The deck was awash with water and when I tried to struggle to my feet the splashing of the sea backward and forward with the movement of the ship caused me to fall down again and be carried yet farther along the deck.

Suddenly I was hurled against the bulwark with such force that for a moment I was stunned out of my senses and could only lie there, helpless and half drowned. Someone rushed past me and a booted foot knocked me out of the way as if I were indeed the bundle of rags or sailcloth that I appeared to be. I heard muffled cries and shouts and above these a wild and eerie whistling sound, which I realized must be the wind through the rigging. I tried once more to get to my feet and slowly, inch by inch, I struggled upright, gripping the edge of the bulwark as hard as I could to maintain my balance.

Although it was afternoon, the sky above me was as overcast as at night. I was aware of a constant movement about me, of figures heaving and tugging at ropes, of the crack and slam of sails being shortened. Somehow I must get below to the safety of the cabins, but how to get across the slippery deck? I shouted, hoping that some sailor would come to my rescue, but my voice was lost in the howl of the wind and the roar of the sea. No one could see me in the dusky half-light and a curtain of spume and spray made for further concealment.

The seas were mountainous. I had never thought there could be waves such as these. Even the dim light could not hide their great slavering jaws as they rose behind the ship like devouring monsters, threatening to engulf the *Lotus Wind* and all who sailed on her in one fearsome gulp.

As I clutched at the bulwark I was trembling with cold and with terror. I remembered that someone had called the Cape of Good Hope the Cape of Storms and I wondered how any ship could weather the promontory in such seas. The waves broke over the side of the ship and the water went swirling about my feet, all but throwing me to the deck again. My cape was gone, carried off in the gale as if it had never been fastened about my shoulders. I was drenched to the skin, my hair loosened and blown into a wet black tangle. There was blood on my face; I felt the taste of it mingle with the salt on my lips.

I thought desperately, I can't hang on much longer, and as

if to prove my words, suddenly a gigantic wave seemed to tumble over the ship and I was swept away in the seething foam of its wake. I seemed to go head over heels along the deck; I felt that I was drowning and I thought how mad I had been to ever venture on deck while such a storm raged. And then, as I gasped for breath, for very life, I was lifted up and held fast against an expanse of wet oilskin. The sailor, whoever he was, tightened one arm about me, and with the other holding on to a line of some sort, the man dragged rather than carried me along the deck, roping us both in as he fought his way to safety.

I was crushed to him in a viselike grip; I could not see his face but I was conscious of a salt-wet beard against my cheek and I began to be fearful as to my rescuer. And then, as abruptly as he had seized me, he let me go, and as he did so he shouted in my ear, in a cold and furiously angry voice, "*Get below* and *stay below*. You'll all be battened down from now on. Goddamnit, Miss Jones, I have better things to do in a storm like this than play nursemaid to a stupid girl who is as foolhardy as she is ignorant," and with a hard and unexpected push he sent me stumbling down the companionway. The next minute the hatchway clanged to and I was left bruised and gasping at the foot of the steps.

I dragged myself to my feet, and with one hand against the wood paneling, supporting my trembling limbs, I staggered to the cabin. At my entry Sylvia sat up with a cry of horror.

"Oh, Megan! Oh, heavens, what has happened to you?" She slid from her bunk and came toward me. "But you are wet to the skin, and where is your cloak? Oh, and your face is all cut and bleeding." She looked so overcome that I had to put my hand out to assist her.

"It is all right," I assured her as I led her back to her bunk. "Foolishly I went on deck, not realizing what a fearful gale was raging, and—and I was thrown down and then could not get up again." My voice trembled to a stop at the memory of that life-and-death moment when I felt I was going to be hurled overboard in the wave that had submerged me. I steadied my voice to add, "But I was rescued and, as you see, am safe and sound. This cut looks worse than it is, I am sure." I helped her lie down and then turned, my teeth chattering, to undress.

"You should have a drink of some kind," Sylvia said. "Ask the steward to bring you a warming posset."

"Yes—yes, I will do that in a few moments."

I dried my long black hair as best I could and bathed the gash on my cheek, which was deeper and more painful than I had supposed. I rang the bell for the steward, but no one came and I realized that the entire crew must be on deck working to keep the ship on course.

I climbed into my bunk only to discover the bedclothes soaked in the water that had managed to break in despite the closed porthole. I found as dry a patch as I could and burrowed down under the damp blankets and fell instantly asleep.

During the next few days, while the storms slowly abated, I remained in my cabin, for as well as being painfully stiff and bruised, I also suffered a severe chill, caused no doubt by the loss of my cloak and the immersion in seawater. Thankfully, Sylvia recovered from her sickness and she was as kind and thoughtful to me as a sister.

Lying alone in the bunk, feeling unexpectedly weak, I thought about Captain Hawkes. I dreaded that he might come to the cabin and inquire after me, but mercifully, any concern he felt was expressed in a brief message by way of Mrs. Meade, who was now up and about again.

I remembered his harsh treatment and the way he had sworn at me, but I could not be angry. I was too thankful to be alive and safe and this I knew I owed to the captain. Strangely enough I remembered very clearly the feel of his wet face against mine and the sound of his angry voice shouting in my ear and the sensation of his crushing embrace as he struggled back with me along the lines to safety.

With the rounding of the dreaded Cape and our emergence into the Indian Ocean we began to feel the true warmth of the tropics. The heat of the sun intensified and a wide awning was put up over the poop deck and here we sat by the hour. The sea was a deep glassy blue and there was seldom a cloud in the sky. By day flying fish skimmed the sea, leaping and falling in the sunshine, and shoals of porpoises plunged through the sea alongside the ship, their bodies black and glistening under the water. At night the stars sparkled and shone more brilliantly than any I had ever seen, and a glittering phosphorescence silvered the foam in the wake of the ship.

Greatly daring, I had hammered a nail into the wood by my bunk, within reach of my hand, and thus was able to keep my Bible and a book of Mr. Wordsworth's poems and Arthur's letters in a small velveteen bag hung on the nail, and often, lying there, I would read the letters over and over again to myself.

Arthur wrote with fluency and gave a graphic picture of life in Macao. After my grandfather's death his letters became warmer and more personal, as he tried to give me comfort in my loss, and in his proposal of marriage he wrote "I have thought of you almost every day since we parted." He told me that he had intended to ask me to marry him on his next leave but that events had precipitated matters.

His letters brought him nearer to me and I felt I knew him well. I loved him as he loved me. I was grateful to him. I knew that had I remained at Hafod Trefeiddan I might have ended my life as an old maid, for I was twenty-six years of age and by no means pretty and single men were few in those remote mountains.

One thing puzzled and disturbed me. The last letters I had received were briefer and less frequent and Arthur wrote of feeling ill. He suffered considerable pain from a tooth abscess and this seemed to affect his health. Dr. Howard, who ran the Mission, was a qualified doctor, but he had gone to Amoy to visit the Mission there and so Arthur had at first treated himself and then had gone to a Portuguese doctor during Dr. Howard's absence. His last letter to me was so vague and evasive on the subject of his well-being that I was anxious for him and only hoped that he was not concealing anything from me.

I had good cause to know Captain Hawkes was a disciplinarian, and now I saw fresh evidence of this in the daily routine. As well as the first and second mates there were a bo'sun and a sailmaker, a cook, a carpenter and a steward, and twenty-four able seamen, of which a third were no more than sixteen years of age. They seemed to spend a great deal of their time clambering up the tall masts to set the royal or the topgallant and the stunsails, or shaking out sails ready to set again, and this went on half a dozen times or more a day.

On every clear day, the deck below and the officers' quarters were cleaned and washed and aired. Even when it was wet or the sky overcast the decks were cleaned just the same. Every other week or so as circumstances allowed, the contents of each man's sea chest and bag and the whole of his bedding were spread out on deck to be freshened in the sun and air. No man was ever allowed to sleep on deck or even lie down when his clothes were wet, which happened often in the sudden storms, or "blow ups," that we ran into from time to time. On Sunday mornings the ship's company mustered and every man presented himself clean and neatly dressed for prayers.

Not content with just the welfare of the crew, the officers oversaw an endless routine of scrubbing and scouring. On moonlight nights, masts and yards would be scrubbed with sand and canvas until they literally shone. And the hard, irksome task of "holystoning" was done with fearsome regularity, the men working on their knees, first scraping the deck and holystoning it thoroughly before putting on a coat of coal tar and scraping and holystoning all over again so that the decks appeared as white as snow.

I marveled at all this and regarded the captain as a martinet. Yet the men seemed content enough and were certainly in good health. Sometimes in the evening the drum and fife would sound and we would know that the men were dancing and amusing themselves in the fo'c'sle. It was a happy sight to see them, woolen cap on head, red or blue shirt tucked into dark trousers, a knife at the belt and barefooted, performing a sprightly hornpipe or a reel.

At Calcutta we anchored in the Hooghly River, where, after landing some cargo, we took on more. We were there only two days and it was so hot and humid that we were all glad when the *Lotus Wind* set sail again.

I was standing by the rail watching the skyline of palaces and white buildings fade from sight when I became aware that Captain Hawkes had come to stand beside me. We had scarcely exchanged a word since the day he had rescued me during the storm off the Cape of Good Hope. I had deliberately avoided contact with him and seemingly his intentions were the same, for apart from a nod of greeting or a brief remark at the dinner table no conversation had passed between us.

Now he gave me a quick sideways glance.

"I see you still bear the scars of your misadventure."

My hand went involuntarily to the weal on my cheek.

"It—it is healed but the mark has not yet faded."

"It will do so in time, no doubt."

I wished he would go away and yet I was constrained to say what had been on my mind for some time.

"I think I owe my life to you. I am very grateful."

He shrugged in his usual indifferent manner.

"Perhaps such an experience will cause you to take more care in future."

I said stiffly, "I am sure it will."

He nodded and with an inclination of his head in lieu of salute walked back to the helmsman.

We had been a hundred days out from England when we passed through Sunda Strait into the Java Sea. The weather had been increasingly sultry, and now, as the *Lotus Wind* moved slowly through the narrow, enclosed waters, we felt a great lassitude. I had little energy to do more than lie back in one of the cane chairs and gaze out at the passing islands, wondering at the lush growth, the tall trees and the trailing foliage that lined the banks. There were many evergreens with broad shining leaves and blossoms of red and pink and white. Sometimes we were so close to the shore that we would hear the chattering of monkeys in the trees and once, an awesome moment, we heard the distant roar of a tiger.

We saw little of Captain Hawkes now, for he was ever on

the watch. The shoals were treacherous and the danger of pirates ever present. I had noticed earlier on the oiling of two small iron guns, and now an assortment of boarding pikes was placed in a rack at the foot of the main mast, while pistols, muskets and even cutlasses were cleaned and polished. Two men were posted on the tall masts above our heads day and night, with rifles on the ready. It was a nerve-racking experience, made the more so by the slow passage of the ship, for Mr. Benson, the first mate, informed us we were now between monsoons and the winds were light. Later, in May, the southwest monsoon would set in and homeward-bound ships would make good speed, but now it was just the reverse.

It was with a sigh of relief that we came to the open seas. Mr. Meade informed us that the dangers were by no means over, but at least the ship had room in which to maneuver.

It was a morning in mid-April when the *Lotus Wind* came to the outer roadstead of the Pearl River and, rounding Barra Point, drew into the shallow harbor of Macao. It was a beautiful sight. Across the bay lay the rolling brown hills of southern China. Above the point stood a tall white lighthouse and as we sailed into the bay I caught sight of an imposing façade of pillars and arches and guessed this must be the ruin of the great church of São Paulo, which had been destroyed by fire nearly twenty years ago. The cross, undamaged, was silhouetted against the blue sky and as I gazed up at it I remembered how Arthur had told me it was the Portuguese who first brought Christianity to Macao. Originally the name Macao came from that of Liang Ma, or A-Ma, as the Chinese called her, the goddess of fishermen. The Portuguese called it A-ma-Gao, or the port of A-Ma.

I stared about me, aware of a rising tide of excitement at the thought that this small rocky peninsula was now to be my home, that soon I would see Arthur again and that, within a week, we should be married.

The ship was already dropping anchor. There was activity and movement everywhere; small boats passed and repassed and I caught my first glimpse of Chinese faces. I was struck by the strangeness of masklike skins and slanting black eyes and queues of black hair swinging under huge conical hats.

A pilot or some such official boat was approaching the *Lotus Wind* and I could see figures in it ready to come aboard. Would Arthur be one of them? I wondered with a surge of excitement.

Sylvia was almost as impatient as I. We chattered to each other, pointing out first this curious sight and then that and all the while I was on tenterhooks over the new arrivals.

I tried not to feel disappointed when I saw that Arthur was not among them. Could I really have expected that? I asked myself. He would not know the actual time of the ship's arrival and he had his own work to do. However, my attention was diverted by a tall stooping man in a black suit who clambered over the rail. After speaking to Mr. Benson, he was taken to Captain Hawkes, who stood on the quarterdeck. I saw the captain turn and glance toward the rail where Sylvia and I stood. He frowned and after a moment left the quarterdeck in the company of the stranger and went up to Mr. Meade. The three of them conferred for some moments, then the captain returned to the quarterdeck, leaving Mr. Meade with the stranger. They seemed to talk together in a confidential manner, and not wishing to seem rude by observing them, I glanced away again to look at the harbor with its fishing junks and scattering of green islands, and beyond, faraway Canton.

From behind I heard Mrs. Meade speak my name and turned to confront her. To my amazement her usually rosy face was deathly pale and her eyes were suffused with tears. She said my name again in a trembling voice and then, taking my hand in hers, she said, "Will you come below with me, my dear. I have something—something to tell you."

Her voice was so serious that I clutched her fingers in alarm.

"What is it, Mrs. Meade? Have you— Is it bad news?"

She shook her head but made no answer, only gently guided me toward the companionway. My heart began to race and thump for I had a sudden and powerful apprehension that Mrs. Meade had bad tidings for me. They could only concern Arthur. What had happened? Was he delayed? Or ill?

The cabin door closed behind us. Mrs. Meade took my other hand in hers and said chokingly, as she drew me down beside her onto the leather coath, "My dear child, "you must be very brave. I—I hardly know how to tell you." She swallowed on a sob. "Oh, Megan, it is Arthur."

I heard myself say with surprising calm, "I guessed as much. What is it, Mrs. Meade? Is he—is he ill? Or has he met with some accident?"

Slowly she shook her head and I saw the tears on her cheeks.

"My dear, it is much worse than that." She paused, staring at me out of grieving blue eyes. Then she said in so low a voice that she was almost inaudible, "Arthur is dead."

I stared back at her in frozen silence. I tried to speak but no words would come. I felt her hands clasping mine more tightly than ever and heard her say as if from a long way off, "May God give you courage to bear your loss, Megan, my dear."

A shudder went through me. Somehow I forced myself to speak, my voice trembling with the effort.

"I—I cannot believe it. Arthur *dead*. When— We—we were going to be married."

Mrs. Meade gave a long, heartfelt sigh.

"I know, dear. This is a terrible thing—a terrible tragedy. The funeral—" She paused and then went on more steadily. "He was buried here in the English Cemetery a week ago."

CHAPTER 3

How LONG I stayed in the cabin with Mrs. Meade I do not recall. I was so stunned with shock that nothing registered. But I do remember Mrs. Meade's motherly kindness, and her tears of sympathy. I did not weep myself; I sat there, talking of Arthur as if he were still alive. And then, how much later I do not know, we disembarked, and I was helped into a carriage with Mrs. Meade while Mr. Meade and Sylvia followed in a second one, for Mrs. Meade had insisted that I should stay with them at their villa on the Praia Grande rather than go to Dr. and Mrs. Howard at the Mission.

"They are the best of people," she explained as the *carroca* made its slow way from the harbor, "but they are as yet strangers to you, Megan, my dear. If you are with us, you are with friends. We wish you to make your home with us until you have decided what you want to do."

I could only let my hand lie in hers and thank her as I stared out at the Portuguese mansions, which were nothing more than a blur of pink and blue and yellow to me as we drove past.

At the villa I was taken upstairs to a cool shuttered bedroom and left to myself.

"Please ring the bell if you wish for anything, my dear," Mrs. Meade said. "I will have some lunch sent up to you. Try to eat something and then lie down and rest. I will be in again later, for you must not be left too long alone."

"You have been so good to me. Thank you."

"It is nothing. Bless you, my dear." And she was gone, her

stays creaking as she tiptoed from the room. Her kindness touched me more than the loss that I had still not fully accepted.

I washed my hands and face in the porcelain basin. Although a little while ago I had felt chilled as if with cold, now my skin was burning. I took off my slippers and lay down on the bed and stared up at the ornately carved ceiling.

"Arthur is dead," I told myself. "You will never see him again. You will never be husband and wife." I said the words aloud, as if to make myself understand. "Arthur is *dead*." And suddenly the tears came and I was weeping into the pillow.

I must have slept, for a sound brought me to awareness again, and as I struggled up onto my elbow I saw Sylvia standing, hesitant and anxious, on the threshold. She said, "Dear Megan, you are awake. I was about to go away again." She came over and sat down on the edge of the bed and leaned forward to give me a gentle kiss. "I do not know what to say. I am so very sorry."

I put my hand in her outstretched one.

"Thank you. It—it is hard to believe."

She turned her head, as if to hide her tears, and said in a low voice, "Mama told me I must not distress you but I wanted so much to come and be with you." She glanced back at me. "One of the servants brought a tray to you but you were asleep. Could you eat something now?"

I shook my head.

"I am not hungry."

"Let me send for some tea. It will revive you. May I stay or would you rather be alone?"

"No. I should like you to stay."

Sylvia's presence, gentle and affectionate, less emotionally charged than her mother's, soothed me. After we had drunk the refreshing tea and she had left me, I felt comforted, and in the heat of the afternoon I slept again.

I think the next few days were harder to bear than the first day of shock and grief, for the full realization of Arthur's death came to me. And with it not only the sadness that we should never meet again but an awareness of my uncertain future.

I had come half across the world to marry a man who had died suddenly and tragically. The farm had been sold; there were no living relatives left in Partrishow. What was I to do? Where was I to go?

As if in answer to my prayers, at the end of the week Dr. Howard called with his wife, to see me.

I was relieved to meet them. There was much I wanted to know about Arthur. I wanted to know about his illness and what he had died of. He had seemed so strong and alive when last we had been together at Hafod Trefeiddan. When I had questioned Mrs. Meade she had shaken her head and answered that Mr. Meade thought Arthur had died of a fever.

Dr. Howard was the tall stooping man I remembered seeing coming aboard the *Lotus Wind* on that fatal morning. He had a sallow complexion and very black eyebrows above deep-set dark eyes; Mrs. Howard seemed not much older than myself and was pretty and delicate-looking with light-auburn hair and light-lashed blue eyes. Hesitantly and somewhat nervously she expressed her sympathy over Arthur's death, which Dr. Howard echoed more emphatically.

After we had spoken together for a few moments I asked Dr. Howard to tell me something of Arthur's death. He frowned for a moment before answering and then said slowly, "He—he died of a fever. That is all I can tell you, Miss Jones. Such disorders are endemic—they come without warning."

"But he had been unwell for several weeks, had he not? He wrote to me of a tooth abscess and of being in much pain. His last letters gave me some anxiety."

Dr. Howard glanced away from me to his wife, as if seeking her assurance.

"Yes, that is true—he suffered much trouble with his teeth." He added uncertainly, "Perhaps that lowered his resistance to illness."

"Were you here when he—he died? I understand you had gone to Amoy and were not able to treat him yourself, which might have helped Arthur rather than the foreign doctor he went to."

"Perhaps. I returned from Amoy two days before he"— again there was the odd hesitation, which in some way made me uneasy—"died. You know that he is buried in the English Cemetery?"

"Yes. Would you—I would be very grateful if you would show me his grave. I wanted to visit it at once—as soon as I—" I broke off, then added, "Mrs. Meade thought it better to wait until I had seen you."

"Of course. I will take you there whenever you wish."

Mrs. Howard, who had been listening, broke in to say in a gentle voice, "What are your plans, Miss Jones? Do you intend soon to return to England? We should welcome you to stay with us at the Mission, if you would care to."

Before I could reply Dr. Howard leaned forward to speak.

"You would be doing us a favor, Miss Jones. My wife has been far from well and I planned to go inland in company with another Mission worker who is coming to join us. If you would come and be with Mrs. Howard it would be of great assistance to me, and who knows, perhaps being so occupied might help to take your mind off your grief." He saw my hesitation and added, "Take time to think it over. We should like to have you. We feel we know you already for Arthur spoke so often of you."

I heard myself sigh.

"I appreciate your thought for me—and your offer. I cannot impose upon Mr. and Mrs. Meade indefinitely and I must somehow make myself independent of other people. But —to stay on in Macao?" I bit my lip. "That is something I had never thought to do with—without Arthur. I must consider it more fully."

"Certainly." He stood up and his little wife rose from her chair to stand beside him. "Shall I call for you tomorrow morning and take you to the cemetery?"

"Please do. And thank you again for your kindness to me."

When, next day, I stood beside Arthur's grave in the English Cemetery I was sad of heart. He had been so happy and so eager, so full of all he intended to do in his work. "We shall carry the word of God far into China," he used to say. "We will found missions and schools and hospitals. I want to help these people in every way I can."

Now, as I laid the flowers that Mrs. Meade had told one of the Chinese gardeners to cut for me on the simple, as yet unmarked, grave, I grieved for the waste of Arthur's life as much as for my own loss.

Dr. Howard had called for me unaccompanied by his wife.

"I hope you will forgive her absence. She wanted to come with me but I thought the exertion too much for her." He lowered his voice as he added, "It is but a few months since she lost our third child."

"I am so sorry."

"His grave is over there. A boy, stillborn."

I said again, "Oh, I am *sorry.*"

As if by common consent we walked to where a covering of blossoms marked the resting place of Dr. Howard's son. As we stood together I said a silent prayer, thinking of the small soul that had returned so swiftly from whence it came and wondering, as I had wondered about Arthur, why these things should happen.

We had come from the Villa Cicadela in a *carroca*, but now Dr. Howard said, "May I put you into a sedan to be taken back to the Meadeses' home? I plan to walk back to the Mission."

I had already observed the strange chairs carried on long poles by the thin brown coolies in their big hats, and though I thought it a harsh form of labor for the poor men I realized that it was an accepted method of travel. I nodded and said, "Of course. Although I should prefer to walk."

Dr. Howard shook his head.

"You are not as yet accustomed to the life here. It is better for an unaccompanied lady to travel by sedan. Also the heat of the day is building up—it would exhaust you to walk from here." He looked down at me. "You will consider my suggestion to come and stay with us at the Mission?"

"Yes. It is very kind of you. I—I am not sure as yet what I am—" My voice trailed off uncertainly.

He nodded his head.

"I understand. It is still too soon." He helped me into a sedan and murmured a few words in Chinese to the coolies and then, standing back with his black hat in his hand, he watched me carried out of sight.

We had scarcely turned out of the cemetery and gone along the quiet tree-lined road when to my surprise the men put down the sedan and one of the front ones came back to speak to me. With clasped hands and a polite bow he said, "Missee likee go glotto? Muchee nicee. Muchee people look see."

I stared in bewilderment at him.

"*Glotto?*" I shook my head. "What is glotto?"

"Glotto muchee nicee." He waved a skeletal brown hand. "Tlees, flowels—muchee pleety. You likee glotto."

A flash of understanding came to me. I remembered something Mrs. Meade had told me when describing Macao, of a garden or grotto built around a statue of Camoëns, the famous Portuguese poet. Apparently he had written part of his famous poem *Os Lusíadas* while living in Macao.

I nodded toward the anxious slanting-eyed face watching me, and because I wanted to be alone with my memories of Arthur and was therefore reluctant to return to the Villa Cicadela, I impulsively said, "Please take me to the grotto. I should like to visit it."

Within a few minutes I was deposited in a small green park, cool and beautiful with trees and shrubs. My guides, bowing and smiling, gestured for me to walk on, while falling into squatting positions on the ground to rest themselves.

It was so quiet and peaceful among the green growing things that I felt increasingly grateful to the coolie for his suggestion. There was a stone seat and I sat down on it and thought of Arthur. Had he walked here? I wondered. Had he too looked at these glossy evergreens, this bougainvillea and sweet-scented jasmine?

Through the trees I glimpsed curving roof tiles and heard the noise of a gong and a thin warbling of flutes, and I realized this must be coming from the nearby Chinese temple. It was a melancholy sound and after a little while I rose and walked on. The trees cast a welcome shade and I had walked only a short way when I came to the Camoëns Grotto. In a niche of rock a statue of the bearded poet, with a laurel wreath about his head, gazed down at the ferns growing on the step. There was an inscription engraved on the stone pedestal, but it was in Portuguese and so I could not read it. For a moment or two I stood staring at the little monument then, listlessly, I turned to walk on. As I did so I heard footsteps coming behind me. Some impulse caused me to look around and to my astonishment I saw, a few paces from me, the tall figure of Captain Hawkes.

Before I could speak he came forward, doffing his peaked cap and giving me a courteous bow.

"Miss Jones. Your servant. I called at the Villa Cicadela this morning and was told you had gone to visit the English Cemetery. On my way there I saw you being carried to the park and I followed you. Please forgive me if I intrude."

I could only stare at him in bewilderment, wondering for what reason he should wish to see me.

"N—no. It is quite all right."

He stared down at me, his eyes grave and darkly blue, then he said in a more gentle voice than I had ever heard him use, "I should like to express my most sincere sympathy. You have suffered a great loss, a great shock."

My own voice trembled as I answered, "Thank you. I still cannot believe it."

"Words are not of much use, but I hope I may be of some practical assistance to you, Miss Jones. I do not know what your future plans are, but if you wish to return to England I can offer you a free passage home on the *Lotus Wind*."

I was taken aback by his suggestion.

"Oh. Oh, that is very kind." I could scarcely credit that this quietly spoken man should be the harsh and arrogant Captain Hawkes. I said uncertainly, "I thank you for your generous offer, but I have not as yet come to any decision."

"Is there an alternative? I cannot help but feel that the wisest thing would be for you to return to England, and although the tea race home will not make for the most comfortable of circumstances, you are a good enough sailor for me not to be too concerned as to your well-being."

"You are very kind." My voice trembled again as I added,

"*Everyone* has been most kind. Mr. and Mrs. Meade and Miss Meade. And Dr. Howard has invited me to stay at the Mission with Mrs. Howard and himself. It seems I can be of some use to them there."

The captain frowned.

"You would do better to return to your own people."

"There is no one left of my family. My home—my grandfather's home—had to be sold after his death. I came out here to be married—to make a new life for myself." I shrugged wearily. "Perhaps I shall stay—perhaps I can undertake something of Arthur's work. I do not know."

"In what capacity, Miss Jones? As a female missionary?" The captain's voice had its familiar sharp edge. "They are few and far between and for the most part elderly spinsters. If you remain on at the Mission that will very likely be your fate."

I lifted my gaze, which had been lowered to the ground, to stare directly at him.

"It will likely be my fate in any case. I am not concerned. God must have some purpose in bringing me here. I try to find comfort in that thought."

He made a gesture of impatience.

"Do not resign yourself too easily, Miss Jones. If you remain with the Meade family you may be fortunate enough to meet one of the well-to-do young men who abound in the warehouses of Canton. Some of them are eager to marry. I gather that is Mrs. Meade's ambition for her daughter."

An icy chill ran through me. I turned from him, saying in a low voice, "I have come these few moments ago from my fiancé's grave."

The silence that fell between us was broken only by the shrill cry of some bird. After a pause I heard him say quietly, "I should not have spoken so. I beg your pardon."

Without looking at him I said, "You are cynical."

"Perhaps I am. Life has made me so. It is my experience that any woman will marry any man if he has sufficient wealth."

I turned to face him, seeing afresh the hard relentless face, the cruel mouth.

"Your experience has obviously been an unhappy one. Do not judge everyone by it."

"I will try not to." His eyes, so dark a blue they seemed almost black in the shadows, narrowed. "You look tired, Miss Jones. And you are not used to this heat. Allow me to escort you back to your sedan."

"I would prefer to remain here."

His mouth tightened.

"As you wish. You are chary of advice it seems, but let me repeat that my offer holds good. I shall shortly be leaving for Whampoa anchorage in readiness for the tea market when it opens. A message sent to the *Lotus Wind* will effect a free passage home." He hesitated. "Can you not return to your fiancé's family? They would surely welcome you."

"My—Arthur's father is married for a second time and has a young family. I am not even acquainted with him. Arthur's brother is in Canada and his two sisters are both married and have children and are living away from Wales. There is no place for me with any of them."

He stared frowningly at me.

"I see."

"I appreciate your generous offer, believe me. As to the advice, I will consider it, though I cannot promise to follow it." I held out my hand. "Goodbye, Captain Hawkes. If we do not meet again I wish you a safe voyage home."

He took my hand in his firm one and said stiffly, "Thank you, ma'am. I wish you well." And releasing my hand from his strong grip, he turned on his heel and walked away down the path.

I stood there, feeling drained and utterly exhausted. A stone bench was placed under the trees and I dropped down onto it with a sigh, and for a few moments sat with my head resting in my hands.

Should I have accepted the captain's offer of a passage home? Would I be forced to in the end? And if I returned to Wales, what would I do, where would I live? If I were to spend the rest of my life in some governess's or companion's post might I not do that as well here, at least for a time?

Perhaps it would be possible to carry on Arthur's work in some form or other, and as that thought came to me I seemed to hear the captain's scornful designation—"a female missionary." Well, why not? If God should deem me worthy to follow Arthur's calling.

When at last I rose to walk slowly back the way I had come I was no nearer to a solution. I could only pray for guidance.

It was Mrs. Meade who finally helped me to make the decision.

"Megan, my dear, there is no cause for you to go and live at the Mission. You may remain with us for as long as you wish. You know you are most welcome and Sylvia will enjoy your company. Since both her sisters married she has felt lonely at times. That is one of the reasons we brought her out here for a visit." She hesitated, glancing at her daughter, then said slowly, "The friendship of someone responsible and a little older cannot be anything but beneficial to Sylvia."

I too hesitated. As usual, this morning they were both beautifully and expensively dressed. Mrs. Meade's gown was of shot-silk lavender with a narrow black fringe on the sleeves. On her still-brown hair was a lace cap trimmed with lavender ribbon. Sylvia wore a dress of beige-and-white-spotted muslin with a fringing of pink and brown on sleeves and bodice. At her throat was a coral necklace, which seemed to echo the flush of pink on her cheeks. She was so pretty and she looked at me so anxiously that I almost accepted Mrs. Meade's warm invitation to stay on at the Villa Cicadela. But as I stood in the handsome drawing room, magnificently furnished, with an ornately carved ceiling and molded fireplace, immense vases and jars of Chinese porcelain set in arched recesses, and shining rosewood furniture, including a grand piano standing near one of the long windows, I saw evidence of wealth such as I had never been accustomed to. It made me realize how different my life had been from that of people like the Meades. In the more Spartan conditions of the *Lotus Wind* we had seemed alike; here I knew that we were worlds apart.

I thought of my parents; my schoolmaster father, learned

but poor, and my mother, the daughter of simple hardworking country folk but proudly independent. As I wished to be. If I remained as a guest at the Villa Cicadela I should be a parasite on other people's lives. I glanced down at the gray alpaca dress I was wearing. Mrs. Meade had wanted to give me a black dress of Sylvia's to wear as mourning for Arthur, but I had refused it. It was a beautiful dress of self-striped black silk, richly elegant, but I preferred to wear my old gray alpaca, for I thought it more in keeping with Arthur and his ideals of simplicity and unadornment.

"Well, dear?" Mrs. Meade interposed gently.

I came to with a start.

"Forgive me, please, if I appear ungracious. You have been so very kind to me and I thank you for your generous invitation, Mrs. Meade, but—but I cannot accept it. I should be grateful to stay with you for perhaps another week, but after that I must leave and go to the Mission. There I can be of use to Dr. and Mrs. Howard. And perhaps—perhaps in time I may undertake some of Arthur's work."

Mrs. Meade frowned.

"It seems so unnecessary, my dear. It will be a hard life for you at the Mission—they live as poor people. It is a trait of their calling."

At the risk of sounding priggish I said, "It is as I would have expected to live." I bit my lip to steady my voice. "As Arthur's wife."

Sylvia came and laid a gentle hand on my arm.

"I wish you might stay. But if you leave us, you must promise to come and see us very often. We are your friends, Megan. You know that and we must not lose touch with one another."

"Thank you, Sylvia. I hope that we may remain friends always."

She leaned forward and kissed my cheek.

"That is a promise."

I stayed not one but two weeks with the Meades, for Mrs. Meade insisted I should do so. She would have been happy to prolong my stay indefinitely, but I had been in touch with

Mrs. Howard and arranged to go to the Mission on a certain day.

Mr. Meade himself escorted me there in his carriage, my trunk and small luggage stacked on the seat in front of us. As we drove along the Avenida Almeida Riberio, one of the main shopping centers, I looked about me. Hitherto I had been too stunned and shocked to have any real awareness of my surroundings, but now, for the first time, I gazed around with some show of interest, knowing that this was where I was to live and work.

The Avenida Almeida Riberio was a wide and handsome thoroughfare with many prosperous-looking shops. As the *carroca* trotted along, Mr. Meade pointed out various noteworthy sights. To the right of us was the hill upon which stood the Fortaleza do Monte, the old Monte fortress and observatory, and just beyond it I glimpsed again the ruined façade of the great Church of St. Paul's, which, so Mr. Meade told me, had been built by the first Japanese Christians in 1602 and destroyed by fire in 1835, not twenty years ago. The original edifice had served as the Jesuit College of the Mother of God.

Some way along the avenue we turned left, leaving the Mediterranean magnificence of tall buildings behind us to drive through narrow streets into the Chinese quarter of the town. I was amazed at the throng of people on every side, at the clamor and shouting of voices. Street vendors stood behind their portable stoves; pig-tailed coolies squatted on the pavement with rice bowls held under their chins with one hand and chopsticks with which to eat in the other. An old black-clad woman sat in a doorway smoking an immensely long pipe; small children went by carrying other children, not much smaller than themselves, in cotton slings upon their backs. Young men and old men, young women and old women, clad in blue or black garments, moved in and out of the crowd, making way for the carriage to pass and yet never pushing or jostling one another, which surprised me. An old man came into sight bent under a long pole upon which were slung several bamboo cages wherein crouched timid and silent birds. I turned to Mr. Meade with a protest at the pathetic sight and at the same moment he spoke to me, saying, "Why there is Hawkes over there. I thought he had left for Canton."

With the words "Oh, the little birds" on my lips, I looked where Mr. Meade indicated and saw Captain Hawkes in the carved doorway of one of the larger houses. His tall figure towered conspicuously above the small one to whom he was speaking, and as the carriage drove past I saw that his companion was a young Chinese girl. I could not see her face, only the top of the embroidered jacket she wore and the shining black hair brushed smoothly from her face and rolled into a knot at the back where it was secured by silver pins that glinted in the sunshine.

Captain Hawkes turned his heaad at the sound of the carriage and, recognizing Mr. Meade, and, in all probability, myself, acknowledged us with a salute of his hand which Mr. Meade returned. I had no time in which to think of the captain or his companion, for the next moment the carriage turned into an even narrower lane and stopped outside a two-storied brick house.

We had arrived at the Mission.

CHAPTER 4

A YOUTH dressed in baggy blue trousers and a knee-length Chinese jacket opened the gate in the wall and, bowing low, gestured for us to enter. While the coachman lifted down the luggage, we walked into an open courtyard with rooms opening out on either side. A wooden door ahead of us stood ajar and on the threshold appeared Dr. Howard, his hand outstretched in welcome. After we had exchanged greetings he led us into a large room with a raftered ceiling and furnished with tall carved chairs set against the walls, with tables placed neatly at intervals between the chairs. There was no furniture whatsoever in the center of the room, a characteristic, I was to learn, typical of Chinese houses.

Here Mrs. Howard was waiting to welcome me, and as we talked, the same smiling boy who had opened the gate brought tea to us. Mrs. Howard was so quiet and gentle a person that I soon felt at ease with her, but when Mr. Meade rose to go, I admit to feeling suddenly very alone. The Meades had become almost like a family to me by now and with Mr. Meade's departure I felt strangely bereft, and longed for Arthur as never before. If he had been alive I should be living here now with him as his wife.

The tears pricked my eyelids and I turned away lest Mrs. Howard should see my distress. Then to my relief, a small, plump Chinese woman came into the room holding a child by either hand, and the next moment I was being introduced to George and Dorothea Howard, aged seven and five, respectively. George was merry-faced and auburn-haired, while Dorothea was small for her age with immense dark eyes in a pale little face. They were friendly, polite children and I knew I should be happy to be with them and teach them all I could.

When the amah had led them away Mrs. Howard showed me the room where I would sleep. It was of medium size and looked out onto a courtyard filled with flowers and shrubs. There was little furniture in the room—a table and a stool and a carved teakwood chest. The bed was fairly ornate, with a wooden canopy of red-and-gold lacquer and hanging curtains. I glanced around at Mrs. Howard.

"Did Arthur— Was this—was this Arthur's room?"

She looked completely taken aback at my question. Her pale face flushed, her blue eyes glanced away from me, and she caught her underlip between her teeth, as if to check the answer she would make. After a moment she said uncertainly, "No—no. Arthur's room was on the other side of the courtyard, a—smaller room. His things are still in it. I thought you might want to send what you thought fit back to his father. Did you know him?"

"No. He lived some distance from Partrishow. He corresponded—he wrote a kind letter to me upon my engagement to Arthur. But my passage to Macao was so quickly arranged that I did not have time to visit him and Mrs. Crosby."

"I understand."

"You were here when—when Arthur died? Did he speak of me? Did he know he would not recover?"

Now Mrs. Howard looked fearful rather than startled. The flush had faded from her cheeks; she was white and strained, and not only did she glance away but she turned from me and walked to the window to stand fingering the shutter as if it concerned her more than my question.

At last she said, over her shoulder, "I was not with Arthur. I—I do not think anyone was. He died very suddenly, you see. We—no one expected it to happen."

I was aghast at her words.

"How dreadful. Oh, poor Arthur, to be alone like that. If only someone had known how ill he was. If only Dr. Howard had been with him. Arthur thought so highly of your husband."

"Yes, I know." Mrs. Howard turned back to me. "I was not well myself at the time," she said nervously. "It wasn't easy— I could not—I grieve for you, Miss Jones. Believe me, we all do." She sighed. "No one will ever know the tragedy of it all."

The note in her voice alarmed me. I glanced quickly at her.

"Is there anything more *to* know?"

"No—no, of course not. I meant—it is just—" Her voice broke. Then she said, as if with a great effort, "You must try to put it behind you now. God will give you strength to face the future and Dr. Howard and myself will be your friends."

"Thank you."

"I will leave you to unpack if you so wish. Or to rest. We eat midday dinner and a light supper early in the evening. Please join us when you are ready, Miss Jones. The children will be eager to see you again."

"I would like you to call me Megan," I said. "And I am very grateful to you for your kindness."

Mrs. Howard smiled but made no answer, merely going quietly out of the room.

I turned back to the window but I did not see the flowers and the shrubs, as before. I seemed only to see Arthur, tall and fair and smiling. Arthur with his zest for life and his eager spirit. That he, of all people, should have died so alone shattered me. And that there was some mystery to his death I was beginning, in an obscure way, to fear.

One sad morning I went through Arthur's possessions and packed them up, ready to send by the next available ship to his father in England. They were pitifully few. Some books, a Bible and prayer book, and the first part of a translation of the Gospel into Chinese characters. The latter I gave to Dr. Howard, and also Arthur's clothes, for they would be given away, through the Mission. There were some bundles of letters, a few from his father, which would be returned to him. My own letters I could not bear to read through; when I started to do so the tears poured down my cheeks. My letters were so full of hopes and plans. In the end I destroyed them. There was a traveling rug, which I kept, placing it across the foot of my bed and thinking how it had lain on Arthur's.

There was no diary or journal, which surprised me, for I had fully expected that Arthur would keep such a thing.

I wrote to his father and to his two sisters and to his brother in Canada and felt that I had done all that I could do.

At first, life in the Mission seemed very strange. There was much to do and to learn, for which I was thankful, for work assuaged grief. Apart from Dr. Howard and Mrs. Howard and the two children, everyone else with whom I came in contact was Chinese. The staff of the Mission was not large. It comprised Wu Chin, the houseboy; Soo Kwei, the cook; and Toh Chung, the amah. In addition there was a man-of-all-work, a coolie named Ah Sing. There was also a young Chinese student teacher named Chao Tsan. He was twenty years of age and tall and good-looking, with clear golden skin, dark slanting eyes, and dark shining hair brushed back from a high forehead and worn in a queue. As he could speak excellent English we soon became friends and he was helpful to me in many ways.

Dr. Howard had followed the example of the early missionaries and had taken in several Chinese children to grow up with his own. It was like a boarding school in miniature, for there were eight of them in all. They learned English and were given teachings of the Gospel, while Chao Tsan taught them Chinese classics in addition to figures.

Mrs. Howard had formerly helped with the children, but since her illness she had been unable to do so except occasionally, as she was required to rest a great deal. I was only too happy to take her place and teach the Chinese children, along with George and small Dorothea. My greatest handicap was ignorance of the Chinese language, but this began to be remedied when Chao Tsan offered to give me daily lessons. I was pleased, for I remembered how diligent Arthur had been in studying Chinese, and he had once told me that the first thing a missionary to China must undertake was to learn the language. Only in this way would one truly understand the people or be able to work in close contact with them. Often it was the missionary who was called upon to act as interpreter for a businessman or diplomat simply because it was he who could write or speak Chinese. Businessmen would not waste time in the difficult study of the language and conducted their dealings through an agent or by the use of pidgin English. It was Arthur who had explained to me that the word "pidgin" was, in fact, the Chinese pronunciation of the word "business."

I had not forgotten Captain Hawkes or his generous offer of a passage home on his ship. I was grateful to him, but as I settled into life at the Mission I had no regrets at not accepting his invitation. Despite my heavy heart and the constant ache of sadness over Arthur's death, I felt I had made the right decision in remaining in Macao.

I unpacked my few possessions and tried to make the room homelike despite the Chinese-style furniture. In my trunk was the linen and the warm Welsh blankets and patchwork quilt I had brought as dowry to my marriage. I could scarcely bear to unpack them for use, but I braced myself to do so. I was not yet used to sleeping on a mat laid over boards, Chinese fashion, and the addition of linen and a quilt gave me comfort.

The simple white wedding dress wrapped in tissue I did not unpack. I did not even unfold it but laid it back in the trunk and tried to stem the tears that fell. Without ever forgetting Arthur I resolved to put my past hopes and dreams behind me.

I did not forget him, but it seemed that Dr. Howard and Mrs. Howard were determined to do so. They never mentioned his name, and I was puzzled and hurt by this. If I made a reference to Arthur or quoted some saying of his, they never responded in kind but, with careful politeness, turned the conversation so that no further reference was made to him. I could not understand it.

Was it because they thought that speaking of Arthur

would grieve me? Did they feel it was better that I should forget him? I did not know, and when once or twice I spoke to Chao Tsan of him, it was to find an even more enigmatic avoidance of my questions.

The house Dr. Howard had rented was large, with ten rooms and two courtyards. One of the rooms facing the street Dr. Howard used as his study and reception room, and the other was used as a schoolroom for the Chinese children. The reception room was furnished in Chinese style, with carved wooden chairs, somewhat hard and uncomfortable, set against the walls, interspersed with tea tables. Many people came daily to speak with him, for Dr. Howard was fluent in the language and could answer their many questions as to the teachings of Christianity. Every Sunday morning he conducted a service in the reception room. The members of the congregation were apt to wander in and out, or would sit somewhat inattentively, tidying their children's hair and talking to one another, and once an elderly woman came in carrying a small dog. But some were sincere converts and all were appreciative of Dr. Howard's care and friendship.

He was a serious and dedicated man, his somber face seldom lightened by a smile. One day he confided to me that his ambition was to take the Mission into the interior of the country.

"Most of the missions are settled on the coast because of the restrictions of the Chinese to foreign travelers. But some have gone inland and opened missions far from here and I hope and pray that I may be one of that band. Three workers are coming out from England next month. One of them will accompany me on the journey to Chen-Lin, and we shall travel in Chinese dress and wear queues." When I stared at him he gave me one of his rare smiles and said, "They will be attached to the inside of our hats, Miss Jones. I fear we cannot grow them."

I smiled back at him.

"And the other two—are they to remain here?"

He nodded.

"Yes, for the time being. They are a brother and sister

who have worked here before and have been on leave in England."

"They—they would have known Arthur?"

As usual he hesitated.

"Yes, but—they were not here when—when Arthur died." He frowned. "It will be a shock to them, as it has been to all of us." He turned away. "If you will excuse me— there are some papers I must attend to."

I stared after him, puzzled and baffled as ever.

There was little time for sight-seeing, but once or twice I accompanied Mrs. Howard on a visit or errand and then I had an opportunity to see something of the strange and fascinating city that was Macao. The architecture was of Mediterranean origin, for the province had been occupied by the Portuguese since 1557. Many of the beautiful and ornate churches built in Portuguese style were now crumbling into decay, but some retained something of their former splendor. The great mansions of the early settlers were better preserved, with shuttered windows and delicate wrought-iron balconies and walled gardens rich in greenery and flowers. The wide tree-lined avenues and spacious formal squares and whitewashed convents gave clear evidence of the time when Portugal was a great maritime power. Immense trade flourished first between China and Japan and later, with the establishment of the East India Company and the headquarters of the Company's powerful Select Committee in Macao itself, with Europe. Here East and West met as in no other city or province of the East.

The Chinese quarter, wherein the Mission stood, was for the most part a congestion of tiny one-room houses opening onto the street where narrow alleys ran upward in flights of steps. Here, from early morning till late at night, sounded the sharp and noisy chatter of Chinese voices. Here old men and old women squatted in the roadway, gambling, while half-naked children with black-fringed impish faces tumbled about them. In this part of the city the temple gongs echoed and the air reeked of sunflower-seed oil and cooking stoves and the burned gunpowder from the fireworks and firecrackers of yet another feast day. It was a world such as I had never known.

One particular day I was on my way back to the Mission when I was halted by the beating of gongs and a drawn-out wailing sound that seemed to alarm every nearby inhabitant. Men and women flattened themselves against their stalls or stoves or the walls of the houses and stood with hands at sides and heads bent in assumed humility. A group of men, brandishing long rattans in their hands, suddenly appeared around the corner of the street. They were followed by another, more authoritative-looking group who flourished chains. I stared in alarm at their menacing appearance and was about to turn and make my retreat when I felt a hand on my arm and a familiar deep voice say in my ear, "Stay where you are. Here comes the mandarin."

I turned to speak to the captain, but he frowned and shook his head. The richly dressed figure in the massive chair carried by eight bearers passed by, and when the sound of the last gong and the noisy wailing had faded into the distance, the street returned to its ordinary activities.

Captain Hawkes released his hold of me and said, "I am sorry if I had to restrain you somewhat forcibly, but it is the custom to stand still when the mandarin goes by."

"Thank you." I could not help adding, "It must be a custom hard for you to abide by."

He shrugged.

"I can be discreet enough if the situation warrants it."

"I thought you might have left for England by now."

"We shall be gone within the fortnight." His blue eyes narrowed as he stared down at me. "I trust you keep well, Miss Jones."

I had forgotten how tall he was, how keen his glance. He towered over me, his blue jacket hooked by one finger over his shoulder. He was wearing white ducks and a freshly laundered white shirt, the peaked cap on his brown hair tipped back at a careless angle. He looked cool and confident and, somehow, formidable. A man equal to any situation that might arise.

"I am well enough, thank you."

"You decided against the opportunity to return to England and have become a missionary after all?"

I said stiffly, "I work at the Mission, yes."

"Are you on your way there now? You should not walk unaccompanied in the streets. I will be your escort, if you will allow me."

"Thank you, but I have not far to go. I had been to the hospital where Dr. Howard gives his services three days a week."

"Why did you not take a sedan? It is the custom."

I answered more primly than I intended, "The chairs are a luxury we try not to indulge ourselves in."

He smiled sardonically.

"Of course. A hair shirt is requisite wear for a missionary."

I halted abruptly to demand in some indignation, "Why do you always speak so disparagingly of a group of people who give their lives to the service of others?"

"If I were to tell you that, we should fall out with each other."

"We are close to doing that now, so speak frankly, please."

"Then I will say this. China is a vast country and it has a culture at once civilized and artistic. It has seen the rise and fall of many empires, from that of Egypt to those of Greece and Rome, and it still remains the only great monument to the past. It is a law-abiding country and no people in the world are more courteous to a stranger. Their architecture is magnificent, their artistic achievements admirable. Into this wholly integrated and self-contained kingdom come a handful of missionaries to begin their pitiful attempts at converting the so-called heathen. In the process they set aside age-old customs and ways of living and do more harm than good. In my opinion such well-meaning busybodies would be better occupied in trying to improve the lot of their fellow countrymen instead of endeavoring to spread the Gospel here. There has been trouble and poverty enough among the working classes of England these past few years. If the energies and funds of the missionaries had been thrown into the struggle for such things as Chartism, the Ten-Hour Bill, and passage of the Factory Acts and the Corn Law Repeal they might have done more good. Let China work out its own salvation."

When he paused for breath I said protestingly, "We are a religious order, not a political one. It is the duty of a missionary to bring the teachings of Christ to those who do not believe. I think you are both prejudiced and mistaken in your criticism of good and self-sacrificing men and women."

He shook his head.

"Your evangelical zeal is wasted upon me, Miss Jones, so do not preach. You asked me to be frank; now you are angry, just as I expected you would be. Shall we walk on?"

I bit my lip and with burning cheeks and head held high walked beside the captain in silence.

Not a word passed between us until we reached the gate leading to the Mission. Then I turned and said, without looking at him, "Thank you for walking with me. Goodbye, Captain."

"Goodbye, Miss Jones. Our views are too at variance for us ever to be on amicable terms, but as it is unlikely that our paths will cross again, that should not matter to either of us. I wish you well." He swung away from me and strode off.

I had been looking away from him so I did not see him go, only heard the echo of his footsteps on the cobbles. Because I was looking in the opposite direction I became suddenly aware of a figure watching me from a doorway. The figure was not near enough for me to see whether it was a man or a woman, but something secret yet alert in the stance made me conscious of being closely observed. The figure moved from the shadow of the doorway and, with one long, backward glance at me, turned and pattered away. My observer was a Chinese girl, a girl in blue trousers and an embroidered jacket. There was something familiar about her and then I remembered. It was the same girl whom I had seen once speaking with Captain Hawkes.

As I turned to the gate, which old Ah Sing, nodding and smiling, had come to open for me, I wondered at the Chinese girl's interest in me. Or was it in Captain Hawkes? Well, it was no concern of mine. I had seen the last of him and for that I was grateful.

CHAPTER 5

By comparison with her strong-minded, resolute husband, Mrs. Howard seemed a shadowy person. But she was gentle and good and one could not help but become fond of her. I was glad I had agreed to come to the Mission, for as May passed into June the weather became increasingly hot and humid and poor Mrs. Howard grew more tried and listless than ever. This distressed her, for she could not be with her family as much as she wished.

"It is a blessing they have become attached to you, Miss Jones. You are so good with children."

"Am I? I have not been used to children, but George and Dorothea are little trouble and it is a pleasure to teach them."

She sighed, lying back in the one comfortable chair. The Mission was sparsely furnished throughout. The few Chinese pieces had come with the rented house; for the rest we made do with boards and trestles in place of tables and we sat on wooden benches for our meals of Chinese food. We ate off bare boards, set with basins and chopsticks, which I soon came to use with dexterity. Upstairs, the bedrooms were equally austere, the beds a simple wooden frame strung with coconut fibers.

"You would have made a good wife for a missionary. You are very capable, and although you are so small, Miss Jones, you seem robust. You are standing up well to the heat, and as well as having the physical stamina that I envy, you have an air of inner strength. It is very sad that—that Arthur should have died."

I was so startled to hear her mention his name of her own accord that I could only stare at her. Then I said quickly, "I wish so much that I knew more of how he died. It seems dreadful to me that he was alone."

She gave me an almost guilty glance and then looked away as she had done so often before. After a moment she said slowly, "I think—I am not sure—Chao Tsan—he—he may have been the last one to see Arthur. But it will do no good—it is better left."

"*Why* is it better left? What is the reason for this mystery?" I demanded.

Mrs. Howard seemed to shrink back against the cushions of the cane chair in which she half sat, half lay.

"I am sorry—I should not have spoken as I did. Dr. Howard would—would not wish it."

She put her hand to her forehead, looking so piteous and bewildered that I said hurriedly, "Please do not distress yourself, Mrs. Howard. It is all right. We will not pursue the matter."

She said again, "I should not have spoken as I did."

"Nor should I. Please rest now, Mrs. Howard. I must go to the children. It is time for their lunch."

"Yes." She laid her head back on the cushions and closed her eyes. "I will be quiet for a little while."

As I walked down the stairs and into the courtyard, where I knew the children would be playing, I was deep in thought and I resolved that at the first opportunity I would question Chao Tsan. I knew that this morning he was in the dispensary, with Dr. Howard, for on the mornings Dr. Howard did not go to the Mission Hospital he saw patients in the dispensary, located in a small building at the side of the house. Sometimes I saw the poor people waiting in the street, suffering from ailments of which there was little hope of cure, only of alleviation. Many of the children suffered from diseases of the eyes and there was much cataract and trachoma. Malaria, dysentery, cholera and typhoid were prevalent, and the remedies mostly the simple ones of quinine, ipecac, calomel and castor oil. All that could be done was done, but, generally, these unhappy people did not come to the dispensary until their illness was well estabilshed and then recovery was often doubtful.

The courtyard was simply laid out. There was a drooping willow tree and three slender bamboos. An apricot tree was in bloom, and near it stood a tall green jar planted with camellias. Nearby was a small tiled pool where goldfish darted to and fro in the shadows. George and Dorothea, who were standing with two of the Chinese children watching the fish, turned at the sound of my step and came running to me, George, boisterous and lively, Dorothea, following after him, more quietly, the other children, Chung Kan and Hai Chutsai, on either side of her. The latter were a bright, merry pair with sparkling black eyes and straight black hair cut short and worn with a fringe over the forehead. Both were in short blue jackets and blue trousers, as were George and Dorothea, for Dr. Howard liked them to wear Chinese dress.

They surroundeed me, babbling in a mixture of languages; George and Dorothea already knew many Chinese words, and Kan and Chutsai were anxious to demonstrate their command of English. I found all the Chinese children with whom I came in contact extremely polite and well behaved and they were quick to learn and assimilate. When we had settled all the problems that beset them we went through the iron gate of the courtyard into the house to find the rest of the children waiting for their midday meal. The food was simple, soup with savory dumplings, rice in bowls, to be eaten with chopsticks of red-painted wood, and, of course, the invariable pot of tea and tea bowls.

When the meal was over I marshaled the children upstairs for their afternoon rest and then decided to go in search of Chao Tsan.

I encountered Chao Tsan on the way to his own room and said hesitatingly that I would like to speak with him privately. He was too polite to reveal the surprise he might feel at this request and merely, with hands hidden in the sleeves of his blue jacket, bowed with an inclination of his head for assent. Opening the door of his room he gestured for me to enter and then, leaving the door discreetly ajar, brought forward a chair for me to sit on.

It was the first time I had been in what was obviously his study-bedroom, for there was a plain wooden desk near the window and many books ranged along the walls. A wooden crucifix hung on the wall over the narrow bed and a large Bible lay on a bedside table.

I sat down on the hard upright chair and Chao Tsan, with a murmured "Permit me to sit," took a small carved stool and sat directly opposite me.

He gave another polite inclination of his head.

"I am honored that the most gracious Miss Jones wishes to speak with me."

I hesitated, biting my lips as I struggled for the words.

"It concerns—it is about my fiancé—about Mr. Crosby. Mrs. Howard told me that—that you were possibly the last one who saw him alive." I leaned forward, my hands clasped tightly, almost imploringly, in front of me. "It has been such grief to me to think that my fiancé—that Arthur might have died alone. Were you with him?"

Tsan's thin, fine-boned face remained as impassive as ever, the dark almond eyes never changed expression. He merely sat there, hands tucked into his sleeves, his head slightly bowed.

After a moment he said quietly, "I was with the honorable Mr. Crosby, but he was not conscious. He did not know that I was beside him"—he dropped his voice a note—"at the last."

I gave a long, heartfelt sigh.

"At least, if Arthur had regained consciousness—he would have had someone he knew with him. Were you—friends?"

Tsan nodded.

"I think you could say that, though I did not know him well. But I held him in great esteem." The black eyes stared at me in calm detachment. "He was a good man. His death was a tragedy. I will say no more."

"Thank you for telling me this. I am consoled by the thought that although Arthur was not conscious when he died, he had a friend beside him. He died of a fever, I understand."

Tsan inclined his head.

"That is possible."

"You do not know what the diagnosis was?"

"I was not told."

"But—" I broke off, aware once again of some obscurity about Arthur's death. "But that is what Dr. Howard said. That he died of a fever."

"Dr. Howard was not here at the time." Tsan leaned forward a fraction and said on a slightly nervous note, "Most gracious Miss Jones, please do not concern yourself further. I have assured you that your fiancé, the greatly lamented Mr. Crosby, did not die alone, as you had supposed. That gives you comfort. Here in the East, men—and women—die suddenly and without warning of an illness that may be hard to distinguish. Accept this fact. It will serve no purpose to pursue the matter."

For a moment we stared at each other. Although the opaque black eyes gazing into mine were expressionless I yet felt as if Tsan's glance transmitted some message to me. Perhaps even a warning.

I sighed, as if with resignation.

"I understand. Thank you, Chao Tsan." I rose from the chair and he too immediately stood up, and walking to the door, pulled it fully open and bowed to me.

"I am honored that the gracious Miss Jones has given me her confidence."

"I'm very grateful to you, Chao Tsan." On these words of courtesy we parted. As I went slowly in the direction of my own room I was aware that the mystery surrounding Arthur's death was as baffling as ever, but that I must do as Chao Tsan had advised and leave it in abeyance.

The hot weeks went by slowly. Dr. Howard was busy with the preparations for his visit to Chen-Lin. The journey was to be made by boat and mule, for the roads were bad from Canton, and indeed, little more than mule tracks. I had seen nothing of the Meades since I left the villa, and then an invitation arrived from Mrs. Meade asking me to visit them and to stay for the night, or longer if I was able to. The thought of seeing the kind Meade family again and, in particular, Sylvia, made me very happy, but I was hesitant to approach Dr. Howard regarding leave from the Mission.

He instantly banished my doubts.

"You must certainly go," he declared. "This is a good moment, before the Crows and Mr. Carter arrive. You have worked so hard you more than deserve a holiday. Write at once and accept Mrs. Meade's invitation."

And so, one morning early in July, I set off in the carriage that Mr. Meade had sent to fetch me. It was a glorious day and I thought the wide avenues of Macao had never looked more splendid, with the white buildings glittering in the sunshine, the tall trees casting shade across the pavements and the gardens full of flowering shrubs and blossoms. Soon it would be unbearably hot and by midday the shallow waters of the harbor would be steaming, the air dancing with heat. But at the moment it was pleasant enough.

As usual there was all manner of sights to capture one's attention, and at my request the coachman drove via the Large do Senado. This square was named when the title "Loyal Senate" was bestowed upon the municipality of Macao by John IV after the restoration of the Portuguese monarchy in 1640. In this beautiful square was the oldest hospital of the province, the original St. Raphael's Hospital, known as the Holy House of Mercy.

The carriage did not follow the curve of the harbor but forked left and went slowly up the Praia Grande, past the handsome baroque houses, colored pink and gold and ocher, surrounded by walls and shady trees.

The Villa Cicadela was a charming rose-pink house, built in colonial style, with long, elegant windows set under graceful fanlights on the ground floor and above these were smaller windows with narrow wrought-iron balconies. It was enclosed by trees, including many palm trees. A short drive led to a flight of shallow steps and handsome double doors standing open under a glass canopy. There were flowers everywhere, blossoms of red and pink and white with glossy green leaves.

A manservant came to the door and led me through the magnificent hall, with its black-and-white-tiled floor and beautiful curving balustrade. The moment the servant opened the door of the drawing room Sylvia sprang up from the damask-covered couch upon which she was sitting and came toward me with hands outstretched in welcome.

"Megan, how lovely to see you again. It has been too long a time." Her soft cheek touched my own and with her hand in mine she led me to her mother, who was sitting with the inevitable embroidery on her ample lap.

Mrs. Meade's welcome was as warm as Sylvia's.

"We have thought about you constantly, Megan, and Sylvia was glad to have your note saying you were settling down at the Mission." She shook her head. "It must be a very different life for you, and hard."

"It is an interesting life and not such hard work as the farm, I assure you. Dr. Howard and Mrs. Howard are very kind to me. But it is good to see you again."

"Sit down beside me," Sylvia urged, "and tell us the things you do. Is it true that you are learning Chinese?"

"Yes. One must try to do so if one is to work among the people." I smiled at Sylvia. "I am told it is difficult to learn the Chinese characters after the age of thirty so I must hurry up."

"I imagine it is not easy to learn such a language," Mrs. Meade said, with a shake of her head. She glanced over her gold-rimmed spectacles at me. "You look a little tired, Megan, and pale."

"It is the heat, I expect."

"Yes. We have come to a trying period of the season. Sylvia feels the heat too."

I looked at Sylvia, thinking she looked as beautiful as ever despite her pallor. She wore a dress of checkered pink muslin with three deep flounces and wide lace-trimmed sleeves, and her curling golden hair was caught up on top of her head for coolness.

Beside her I felt I presented an austere figure in the simple lilac print dress that had been made up for me by Mrs. Howard's Chinese dressmaker because my two other dresses were now too warm for the climate.

While I told them something of life at the Mission a servant came in with a tray of refreshing tea and thin biscuits made with rice flour.

"I have planned an excursion for us," Sylvia said. "Later, when it is cooler, we are to ride up Penha Hill and see the view. We are taking a picnic supper, and Papa is coming with us and also two other friends. You will enjoy it, Megan."

"I am sure I shall." I felt quite dazzled by my surroundings and by Sylvia's charm and grace and Mrs. Meade's motherly kindness.

After we had drunk the tea Sylvia suggested that she and I should take a walk through the garden.

"It is cool under the trees."

"Yes, I thought the garden looked inviting when I arrived."

The garden was indeed a pleasant place, laid out in the European fashion rather than in the Chinese, with drooping trees left untrimmed and cool lily-filled pools into which water trickled enticingly. The silence was broken only by the soft cooing of doves, for the heat was now so soporific that most of the other birds were silent.

Sylvia indicated a seat of wrought iron carved in a delicate lacy pattern.

"Let us sit and talk." She turned to me as we sat down together. "I have thought of you often and often, Megan. I think you have been very brave, choosing to work as you do. Have you recovered a little from the sad death of your fiancé?"

I said slowly, feeling this to be now true, "I have accepted it."

She sighed deeply and I saw the wistful expression in her lovely eyes.

"We have much in common, Megan. We have both lost the man whom we loved. Arthur through death and Henry, just as surely, by unhappy circumstance."

I touched her hand with mine.

"Whilst you are both in this world, you may hope."

She shook her head.

"You do not know my father. He can be stern and un-yielding when his mind is set against something. If only Henry and I were not so far away; if only we could write to each other. But my father overlooks the correspondence that comes to the house before anyone else and would never permit me to receive a letter from Henry." Her voice trembled to a stop and a tear rolled down her cheek. "Oh, Megan."

"Sylvia dear." I did not know what to say to console her and we sat in silence for a few moments, our hands clasped together. Then, abruptly, she shook her head and stood up.

"I am not going to spoil your visit with us, Megan. For-give me. But you are truly my only friend here. Oh, my parents know all manner of people—half the wives and fami-lies of the Company, and we are sociable enough. But there is no one else in whom I can confide but you. Only you, who have suffered so much more than I, can understand something of what I feel."

"I think I do a little."

We continued our promenade along the winding paths of the garden and then returned to the house for a glass of Madeira. Mr. Meade had returned from some business con-nected with the East India Company's Select Committee, which had its headquarters in the Camoëns Gardens. He greeted me kindly enough and I found it hard to believe he could be as harsh in his treatment of Sylvia's love affair as she had confided in me. Yet, glancing at him unobserved, I thought I saw obstinacy in the set of his pursed mouth and a certain look of despotism in his pale eyes.

After a delicious Portuguese-style meal I was taken to a cool shuttered bedroom where I was commanded to have a siesta as everyone else did at that time of day, and I fell asleep thinking about how cruel it was that Sylvia should be parted from her beloved Henry.

It was arranged that we should ride up to the summit of Penha Hill. Sylvia had changed into a simpler, more suitable dress for horseback, but she assured me that our mounts would only go at walking pace and the dress I was wearing would do perfectly well. So, in shady hats, and with a small pony laden

with picnic fare, we set off, Mr. Meade, well in advance, on a
tall horse, with Sylvia and myself following behind on sturdy
ponies, while Mrs. Meade elected to be carried in a sedan with
eight bearers instead of four for the task of transporting her
stout frame.

Mr. Meade halted to indicate an imposing residence set
among fine trees.

"That is the seat of the present governor of Macao—
Isidoro Francisco Guimarães. He was elected three years ago.
He is a good man." He gestured with his whip to the tall
church set on the peak of the hill. "And there is Penha Church
and the bishop's residence. We shall see them more clearly as
we ascend."

We were little more than halfway up the hill when we
came upon three people who had dismounted from their
horses and were evidently awaiting our arrival. The ponies
were glad to rest and the coolies bearing Mrs. Meade in the
sedan even more relieved. As we halted I heard Sylvia give an
exclamation, and turning my head, I saw that she looked as
dismayed as she sounded.

"Oh. Oh, it is Mr. Henshawe with the Barretts. He will
spoil everything."

I looked in the direction of the three people who were
waiting to greet us. There was one lady and two gentlemen
and all three looked agreeable and harmless enough, especially
the tall, thin man who was advancing toward us with a smile.
He had a pale complexion and fine aquiline features and dark-
gray eyes and seemed both handsome and distinguished. Yet
when he presented himself and bowed to Sylvia with a courteous, "Good day, Miss Meade. I trust I find you well," she all
but tossed her head in disdain as she answered stiffly, "Thank
you, I am well enough. Megan, may I present Mr. Henshawe,
an acquaintance of my father's. Mr. Henshawe—Miss Jones."

Mr. Henshawe inclined his head, smiling pleasantly.

"I am happy to meet you, Miss Jones." He glanced back
to Sylvia. "And to be invited to the picnic. It is cooler now,
and when we reach the top we shall find a welcome breeze, I
think."

As he was speaking, his companions sauntered across to us and I was introduced to them. Mrs. Barrett was in her late twenties and pretty, with dark curls showing under her wide-brimmed hat and with sparkling dark eyes, while Mr. Barrett was of medium height and stockily built, with fair hair and blue eyes.

Sylvia was more friendly in manner to Mr. and Mrs. Barrett than to Mr. Henshawe, whom she all but ignored, and when the three moved away to remount their horses, she turned to me and said hurriedly, in a low voice, "Come, Megan. Let us start off right away or Mr. Henshawe will ride with us the rest of the way." She flicked her pony's reins in such a manner that it started up in surprise and set off up the hill at a brisk pace, and after a moment's delay I followed.

I caught up with her to say, "What is amiss with Mr. Henshawe? He seems a pleasant man."

Sylvia glanced around at me, her brown eyes flashing.

"He has one great fault. He is not *Henry*." As I looked in some bewilderment at her she added impatiently, "Megan, can't you see? Mr. Henshawe has been invited to the picnic at my father's instigation. He is with the Company and he is wealthy and a widower. His wife died in childbirth a year ago."

"Oh, but that is sad. Poor man."

"It is very sad, and I am very sorry for him. But not sufficiently to encourage his attentions. It is *Henry* I love and always shall, and it is useless for my father to present these unattached men to me as he has now started to do." She looked at me quite fiercely and I was startled by the change in the usually gentle Sylvia. "Megan, you are *not* to leave my side. Do you hear? You are not to leave me alone with that man, for though he appears to be well mannered and polite, he is also remarkably persistent."

Sylvia's command was not easy to obey during the time spent on Penha Hill. I felt intrusive and uncomfortable in Mr. Henshawe's company, for, just as Sylvia had warned me, upon arrival at the picnic site he quickly attached himself to her. His courtesy and good manners were not to be faulted; he included me in the conversation and deferred in the politest way. Yet I was aware of a faint surprise in his glance, a puzzlement that I should remain so obstinate a duenna.

Although I was not diverted in my loyalty to Sylvia, I took pity enough on poor Mr. Henshawe to turn away and gaze at the view on several occasions. It was magnificent. Far below were the splendid white houses, half hidden by the rich green of the terraced gardens. All around me lay the sea, a deep, shining blue in the golden light of evening, with distant islands, bare brown cones for the most part, rising straight from the water. Few had habitation upon them; only the larger islands of Taipa and Colowan showed the green of vegetation. Some junks were at anchor on the harbor waters, their square sails hanging limp and still in the somnolent air.

Turning to look inland toward Canton I glimpsed a tall pagoda, all but concealed by trees, and past that, the sandy beaches of the coastal road leading back to the Praia Manduco and the Inner Harbor, where the tall masts of the junks and sampans jostled one against the other.

Sylvia called to me, drawing my attention to the picnic supper spread out for us on the cloth-covered grass. When we walked over to join the rest of the party I observed that she quickly found a place for herself between Mr. and Mrs. Barrett, leaving Mr. Henshawe to her father's company.

It was almost dark by the time we rode back down the hill, and lights shone between the trees and glittered like fireflies upon the shadowy sea. There were fugitive scents and sounds, the smell of freshly turned earth and the perfume of unseen flowers, the echoing boom of a temple gong. To Sylvia's chagrin, Mr. Henshawe and the Barretts were invited to the villa for a last glass of wine. This was no sooner served in the drawing room, doubly elegant at night with heavy gold curtains and the beautiful cut-glass chandeliers reflecting the many candles, than Sylvia made an excuse of a headache to retire early to her room. I could not accompany her and so remained making perfunctory conversation with Mrs. Barrett, who, upon learning I worked at the Mission, soon lost interest in me. Mr. Henshawe, his thin face shadowed by melancholy, lapsed into silence in his chair, so it was a relief to all when the evening broke up.

When, next morning, I reproached Sylvia for her cavalier treatment of Mr. Henshawe, she shook her head and defended herself, saying firmly, "I am being cruel to be kind. It is pointless to encourage Mr. Henshawe for I have not the slightest interest in him, and the sooner he accepts this fact, the better. But I blame my father, for I am sure he persists in raising Mr. Henshawe's expectations instead of telling him that my affections are already given to someone else." She tossed her head defiantly. "If the occasion arises I shall tell him so myself."

As before, Sylvia and I spent a pleasant morning in the garden and then, as the day advanced, retreated to the shuttered sitting room to sit in shadowy coolness. After luncheon, there was a short siesta before tea was served and the carriage was called for my departure.

"I cannot tell you how much I have enjoyed my visit," I told Sylvia as we said our reluctant goodbyes.

"And I, too, dear Megan. So I have another plan for us," she confided. "Papa returns to Canton in a little while and there is a scheme for some of us, that is, the wives of the Company and their families, to visit Canton and stay for a few days. You know how difficult this still is, despite the promise of concessions from the Chinese, but I think it will be arranged in the end. And if it is, I shall insist that *you* come with us. Perhaps with Dr. and Mrs. Howard—if Papa will invite them. But certainly *you* must come, Megan. It will be at the end of the summer I think."

I stared at her in amazement.

"Stay in Canton? But—would it be possible? I have my work at the Mission, and your parents might not . . ." My voice trailed off.

"Of course it is possible," Sylvia said firmly. "And you cannot work every day of the year." She leaned forward to kiss me. "You will see, Megan. This is only *au revoir*."

I kissed her and was clasped in Mrs. Meade's motherly embrace before being helped into the carriage. I had said goodbye to Mr. Meade earlier, for he had gone out on business matters but had insisted that I should be driven back to the Mission.

As we turned out of the gates of the Villa Cicadela and trotted up the avenue leading to the Praia Grande, my head seemed to whirl from the pleasures of the last two days. I was touched by the kindness shown to me by Mr. and Mrs. Meade. And despite my doubts as to the possibility, I could not help daydreaming a little of going to visit the great city of Canton, of which I had already heard so much.

CHAPTER 6

A WEEK LATER Miss Crow and her brother, Hubert, accompanied by Mr. Carter, arrived, and preparations for the departure to Chen-Lin were accelerated. The morning came when Mrs. Howard bade her husband a tearful farewell, and to the accompaniment of waving children, bowing servants, and the good wishes of Mr. and Miss Crow and myself, the party set off, dressed in Chinese garb, and each carrying packs and a roll of bedding.

The house seemed strangely quiet after they had gone and for a while I sat with Mrs. Howard, who was convinced she would never set eyes upon her husband again.

"Yet I would not wish to accompany him if I could," she confided to me. "The fact is, Miss Jones, I do not care for the Chinese people. I know it is wrong. They are good people, but I do not like foreigners of any kind." She sighed, shaking her head. "I try to hide the fact from Dr. Howard, but I fear that at times he suspects and I feel that I have failed him as a wife. He should have married someone who would share every aspect of his life with the Mission. Someone like Miss Crow."

I tried not to smile at the idea of Dr. Howard marrying Miss Crow. Or any man, for that matter, for she was the queerest, ugliest little woman I had ever set eyes upon. Her face was long and horselike, with heavy features and sallow skin. Her eyes, behind thick pebble glasses, were a pale indeterminate gray, and sadly, she suffered from a curvature of the spine, so that her neck appeared to be sunk between her shoulders.

And yet I discovered in the short time we had been acquainted that she was the soul of goodness. An aura of kindliness and simplicity surrounded her, so that despite her unprepossessing appearance, one was drawn to her. The children loved her, as did the Chinese servants, and the people who came to listen to the Bible readings or to visit the dispensary called her "Elder Sister" in the most respectful and affectionate way.

Mr. Crow, like his sister, was middle-aged, and was a quiet scholarly man, who spoke and wrote fluent Chinese. He had already translated the Gospel of St. Matthew into Chinese and was now working upon the Gospel of St. John.

Both he and Miss Crow expressed their grief and sympathy to me over Arthur's death. I could see that it was a great shock to them, and once Miss Crow took my hands in hers, and looking up at me, for though I was not tall, she was even less so, said in the gentlest manner, "My dear Miss Jones, my heart aches for you in your loss. But God has given you courage and you will carry on Arthur's work, I am sure. I will pray that you will be given help and guidance."

"Thank you." I did not know what else to say. I knew that I wanted to work at the Mission and yet I doubted in my heart that I was sufficiently dedicated to become one of them. I looked at Miss Crow and then I looked quickly away. I admired her so much, but I did not want to become like her. I had come to Macao because I loved and was loved. I should have been wife now to Arthur. In my mind, I seemed to hear the echo of Captain Hawkes's disparaging remarks about female missionaries and elderly spinsters. I had answered him with some bravado, but standing there, with little Miss Crow gazing up at me with such intensity, I knew that my heart was divided. I was not yet ready to accept my destiny at the Mission.

July passed into August, and one day, returning from a walk with the children, I became suddenly aware that the sky had grown overcast and was colored a strange metallic hue, that the wind had risen and was blowing in spasmodic gusts. I guessed it presaged the torrential rain that sometimes came with scarcely a warning.

Holding Dorothea's small hand in mine I urged the children to hurry, and with a quick patter of feet over the cobbles we all but ran down the lane that led to the Mission.

The first heavy drops of rain caught us as we came to the gate, which, almost before I had reached my hand to the bell, was opened by Chung Ling, an old servant long attached to the mission, gesticulating for us to enter so that he might lock and bar the gate behind us.

I stared around at him in surprise, but he shook his head and said, "Plentee big stolm come by-by." One wrinkled hand described a circle. "All alound—bang—bang. Lain evelywhere. Ah Sing closee gate—closee door. No come in—no go out."

We went into the house, which was in virtual darkness and stiflingly hot. The candles had been lit and also small lamps burning bean oil. Mrs. Howard, obviously relieved to see us safely home, told me that Mr. Crow was at the hospital, visiting a sick convert.

"I do not think he will attempt to come home until the storm has passed. *Oh!*" She gave a start as a clap of thunder, loud as a cannon roll, sounded above our heads. "Oh, dear, I hope there will be no damage. Once the windows were blown in, but Dr. Howard was here to see to matters."

"I am sure it is only a summer storm and will soon be over," I said consolingly. But in my ignorance I was wrong, and almost upon my words the storm broke with a noise and violence such as I had never experienced. The entire building shook under it, and the shuttered windows rattled and banged as if at any moment they would burst open.

We had gathered together in the downstairs room used habitually by Dr. Howard. Timid little Dorothea crouched on my knees, her face pressed into my shoulder, while George, trying hard to be brave, knelt at his mother's feet. Miss Crow and her pupils, both the resident children and the several Chinese who had been attending a lesson, huddled in a group beside us.

Ah Sing came running downstairs to say that one of the shutters had broken loose and called upon Soo Kwei, the cook, and old Chung Ling to help him repair matters as best they could. There were thumps and bumps and crashes from outside and the sound of the water cascading down the walls of the house and splashing onto the paving stones in a torrent.

After a while, putting Dorothea gently into her mother's arms, I went upon a tour of exploration. In the room upstairs Ah Sing and the other servants had managed to close the shutter and mop up the water that had poured in, but for the time being nothing could be done about soaked curtains and hangings. Rivulets of water appeared to have penetrated everywhere, even though the shutters were tightly shut, for the force of the wind had driven the rain through every crack and fissure.

As I retraced my steps downstairs, I heard a noise that seemed to penetrate the other sounds of the storm. It was a knocking, but so persistent and regular in its rhythm that I was convinced that someone was at the outer door.

I called to Miss Crow, who came to stand in the hall and listen with me.

"It must be someone trying to obtain an entry," I said in alarm. "Can it be your brother? We must unlock the door to see."

Miss Crow frowned anxiously up at me.

"It would surely not be Hubert. The storm has been going on for three hours or more. If he had left the hospital he would never attempt to come through to the Mission, for he knows too well what weather conditions can be at such a time. It must be a loose shutter or door that we hear."

I listened again and above the fierce onslaught of the wind I thought I heard a shout and after that a renewed knocking. Then, abruptly, it ceased.

For what seemed a long period of time Miss Crow and I stood in the hall, alert and listening. The screech of the wind continued, but the insistent knocking had finished.

Miss Crow gave a sigh of relief.

"It must have been a shutter upstairs and one of the servants has repaired it. There is no one at the door."

"Or they have gone away," I said slowly.

The storm raged for another three hours, ebbing at intervals and then returning to the attack. Gradually the last rumble of thunder faded and the rain dwindled to a patter and finally ceased. Long before the storm was over, the house had become a scene of activity, with rooms being mopped and cleaned and the soaked curtains and hangings dried as much as possible.

My own bedroom had withstood the force of the storm well, and apart from the rivulets of water that had penetrated between the shutters, the bed and curtains were only slightly dampened.

Miss Crow went to supervise a meal of tea and rice for the children and for the people from outside who had remained to shelter with us. I was about to assist her in this when I saw that Chung Ling was at the front door unfastening the shutter and on impulse I went to look outside.

The courtyard presented a scene of wreckage, with leaves and twigs and branches scattered across the paving. One of the bamboos was split halfway down and the willow leaned over at an angle, while the apricot tree had scarcely a leaf left on its branches. The green ceramic jar was shattered and the camellias blown to the four winds. I could only stare in dismay at the sad spectacle and wonder how it would ever be put to rights.

Chung Ling went back into the house with a shake of his head and a grunt of lamentation and I turned to follow him when I noticed that the gate in the wall stood ajar, as if it had been forced open. Perhaps it had swung to and fro in the night and this had been the cause of what I thought of as someone knocking?

It surprised me that Chung Ling had not gone to close it, and then I remembered that his filmy old eyes were far from sharp and he had in all probability not observed that it was open.

I walked across the courtyard, and as I put my hand on the latch, I saw that the gate now hung on its hinges as if indeed it had been damaged by the wind blast. It was difficult to close and I was struggling to adjust it when my glance was caught and held by what looked like the fallen trunk of a tree lying in the gutter only a few feet away from the gate. Staring harder, I saw that it was not part of a tree but a bundle of rags.

Something forced me to step into the roadway for a closer glance and then I halted, staring in horror at the emaciated form of a man lying with leaden-hued face staring up at the sky.

The livid features were skull-like in their gauntness, one claw-shaped hand was outstretched on the mud, the long, attenuated fingers stained as if with some dye. I knew, even without touching the poor creature, that I was looking at a corpse.

Thoughts and fears raced through my mind. Was it possible that this unhappy soul had come to the Mission door last night and knocked so persistently? And had he turned away in a final extremity of despair only to fall and die a few yards from the gate, which, being blown open by the wind, had promised him shelter?

I turned to go back to the house and fetch help when from a doorway some distance down the lane a figure emerged and advanced slowly toward me, and I saw, with a start of surprise, that it was the girl I had seen before, once with Captain Hawkes and once in this same roadway.

I said in my halting Chinese, "I think this poor man is dead. Do you know who he is?"

She gazed at me out of slanting black eyes and then, after a downward glance at the wasted face, nodded and said something in Chinese which I did not understand.

I shook my head.

"I am sorry . . ."

And to my surprise she answered in pidgin English. "Him plentee beggar man. Live alongee allee place." She shrugged. "Him die along too muchee opium smokee."

Opium. I shuddered, seeing the ghastly-hued skin, the stained fingers, and knowing, from what I had been told, that the girl was correct. He had died of the fearful opium drug.

I said slowly, hoping she would understand me, "I think he came to us at the Mission while the storm was on, perhaps for shelter. We heard knocking and thought it was a door or window banging." I bit my lip. "Perhaps he has died of exposure. His clothes are soaked through."

She shrugged again, and despite my sorrowful preoccupation I thought how graceful she looked in her black cotton jacket and trousers. She was beautiful too, with a skin of porcelain delicacy and glossy black hair pinned high on top of a long and slender neck. Tiny gold earrings were worn at the small, shell-like ears.

"Him no good. Too muchee opium."

"How dreadful," I said.

She gave me a sideways glance.

"Samee along him at Mission. Muchee opium."

I stared at her in astonishment.

"Someone at the *Mission?* What do you mean? Opium?"

"Plentee spokee opium. He die same along him." And she gestured toward the corpse at our feet.

"You mean someone at the Mission has died from *opium?* That is impossible. No one has died—" And I broke off, while a wave of trembling fear swept over me. Arthur had died. Arthur was the *only* person who had died at the Mission.

I turned on the girl angrily.

"Please do not say such a thing. It is very wrong. It is untrue and you must not speak in this way. I am going to fetch someone from the house." Without a backward glance I ran on shaking legs back to the courtyard and into the house.

I would not think of what the girl had said. I would not even remember it. In a frenzy of action I sought out first Miss Crow and then Mrs. Howard. On their instructions, Chung Ling and Ah Sing were commanded to bring the dead man into a room near the tiny chapel Dr. Howard had improvised at the back of the house. In the midst of all this Mr. Crow returned to the Mission and, thankfully, matters were put into his hands, and Ah Sing was sent to fetch one of the Portuguese police force.

It was confirmed that the unfortunate beggar had died from the taking of opium and that the storm and exposure had only hastened his death. No one could discover why he had come to the Mission, and it was thought he must have been seeking shelter or help of some kind.

Despite my firmest resolutions I could not stop myself thinking of the Chinese girl's words, and all the doubt and puzzlement over Arthur's death returned to me. And yet I knew it was inconceivable that he would ever take opium. For what purpose? One moment I was trying desperately to put it out of my mind and the next I was wondering whom I could question on the matter. I could not worry Mrs. Howard again and the Crows obviously knew no more than I did. The only ones who might tell me the truth were Dr. Howard or Chao Tsan.

Such dark thoughts seemed disloyal to Arthur. Arthur, who had been the soul of uprightness and integrity. No, it was impossible that he could ever have been involved in the vile traffic that was the curse of China. Finally I decided, seeing old Chung Ling shuffling around the house, that there must have been a servant at the Mission who had resorted to opium smoking and died of the drug. Thus consoling myself, I worked harder than ever in an endeavor not to dwell upon the incident, teaching the children and reading to them the simple Bible stories that held them spellbound, though I sometimes thought they regarded them as being similar to the numerous Chinese fairy tales so popular with professional storytellers.

I worked hard too at my study of the language and bent laboriously over my desk, painstakingly copying the Chinese characters with a brush, so that I might learn better how to communicate with the people. I suppose I had inherited a little of my father's scholarly aptitude, for the learning of the Chinese language and characters did not prove as daunting as I had expected. Or perhaps I applied myself the more diligently because my life was empty of other ambitions.

The better I grew to know the Chinese, the more I liked and admired them. I found them good-tempered people with a great sense of fun. They were calm and unhurried, seldom displaying impatience, and their courtesy was remarkable. I thought often of a saying I had learned from them: "Deal gently with the stranger from afar."

I learned that ancestor worship was the foundation of the Chinese religion and this accounted in good measure not only for their love of children but for their intense desire for them, above all, for sons. A man did not fear death, but he feared to die without leaving sons to worship at his shrine. If a man died childless, he left no one on earth to sustain him in heaven. He would be condemned to wander, a lonely ghost, hungry and forsaken, because he had no sons. There was another saying I learned: "If one has plenty of money but no children he cannot be reckoned rich; if one has children but no money he cannot be considered poor."

To these people, anxious and fearful of mortality, came the missions, with their teachings of the Resurrection and the life everlasting. The missionaries had come to this vast land following the command of Christ, who had said, "Go—teach all nations," and if I was not as yet a proselyte, I could not be other than an admirer of their dedication and self-sacrifice.

Dr. Howard, I knew, was resolved to found inland missions; to settle along the coast and in the ports were not sufficient. The Gospel must be taken to the interior, so far little known and scarcely visited except by the early Jesuits and other Catholics. There had been opposition and even persecution of Christians by the country people, but there was a feeling abroad that China could not remain forever the secret "Middle Kingdom" that it had been for so long.

In September Dr. Howard and his party returned to Macao. It was a day of great rejoicing when the weary travel-stained figures in shabby Chinese costume appeared in the courtyard. We were all eager to hear of their adventures.

Dr. Howard was high in praise of the people of Chen-Lin.

"We have been well received and I have every hope that we shall found our first inland mission there. Mr. Carter has remained behind to work and live with the people who so kindly gave us help and hospitality." He shook his head, his black brows knotted in a frown. "But there is much to do and we need many more recruits. I shall be writing to London on this matter."

For a few days after his return there was much talk and movement, and then the Mission settled down to its routine again. The weather was still hot but less oppressively so, and as the days passed, all felt more lively and energetic. In the courtyard the seedpods of the golden rain tree shone purple in the sunshine, and furry brown bees plundered the blossoms as if aware that summer would not last forever.

There were times when I looked first at Dr. Howard and then at Chao Tsan and was tempted to ask the question that, against every resolution, nagged at me. But, after hesitating, I would turn away. And then, one day, Tsan gave me the opportunity to speak.

We had just returned from the hospital together. I had been visiting a patient and Tsan had been helping Dr. Howard in his work. As we came through the gate to the courtyard, Tsan for the first time noticed the panels of new wood that had replaced the broken slats, and he said, "Was this another casualty of the storm?"

"Yes, it was broken from the hinges and some of the wood splintered."

"It must have been a bad night."

"It was very bad." I glanced at him and then the words seemed to burst out of me. "You know we found a man dead in the roadway? He had died from taking opium. Someone said—a Chinese girl told me that—that another man had died in the same way. A man from the Mission." I looked directly at Tsan. "It couldn't have been—it wasn't—*Arthur*? Oh, forgive me, there has been such mystery over his death. But I wondered—I could not help it." I broke off and after a moment said as calmly as I could, "Please tell me the truth."

Tsan gazed back at me, his black eyes expressionless. There was a long silence and then he said, "Most gracious Miss Jones, it is hard for me to speak of this, but you ask for honesty. It is true that the honored Mr. Crosby died from the taking of opium. Only I knew, for only I was with him." He saw the effect of his words, and without touching me, but with an almost imploring gesture, said quickly, "Please to sit down, Miss Jones. Please rest to recover yourself," and he pushed nearer to me the garden seat he had indicated.

I sank down onto it, aware of a shivering as if with cold. I closed my eyes against the horror of what I had heard. *Opium.* That vile and dreadful drug.

At last I managed to speak.

"But how? *Why?* And how is it no one else seemed to know of this dreadful occurrence?"

Tsan stood before me, his head bowed, his hands hidden in the wide sleeves of his jacket.

"It is something that has happened before to other people. Like the greatly lamented Mr. Crosby, a person takes a dose of opium against some pain or illness. Your honorable fiancé suffered a distressing toothache and resorted to the drug for relief. Certain constitutions succumb more quickly than others to the power of the drug and are unable to withstand its terrible consequences. So it was with the unhappy Mr. Crosby. In a short time after his introduction to opium he became a victim." He paused, frowning, and shook his head. "If we had known the facts, if we had realized what was happening, steps might have been taken to effect a cure. But alas, nothing could be done."

I sat with bowed head, my trembling hands clasped on my lap as I listened to Tsan's sad account of what had occurred. When he finished speaking I could find no words with which to answer him. I was utterly shattered by the double tragedy of Arthur's death. It was sorrow enough that he should have died so young; it was more grievous still that he should have died in such circumstances. I felt as if I were living through the heartbreak of it all over again.

Tsan stood silent before me. At last I lifted my head and said slowly, with tear-blurred eyes, "You said that you knew the cause of Mr. Crosby's death. Was Dr. Howard aware of it?"

Tsan shook his head.

"Not until the end. He had been away, in Amoy. When the honored doctor returned the day after the demise of your honorable fiancé, I acquainted him with the truth. It was decided between us that no purpose would be served by revealing the sad details of the esteemed Mr. Crosby's death. The honored Dr. Howard signed the death certificate and the cause of death was attributed to the fever and emaciation from which Mr. Crosby suffered. It was thought better that the reason for the fever should not be stated. Do you not think that it was kinder and wiser not to, as you say, dot every *i* and cross every *t*? There was his father in England to consider, as well as yourself, most gracious Miss Jones."

I sighed heavily.

"Yes, it was the kindest thing to do, although an evasion of the truth." For a few moments I was silent and then I looked again at Tsan. "The man who died—the beggar—in the road outside—do you think he had any connection with Mr. Crosby? It seems so strange that an opium addict should come here like that."

"I think it is very probable that he knew the late lamented Mr. Crosby," Tsan said slowly. Your esteemed fiancé would need to obtain the drug from someone outside, for although he resorted to opium in the first place for medicinal purposes, when the drug took a hold upon him, as evidently it did, he must have sought further supplies in secret. That is why no one here had any idea of what was happening until it was too late." He bowed his head. "I regret deeply that I am the unfortunate person who has had to reveal these facts to you, Miss Jones. I should prefer that you had remained in ignorance, as Dr. Howard wished that you should."

"And Mrs. Howard—did she know the truth?"

"I do not think she was told in so many words, but she may have guessed there was some instance that her husband preferred to remain silent upon."

I nodded, remembering Mrs. Howard's nervous manner with me, her evasive glance when I had questioned her.

"I prefer to have learned the truth." I sighed again. "It has made me more deeply aware than ever of the horror of the opium trade in China. Until the day I die I shall do everything I can to help fight it. It has been condemned by all good and thinking people in my country as unchristian, but we must protest even harder and fight against the evil of it."

"Do not reproach yourself too greatly, most esteemed Miss Jones. The fault is with my people as much as yours," Tsan answered. "Every business house and bank and shop here of any substance possesses its opium room, with the lamp lit, ready for the guest. These opium rooms are the equivalent of your own smoking rooms, and with us a whiff of opium takes the place of the glass of wine or brandy such as your traders indulge in."

"If that is true, there are less tragic consequences for us," I answered. "I know all too well that the only reason for the smuggling many of my countrymen indulge in is for the acquisition of the wealth it may bring them. It is a cursed trade and some say one that brings disaster and ill luck to those who indulge in it. I pray to God that one day it will end." I stood up. "Thank you, Tsan, for being honest with me. I shall not speak of this to Dr. Howard. I know the truth now of my fiancé's death, but it will remain a secret as far as I am concerned. I will leave you now," and slowly, and with heavy heart, I turned and walked away from him.

The knowledge of Arthur's sad death lay like a shadow over me for several days, and then gradually it lifted and once again I found consolation in my work at the Mission. As the month went on, the weather was less hot and tiring and sometimes we even felt a slight breeze on the September air.

One day, to my surprise, Mrs. Meade and Sylvia arrived at the Mission. They were taken to Mrs. Howard and I was sent for, and after the usual warm and affectionate greeting from them both, the reason for their visit was revealed. They brought a personal invitation to Dr. and Mrs. Howard and myself to go with them on the expedition to Canton.

"We shall stay several days," Mrs. Meade informed us. "The Company is to give a big dinner party one evening and there will be other entertainments. Of course, we shall not be permitted to visit the city of Canton, which is a great pity, but I am told that the sail up the Pearl River is both interesting and pleasant and we shall meet residents of the other hongs. Please say you will come, Mrs. Howard, and bring Megan with you."

Mrs. Howard's small face was pink with a flush of excitement and I had a glimpse of how pretty she could be.

"It is a delightful suggestion. I should so like to accept your kind invitation, Mrs. Meade, but, of course, the decision must rest with my husband." A frown puckered her forehead.

"And there are the children to consider. I do not know if we can leave them."

"It would be for only a few days," Mrs. Meade answered. "I hope Dr. Howard will consent. He will find it of great interest to himself, I am sure, and may form useful connections that will help the Mission."

Sylvia was sitting beside me and I felt the touch of her fingers on mine as she whispered, "No matter what, Megan, *you* are to come. The other members of the party are all married and I shall not enjoy it the same without you. I shall plead with Dr. Howard myself, if need be."

As it so happened, she had no need to go to such lengths or persuasion, for after a little while Dr. Howard joined us and, upon being approached about the matter, gave his immediate approval and acceptance of the invitation.

"I am sure Miss Crow and Hubert will take good care of George and Dorothea for us," he assured Mrs. Howard, "and we shall be away little over a week. As for Megan"—he turned and gave me what passed as a smile on his serious face—"she has helped to hold the fort for me while I was in Chen-Lin and is looking a little tired, so a short holiday for her seems clearly indicated."

Thus arrangements for the expedition were made and a date was fixed; during the last week of October we should leave Macao and travel by boat up the Pearl River to Canton. The party was to consist of Dr. and Mrs. Howard and myself and Sylvia and Mrs. Meade and two married couples: Mr. and Mrs. Barrett, whom I had met before on the picnic to Penha Hill, and another couple of middle age, a Mr. and Mrs. Dennison. Mr. Meade had returned to Canton some weeks before and would be waiting to welcome us when we arrived at the great hong of the East India Company.

It was a clear, bright morning when we sailed from Praia Manduco and, rounding Barra Point, sailed into Canton Bay on our three-day journey. I was excited and yet, as I looked back to see the green of Penha Hill and the towers and spires of Macao's many churches fade from sight, I felt the sense of sadness return. I remembered that first morning in April when we had arrived at the Baia da Praia Grande in the *Lotus Wind* and I had seen it all for the first time. I remembered my joy at the thought that within a few hours I should be reunited with Arthur, and that soon I should be his wife. And then the shattering news that he was dead. For a moment there, standing by the side of the ship, I could have put my face in my hands and wept for all that might have been.

Fortunately for my self-control, Sylvia came to stand beside me, full of comment and interest in the scene before us, and she was so eager to point out first this strange sight and then that one, that I found time in which to recover.

"What a lot of islands and some are quite green. Papa says later on we shall pass close to the Nine Pins. Oh, Megan, look! There is a picturesque sight—I have never seen such a splendid-looking junk."

I glanced around and saw a much-decorated ship looming over us, its great poop deck ornately carved, the muzzles of its guns painted an alarmingly bright red, as if the color itself must frighten off invaders. Streamers and dragon banners hung in all directions and upon her towering stern were painted three tigers' heads.

"It is impressive enough," said Dr. Howard, who had come up to us, "but most of these old ships are quite rotten within and they are gradually disappearing from the seas."

We watched it move somewhat cumbersomely out of sight and then directed our gaze to the many other craft that plied the vast river. The sampan that was taking us to Canton made steady progress and the Chinese crew busied itself moving the huge mainsail and sometimes taking a turn with the oars. A fire had been made in the stern and over this the cooks prepared a meal for us and very good it was. There were small dumplings made of prawns and whitefish, and ham chopped with parsley cooked in a chicken broth, followed by rice and noodles with bean sprouts and lychees, and tea. I could not imagine how such delicious food could be produced in so limited a space.

The first day passed idly but pleasantly and the panorama of the river provided ample entertainment for us.

Mrs. Howard, after her initial anxiety over George and Dorothea, settled down to enjoy the voyage up the river and by the following day already looked rested. Her usually pale cheeks acquired a becoming tinge of color and her blue eyes looked darker and brighter. She and Mrs. Barrett became friendly and sat talking together and sometimes I even heard Mrs. Howard's soft laugh.

It was expected that we would reach Canton by nightfall of the third day, for we had passed Old Duck Fort during the morning, and sure enough, that evening we reached Jackass Point and saw the lights of the city twinkling and shining ahead of us. Innumerable lanterns shone from the hundreds of sampans on the river, and the great factories of the hongs reared themselves against the dark night sky, glittering with lights so that the sky seemed ablaze with their reflection.

The sails were taken down and the Chinese crew paddled us slowly to the shore through a mass of boats, every one of which was lit by lamp or candle, tied up near the banks of the river. Here a gangway was placed in position and one by one we were helped ashore while a gathering of servants and coolies from Soo hong, where we were to stay, arrived to deal with the luggage.

We crossed a courtyard lit by lanterns and flares and in a few moments were being welcomed by Mr. Meade and several other gentlemen belonging to the Company. Then we were taken to our apartments to rest and refresh ourselves before dinner.

Sylvia and I shared a large, rather gloomy room looking out onto a courtyard. The furniture was of rich heavy mahogany with a four-poster bed hung with net and brocade curtains, very much in English style.

Sylvia had insisted on lending me a dress for the dinner party, which was to be held the following evening, and as, with a rustle of silk, I shook it out, I turned to thank her again for her generous thought.

"I have never possessed anything so beautiful," I said, smoothing the folds of Parma-violet-hued taffetas. "I will take great care of it."

Sylvia smiled.

"It is your dress—a gift from Mama and myself. Now do not frown in that way, Megan, and look so fierce. It is a roll of silk Mama had which she did not want. We thought you would not wish for a bright color and this seemed suitable in every way, so whilst a dress was being made for me we had this one sewn for you. We are almost the same size, though I am taller." She waved a graceful hand. "It was not difficult to arrange."

"Oh, Sylvia" was all I could say.

We did not dine with the Company that night, but with our own party in a comfortable paneled room obviously used for informal occasions. Mrs. Howard, feeling weary, soon retired, and after a short while Sylvia and I followed her example.

When we crossed the inner courtyard to our room it was too dark to see anything clearly. I could make out, by the light of the lanterns, a tiled floor and some shadowy pieces of sculpture; above our heads the sky glittered with stars and with the glow of lights from the great city that stirred in faint sound not a mile from us.

The dinner party given by the East India Company next evening was the most splendid occasion I had so far experienced. The reception was held in a handsome room hung with glittering chandeliers and furnished in mahogany and rosewood. The guests for the most part were male, for we were the only party of ladies, and so we were much fêted. As well as members of the Company there were guests from the Spanish, French and Portuguese hongs, a few of them resplendent in faded uniforms.

I felt shy and somewhat at a loss in such distinguished company, and so stayed close within Mrs. Meade's motherly orbit. I was grateful indeed for her generous gift of the new dress. I had never thought to look the least bit pretty, but tonight my black hair and dark eyes and pale skin were set off to advantage by the shot-silk violet of my dress, and the very rustle of its sweeping skirts gave me a confidence I would otherwise had lacked.

A tall figure came to stand before me and to my surprise I

recognized Mr. Henshawe. Perhaps I should not have been surprised, for he worked in the Company, but I was so pleased to see a familiar face that my acknowledgment of him was extra friendly.

As we spoke together I glanced across the room to where Sylvia stood surrounded by a bevy of admirers. As usual she looked beautiful and her white dress trimmed with gold lace, with gold fringe on the tiered flounces, set off her shining hair to perfection.

Mr. Henshawe's gaze followed my own and he said, with a wry smile, "Miss Sylvia is positively besieged. I could barely exchange a greeting with her. We are all in the same state of deprivation—lacking the charms of feminine company. Though I think," he added, "Miss Sylvia would command the same homage even if we were surrounded by our wives and sweethearts."

"Yes, I am inclined to agree."

He stared across the room, his gray eyes somber. After a moment he sighed.

"She is very young."

"Yes."

Conversation lapsed between us and then there was a rustle and movement among the guests and I saw that we were to go in to dinner.

Mr. Henshawe proffered his arm. "I think we are sitting near each other. May I escort you in, Miss Jones?"

"Thank you." We allowed for the protocol of the important guests going into the dining room ahead of us and then walked slowly into a vast room paneled in rich dark wood and lit by immense candle-filled chandeliers. A long table covered in shining damask and sparkling with silverware and cut glass took up much of the space, and a servant stood behind every chair. Grace was said by the Company's chaplain and after the amen we took our places for dinner.

I saw that Sylvia was seated on Mr. Henshawe's other side, and turning my head I glanced to see who was my other dinner companion and saw, with some surprise, that the chair was empty.

Mr. Henshawe was speaking to Sylvia. I waited until he

had finished and then looked around to comment on the empty chair, but at the same moment I saw him glance upward and smile and I sensed the movement of someone taking the seat beside me.

I heard Mr. Henshawe say, "We thought you had forsaken us, Hawkes," and at the last word I felt myself give an uncontrollable start. Without raising my gaze from the gleaming tablecloth, I heard a familiar voice say, "I was delayed coming from Whampoa. I have just made my apologies to Mr. Brocklebank," and then, on a drier note, "Good evening, Miss Jones. I did not know I was to have the pleasure of your company this evening." Forcing myself at last to look around I encountered the formidable blue gaze of Captain Hawkes.

CHAPTER 7

FOR WHAT SEEMED a long moment we stared at each other without speaking, myself because I could not find the words with which to answer his sardonic greeting and the captain because he chose to regard me with a hard, assessing look, frowning the meanwhile.

I collected myself sufficiently to say, "It is as much a surprise to me as to you, Captain. I did not know you were returned to China."

"My ship anchored at Whampoa but three days ago, and upon reporting to the Company I found myself invited to this novel occasion."

"I did not know you were connected with the East India Company, and why do you refer to this occasion as novel?"

"Because it is a great rarity for any ladies to visit Canton. The last time was a year or so ago I believe." He added in the driest manner possible, "You can imagine the feverish state of pleasure that has consumed us at the prospect."

I said stiffly, "You choose to exaggerate, Captain Hawkes."

"A little perhaps, as regards myself, but not, I am sure, for the rest of the gentlemen. They suffer a greater deprivation than I do, being incarcerated within these walls for weeks, months at a time. Do you know that the members of these trading companies are permitted by the Chinese authorities to venture beyond the boundaries of the warehouses only three days a month, when they are allowed to take exercise in the flower gardens across the river? And this only in limited numbers and always accompanied by a Chinese interpreter."

I looked at him aghast.

I did not realize the rules were so stringent."

He shrugged.

"The authorities will be forced to show greater leniency in time. It is absurd that members of the companies should be forbidden their wives here. When I add that members are even forbidden to row upon the river you will understand how carping the rules seem."

"I thought you wished for China to retain its old ways and not be changed by foreign intervention."

I half expected him to be annoyed at the reminder of his earlier statement to me, but to my surprise he smiled. Only slightly, but a quiver of amusement touched the firm mouth, and I was aware, as I had been at first sight of him that evening, that he looked both handsome and distinguished. He was wearing full-dress uniform, the dark blue of the double-breasted tailcoat set off by gold epaulets and gold buttons. Above the rim of white collar his skin was smooth and brown, the lean jaw scarcely hidden by the trim brown beard and brown sideburns. From under the level brows his eyes shone, deep-set and jewel bright.

"Within moderation, Miss Jones. The ways of commerce may influence for the better where the discourse of the missionaries only proves a handicap."

"I cannot agree with that," I said quickly.

He shook his head.

"I fear I must abandon the argument. Your other dinner partner appears to be waiting to address you," and with a slight inclination of his head he turned away to the elderly man on his other side and I found myself talking once again with Mr. Henshawe. Sylvia, on Mr. Henshawe's other side, was in animated conversation with a fair-haired young man who gazed at her in a trance of admiration.

The dinner was splendidly cooked and served and predominantly British in preparation, if not in origin. We ate lavishly of bird's-nest soup and a delicate-tasting local fish flavored with ginger. To follow there was roast mutton served together with ham and sweet potatoes and beans and chicken boiled in oyster sauce, and after this, bananas cooked in a sugary, buttery sauce and served so fiery hot that each spoonful had to be dipped in ice water before being eaten. The fruit immediately candied so that it turned into a deliciously crunchy confection. There was a different wine to drink with each course, but I was sparing of these for I was unaccustomed to wine. Indeed, the entire evening was something such as I had never experienced in my life before.

Afterward, finger bowls with rose petals floating on the surface were placed before us while attendants proffered warm scented towels with which to dry our fingers.

My conversation during dinner was addressed more to Mr. Henshawe than to Captain Hawkes. My sympathy was with the former, for Sylvia was sparing of herself and talked more often to her fair-haired admirer than to poor Mr. Henshawe. In consequence he turned frequently to me, so that it would seem to an onlooker that we were on more intimate terms than was actually the case.

When at last dinner was over, the ladies of the party retired to the drawing room, leaving the gentlemen to their port.

Tonight Mrs. Howard appeared a different person and was positively animated as she talked with Mrs. Meade and Mrs. Barrett. She was wearing a gown of eau-de-Nile silk in which she looked surprisingly young and pretty. I was so glad, for she had often seemed to me sad and withdrawn from life.

Sylvia, on the contrary, after being markedly vivacious at dinner now sat quietly on a low chair, her head with its silky golden curls bowed over the fan she held between her fingers. I would have gone over to speak to her but Mrs. Meade held me in conversation. When she turned away to address Mrs. Dennison, the gentlemen came in to join us.

Captain Hawkes was in deep conversation with the tall, burly man with gray hair and gray sideburns who had sat at the head of the table at dinner. He was a director of the East India Company at Canton and I had been introduced to him at the reception. As he and Captain Hawkes stood talking together I found my gaze straying back to the lithe figure in the dark naval dress, his brown head bent slightly toward Mr. Brocklebank's, for though the latter was tall, Captain Hawkes was even taller. Perhaps he became aware of my reluctant interest, for suddenly he turned and caught my glance and for a brief moment held it with his own penetrating stare. I felt my cheeks warm and looked quickly away and found myself surrounded by a small coterie of gentlemen, each one as agreeable as the other as they vied for my attention.

It was a new role for me, to feel almost a belle, but it must be admitted that the other five ladies were equally surrounded. Even Mrs. Meade had four gentlemen in attendance. Sylvia, as usual, was a magnet of attraction, and after sitting so pensively alone was now smiling and sparkling. Mr. Henshawe hovered on the perimeter of her admirers, seldom speaking, but watching her animated face in a bemused fashion.

After an interval, cups of delicate amber tea were brought in and served and the company dispersed a little, the men gathering among themselves in small groups, leaving the feminine members of the party with some favored companions.

To my surprise the tall figure of Captain Hawkes came to stand beside my chair and, with a bow, inquired if I would like more tea.

"Thank you. I should indeed. It is one of the most delicious I have ever tasted."

He gave me one of his ironical half smiles as he took the cup from my hand.

"This is green tea, from the province of Kiangsi, and it is called *Wun Mo Chaah*, which means Cloud Mist Tea. It is grown at such an altitude that men cannot climb to that height and so monkeys have been trained to pluck the leaves and fill baskets and carry them down to the men below."

"Monkeys?" I was astounded. "Is that possible?"

"Everything is possible in China. It is a strange and extraordinary land," and turning away he took my cup to be refilled.

When he returned I said, as I took the cup from him, "Thank you. *Cloud Mist Tea.* Do all the teas have such beautiful names?"

"Descriptive would be more accurate. From the province of Kwangtung come teas with scarcely less beautiful names— *Sao May Chaah*, which means Eyebrows of Longevity Tea, and one with the perhaps more picturesque name of *Loong So Chaah*, which is Dragon's Beard Tea. Both are green teas. A good red tea is *Ching Yuen Chaah*—Clear Distance Tea."

I shook my head.

"I have never seen tea growing. What is it like?"

"The bush is about three to five feet high with shining dark leaves and waxy white blossoms. It thrives in poor soil and it grows for three years before the leaves may be plucked. There are three pluckings a year, but the first is the finest. It is ready in April."

"And that is why in May there is the rush to open the tea market and every ship wishes to be the first one away?"

He shrugged.

"The first to sail is not necessarily the first to dock in London. But, yes, we are all set to heave anchor once the market is open."

I find it very interesting," I said. For the first time I was enjoying a conversation with Captain Hawkes, which surprised me.

But my gratification was soon marred for, glancing down at me, he said, "You appear to be having a pleasurable evening. I observed you besieged by admirers."

I colored under his sardonic gaze and answered stiffly, "As you said yourself at dinner, the gentlemen here lack feminine society, and, in consequence, when we are present, we are much in demand."

"Perhaps so. But I think one gentleman in particular seeks you out for another reason. You appear to be on very friendly terms, which augurs well for your future together."

I could only stare at him in astonishment, for I did not know to whom he referred. And something in the tone of his voice was already stirring me to a familiar resentment. I said coolly, "You put me in a quandary, Captain Hawkes."

The keen blue eyes narrowed.

"Come, Miss Jones. You know full well of whom I speak.

Coyness is not your style. As a matter of fact, in the past I have rather admired your forthrightness."

My irony matched his.

"You flatter me."

"So you will not admit that a certain gentleman whom I will not name but with whom at dinner you were animatedly discussing gardens and picnics and all manner of pleasant recreations is not attracted to you?"

"You don't mean—Mr. Hensh—" I broke off, lowering my voice to a more discreet note. "You are quite mistaken. We are not—it is—" I was going to say, "It is Miss Meade he admires," but thought better of such candor and added, "We are acquainted through Mr. and Mrs. Meade. He joined us on an excursion to Penha Hill. That is the extent of our acquaintance, so please do not speak in this way again."

The captain's thin mouth curled mockingly.

"Forgive my assumption. A natural enough one when the parties in question are a widower and a spinster and marriage is a problematical thing out here, where there are so few eligible women." He shook his head. "If you are not looking for a husband in Macao, Miss Jones, you would have done better to have gone home, as I first suggested." He gave me a considering look. "This climate soon ruins a woman's looks."

I said tartly, aware of a flurry of anger rising within me, "As I had little pretensions to those in the first place, I have small cause to be concerned now."

He shrugged.

"Perhaps not. But you have a remarkably pretty complexion—it was the first thing I noticed about you." He added, as if aware of my discomfort, "And expressive eyes."

I was taken aback. First he criticized my appearance and then he paid me a compliment.

"Your gallantry is somewhat double-edged, sir. I am scarcely flattered by it."

"That is as well, as I was about to add that you must make the most of your charms while they last if you wish to acquire a husband."

I said through gritted teeth, "You are obsessed by the idea

that all women wish to acquire husbands, but I assure you I am *not* one of them. Once, perhaps. Not now." I saw his expression change, a flicker of something in the depth of the hard blue eyes. I added, lest he should think I sought sympathy, "What of yourself, Captain? I might well inquire as to why you, an eligible bachelor of—what?—thirty or more years, have not long ago fulfilled the heartfelt aspiration of some lone female."

He smiled grimly.

"As you are aware, Miss Jones, I am a hardened cynic and so am well armed against predatory schemers. I am also incapable now of losing my heart to the prettiest and most charming of young women to be presented to me, in however favorable a light." His mouth tightened as he added, "If you are one of the rare women who do not seek a husband then I am a man no less determined never to acquire a wife."

It was my turn to shrug my shoulders as I said lightly, "We have found something in common at last, Captain." I broke off as Mr. Dennison came up to us accompanied by a tall redheaded young man who had regarded me several times across the dinner table and was now to be presented.

Captain Hawkes gave me a sardonic smile, a smile that seemed to say, "You see? Here is yet another opportunity for you," as he bowed politely before moving away to another part of the room.

I did not speak with him again that evening, save for a few words of leave-taking when he came to say good night to the Meades and Sylvia as well as myself.

Sylvia was strangely quiet as, after we had retired to the chamber we were sharing, we made ready for bed. I thought perhaps she had exhausted herself with chatter and vivacity, for now she looked pale and tired. For a long while she knelt by the low wooden bed saying her prayers, and when, finally, she slid under the covers, I heard her sigh, but whether from weariness or from the melancholy that overcame her at times I did not know.

We woke to a bright, clear morning and Sylvia seemed to have recovered her spirits, at least in part.

"We are to be taken in a party across the river today," she told me. "Did you know? Only nine of us are permitted to go." She frowned. "I hope Mr. Henshawe is not to accompany us. He is so persistent a companion and not in the least entertaining. I hope Mr. Johnson or Mr. Mackie will come; they are both amusing. Whom do you favor, Megan? Is it the auburn-haired young man I saw you talking to for a long time, or is it Mr. Hill, who seemed to admire you a great deal?"

"I do not mind in the least who escorts us. My chief interest will be to see something of the mainland. I thought it looked delightful from the courtyard yesterday."

"I am afraid you will not see much of it—our excursions are restricted, from what Papa tells me. But it will be a pleasant outing I am sure."

Sylvia's words proved true. Shortly before midday we made our way across the courtyard to the stone stairway where a small boat was waiting to take us across the river. We were objects of much interest to the many sight-seers who had gathered each day to see the comings and goings of the "foreign devils," as we were termed. Old and young sat squatting in the sunshine, the old men with lit pipes and open fans, watching us with curious eyes, the boys grinning at such grotesqueries as tight-fitting suits and stovepipe hats worn by men who, in their eyes, possessed ugly long noses and strange blue eyes and, above all, reddish hair or whiskers, which repelled them.

As for we ladies, they could only stare in wonderment, for many of them had never seen a foreign female before.

I was amazed at the traffic on the river. There were vessels of every description—large junks, sampans, chops and small Tanka boats passing and repassing in every direction—and a shouting and hubbub of voices surrounded us on all sides. The junks, with their towering sterns, looked like floating fortresses, while on the other craft whole families appeared to live upon the great Pearl River. I could see cooking fires in the well of the Tanka boats and caught a glimpse of an old black-clad grandmother bent over one fire. Sampans passed us, piled with reeds and vegetables and fruit. One was loaded with a crate of loudly quacking ducks and a silent staring pig. Many of the vessels had eyes painted upon then and Dr. Howard told me that the superstitious Chinese thought that without an eye a boat would not be able to see its way and quoted to me an old sailor who had told him in pidgin English, " 'Wanchee walkee water.' Have eye, can see; no have eye, no can see."

The boat tied up in a small inlet where we were allowed to land and walk in the laid-out pleasure gardens. There was a profusion of trees and glossy-leaved shrubs and low feathery bushes. Amidst this greenery were set strangely carved figures: a lion or a crouching dog, a queer gargoyle-faced water god presiding over a small lake. Shallow flights of steps led this way or that between the trees and gave a view of the countryside beyond the gardens. The land looked green and fertile; there was a scattering of small hamlets with white houses and red-tiled roofs. Turning to look in another direction I could see the walls of Canton and a haze of blue smoke drifting up from the harbor.

To Sylvia's chagrin, Mr. Henshawe was one of the three gentlemen of the party, Mr. Barrett having elected not to come. Although Mr. Henshawe was too courteous a man to devote himself to Sylvia to the exclusion of the other ladies, I observed that he attached himself to her whenever he could politely do so. A picnic meal had been brought for us and this was served and eaten beside a shining blue pool covered with lotus blossoms. The sun was warm but not unpleasantly so and a pagoda within the gardens was outlined against the pale-blue sky.

Mr. Henshawe, having been rebuffed by Sylvia, came to sit beside me, and when I put a question to him concerning the pagoda, he said in answer, "They are really towers built in tiers, or stories, and are invariably set at an important point in the landscape. They are usually connected with some astrological purpose and are considered to have a good influence on their surroundings." He gestured. "That pagoda, five stories only, is small, but large and important ones are erected to guard a city. One I heard of was placed over a subterranean monster—a dragon, I think, which threatened the safety of the nearby river and countryside. So an immense pagoda was placed upon the head of the creature so that it should not break free and bring ruin to everyone nearby."

I shook my head.

"China is full of the most fascinating legends and superstitions. I have never known such a strange land." I smiled wryly. "I have never known any other country but Wales, not even England."

Mr. Henshawe smiled back at me in his shy reserved way.

"I think that Wales too is a wild land and not without its legends."

"But we are not superstitious. At least not unaccountably so. We are too religiously minded for that."

"The home of Methodists. Your society has done much good in the world, Miss Jones. I was present in the House of Commons ten years ago when Lord Ashley spoke in support of the petitions raised by the Wesleyan and Baptist missions, in connection with a group of Quakers, to protest against the opium monopoly. I remember that it was condemned as, and I think I may quote, utterly inconsistent with the honor and duty of a Christian kingdom.'" He shook his head. "Yet the traffic continues to increase and the smuggling is ignored by both British and Chinese authorities. It is a trade of death, yet immensely profitable to all who deal in it."

At his words something went out of the bright day. I saw again, as if in a dream, the staring yellow face of the beggar on the roadway outside the Mission and I tried not to think that Arthur had died in the same fashion. For a moment I could not speak, only sit in silence staring at my clasped hands. And then, with a murmured excuse to Mr. Henshawe, I walked over to sit by Mrs. Meade and let her easy, comfortable chatter pass over my head until it was time to board the boat again.

If I was preoccupied by my thoughts on the journey back, Sylvia was no less so. Back in our room she lay down on the bed, staring up at the raftered ceiling without speaking, and when, having taken off my dress and put on a wrapper, I lay down beside her, she closed her eyes as if to make sure of my silence.

That night we dined again with the company, but with less ceremony and minus the outside visitors. The meal was not as elaborate as the night before but none the less excellent. I was seated between two of the younger clerks, and their company, lively and amusing, relieved me of my melancholy. Sylvia, I saw, was placed next to the fair-haired young man of the previous evening, with Mr. Barrett on her other side. Mr. Henshawe, seated between Mr. Dennison and Mrs. Meade, was left to gaze mournfully across the table at Sylvia.

When dinner was over and we had left the gentlemen and gone into the drawing room, Mrs. Meade turned to me and said, "Have you heard that we are to dine with Captain Hawkes on the *Lotus Wind* tomorrow evening? A message came for Mr. Meade this morning, while we were across the river."

I felt a tremor go through me, but whether it was of pleasure or the reverse I could not say.

"With Captain Hawkes?" I echoed.

"Yes. His ship is at Whampoa, you know. There will be eleven of us in all, including Mr. Brocklebank. The *Lotus Wind* is to send a boat to take us at four o'clock and bring us back before the night restrictions on the river come into force."

I could only say "Oh," and I wondered at the mixture of anticipation and dread that filled me. Was it because I looked forward to being on board the *Lotus Wind* again or did I fear the captain's caustic tongue in fresh argument? I did not know.

Sylvia, who had caught the last few words of her mother's remark, came closer to say, "What is this you say, Mama? We are to go on board the *Lotus Wind*?"

"Yes, my dear." Mrs. Meade repeated the invitation and ended by saying, "I think the captain will be away to sea again very soon."

Sylvia frowned, as if considering something.

"Does he sail for England?"

"I expect so. It will be pleasant to be aboard the *Lotus Wind* and know we have not to sail ourselves." Mrs. Meade shook her head. "I really do not care for sea voyages."

The following morning it was arranged that, as we were

not permitted to visit Canton City, some shopkeepers would bring a selection to the Soo hong for our inspection. In one of the large reception halls a breathtaking display was set out for anyone who wished to make a purchase. There were lengths of shimmering silks and embroidery, silver filigree jewelry, and some rare and beautiful jade ornaments. Exquisite porcelain bowls and jars and vases were set out for us to see and plates and dishes and wine cups of famille rose chinoiserie. There were teapots of shadowy gray china and tiny frail cups without handles, many delicately carved ivory figures and, lastly, some paintings on silk, which caught and held my eye with their beauty. Birds and flowers and strange gods and landscapes of haunting loveliness were depicted in the most perfect fashion.

I could afford to buy little myself, but I had saved some money from the token salary that Dr. Howard had insisted on paying me at the Mission. Delightedly, I found I was able to buy a present for Mrs. Meade, as a gesture of appreciation for all her kindness to me. This was a small but charming painting of poppies upon silk. Like scarlet birds they appeared to float upon the soft surface of the scroll and I felt sure, that with her love of color, they would appeal to Mrs. Meade.

When Sylvia and I returned to the bedroom before luncheon I showed the painting to her and she exclaimed in admiration, "Mama will love it, Megan, and treasure it, I am sure. And all the more because she knows how few things you have for yourself. It is generous of you." She turned to the dressing table and picked something up and held it out to me. "I have brought a little gift for *you*, Megan."

I unwrapped the package she placed in my hands and found, in a small box, a pair of tiny jade earrings. I caught my breath at the sight of them, so pure and translucent a green. I did not possess any earrings, or in fact any jewelry beyond a ring that had belonged to my mother and a cameo brooch set in gold.

"Sylvia—they are *beautiful*. But I cannot accept such a valuable gift."

"Of course you can. It will make me so happy if you do."

She hesitated, her gaze fixed on mine. "Really, they are in the nature of a bribe. I wish to ask a favor of you."

"I hardly know how to thank you for such a lovely gift. And you know you do not need to bribe me to do anything you ask. Just tell me what the favor is."

For a moment she stared at me in silence, her lip caught between her teeth. Then she said slowly, "It is to take a letter to Captain Hawkes."

"*Captain Hawkes?*" I could not believe my own ears.

She half smiled.

"Do not look at me like that, Megan. It is not a *billet-doux*." Her expression changed and she frowned, her brown eyes almost pleading as she gazed at me. "Please listen carefully. This is terribly important to me. You know we are to dine on the *Lotus Wind*. Mama says Captain Hawkes will be returning to England quite soon. I am going to write a letter to Henry and I want you to give it to the captain this evening and ask him to post or deliver it to Henry when he reaches England." I must have looked as alarmed by her words as I felt, for she added quickly, "It must be done this way, Megan, for my parents have forbidden us to write to each other and all my correspondence is scrutinized. But I must write to him; I must know if he still feels the same way about me. I dare not take a letter myself to Captain Hawkes—my father might see or hear something and the captain might betray me."

"But, Sylvia—it is wrong. You cannot deceive your parents in this fashion. They will be hurt and angry if they find out and they will never forgive me for betraying their trust."

Sylvia almost flung herself at me, seizing an arm in each hand, so that I was imprisoned by her grasp.

"Megan, please, I beseech you. It is my only chance—my one hope of escape. You do not know what I have had to endure. My father is set upon my marraige to Mr. Henshawe. Oh, yes, I know this for a fact. My mother has told me that he has approached my father upon the matter and Papa had given his consent. I dread that Mr. Henshawe will address me and I shall be forced to refuse him and then Papa will be so angry and I shall not know what to do." She was almost weeping in her distress and I pulled one arm free and, placing it about her slender shoulders, said gently, "Surely your father will understand if you tell him you do not wish to marry Mr. Henshawe. He will not force you to do something against your wishes."

Sylvia lifted her bowed head to gaze at me with tear-filled eyes.

"Papa thinks he knows what is best for me—for us all. He chose both my sisters' husbands for them. Oh, they are not unhappy. Geoffrey and George are both good men, but neither of my sisters was in love with anyone else at the time. I *cannot* love Mr. Henshawe or any man when my heart is given to Henry. Do you not see that? Could *you* have married anyone other than Arthur once you knew and loved him? Of course not. And so it is with me."

"But, Sylvia dear, if your father is so set against Henry, how can sending a letter to him in England now alter your father's decision?"

"Because I must know if Henry still thinks of me as I think of him." She shook her head despairingly. "I am trapped here. I cannot escape back to England. But if I could only have a letter from Henry, some word of hope that one day we should be together, I feel I should have the strength to withstand my father's wishes. We shall not be in Macao forever— one day Mama and I will go back. The climate does not suit her for long spells at a time—she will have to return to England for her health." Her hand moved down my arm to clasp my hand tightly in her own. "Megan, help me. Give the letter I have written to Henry to Captain Hawkes tonight for safe delivery in England. Please say you will."

I was torn between loyalty to Mr. and Mrs. Meade and the love and sympathy I felt for Sylvia. Unable to come to a decision, I delayed by saying, "But even if Henry receives the letter, how can he reply to you? You tell me your correspondence is checked, so how would his answer get to you?"

She looked away from me and said in a low voice, "Oh, he will manage something. I am sure of that. All I ask is that you will take my letter to Captain Hawkes. Of course you must tell him it is to a friend of *yours*—just in case my father should overhear or suspect anything." She said again, with a touching wistfulness, "Please do this for me, Megan."

Against all my better judgment I found I could not refuse the soft pleading of her lovely eyes, the yearning in her voice. I could not bear to think that Sylvia might be forced into a loveless marriage. And so, uncertainly and in some trepidation, I nodded and said slowly, "Very well, Sylvia. I agree to your request. But this once only and never again."

Her two arms came about me. She hugged and kissed me.

"Oh, you are good. I know what it costs you to go against Mama and Papa, but you are giving me one last chance to find happiness in this world. If it fails, then I must resign myself and submit to Papa's wishes. I shall not care whom I marry then, or if I ever marry at all." She turned and, in her impulsive way, dragged open a drawer and ferreted beneath a pile of clothing. "Here is the letter, Megan. Keep it very carefully and let no one see it save Captain Hawkes." She gave an enormous sigh. "It is a matter of life and death."

If I had not been so filled with guilt and distress at the action I was about to take I might have smiled at Sylvia's dramatic declamation and the intensity with which she expressed her emotions. Instead I took the letter in my hand and placed it carefully in the vanity bag which I should be carrying with me that evening.

She came and stood beside me and said quietly, "I am very grateful, Megan. I shall never forget how you have tried to help me."

I looked down at the jade earrings on the dressing chest. A gift, or a bribe, as Sylvia herself had said. Sylvia was so generous and warmhearted I guessed she would have bought them for me in any case. But I wondered if I should ever wear them with a clear conscience.

The feeling of guilt was no less strong when, later on, I presented Mrs. Meade with her gift. When she kissed me and thanked me so warmly I wished with all my heart that I had not promised to help Sylvia deceive her parents and my manner was so nervous and awkward with kind Mrs. Meade that she inquired anxiously if I was feeling well.

After luncheon we rested as usual and then at four o'clock set off in the boat that was to take us to Whampoa anchorage, a few miles down the river. I was again wearing the violet silk dress that Mrs. Meade had given to me and in my hands I clutched the small reticule that held the letter addressed to Henry Rochford. I felt that everyone must see the envelope lying between my lace-edged handkerchief and a tortoiseshell comb, and when Mr. Meade addressed a remark to me I crouched over the bag as if to hide it from view. I was preoccupied too with wondering how, when I went aboard the *Lotus Wind*, I would be able to speak privately with Captain Hawkes.

In consequence I took little notice of the traffic upon the river and scarcely observed in which direction we were going. But at Whampoa, a dozen or more sailing ships moored in the river, their sharp, clean lines and tall masts outlined against the sky, caught my attention. They were clippers, their black hulls shining smooth and glossy, the brasswork of bulwark rails, stanchions, capstans and binnacles glittering in the last of the daylight. They looked so swift and strong, their carved and painted figureheads seeming ready at any moment to breast the waves, that my heart leaped with excitement and for a few moments my problems fell into abeyance. Flags and pennants fluttered in a gentle wind, the Union Jack on one mast, the Stars and Stripes on another, and beyond these the tricolor of France. The Chinese crew bent to the long sweeps and in no time at all we came alongside the *Lotus Wind*. Above our heads rose the familiar green and gold of the painted figurehead, a goddess of unknown origin with hands clasped upon her bosom. Despite being so recently returned from her long voyage, the clipper looked spick-and-span, her copper sheathing oiled and polished, her topsails neatly reefed.

A narrow stairway of rope and boards hung over the side and onto this, with the aid of a Chinese seaman, we were helped in turn. A handrail of soft waterlogged rope was the only support as I clambered up the swaying gangway, my long skirts clinging about my legs in most unladylike fashion. A sturdy British sailor lifted me over the side with a grin and a gruff "Take care, missy," and the next moment I was standing on the deck of the *Lotus Wind*, not a few paces away from the tall figure of Captain Hawkes, who was waiting to welcome us aboard.

CHAPTER 8

WE WERE TAKEN to the captain's cabin, which had been put at our disposal, and there we left shawls and wraps. I could not help glancing around in some curiosity. It was more comfortable than I would have expected from the austere Captain Hawkes. The dressing chest was of fine old mahogany and above it hung an oil lamp of heavy shining brass. Several maps covered the paneled wood and a pile of books stood on a small circular table. Most surprising of all was the four-poster bed in place of a bunk, across which lay a handsome fur rug. I could only suppose that the captain had inherited the furniture from his predecessor aboard the *Lotus Wind*.

In the saloon, the captain's steward came around with a tray of sherry-filled glasses. Mr. Meade was in an expansive mood but deferred politely to Mr. Brocklebank, who was his senior in authority if not in years. Mrs. Meade beamed and smiled, but Sylvia, looking paler than usual, glanced anxiously at me from time to time as if to say, "Do not forget what you have to do."

The other members of the party were happy and relaxed, even the usually solemn Dr. Howard and wistful Mrs. Howard. To Sylvia's relief Mr. Henshawe was not one of the dinner guests. There was some reminiscing on the part of those who had been passengers on the *Lotus Wind*, and Mr. Meade recounted to Mr. Brocklebank, the Dennisons and the Barretts our experience of the storm at sea. While he was doing so I became aware that Captain Hawkes had turned his head in my direction, and when I met his glance, he raised an eyebrow as if to remind me of my narrow escape from being swept overboard.

Tonight the dinner was Chinese style. First a selection of small appetizing dishes such as chicken livers, shrimp balls, mushrooms and melon seeds was put before us, then followed diced fish and peppers in black-bean sauce, and after that a famous Cantonese dish of chicken with snow peas and black mushrooms. We used chopsticks and I was glad that I was now proficient with them. Dessert was simply sliced oranges and fresh pineapple slices, and we drank a French wine in place of Chinese. Captain Hawkes explained that although in China wine had been made from grapes even before the Christian era, an edict was later passed prohibiting the growing of vines because the authorities felt that the land should be used for edible crops in view of the vast population that had to be fed. Certain wines were still produced, but these consisted mainly of herbs, honey, sugar, fruit and flavoring and were named after the chief ingredient used, such as quince, cherry, pine nut, ginger or cinnamon.

I was too preoccupied with the problem of how best I was to approach Captain Hawkes in private to truly enjoy my dinner. He was seated at the head of the table with Mrs. Meade on his right hand and Mrs. Howard on his left. I sat farther down the table from him and so was able to observe that although with scrupulous politeness he addressed remarks to each lady in turn, his narrow blue gaze lingered on Mr. Barrett and Dr. Howard when these two gentlemen exchanged words across the table, as if he would have preferred to be conversing with either of them.

After dinner, tea was served and then, during a pause, Mr. Brocklebank suggested that as it was a fine night a stroll upon the poop deck to look at the lights of Whampoa would make a pleasant interlude.

Mrs. Meade and Mrs. Howard with Mrs. Barrett remained in the saloon, but Sylvia and I seized the opportunity to leave the cabin accompanied by Mrs. Dennison. As we went up the companionway Sylvia lingered behind to whisper in my ear,

"Try to see him now, Megan. I will keep the others engaged on deck."

I opened my mouth to protest that I could not pursue Captain Hawkes, but remembering my promise I nodded and whispered, "I will try."

I walked slowly a few paces behind the rest of the party wondering how best I could gain my ends. One idea after another passed through my mind, but none seemed satisfactory.

The night was cool and windless. There was no moon, but the stars were big and bright in the dark sky and all around us lights glittered and shone from the many ships upon the river. The clippers hung lanterns fore and aft and from their tall masts. Against the riverbanks shone hundreds of lights from the boat people, the floating population of the great Pearl River. Lanterns and candles twinkled like so many glowworms and from where I stood near the ship's rail I could see a Tanka boat family eating its supper by the light of a lantern slung on an oar.

Sylvia, with a meaningful glance in my direction, elected to stay with Mr. Brocklebank and Dr. Howard and on some pretext she led them a little way along the weather deck so that they were out of earshot. Mr. Dennison and Mr. Barrett and myself remained upon the poop deck while, a few feet away, Captain Hawkes stood beside Mrs. Dennison, who was questioning him on the various nationalities of the nearby clippers.

Upon overhearing this, Mr. Barrett moved nearer to the captain, and after a moment Mr. Dennison, with a murmured "This sounds interesting. Shall we join them?" gestured for me to walk forward.

I took a few steps and then paused on the perimeter of the group. I did not want to become so involved that I could not follow after the captain if he moved away. My watchfulness was rewarded, for after a somewhat lengthy discussion Captain Hawkes glanced restlessly about him and, with a few words of excuse and a polite inclination of his head, turned to go down the steps to the weather deck. The rest of the party remained together, pointing out this or that object upon the shadowy waters, while I quickly followed after the captain.

He turned as I spoke his name and paused at the foot of the steps to hand me down.

"Miss Jones?"

I swallowed and said breathlessly, "May I speak with you alone, Captain? I wish to ask something of you."

He gave me a keen blue glance.

"Certainly."

I hesitated. A few feet above us were the Dennisons and Mr. Barrett; a little way along the deck was Sylvia with Mr. Brocklebank and Dr. Howard. At any moment either of these groups might come within earshot of us.

"It—it is a personal matter."

"I see. We had better go below." He gestured toward the companionway and, going first, handed me down the five steps. In the narrow passageway leading to the saloon I halted.

"Mrs. Meade—the other ladies—" I began, but he reached over my head and pushed open a door on the left.

"We shall be undisturbed in here."

I hesitated and then went in followed by the captain, who closed the door behind him. I saw that we were in the cabin that Sylvia and I had shared on the voyage out to Macao, but now it was stripped and empty of occupation.

Captain Hawkes loomed over me in the confined space, a formidable, almost frightening figure. His eyes, a cold dark blue, stared down at me.

"Well, Miss Jones?"

I bit my lip, clutching the vanity bag, wondering how to explain my errand. With trembling hands I opened the bag and took out the letter.

"I wondered if—I wanted to ask you—" Then, as I met his impatient glance, I said with a rush of words, "Would you please take this letter back to England and see it is safely delivered? It—it is very important. Mrs. Meade told me that you were due to sail again soon and I wanted to give it to you at once. And"—I paused—"and I would prefer that—that you do not speak of this to anyone else."

He took the letter in firm brown fingers and glanced down at it. The hard mouth curled almost sneeringly as he read the address.

"Sherborne. I know it well. I will do my best to see that this is safely delivered to your correspondent, but I am afraid it will not be by *my* ship. I am due to leave for Bengal in a few days. However, a friend of mine sails for England the day after tomorrow. I will give this into his hands and explain that it is an important and urgent letter." His eyes narrowed. "Shall I tell him it is to be a secret one too?"

I felt my cheeks color under his sardonic gaze.

"It is not—not secret," I stammered. "Only—I did not wish Mr. Meade—or Mrs. Meade . . ." My voice trailed off.

"Mrs. Meade would not approve of your correspondent. Is that it?" He glanced at the envelope again. "He sounds respectable enough. 'Henry Rochford, Esq. The Parsonage. Milford Abbas, Sherborne. Dorset.'" He lifted a cynical eyebrow. "You do well for yourself, Miss Jones. A missionary lady with a clerical gentleman."

"It is not like that," I began furiously and then I stopped. There was nothing to say, nothing I could explain. I said stiffly, "Will you do this for me, please?"

He jerked his head in acquiescence.

"By all means. Your servant, ma'am."

He was mocking me, as usual. I was about to protest when, as I stood with crimsoning cheeks and angry stare, the door behind Captain Hawkes opened slowly and silently and in the aperture stood a figure.

I almost gasped aloud, for I recognized the Chinese girl. The one I had seen before with Captain Hawkes, the one who had come upon me the morning after the storm when I discovered the body of the dead man outside the Mission.

For a long moment we stared at each other, the slanting black eyes inscrutable on my own, the smooth pale face expressionless. She was more elaborately dressed than formerly, for in place of the cotton jacket and trousers I had seen hitherto, she wore a soft wide-sleeved coat of green satin embroidered with birds and flowers over a black satin skirt. In her shining black hair were pins of jade and seed pearls. She looked exotically beautiful.

At my involuntary gasp the captain swung around with lightning swiftness and said, in a voice so sharp that it cut the air like a saber, "Te Ling! *Go!*"

As silently and softly as it had opened, the door closed upon her.

I said quickly, "I know that girl. I have seen her before— several times. She came to the Mission that morning—" But I could not go on to describe what had happened. After a moment I said, "I have seen her with you—in the street. What is she doing *here?* Is she—has she come to help cook the Chinese dinner?"

The captain shrugged.

"Perhaps. She has a cousin who helps in the galley."

I frowned. "But she is dressed so elaborately."

"Do not concern yourself, Miss Jones. Who is aboard this ship is my business."

I stared at him, gaped rather, and a blinding flash of insight revealed to me the connection between the Chinese girl, Te Ling, and Captain Hawkes.

The words were spoken before I realized, the thought expressed aloud.

"She is your mistress!"

He gave me so fierce a glance that I stepped back a pace against the bunk.

"You are singularly outspoken for a missionary miss. But in view of your desire for privacy concerning your correspondent in England may I say that there are matters of my own that I do not wish to discuss." He slid the envelope into the breast pocket of his jacket. "I will see that this letter arrives safely in England and I will honor your confidence." He pulled open the door and added sternly, "You would do better to return to the saloon with the other ladies." He gave an abrupt inclination of his head, saying, "Your servant, ma'am."

I walked slowly along the passage to the saloon in a state of great confusion. I was relieved that Sylvia's letter was safely disposed of, but I wished fervently that I had not been so outspoken with Captain Hawkes. It was none of my business and yet I was aware of a sense of shock, and something else, more difficult to explain—disappointment. Had I expected him to be so different from the many other men who, in foreign countries, took a mistress in place of a wife? I knew, from remarks passed at the Mission, that the workers there despaired of teaching the Chinese girls English because as often as not that was a guarantee that they would be quickly taken up by a naval man or a merchant from Canton. It had even been known that on rare occasions some British or foreign merchant had married a Chinese girl. Such a marriage was frowned upon, the man in question threatened with dismissal. Yet illicit liaisons were ignored.

Shaking my head I opened the door and went into the saloon, where Mrs. Meade sat comfortably gossiping with Mrs. Howard and Mrs. Barrett. She looked up and smiled at me, saying, "There you are, Megan. Surely the others will be returning soon? It must be cool up on deck."

I hung my shawl on a chair and sat down beside her.

"It is fresh but pleasant." I could think of no more to say, for my thoughts were still in a turmoil.

It was not long before the rest of the party rejoined us and soon afterward preparations were made for us to embark for Canton. As soon as Sylvia came into the saloon she glanced anxiously across to where I sat, and imperceptibly I nodded and I saw, rather than heard, the sigh of relief that stirred her breast.

When Captain Hawkes put in an appearance I carefully avoided looking in his direction and he seemed equally determined to ignore me. But as we took our leave I was forced to put my hand out to him with a murmur of thanks. I had not the slightest intention of looking at him, and yet something forced me to glance upward. The blue eyes, hard and narrow, stared several inches above my head, the cool fingers scarcely touched my own, but at that contact, a shock ran through me, as swift and scorching as a flash of lightning. I was overwhelmed by the sensation; then I collected myself and turned stumblingly away.

I had no time in which to dwell upon the experience for I was being lifted over the bulwark onto the rope gangway. By the wavering light of the oil lamp the disembarking seemed even more hazardous than our arrival, and I had to clamber down the stairway to where the sampan bobbed wildly up and down upon the rushing currents of the river. I jumped across the gap of water into the arms of the waiting boatman and was thankful indeed to find myself safely ensconced on a seat in the bow beside Sylvia.

She reached for my hand and whispered, "It has gone?"

"Yes. I will explain later."

She nodded and we sat in silence while the boat made its way upriver to Canton. I was still trembling, but whether that was from the adventure of disembarking from the *Lotus Wind* or from the strange sensation caused by Captain Hawkes's handclasp I could not have said.

Soon the lights of the great city shone against the sky and the Soo hong glittered a welcome from across the courtyard as we came ashore.

When we reached the bedroom Sylvia turned and flung her arms about me.

"I am so grateful, Megan. It cannot have been easy. I dreaded that you would not find the opportunity to speak alone with Captain Hawkes and give him the letter."

"No, it was not easy," I answered, but I was not referring to the difficulty of seeking out the captain. Instead I was remembering the animosity in his hard blue eyes as he dismissed the remark I had made to him. Whatever had made me speak so bluntly? And then I thought, But it is not *I* who am in the wrong. It is Captain Hawkes for having the Chinese girl aboard his ship. Especially when he was entertaining English guests.

I did not speak of this to Sylvia. The captain had promised to keep the letter secret and so in turn I felt I could not reveal the presence of the girl, Te Ling, aboard the *Lotus Wind*.

The journey back to Macao was as pleasant as the sail had been up the Pearl River. It was now the last day of October and the weather was blue and calm. We passed through the anchorage at Whampoa and the following day sighted the great Bogue Forts that stood guard over the mouth of the Pearl River. For another forty miles or so the boat made its way along the western shores of Canton Bay and soon we were in sight of Macao. But before we glimpsed the spires and towers on the skyline we came to the gilded "flower boats" where painted faces smiled and beckoned and forced us to turn away in well-bred consternation. I knew that these boats were intended for the pleasure of the Chinese alone, that any foreigner who dared to venture upon them would be tossed overboard and drowned in the river. It was an aspect of life of which I knew nothing and as we were carried by on the strong current I tried not to think of the association of Captain Hawkes with the girl, Te Ling. But the remembrance persisted and I knew I must accept the fact, as the Mission accepted these harsh truths of life in China. But I knew that, disproportionately perhaps, the idea troubled me.

A warm welcome was waiting for us at the Mission. George and Dorothea rushed to greet their parents with laughter and excitement, a straggle of Chinese children in their wake. Little Miss Crow appeared, quaint and dwarflike, her gray eyes behind the thick glasses beaming with kindliness. Mr. Crow came forward to express his pleasure at seeing us again, and close behind him, Chao Tsan, his black eyes bright as jet, his usually impassive face wreathed in smiles. After the richness and spacious comfort of the Soo hong, the Mission seemed a sparse place, but it was home to us all and we were as happy to be there as the children and our friends were to receive us.

The time drew nearer to Christmas and everyone became involved in preparations for the festivities. The children, and particularly the Chinese children, loved to hear the story of the Christ Child and the stable in Bethlehem where Mary and Joseph sought shelter, and how He lay, as a tiny baby in a manger, among the beasts of the field. They loved, too, to hear of the Three Wise Men who journeyed from afar to bring Him gifts, for Chinese children had great veneration for the elderly.

The children who had come to us were mostly orphans, but some of them had parents in Macao who had been converted to the Christian faith. These, with many other converts, came eagerly to the special Christmas services held at the Mission and sang such hymns as "Silent Night" as joyously as we did. The rest of the Chinese did not keep Christmas, of course, but looked eagerly forward to their own celebration of the New Year.

Mr. and Mrs. Meade and Sylvia visited the Mission during Christmas week and brought gifts for the children and for us all. I had not seen Sylvia since our excursion to Canton and so we had much to say to each other. The day she came to see us she looked lovelier than ever in a velvet jacket and skirt, the jacket cut on basque lines, which set off her graceful figure. The color, a soft honey gold, matched her beautiful hair and deepened the pansy brown of her eyes. Yet her expression held the same shadow of pensiveness as before.

She spoke to me of Henry, saying that he would soon receive her letter and perhaps before long she would have his answer.

"I have told Mr. Henshawe my affections are engaged elsewhere. He was about to propose to me, but I forestalled him. It was a most embarrassing moment, Megan, I cannot tell you. But somehow I fended him off."

"It must have been very difficult. What did he say? Has he given up hope?"

She frowned.

"That is the problem. He has not. He said that he was prepared to await the outcome. He told me that my father had hinted to him of a former attachment but that I was very young and it was not impossible that I might change my mind." She shook her head vigorously. "But I never shall, Megan. You know that."

I touched her hand gently.

"I pray that you will be reunited with Henry one day."

"Thank you, dear Megan."

After Christmas came *Sun Neen*, the celebration of the Chinese New Year, which began on the last day of the

Twelfth Moon. All business came to a standstill while the people, dressed in their best, paid their respects to parents, grandparents, friends, neighbors and deceased ancestors. In the evening there was a celebratory feast called "bidding farewell to the year," and for three days festivals and entertainments were enjoyed by all. Gifts were exchanged, protestations of friendship made to everyone and quarrels patched up. Lastly, before the dawn of the New Year, debts were settled, thus bringing good fortune in the coming year to the borrower and his family.

It was a happy time for everyone, but even more exciting was the Lantern Festival, which occurred on the fifteenth day of the First Moon. *Dung-Loon Jeet*, as it was called, was a general holiday and for several days everyone celebrated the return of spring and longer daylight hours. Macao was ablaze with light. Mr. Crow, Miss Crow and myself, with Chao Tsan, took George and Dorothea and the other children down to the Praia Manduco to see the lanterns hung from the masts and rigging of every junk and sampan. Everything glittered and shone, and as we came back through the city we saw strands of lanterns hung from huge poles and strung across the streets. The lanterns were of every size and description, mostly hexagonal in shape, with panels of fine silk or paper framed in painted or gilded wood.

I was enthralled by the spectacle, but my wonderment was as nothing compared to that of the children, who gazed about them as if transported to a world of fairyland. A procession came by with people wearing fantastic costumes, their faces hidden by masks, and little Dorothea's hand tightened on my own and she turned her face into my skirt in alarm, but Hai Chutsai, who was holding my other hand, let go of it and jumped up and down in great glee, clapping his hands. George, standing beside his friend Chu Yi-Chun, was equally excited and his eyes widened in amazement as an enormous dragon came weaving and dancing its way through the noisy crowd. It was at least a hundred feet long and was shouldered by men hidden under the paper sides so that only their legs showed. At the same time, fireworks were released and a rain of stars and flowers and rockets lit up the sky above our heads.

The children could scarcely contain themselves, though Dorothea's timidity dimmed her pleasure. Miss Crow, who had seen many such processions, nodded and smiled in approval, her long, ugly face somehow beautified by the beaming happiness of its expression. The Chinese children clustered about her, each one eager to take her hand, and she spoke to them in turn, listening to every remark, answering every question. Mr. Crow and Chao Tsan stood guard on either side of us, so as to prevent our being crushed or tumbled over, but the crowd was good-tempered and civil as only the Chinese can be.

I had seen few Chinese women with bound feet in Macao, for the women in the environs of the Mission, being in one of the poorer districts, were peasants, who left their feet unbound. Those of high degree seldom appeared on foot in the streets, but were carried everywhere by sedan chair or litter. But now, as reluctantly we made our way homeward, we were halted by an important-looking official and we were forced to pause in the roadway while two Chinese ladies came out of a gate in a high wall and with tiny, tottering steps crossed the pavement to the waiting sedans. They were beautifully dressed in soft silken robes, high-waisted and with flowing sleeves; their shining black hair was interwoven with pearls and flowers and their creamy skin was porcelain smooth. I gazed entranced until, as one took her place in her sedan, I glimpsed a satin-shod foot so incredibly tiny as to be deformed and I shuddered at this proof of pain and discomfort that had to be endured to conform to a bizzare fashion.

They were gone, like bright birds or butterflies, and as we walked on, the children lagging behind with weariness, the city behind us continued to celebrate the Lantern Festival.

Dr. Howard was busy making plans to visit Amoy, a port situated on an island just off the coast of southern China. The missionary there was a friend of his, but he had been ill, and as his wife was anxious that they should go home on leave for a few weeks, Dr. Howard had offered to take over the Mission during their absence.

To my surprise, he suggested that I should accompany

Mrs. Howard and himself and the children, George and Dorothea.

"You would be a great asset, Megan," he told me. "You have mastered the language tolerably well and can help teach the Chinese, and at the same time will be a helpful companion to Mrs. Howard and to the children. Miss Crow and Hubert will remain here with Chao Tsan. We shall not be gone long— a few months at most. What do you think of the idea?"

"Thank you—I should like it. I would enjoy seeing something more of China. Is it a pleasant island?"

He shook his head.

"Somewhat barren—and granite, but the people are not as averse to foreigners as are the Cantonese. It will be an experience for us all, I am sure."

"When do you expect to leave, Dr. Howard?"

"As soon as I have arranged a passage. The voyage will take about three weeks."

We were all excited at the prospect of the trip, although Mrs. Howard as usual was more apprehensive than pleased.

"It is a bad time of year—early April. There will be plenty of rain I expect, perhaps even storms."

"At least the typhoon season is over," I said consolingly.

She shook her head.

"One never knows what may happen."

I packed the children's clothes and their favorite books and toys and gathered together my own few things, for Dr. Howard had told us we must be in readiness to leave at short notice.

So it proved. A few days later he came home unexpectedly, his dark face animated and alert.

"It is all arranged," he told Mrs. Howard and myself. "We must be ready to sail the day after tomorrow. I have this morning met up with Captain Hawkes, recently returned from Bengal, who has a cargo to discharge some way up the coast past Amoy. He has offered us passage on the *Lotus Wind*. What do you think of that?"

We could only stare at him in dismay, Mrs. Howard in alarm that we were to depart so soon and myself in growing consternation. To sail again in the *Lotus Wind*. To sail again with *Captain Hawkes*. The mere idea of it filled me with misgiving. And something more than that. I had a strange and unaccountable premonition that the voyage would bring disaster in its wake.

CHAPTER 9

WE SAILED from Macao on a fine April morning. The two children were excited by the prospect of the voyage. George had come out from England when he was three, but he remembered little concerning the trip, and Dorothea, who was born in Macao, had never been to sea in her life. They were very much in my charge, for Mrs. Howard, exhausted by the rush of departure, rested in her cabin for the first few days.

Aware of Captain Hawkes's stern discipline, I was careful to keep the children out of sight as much as possible. In the mornings I gave them lessons and in the afternoons, after their rest, we played quiet games on some part of the deck. George was fascinated by every aspect of life aboard and, if he could escape me, would follow one member or another of the crew and pester him with his endless questions. The seamen for the most part were kindly and patient, and Dorothea, with her big dark eyes and shy charm, was a favorite with them all.

Captain Hawkes and I scarcely exchanged a word; a brief greeting when I first came aboard and an abrupt bow over my hand, a nod or a stiff smile when we passed each other on the deck. He did not dine in the saloon but took his meals in his cabin; this, I presumed, was to avoid the children's chatter. Sometimes I would see him in conversation with Dr. Howard, but even these communications were limited and infrequent.

The curious thing was that the more aloof and enigmatic the captain seemed, the more often I found myself thinking of him. He puzzled me. I knew so little about him, only that he was cynical and a confirmed bachelor. I wondered why he was so adamant on that score. Was it because he had been disillusioned by a woman? I wondered about Te Ling and the extent of his association with her. He was cold and harsh as a man, yet brave and disciplined as a sailor. His men esteemed him even when they feared him. He could make a generous, thoughtful gesture, as the time he had offered me passage home after Arthur's death, and then he had marred the kindness by a cruel outspokenness. He was a contradiction in terms. I had been told he was of good family, and yet he sailed the seas in a China clipper, living dangerously and austerely, caring little for the niceties of life. He was handsome, but the hard, keen eyes and unyielding mouth spoiled his good looks. He had, however, a steellike strength that drew me toward him like a steel magnet. I could not understand it. I was not sure I even liked him.

We had been at sea a week, sailing uneventfully through rough blue waters, when one morning I discovered George and Dorothea crouching, almost hidden, among a pile of ropes.

"So there you are. I have been looking everywhere for you, children. George, you know better than to bring Dorothea so far along the deck."

He scrambled to his feet, a small, sturdy figure in his white sailor suit and round sailor hat.

"Don't be cross, Megan. We were only playing a game."

"I can see that," I said resignedly, brushing his dusty back. "Come, Dorothea, let me look at your dress." I stopped and stared at her. "What are you both eating? It is nearly lunchtime and here you are with cakes in your hands. Or are they biscuits?" Gently I removed a half-eaten sticky sweetmeat from Dorothea's fingers. "This will do the fishes more good than you," and I threw it over the side of the ship.

Dorothea's face puckered as if to cry.

"The lady gave them to us. She said we would like them. They are nice."

"The lady?"

George frowned at his sister and said quickly, "She asked us not to tell. Now you have spoiled everything."

Dorothea started to wail.

"I haven't. I *haven't*."

"You have."

"Children, please." I took Dorothea's small hand in mine. "Don't cry, Dotty pet. You have not done anything wrong. But, George, *you* had better tell me who this lady is and where you saw her."

"We said we wouldn't," he mumbled, his face scarlet.

"If you do not tell me, you will have to tell your father."

George bit his underlip. Then he said slowly, "She is the Chinese lady. We met her here two mornings ago. She is very pretty and nice. She asked us not to tell anyone we had seen her."

The Chinese lady. *Te Ling.* I could scarcely believe it. Te Ling was here. Had Captain Hawkes the effrontery to bring his mistress aboard the *Lotus Wind?* I could not imagine what Dr. Howard or Mrs. Howard would say if they were to learn of this. They would be even more shocked than I was, if that were possible.

George gazed anxiously up at me.

"You will not tell my father?"

I hesitated, then shook my head.

"No, not for the moment. Keep your secret, children, and do not speak of this to anyone else."

"Why does the Chinese lady not want anyone to know about her?" George asked.

"That is what we must find out. Come along now, both of you. It is time to wash your hands and tidy before lunch."

If outwardly I was calm and unconcerned by George's revelation, inwardly I was more angry and indignant than I would have imagined. I felt I could not betray Captain Hawkes to Dr. and Mrs. Howard and yet I seethed at the way he was deceiving everyone. But perhaps it was no business of ours. Many a sea captain brought his wife on a voyage. Why should one not bring his mistress? Yet I knew that morally and ethically it was wrong.

The day passed without incident, the children quieter than usual. When I had put them to bed in the top bunk which they shared, while I slept in the lower one in the same cabin, I took my shawl and went up on the poop deck. The night was dark and starless, the sea choppy with small waves. I stood by the rail lost in my thoughts.

Voices caused me to turn in dismay and see Dr. Howard coming along the deck with Captain Hawkes at his side. In no mood for a confrontation I continued to stare long and hard at the horizon.

I heard Dr. Howard say, "If you will excuse me now, Captain, I will go below to join Mrs. Howard."

"Certainly."

There was silence and I thought perhaps they had both gone below. I turned and, looking over my shoulder, saw the dark bulk of Captain Hawkes standing a few feet behind me, the pinpoint of a cheroot half lighting his dark face.

When he caught my glance he waved a casual hand and said, "Do not let me interrupt your meditations, Miss Jones."

A spark of anger jerked me into speech.

"Not at all. Do not let me interrupt any tête-à-tête you may be anticipating," and gathering the shawl about my shoulders I made to walk past him to the steps.

Without appearing to move, he blocked my way, saying, "Tête-à-tête? With whom, may I ask?"

"That is for you to answer," and at his blank stare I added sharply, "I had better tell you that I have learned that the Chinese girl, Te Ling, is aboard your ship."

"The devil! I beg your pardon. How do you know this? She has strict instructions to keep to her cabin except when I say she may quit it. Where did you see her?"

"I have not seen her myself, but the children have met her twice, perhaps three times, on the main deck forward. She made them promise not to reveal her presence to anyone." I met his frowning look and a rush of words broke from me. "Do you not realize the impropriety of your conduct? To bring the girl aboard your ship like this? Do you deny that she is your mistress?"

He stared with an implacable coldness at me.

"Certainly not. At the risk of scandalizing you further I will add that a man has needs which a woman satisfies, but it is not every man who wishes to acquire a wife for that purpose. I choose to have a mistress."

I was so appalled by his frankness of speech that I could only stare at him in horrified silence. His lip curled as if in sardonic amusement.

"Now, Miss Jones, you see you have bitten off rather more than you can chew. Standing before you is an out-and-out reprobate whom no amount of missionary zeal will reform, so you had better cease your preaching."

I said sharply, "You choose to mock me. Your morals are no concern of mine, but I am distressed that you should embarrass Dr. Howard and Mrs. Howard in this manner. They are high-minded, good-living people who would be deeply offended by the presence of Te Ling in these circumstances."

"Then you must refrain from running to them with tales out of school so that they may remain in happy ignorance."

"Have you *no* compunction? Your attitude is disgraceful."

His eyes narrowed to glittering blue slits.

"And you are not giving me the least benefit of the doubt. It is stupid of me to attempt to defend myself, but so that your delicate scruples may be put at rest I will tell you this. Te Ling is not on the *Lotus Wind* at *my* invitation. She shipped herself aboard as a stowaway and was found by a member of the crew when we were four days out."

My hand went to my mouth in dismay. I was taken aback by his statement and could only say stammeringly, "I am sorry. I—I did not know."

"Do not be sorry, Miss Jones. Nothing has changed. Te Ling remains my mistress, but at least I did not openly invite her to join a pack of missionaries on the voyage to Amoy."

I felt my cheeks warm at his scathing tone of voice, but I forced myself to say, "How will you explain her presence on board to Dr. and Mrs. Howard?"

He lifted his glance as if in exasperation.

"Why should I explain it at all? There have been women, both white and Chinese, on board ships before. As it so happens, Te Ling has a cousin working in the galley—that should provide sufficient reason. For the most part she will remain discreetly in the steward's cabin, which has been allocated to her. Does that satisfy you, Miss Jones, or is there to be a further inquisition?"

I turned away, clutching my shawl about me, shivering a little in the wind. I said in a low voice, "You have put the case very clearly. Good night, Captain Hawkes," and before he could answer I moved to the steps leading from the poop deck and went quickly below to the cabin.

The children were asleep, auburn head and dark head side by side upon the pillow. I sat down on the leather couchette and clasped my trembling hands tightly together as if to calm myself. Once again Captain Hawkes had made me feel as if I were in the wrong, and not he. As if I had erred in confronting him with what I felt to be most questionable circumstances. But though he was guiltless of inviting the Chinese girl to accompany him on the voyage, as he had said so cynically, "Nothing has changed. Te Ling remains my mistress." My cheeks burned. His conduct was shameless; I could not forgive it.

A few days went by during which there was no sign or sight of Te Ling. George was regretful.

"The lady doesn't come anymore." He shook his head. "They were such nice biscuits." He looked inquiringly at me. "Where has she gone, Megan?"

"I do not know, George," I answered in perfect truth.

A night or two later, as we sailed on, the sky became lit by intermittent flashes of lightning. There was no rain or thunder, only streaks of blue-white flame slashing the dark sky. It was eerie and I was glad that the children were asleep with the curtain drawn across the porthole so that they would not see so alarming a display. Leaving Mrs. Howard at her crochet in the saloon, I went up on deck to join Dr. Howard, who was standing against the rail.

"It is only a tropical storm," he told me. "Unusual at this time of year, but out here the weather changes rapidly and without warning." He gestured. "There seems to be a great deal of activity down there."

I glanced along the main deck and saw in the lantern light

the shadowy figures of men moving quickly to and fro, some reefing sail, others tightening stays. I heard Captain Hawkes's curt voice rapping out a command, to be repeated by Mr. Benson, the first mate.

Somewhat nervously I looked down at the sea, but it lay smooth and dark in the half-light, the waves of a few days ago calmed down.

"The sea seems quiet enough," I assured Dr. Howard.

He nodded.

"Yes. These are precautions I expect. The captain is very thorough and conscientious; he leaves nothing to chance."

For a little while we watched the panorama of the skies and then Dr. Howard yawned and said politely, "Please excuse me, Megan. I think it is time to rejoin Mrs. Howard and go to our cabin."

"Yes. I will come too." And with a last glance at the sheets of blue-white lightning illuminating the horizon in startling glare, I turned to go with him.

I had been asleep in my bunk for little more than an hour when suddenly I found myself sitting up, wide awake, with my heart thumping against my side, as if echoing the tremendous crash that still reverberated in my ears. At the same moment the *Lotus Wind* shuddered mightily from stem to stern, as if smitten by a giant hand.

Dorothea began to wail, and George sprang down from their bunk, crying, "What is it, Megan? What was that bang? Oh, look, the floor is sloping down to one side—I can't stand up straight."

I climbed out of the lower bunk, dragging my dressing gown about myself. George was right. The cabin was tilted at a queer angle so that furniture was sliding or had already slid to one side.

I said with more assurance than I felt, "Don't worry, children. Perhaps the ship is turning around or the wind has come up. The noise might be something that has moved." I leaned over Dorothea and put my arms about her. "Don't cry, Dotty pet. It was just a nasty bang. Stay here quietly with George while I see what has happened." I kissed her and turned away, clutching the gown about myself. At the door I paused to say warningly, "No, George. You cannot come with me. Be a good boy and look after Dorothea. I will be back in a few moments."

The passage and companionway listed heavily and it was with some difficulty that I clambered up the steps. When I pushed open the door onto the deck I was confronted with a most terrifying sight.

An enormous blue-black cloud enveloped the *Lotus Wind*, which was lying almost on her beam-ends. The mizzenmast had crashed onto the poop deck, smashing in the skylight and breaking part of the ship's rail. The sound of its fall had been the sound that had waked me. As I stared in horror at the devastation, I heard Captain Hawkes shouting from the quarterdeck, "Get the royal in, damn it," but the great yards, volleying like thunder above his head, all but drowned his voice. Some members of the crew were struggling to haul in the mainsail and the crossjack, but even as I watched, the sails were shredded to pieces by the force of the wind.

Remembering my earlier experience I knew better than to stand any longer at risk, and turning quickly I stumbled down the companionway, to find Dr. Howard, a striped dressing gown over his nightshirt, waiting at the foot of it.

"For heaven's sake, what was that appalling noise? My wife is in a state of hysteria; I feared to leave her for more than a moment. What has happened?"

As quickly as I could I described the scene of devastation I had witnessed, and with a frown and a shake of his head he said, "We are best keeping to our cabins for the present. Are the children all right?"

"Yes. Dorothea was upset, but George was very brave and good and will have calmed her, I am sure. Shall I go to Mrs. Howard?"

"No. Stay with the children. If I need you I will come to you. For the moment Mrs. Howard is better alone with me than having the children about her."

"Will—will Captain Hawkes be able to put matters right? I cannot tell you how dreadful everything appears."

He is a brave and resourceful man. With God's help he will save us from further disaster. Pray for him and for us all, Megan," and he turned and hurried back to his wife.

I had reached the cabin and had my hand on the latch when I heard a slight sound behind me and then a voice said whisperingly, "Please—please, what is long? My hear muchee noise—my muchee flight."

I swung around to see the Chinese girl, Te Ling, leaning against the wooden side of the passageway, her black eyes filled with alarm, her porcelain skin tinged with ashen gray. Her mouth trembled so much that she put up a trembling hand to cover it.

"There has been an accident to one of the masts. It broke and falling on the deck made the noise that woke us all."

"But the ship sink—it is all-ee one side. No savee fall along sea."

I said as confidently as I could, "No—it is just listing for some reason. I am sure Captain Hawkes will soon put things to rights."

"My go long him—go long findee captain," she said. "Am muchee flaid stay alone."

I put a hand out to her, and then I remembered that Chinese people do not touch others or like to be touched themselves, so I drew back. Her association with the captain seemed no longer of importance. She was just another girl, younger than myself, looking for help and reassurance.

"Would you like to come into the cabin? The children are there. You have met them, I think. They call you 'the lady.' "

She hesitated, staring as if in disbelief.

"My come along you? My come along you and the children?"

"Of course. They will like to see you again." And pushing open the cabin door, I gestured for her to walk in.

Timidly, almost reluctantly, she went into the cabin, and George and Dorothea, after a momentary surprise, ran to her.

"Where have you been, Chinese lady?" George asked. "We waited for you to come and be with us again. Have you not been well?"

Te Ling shook her head and I indicated for her to sit on the bunk beside me, for the couchette, on the other side of the cabin, was tilted at such an angle she would have immediately fallen off it.

"My have been—lesting," she told George and something of the fear and strain went from her face as she met his friendly upturned glance.

"I am glad you have come to be with us. Have you brought some more biscuits?"

She shook her head.

"Vellee solly. All along gone." She was silent and then, after gazing at me for a moment, said slowly, "My thank you come sit here. My vellee glad have companee along you and Golge and Dolotea." At the mispronunciation of their names the children could not forbear to giggle and the trace of a smile softened her pale face.

We huddled uncomfortably together upon the bunk, the children seated between Te Ling and myself. I was as frightened as Te Ling, though, for the children's sake, I did my best to disguise my fear. The ship listed alarmingly and rolled continuously in the rough sea. The lantern above the bunks swung so dangerously that I extinguished it and we sat in darkness, lit only by the faint light coming in at the porthole. All the while a constant banging and hammering sounded over our heads, and we could hear footsteps up and down and the rattle of chains and other gear. Despite this we must have slept, for I was waked suddenly by a tap on the cabin door.

I scrambled off the bunk and went dazedly to answer the summons while Te Ling and the children came after me.

It was Bates, the steward, with what looked like a large picnic basket in his hands. One eyebrow shot up in a look of surprise when he saw Te Ling, but his voice was as impersonally polite as usual as he said, "Good mornin', miss. Cap'n's orders, and if you please, vittles to be taken in the cabin until the broken glass in the saloon be repaired and a tarpaulin put over the skylight. There be sufficient for breakfast an' midday meal in here. I'll be along agin later, miss."

I took the basket, which was surprisingly heavy, from him.

"Thank you, Bates. Is—is everything else all right?"

He grinned wryly.

"Depends what you means by all right, miss. What ain't soon will be. The cap'n 'ull see to that. There was a bit of a blow last night, see. Just you all stay comfortable down here and don't none of you fret." And with a jerk of his head, he closed the cabin door after him.

Comfortable was hardly the word, I thought, staring around in dismay at the cabin, where half our possessions had found a home on the floor and others were jumbled up in a heap against the side of the bunk where we sat. I felt as if the whole world had turned topsy-turvy and said as cheerfully as I could, as I lifted the lid of the basket, "Look what's in here, children. Bread and butter and some cold ham and biscuits and cheese and, oh, how good, a big pot of tea wedged into this corner. Now let's see if there is any water left in the jug or if it has all been spilled. No, there is enough to wipe your hands and faces and then you must get dressed before we have our breakfast."

To my surprise Te Ling came forward and indicated that she would see to the children and I watched her gently wipe Dorothea's upturned face before I began to dress, as discreetly as I could, under the shelter of my robe.

The children were intrigued by the picnic aspect of our meal and foraged in the basket, discovering apples and oranges and a piece of cold tart, but the latter I insisted should be left for our lunch and not eaten as breakfast fare.

When we came to the end of the repast Dorothea tugged at my arm.

"Where's Mama? I want to see Mama."

"You shall, darling. Just finish off your bread and butter. You too, George. And then we will go and see if Mama is awake."

Te Ling put her two hands together and said with an inclination of her black head, "Food vellee good. My thank you. My go now. My go wait along samee cabin."

"Yes, of course. But come back to us if—if you feel lonely."

She made no answer, only bowed, and, smiling at the children, left the cabin.

The children went alone into Mrs. Howard's cabin, cautioned by Dr. Howard, who came out to greet me, saying that the disturbance of the night had left Mrs. Howard with a severe headache and it would be best for the children to remain with me, after they had seen their mother.

He shook his head gloomily.

"I went up on deck earlier on. Everything seems to be chaos and the men have been at the pumps all night. But I think the ship will be under sail again before long."

"It is not listing quite so badly."

"No. We must hope and pray, Megan. Hope and pray that we shall safely reach Amoy." He sighed. "Meanwhile, I had better go and eat some of the breakfast the steward brought us. My poor wife will take nothing but a cup of tea."

"Is there anything I can do to help Mrs. Howard?"

"Thank you, Megan, but no. She is best left quiet. Just see after the children, if you please." He gave me a strained smile. "That is a task sufficient to itself in circumstances such as these. I will send them back to you in a few minutes."

I went back into the cabin and made some attempt at tidying it. The ship's list was definitely less pronounced and suddenly I became aware, by the shifting and creaking of the timbers, that we were getting under way again. I breathed a sigh of relief as I folded Dorothea's cotton nightdress.

The door opened and I heard her voice behind me.

"Papa says to tell you we are sailing again."

Without turning from my task of straightening the bedclothes I said, "So it seems. How is your mama?"

"Mama is poorly. She does not want to talk to us."

"Never mind. She will feel better soon. When I have finished putting things right, shall we read together? George, see if you can find the books."

There was no answer from him and I swung around to find only Dorothea staring at me, a finger in her mouth.

I said sharply, "George. Where is George? Is he still with your mama? Tell me—Dotty—quickly."

Dorothea went on staring at me, her dark eyes widening in alarm at the tone of my voice, and I said, more calmly, "Is George with your mama and papa?"

She shook her head slowly from side to side without speaking. Then she said, "The lady. He went to find the lady."

"Te Ling? Do you mean he has gone to Te Ling's cabin? Dotty, stay here, darling. Don't move. Do you understand? Just sit there while I go to see if George is with Te Ling. I shall be back in a moment."

Without giving Dorothea time to protest I dragged open the door, closed it as swiftly again, rushed across the passage-way to the steward's cabin, which was next door to the pantry, and rapped sharply on the door, calling, "Te Ling. Te Ling, is George with you?"

The door opened and a bewildered Te Ling stood there, shaking her head.

"No Golge. Golge no come long me."

I bit my lip.

"He must have gone up on deck. I shall have to find him. Oh!" I broke off in dismay. I had thought to make sure the cabin door was shut, for Dorothea was too small to reach the handle, but obviously in my haste I had been careless, for now Dorothea's small figure stood in the passageway behind me, and as I turned, she ran to clutch my skirts, wailing, "I want to be with you, Megan. I don't want to be left alone."

I picked her up in my arms.

"All right, darling. We'll go and find George together."

Te Ling had been watching and listening and, with a shake of her head, she said, "*Fie dee. Fie dee*," which I knew meant "Hurry." She almost ran along the passage, and as I followed more slowly, with Dorothea's arms tight about my neck, she was gone, swift as a bird, up the companionway and onto the deck.

The next few moments were a nightmare I shall never forget. I came up onto the deck, carrying Dorothea. Every-where there was activity. The mizzenmast lay along the weather deck, some men carefully hammering it. Beyond them other members of the crew were repairing the broken jib-boom, while above my head boys swarmed in the rigging reefing the topsails.

The wind had come up, and with the mainmast intact, it was obvious that Captain Hawkes was anxious to make what speed he could. As I looked around in dismay for George, fearing the captain's wrath if he should see him, I caught a glimpse of a white sailor suit. I put Dorothea down and holding her hand tightly in mine moved across the deck to where George stood watching some of the sailors.

They went on with their work, seemingly unaware of his presence. Te Ling had seen George almost at the same time that I had, and now, unhampered by Dorothea's clinging hand, she went the more quickly toward him.

At that moment the wind tore the main upper topsail and the main gallant in a sudden gust so that they billowed out afresh and the ship rolled to the port side.

The movement caught George unaware. He was thrown off his feet and went spinning across the deck, and to my horror, I saw for the first time that part of the bulwark had been washed away. I rushed forward, screaming his name, dragging Dorothea in my wake, but I knew I would never reach him. One of the sailors heard my scream and jumped up to see the cause, but he was too late to stop George as he slid toward the opening.

Te Ling had seen him. In that moment she raced forward and in one stupendous effort caught him around the waist and flung him clear of the gap. But she was too late to save herself. The ship still listed and now it dipped down farther, to almost touch the waves, so that the Chinese girl was swept off her feet as George had been, and before anyone could help her, she disappeared through the gap into the tumultuous sea.

CHAPTER 10

THERE WAS A CRY of "Man overboard—man overboard." A
seaman ran to the bulwark and looked over, calling to someone
behind him. But before either of the sailors could effect a
rescue a tall figure dashed to the side, unfastening his jacket,
wrenching off heavy boots almost in one movement. Then he
dived from the side and a second later I saw his arms flailing
through the racing sea-green waves.

I did not know where to look first. To poor little George,
bruised and shaken, being lifted to his feet again by one of the
crew, or to the seal-wet head of Captain Hawkes disappearing
and reappearing as he dived and came up for breath and dived
yet again. Dorothea was crying and I lifted her up to comfort
her while at the same time the seaman carried George back to
me with a rough, "You'd best mind him, ma'am. He ain't
much the worse for his tumble, but he's caused a powerful
amount of trouble."

"I am sorry—I did not know he had come up here. Oh,
George, you have acted so foolishly and disobediently. This is
a terrible thing to have happened. But they will rescue her,
won't they? Captain Hawkes looks to be a very strong swim-
mer."

"Ay—an' he'll need to be. The sea's like a whirlpool arter
the storm—ain't settled down agin yet and there's no tellin'
what currents is running underneath." He saw distress in my
face and amended his tone to add, "There's two more gone to
help the cap'n—both on 'em good swimmers though none can
dive like him."

George was crying, and holding Dorothea with one arm I put the other about his shaking shoulders while he pressed his face into the folds of my skirt and I felt his hands clutch at my waist.

I wanted to remain on deck; I wanted to see Captain Hawkes bring Te Ling to the surface and swim back to the ship with her. I stood as long as I could, staring with fixed eyes toward the patch of water where she had gone down, watching the three men swim around, and the captain dive through the waves time after time.

But George's lip was bleeding and Dorothea was crying and I could not neglect them for a moment longer, so with one last despairing glance over my shoulder I forced myself to walk away, carrying Dorothea and holding George by one hand.

When I had cleaned his face and put some ointment on the torn lip and taken off his stained suit, I went to knock fearfully on the door of his parents' cabin to bring Dr. Howard into the passage so I could explain what had happened.

"Please do not punish him too harshly," I pleaded at the end of my account. "It is punishment enough that—that this girl is washed overboard. He is very frightened, and very sorry, aren't you, George?"

George could not speak, but only nod, cowering away from his father's stern look, and the harsh voice that admonished him, saying, "I am afraid George must suffer some chastisement for such folly and disobedience. Go to your cabin, sir, and remain there. I would have you under my supervision except that your mama must not be upset by the knowledge of what has occurred." He frowned at me. "Who is this Chinese girl? I have not heard or seen anything of her. What is she doing aboard the ship? Is she a passenger?"

I hesitated and then said as calmly as I could, "She—she is related to some member of the crew, I understand. Perhaps on that account she was—was given passage on the ship."

Dr. Howard still frowned as he shook his head.

"Poor girl. Let us hope she has now been rescued. See to the children, Megan, and for pity's sake, do not let them out of your sight. I will go up on deck to learn what has further transpired."

I wanted to go with him. I longed desperately to know if Te Ling was safe. But I could only turn away, saying, "I would be grateful if you would come and tell me any news you have, Dr. Howard."

It was midday but none of us could eat any lunch. George was silent and subdued; Dorothea, tearful and asking to go to her mother. Time passed and we seemed to have been sitting in the cabin for hours. The ship, which earlier had been under way, had come about and been laid to. Then, suddenly, I felt a shiver run through her and she came to life once more. I sprang up from the bunk with the wild hope that Te Ling had been found. I dared not leave the children, but a few minutes later I heard a tap on the door and Dr. Howard's voice calling my name.

When I opened the door he said hurriedly, "Leave the children and come out," and as I closed the door behind me he shook his head solemnly and said, "I am afraid all hope of a rescue has been abandoned. Captain Hawkes has exhausted himself diving, and though some other men went in with the two who were already helping the captain, they have found no sign of the girl."

I clasped my hands together but I could find no words. Te Ling, I thought. Young and beautiful and kind. She had given her life for George.

As if Dr. Howard could read my mind he said gently, "You are shocked as I am by the tragedy. Bring George to me and I will take him away on his own and break the news to him. It will be punishment enough for the boy to learn what has happened. I understand that if the girl had not acted as she did it might have been my son who was lost. God rest her soul, even if she died a heathen."

For a moment the words jarred me. And then I thought, But that is true—in the eyes of the missionaries. I turned back to the cabin and called to George to come to his father.

I could not do other than reproach myself. I should have kept George with me all the time. Yet when he went to his mother I never thought but that he would return to the cabin with Dorothea. If only Mrs. Howard had not been indisposed. If only, I thought, if only—if only.

I was sad for Captain Hawkes. Whatever his association had been with Te Ling he could not be other than deeply grieved that she had met with such an end. He would blame poor George—most certainly he would blame me.

The long, weary day passed. The list of the ship appeared to be almost righted and Bates appeared with a supper tray instead of a basket, as he was now able to carry on the level. But we could eat little—only some soup and bread.

I settled the children down to sleep and lay down on my own bunk reading my Bible for a while. The movement of the ship seemed sluggish, perhaps the wind had dropped again. For a long time I neither read nor slept. A little before midnight I slid from the bunk, and observing that George and Dorothea were sleeping the sleep of exhaustion after the sad events of the day, I picked up my dressing gown and stole quietly out of the cabin and up to the deck. I could no longer stand the claustrophobic sensation of being cooped up with my melancholy thoughts.

All was quiet on deck, the hammering and activity of the previous night having been abandoned until daybreak. I forced myself to look across to the gap in the bulwark, but it was repaired and in the dim light I could not make out where the break had been, for which I was thankful. I turned along the poop deck but kept out of sight of the lonely helmsman, who stood at the wheel, his gaze constantly lifted to the drooping sails ahead of him.

The ship seemed scarcely to be moving. As I had thought, the wind had dropped. For a long while I stood at the rail, staring at the dark sea, and then, at last, feeling chilled in my thin robe, I went below again.

I had reached the cabin door when I caught sight of Captain Hawkes emerging from his cabin at the end of the passageway. He was about to go up the steps that led to the helmsman when he must have heard some sound I made, careful though I was. He swung around and saw me. For a long moment we stared at each other without speaking. I, because I could find no words, and he, because of some frowning uncertainty that darkened his hard face.

Then, to my surprise, he came toward me and said in a low voice, "You are abroad very late, Miss Jones."

"I could not sleep."

He shook his head.

"Nor I."

I looked up at him and saw the deep lines on either side of the hard mouth, the shadowed weary eyes, the exhaustion that had found no rest. He wore no jacket, only a white shirt open at the neck and dark trousers belted about his narrow waist.

I said on the impulse of sympathy that swept over me, "I am sorry. I am so very sorry about—Te Ling. She gave her life for George. We shall always remember her. I—I feel in some way responsible for what happened, and yet I—it was out of my hands. George was with his mother—he had been told to come straight back to his cabin. Instead he went up on deck."

"Do not reproach yourself, Miss Jones. These things happen. A child cannot be kept on a rope, like a dog." His mouth twisted. "More's the pity, perhaps. Te Ling was concerned for George. It seems the children were fond of her, as she was fond of them. And you were kind to her. I am grateful to you for not leaving her alone when she was frightened."

"You knew she was with us?"

"She told me in the few words we exchanged when I went to see if she was all right."

I bit my lip.

"I am sorry if I ever sounded—uncharitable regarding her. She was a beautiful, gentle girl and you—you must feel sad at heart that you could not rescue her today."

His mouth tightened.

"It was impossible. I knew it almost at once, but we kept searching as long as we could. Then I had to get under way. These are dangerous waters in which to linger." He paused and then said slowly, "Yes, I am sad at heart. Thank you for your sympathy, Miss Jones. Good night." And he turned and disappeared up the companionway.

I crept quietly into the cabin to find the children still sleeping soundly. There were tearstains on George's cheek as if he had wept in some dream. I pulled the sheet gently over them both and lay down in my bunk. Saddened at heart as I was over Te Ling's death, a burden had been lifted from me in that Captain Hawkes had not censured me for my carelessness. After a while, surprisingly, I slept.

Next morning breakfast was served in the saloon, darkened by a tarpaulin stretched over the skylight. George was a sad, silent little boy, his lively spirit subdued. He spent most of the day with his mother in her cabin, for Mrs. Howard, now recovered from her indisposition, had been told of the tragedy and was grieved for her son.

"When do you expect that we shall reach Amoy?" I inquired of Dr. Howard when we met in the saloon again at midday.

He frowned.

"That I cannot tell you. We are twelve days out from Macao, nine from Hong Kong. In the ordinary way we would have expected to reach Amoy in another two weeks, but the ship is making slow progress despite the good wind. The mizzenmast is not yet repaired, although the captain hopes to have it up again and the sails reset within a day or so. Then with good fortune, we shall make up lost time."

"That sounds hopeful."

"Yes, I think we shall all be glad to arrive at Amoy." He glanced across at his wife. "You, not the least of us, my dear."

"Yes, indeed. I have never cared for being at sea and the events of yesterday have cast a dreadful shadow over everything. That poor Chinese girl—and—and poor little George."

Dr. Howard leaned forward and patted her hand.

"Now, my dear, we must try to put it behind us and turn our thoughts instead to the work to be done at Amoy."

"Yes, Daniel."

I did not encounter Captain Hawkes that day, which was spent with Dorothea, mostly in the cabin or in the saloon, where I gave her a lesson and read to her. We retired early, for the shock of the previous day had put a strain upon us all.

That night, as soon as I put my head upon the pillow, I fell into a deep and dreamless sleep. Little did I know what the next day was to bring and that this would be the last peaceful night I would know for many weary months.

I woke to find the cabin filled with the pearly light of dawn and George already wide awake. It must have been his voice that roused me, for he was calling my name excitedly.

"Megan! Megan, come and look. There are such a lot of boats out here. They are the big Chinese ones."

I slid from the bunk and came to stand behind where he crouched, peering out of the porthole.

Sure enough, upon the shining morning sea a fleet of junks, with some sampans scattered about them like chickens around a hen, advanced slowly toward us.

"It will be a fishing fleet from some village on the coast," I began and then broke off in alarm at the sound of sudden gunshot.

"Oh," George cried. "Oh, a man has fallen into the sea."

We both stared at the figure floundering on the surface of the water and I turned my head away, seeing in this sight a repetition of Te Ling's death.

Another sharp explosion sounded overhead, and as I forced myself to look back at the sea, I saw a puff of smoke evaporating on the air. I was filled with a growing fear that I would not let my mind put into definite thought. Leaning down to comfort Dorothea, who was clinging to my hand, I said firmly to George, "Come away from the porthole, George. One of those ships may fire back at us."

"No, I want to see," George protested, but when I said sternly, "George! Remember, you are to mind what I say," his small face flushed and he scrambled down immediately.

"We must get dressed at once, children. I do not think the people on those boats are friendly toward us. There is no need to be frightened. The captain will soon send them about their business, but we must be prepared for some noise and upset. Come, Dotty, let me wash your face and hands."

My own hands were trembling as I helped her dress and I was trying hard not to admit to myself what I dreaded: that the ships still advancing remorselessly toward the *Lotus Wind* were manned by pirates. *Pirates.* I shivered at the word, for I had heard terrifying stories of their deeds, and glancing out of the porthole for a second, it seemed to me there was an alarming number of junks surrounding us and all seemed to be heavily manned.

The gunfire was now noisy and constant overhead. I heard shouts and cries, strange thumps and bangs, the thunder of a cannon which rocked the *Lotus Wind* but which I sensed was fired by her at the invaders, rather than the reverse.

Finishing my own dressing as hurriedly as I could, hindered by my shaking fingers, and pinning up my hair in some semblance of order, I delayed no more, but seizing each child by the hand, all but ran out of the cabin to the one where Dr. and Mrs. Howard slept.

Or rather, had slept, for both were awake. Dr. Howard was in trousers and shirt sleeves, and behind him, I could see Mrs. Howard leaning against a bunk, still in night-robe and dressing gown.

"We are surrounded by pirates," Dr. Howard said, without more ado. "Help my wife, if you will, Megan. She is too nervous to do much for herself. George, Dorothea, sit on the sofa and do not move from there until I give the word. Don't cry, child. All that noise is to frighten these men away. Now, I will go and—" The words died on his lips as the *Lotus Wind* shuddered under a tremendous impact and Dr. Howard had to catch hold of the door lintel to keep himself from falling.

I had my arms about Mrs. Howard, who was in an almost fainting state. She pressed her face into my shoulder, murmuring, "Oh, God help us all."

But this was only the beginning of the disasters. The shouting overhead was now a frenzy of sound as the pirates attempted to board the *Lotus Wind*. We heard scuffling sounds, the report of pistol and musket, and a constant banging against the bulwarks as the junks and sampans came alongside.

Bewildered and terrified, we looked at one another helplessly, not knowing what to do, where to go. Dorothea was crying, but George only sat in numbed silence. I helped Mrs.

Howard to the sofa, hoping that by comforting the children her own fears might be diminished.

"It will do no good to go up there in that melee," Dr. Howard said. "We must remain in the cabin until the Chinese are repelled. Let us pray together—remembering that we are in God's hands."

We bowed our heads over our clasped hands, listening to his slow, steady voice, but I admit I was listening also to the noise above my head, which seemed to have risen to maniacal porportions.

And then suddenly, in the midst of the Lord's Prayer, the cabin door burst open and Bates, the steward, stood on the threshold, his jacket ripped from his shoulders, his face burned and black with gunpowder.

"You're to come with me," he said tersely. "Cap'n's orders. They're gettin' a boat ready, and cap'n says while he and the others fight these bleeders—pardon—off, you'll be got away. No time for luggage nor nothing. Just pick up yer warm clothes and a blanket or two." And without further delay he came into the cabin and started lifting some bedding from one of the bunks. He caught my startled gaze and said, "Hurry up, miss. Get them kids movin', and you, sir, see after the lady."

As in a nightmare, we did as we were told and within a matter of minutes were being led up the rear companionway to the poop deck. Here a terrible sight met my eyes, for the poor helmsman lay spread-eagled below the wheel, his face a mass of blood. I dragged the children past him, saying, "Don't look—don't look." I heard Mrs. Howard's faint scream and then all I heard and saw was the inferno on the deck below. The crew were fighting hand to hand with their attackers, but these were so many in number that they were in danger of being overcome. Everywhere I looked fierce figures in blue were swarming over the ship's sides, scrambling along bulwark and mast, climbing on top of the deckhouse and galley, and jumping from the rigging. Some had axes in their hands; others, murderous-looking cutlasses. The crew of the *Lotus Wind* were firing from muskets or pistols, but not all were armed, for the attack had been so sudden and so early in the morning that many of the crew had only a cutlass or knife with which to defend themselves.

We were on the poop deck and below us, fighting with sword and pistol, was Captain Hawkes. Even as I looked I saw him slash at one of the pirates and saw the Chinaman fall with a crash onto his back. In the split second before another invader made to attack him, the captain glanced over his shoulder, shouting to Bates, "Get them away in the boat—God knows how long we shall hold these beggars," and then he turned back and fired the pistol at a man creeping over the yardarm and the man fell with a cry into the sea.

Bates was urging us over the ship's side from where a rope ladder dangled dangerously. Below this was the longboat with men at the oars and two others waiting to catch us as we jumped. One of them called up to me, "Throw us the little 'un—and then the lad."

Before Dorothea could realize what was happening I had lifted her over the rail and released her. She fell like a white dumpling through the air and was caught in the brawny arms of the sailor below, and I heard myself gasp in relief. George was next. He was ready to go and scrambled onto the rail without much assistance. For a moment I steadied him and then, bravely, he jumped and the next moment was crouched beside Dorothea in the well of the boat.

I heard Dr. Howard say, "Now, my dear," and I turned to help his wife over the side.

The pallor of her face was extreme and I half expected her to faint, but though her hand trembled as I helped her onto the rail, she gave me a steady look and murmured, "You must be next, Megan."

Dr. Howard had his arm ready to lift me when something prompted me to glance backward at where the captain fought so bravely to keep the pirates from getting at us before we left the ship. The scene before me was etched in my mind forever. With the impact of a Dürer painting, or the phantasmagoria of a nightmare, I saw a vicious yellow face peering down from the rigging above the captain, who was surrounded by three or more pirates. As fast as he struck at one with his sword another slashed at him with the broad blade of a cutlass. He fired the pistol, but it must have needed reloading, for it went dead in his hand. I saw him fling it away and pull out a knife in an attempt to hold off his attackers. He had not reckoned upon the unseen assailant, and even as I screamed a useless warning, the man hurled himself from the rigging and flung the captain to the deck. The next moment the others were upon him.

Dr. Howard dragged at my arm.

"For God's sake, hurry, Megan. We cannot delay a second longer. The boat is ready to pull away."

"No—no. I cannot. The captain is struck down. He is lying there—he is being murdered. Oh, God help him."

Dr. Howard gave one swift glance over his shoulder and then said harshly in my ear, "There is nothing we can do. There is still time for us to get away before those men turn upon us too. Hurry." And he struggled to lift me over the rail.

I fought him as fiercely as I might have done one of the invaders.

"I cannot go. *You* must go—they are waiting for you—your wife and children. My life is not important. Leave me—leave me, please." Somehow I urged him onto the rail, and before he could turn to protest, I gave him a strong push so that he fell to the boat below. At the same moment I ran from the rail and down the steps to the deck where the captain lay as one lifeless.

Only a few feet away a British sailor was struggling with one of the attackers.

I fell upon my knees beside the captain. There was blood on his head, blood on his face and blood on his torn shirt. My own heart seemed to stop beating as I put my hand on his chest to feel for his heartbeat, and I bowed my head in trembling thankfulness as I felt a weak but perceptible throb.

He was alive. And I knew in that moment why I had refused against all sense and reason to leave the *Lotus Wind.* If the captain were to die, I would gladly have died with him.

The maelstrom around me was so fierce that no one

seemed aware of my presence. I bent over Captain Hawkes, carefully wiping the blood from his face with a strip of torn petticoat, but the flesh around his left eye was so lacerated and swollen that I hesitated to touch it in case I injured it further. I laid a strip of linen across the wound and bound his head as best I could. As I did so, he opened his good eye and stared up at me in a blurred, unfocused way. He frowned and tried to speak and I bent nearer to him and in my relief could say nothing more than his name.

"*Robert*. Oh, Robert."

He said whisperingly, "Megan? What—what are you—" and then he broke off. At the same time the sailor behind me gave a loud cry and I sensed rather than saw his body crash to the deck. Looking swiftly over my shoulder I saw his assailant creeping toward us with a murderous-looking kris in one claw-like hand.

I think I screamed. I was not so ready to die now that I had discovered that Robert lived. An instinct stronger than reason or courage caused me to grab the cutlass that had fallen from the dead sailor's hand and hurl it in the direction of the advancing Chinaman. It caught him full in the chest. A terrible groan issued from his lips and the kris clattered onto the deck as he clutched at himself with both hands. I did not know whether I had killed or wounded him; I only knew that he could no longer harm us.

Robert's eye was wide open and staring and then, as I bent over him again, he gave me a long look before sinking back into unconsciousness.

I did not know what to do. Robert had fallen at the foot of the steps leading to the poop deck. Carefully and with something of a struggle, I managed to drag him a few feet to the side and under the shelter of the steps. Here I crouched, helpless and terrified, wondering when one of the pirates would catch sight of me and turn to kill us. One of Robert's legs was bleeding and I saw there was a deep wound in the calf and I bound it up as best I could.

I realized, after a time, that the battle was all but over. The crew of the *Lotus Wind* were dead or wounded. Perhaps some had escaped by boat. The pirates began to loot the ship, and from below, a procession of figures appeared, carrying such cargo as they could find. There seemed to be boxes and boxes of some sort, and while one party plundered the hold, another began systematically to strip the *Lotus Wind* of everything that could be of use.

The moment came that I had dreaded. One of the pirates, looking about to see what next to purloin, glimpsed me and with a cry sprang toward the steps. He shouted over his shoulder at another figure not far behind him. I saw the knife in his hand, the triumphant grin upon his face, and I flung myself across Robert's body, calling out desperately in Chinese, "*No!* No, please. He is wounded. The captain is wounded. Spare him, *please*—spare us both."

He halted abruptly, a puzzled look on his face at being addressed in Chinese. And as he paused, the man he had called to came up alongside. He was tall and more strongly built than the other men. By his dress, a jacket covered with tarnished embroidery and a yellow scarf tied about long black hair worn loose instead of in a queue, he appeared to be the pirates' leader.

The first man spoke to him, but I could not understand the dialect. Then the leader addressed me.

"You say man lying here is captain of the ship?"

"Yes. He—he is wounded. Do not kill him—do not kill us."

He frowned.

"Where is the ship bound for? Where do you go?"

"To Amoy. We—we are missionaries. The captain was taking us to Amoy and then going on—I do not know—to another port."

He nodded, as if I had confirmed something in his mind.

"The other passengers—they go in boat." He shrugged. "Maybe saved—maybe not. You stay with captain. Why?"

I stared up at him, still shielding the captain's unconscious body as best I could. I said the first thing that came into my head.

"I am his wife. Please do not separate us."

He still frowned, as if trying to make up his mind about something. Then he turned and addressed the man at his side, speaking in the dialect I could not understand, but I heard the word "*ladban*," which meant captain, and also "*yang kweitye*," which I knew was "foreign devil." There was another word uttered several times, but I was not sure of its meaning. Was it "prize"?

The other man nodded and the leader, looking back at me, said, "We take you as prisoners."

I heard my own shuddering gasp of relief. But my relief was short-lived, for at a signal, two more pirates came up to us and without ceremony one dragged me off from Robert while the other two lifted him by head and feet and started to move away down the deck while the leader looked on.

I struggled desperately in the grasp of the Chinaman, panting out my protests.

"Don't take him away. Please don't part us. He is wounded—he will die if he is not looked after." I cried imploringly once again, "I am his wife."

The leader gestured to the man holding me and said something and then addressed me.

"You go with him. You are prisoners. We take you away now."

"Where are we going? Where are you taking us?" I screamed.

He ignored me and, half dragged, half pushed, I was taken in Robert's wake to where one of the pirate junks lay alongside the *Lotus Wind*. Robert was lifted, none too carefully, over the side and I was bundled after him, and we were deposited at one end of the junk and were left alone. In fear and trembling I bent over Robert, smoothing his hair away from the blood-soaked bandage, examining carefully the equally stained strip across the injured eye. His pulse was weak, his body chill to my touch. I put my arms about his shoulders and, holding him against me, tried to cover him partially with a piece of sacking I found lying nearby. I was numbed with terror and exhaustion. I thought, Perhaps we shall die together, and I closed my eyes and prayed. I prayed for us both and I prayed that Mrs. Howard and little George and Dorothea and Dr. Howard and the members of the crew who were with them would somehow reach safety. Their chances were little better than Robert's and mine. We were all in God's hands.

The junk was pulling away from the *Lotus Wind*; the movement of its long sweeps brought me back to the realities of the moment. The other junks had already moved well clear of the ship and were making their way north, their huge square sails like birds' wings against the horizon.

Suddenly, terrifyingly, there was a tremendous explosion from the *Lotus Wind*, shattering the sparkling sea, causing the junk to rock perilously from side to side. I held Robert as steady as I could and then, as the sweeps of the pirates took the junk even farther away from the abandoned ship, I saw sheets of flame envelop her. Everything burned at once. The masts broke and fell to the decks; the whole ship was alight. And then, as I looked back over the widening expanse of water, I saw the beautiful clipper heel slowly over and sink beneath the sea.

I gasped. I could not believe it. One moment the *Lotus Wind*, battered but still seaworthy, had been afloat, and the next, burned out and shattered, she was gone to her grave, fathoms below.

At least, I thought, as I wiped the tears from my cheeks, Robert had not seen the death of his beloved ship. Hard and unfeeling as he might sometimes appear, I knew that the *Lotus Wind* had meant a great deal to him.

Time passed. The sun was now high overhead so I guessed it was past midday. Fortunately, we were under an awning, so the heat was not as intense as it might have been. A thin youth brought tea and a bowl of rice. Robert could eat nothing, but I moistened his lips with the cooled tea and asked the boy to bring me water. In this I soaked a fresh strip torn from my petticoat and managed to swab the head wound. The injured eye was a mass of congealed blood and I hesitated to interfere with it until, if ever, we reached some place where facilities were better.

I dozed uneasily, waking at every unexpected sound.

Robert's body gradually felt less chilled; his heartbeat was feeble but steady. I laid him flat on the deck, except for his head, which rested on the folded sack. The sun sank quickly in the west and the sea was suddenly shadowed and dark. I wondered, in an inertia of weariness, to what unknown destination we were being taken.

PART TWO

THE PEARL PAGODA

CHAPTER II

THE LONG, endless-seeming night passed. Robert slept heavily, turning onto his side, away from the fitful lantern light, his knees drawn up uncomfortably. I lay awake, my mind in a turmoil, wondering what was to happen to us, who our captors were. At least if we were to be held as prisoners we were not to die. I was desperately anxious for Dr. and Mrs. Howard and the two children. Had they gotten safely away? And if they had, would they, and the members of the crew with them, reach harbor somewhere? I knew, by experience, how hazardous were the China seas, and the boat they had escaped in was a small, frail vessel by comparison with the *Lotus Wind*.

I shuddered, remembering the fate that had overtaken the clipper. To burn and scuttle so beautiful a ship seemed a double murder, but I had heard that it was the custom of the pirates.

When morning came I found we were anchored at the mouth of a small creek. Beyond it were low trees and the green of paddy fields and distant brown hills. The Chinese boy came with tea and bowls of hot millet. Robert lay inert; when I tried to make him take a little tea it trickled from his dry lips. I wiped his face and laid a damp cloth upon his forehead, for the boy, at my request, had left a bucket of water beside me.

I was now filled with dread for Robert, for he was so deeply unconscious, I feared he was concussed and I could not remember what should be done in such cases. But I learned that somehow he must be made to take fluids and common sense dictated that his head must be kept cool.

I was doing my best to attend to him when suddenly the pirate leader appeared under the awning and with a frowning look in Robert's direction said curtly, "We go now. Go in sampan up river," and at a gesture two men came forward and lifted Robert onto a piece of sail.

I cried, "Oh, please. Please be careful. He is ill, *very* ill."

The men ignored me and moved away with Robert, and the pirate leader jerked his head in my direction and said, "You go. Go in sampan."

I followed as quickly as my stiffened legs and body would allow. I was helped into the boat in which Robert already lay and without more ado it was cast off and we moved slowly up the creek.

It was still early morning—there was a mist on the paddy fields and among the bushes bordering the stream. I could see small houses built of earth and thatched with rice straw. There were water buffalo, enormous wrinkled beasts, being driven by small boys. A group of men in wide straw hats paddled knee-deep in mud.

Progress was slow up the river. I was glad of the strip of matting overhead for the sun was hot. From time to time I wet the cloth and laid it on Robert's forehead and moistened his lips with cold tea but still he lay inert. I began to wonder if he would die before we reached our journey's end.

Worse was to come, for late in the afternoon the sampan moored at a small pier, and, to my horror, Robert was lifted into a sort of wicker cage in which he sagged, half sitting, half lying, while I, struggling and protesting, was placed in a similar one. The cages were slung on long poles which were taken upon the shoulders of the pirates who had brought the sampan up the creek. Then, with the leader loping ahead, we set off along a narrow track through thick undergrowth and banyan trees, which wove a curtain of green overhead.

I was crying in my distress, not so much for myself as for Robert, crushed so pitifully into his prison. The cage, or basket, swayed with every movement of the men as they jogged along the rough path and I feared what harm might be done to him in such harsh circumstances. If he survives this, I thought despairingly, he will survive anything.

It was soon dark, but the men plodded on, following their leader, who seemed to know his way even in the gloom. Suddenly I heard the baying of dogs and a few minutes later we were surrounded by shouting men. Escorted by this noisy crew we were carried for a farther distance and then, none too gently, deposited on the ground. My cage was unfastened and I was let out. For a moment I could scarcely stand upright and when I turned to look around it was to see Robert lying on a cushioned litter. I took his flaccid hand in mine and felt for his pulse. It still beat faintly, but his face was a ghastly color and the wound in his head looked as if it had started to bleed afresh.

I turned fiercely on the servants who came to lift the litter.

"Please take care of this man. He is gravely ill. He must have attention at once. Where is your master? I must speak with him."

They stared at me without answering. I looked for the pirate leader but there was no sign of him. We had arrived in a lantern-lit courtyard filled with shurbs and drooping trees. Someone touched my arm and a voice said in Chinese, "*Chang nay*," meaning "Please," and looking down I saw a small elderly woman in a black satin jacket and trousers. She said again, "*Chang nay*," and bowed for me to walk toward the moon gate ahead of us. The servants had already lifted Robert; when I went forward they came after me. The fierce and tattered figures of the pirates seemed to have vanished.

We crossed another paved courtyard to a second moon gate. There were buildings on either side, glimpsed through trees, and yet another gate, and then before us rose a pavilion, so immense it was like a palace, with double curving roof and latticed windows glowing from the lantern lights behind them.

We entered a marble hall, empty of furniture except for a row of carved chairs set against the walls on each side. At the far end rose a flight of marble stairs, and as I glanced upward, four men came down them and stood two on either side, at the foot of the stairway, as if waiting for someone. A moment later an imposing figure dressed in a long blue embroidered gown and wearing a round black hat appeared and slowly, and with great dignity, descended the stairs. He paused at the foot and the elderly woman bowed and gestured for me to go forward.

When, somewhat hesitantly, I did so, the Chinaman, with hands hidden in the wide sleeves of his robe, bowed and said, in the Cantonese I understood, "I bid you welcome to my house, Honored Lady. I am Mr. Yao." The narrow black eyes in the wide fleshy face scrutinized me. He lifted a hand out of his sleeve and the servants quickly picked up the litter and placed it at his feet. The man bent slightly forward to stare at Robert's white unconscious face, then, lifting his head, he addressed me again.

"Is it correct that you are Number One Wife of Illustrious Captain?"

"I am his—his wife, yes," I said stammeringly. Then, with more courage, "Captain Hawkes is extremely ill. He may die if he does not have immediate attention. I—I must ask that he should be seen to at once. I can nurse him myself if you will give me the facilities."

He nodded impassively, his black mustache and short black beard disappearing into the folds of chin.

"He will be taken care of. My physician will attend to him. Please go with Wei Liang, Lady."

I hesitated, and when the servants lifted the litter and started up the staircase I made to go after them. Mr. Yao frowned and lifted his hand and immediately two of the servants came forward and placed themselves before me, blocking my way.

I turned in protest.

"I—I must go with my husband. We must be together. He is concussed—I am sure of this—and his eye is so badly injured that I fear for the sight of it."

Mr. Yao gazed calmly at me.

"I regret it would not be seemly for you to be in the men's quarters, where your husband will reside. You will be taken to an apartment in one of the women's pavilions. It is our custom that men and women dwell separately."

"It is not our custom. We are Europeans. Husbands and wives remain in each other's company."

Mr. Yao shrugged.

"You are foreigners. You will follow my ways while you are in my house. Please go with Wei Liang, Lady. Your honored husband is in good hands."

The litter moved slowly out of sight. I was frantic at being separated from Robert but there was nothing I could do. The small elderly woman stood beside me, her black eyes kindly in her wrinkled brown face.

"Please to come with me, Honored Lady."

After a last despairing glance toward the staircase and a brief bow in Mr. Yao's direction, I followed her through a door at the far end of the room and into a courtyard. Crossing this we came to a handsome pavilion with a curved roof of green tiles and a pillared balcony set above the ground floor. Wei Liang, with another bow and smile and bow, gestured for me to ascend the few shallow steps to the painted door, which opened even as I approached it. I went into a lantern-hung hall where another woman servant bowed and greeted me.

I was led up a flight of stairs to an upper room and here Wei Liang gently assisted me out of my torn and filthy clothing. I was as a child in my docility as she proffered warm perfumed water in a porcelain bowl and helped me with my toilette. Dazed and weary from the terrifying events of the day I could no longer think coherently or conjecture further on what was to happen to Robert and myself. As in a dream I felt Wei Liang slip a cool cotton night-robe over my head and guide me to a low wide bed set in a latticed recess. A bowl of thin chicken broth was brought to me and I took a few spoonfuls, but before I had half finished it, I fell back onto the small hard pillow and was engulfed in sleep.

I woke at dawn. A gray light filtered through the latticed windows. The bed was half enclosed by a carved trellis. From the recess in which it stood I could make out a few pieces of single but elegant furniture: an armchair, a table with curved legs, and, beneath it, a small lacquer stool. A lacquer dressing table with a mirror stood against a wall, and a tall cabinet in a corner displayed a few ornaments on open shelves.

My first thought was for Robert. Where was he—and how

was he? Had someone cleansed his wounds and bandaged the injured eye? Had he been given some restorative drink or did he lie in a distant room weak and dying?

I felt dizzy as I slid from the bed, as if the effects of the day before still affected me. I sat for a moment to steady myself and then I padded slowly over to the paper-filled window. Opening it, I looked out. Below me was the flower-filled courtyard, and beyond the tiled walls, a mass of trees stretching as far as the eye could see. I surmised this was the parkland we had come through the night before. Among the distant trees I glimpsed something tall and silvery, and staring the harder to see what it could be, I made out the topmost tiers of a pagoda. I was caught and held by the spectacle. In my present state of light-headedness the curving roofs seemed to float above the trees, mysterious and ethereal, strange and fantastically beautiful in the dawning light.

With a start, I returned to the reality of the moment, to my fears for Robert. Somehow I must go to him today. I would insist upon that. Even if it were not permitted for me to sleep under the same roof, surely I would be allowed to visit him. I felt helpless and despairing and when I wished to get dressed I was appalled to find nothing but a silken robe hanging against the trellis that concealed the bed, only that and the nightgown I was wearing. There was little I could do but return to my bed.

An hour or more passed. I lay awake, remembering all that had happened during the past few days. The storm and Te Ling's tragic death; the pirates' attack; the hurried escape of the Howard family—if they had escaped. But yes, the crew of the longboat were brave and resourceful; surely they would make for safety or be fortunate enough to be picked up by some friendly ship.

I thought of how Robert had been struck down and in my mind's eye I saw again the pirate rolling over after I had flung the cutlass at him. Was it possible I had killed a man? I shuddered at the thought, evil and dangerous though the pirate had seemed in that terrible moment when he advanced toward us.

Now we were here in this strange pavilion. Why had we been brought here? It was as if Mr. Yao had been expecting us. The pirate leader had called us prisoners. Were we *his* prisoners or were we the prisoners of Mr. Yao? The entire situation frightened and bewildered me.

Wei Liang glided quietly in bearing a tray of tea, a bowl of millet and some fresh fruit. She nodded smilingly at me.

"You are awake, Lady. You feel better?"

"Much better, thank you. I wanted to get dressed but you have taken my clothes away."

She frowned, shaking her head.

"Dress, no good. Nothing left good. I bring you new dress, new thing to wear. See?" She reached into a tall cabinet and brought out a long robe of embroidered gold silk. "You wear Chinese dress."

There was nothing else for it. After I had drunk the refreshing tea and eaten some of the fruit, I performed a toilette made elaborate by Wei Liang's ministrations. Then I put on silk underthings, the soft and beautiful robe, and a pair of brocade slippers.

"Now I wish to be taken to my husband," I said firmly, at the end of it all.

Wei Liang shook her head again.

"Not see honored husband without permission of great and esteemed master."

"Then take me to him at once."

"Great master not wish to be disturbed. You wait little while. Later perhaps give permission to visit honored husband."

Once again it was deadlock. There was nothing I could do but pace about the apartment or sit, fretting and worrying, until such time as Wei Liang deemed it politic to go and make an inquiry of Mr. Yao.

According to Wei Liang I was in a guest pavilion close by the Pavilion of the Wives. There was also a Pavilion of the Daughters.

"My honored master's sons live across courtyard, in Pavilion of Men. Not good for son to be with women after certain age."

"So I have heard. Please, Wei Liang, will you go now and ask your honored master to give me an audience?"

She seemed to be gone a long time, but the Chinese never hurried, as I knew. When she returned after what seemed an endless interval it was to bow and say, "My great master will send for you to visit honored husband in little while," and so I had to content myself again to wait.

I waited two days. On the third day Wei Liang came to me and said that a servant had come to escort me to the Pavilion of the Men. By now I was desperately anxious about Robert and only a physical reaction that had set in after the ordeal of the previous days, causing me to feel tired and listless, had prevented me from taking more energetic measures to seek him out.

I followed the manservant through a maze of courtyards and into the big reception hall where we had first arrived. He led me up the staircase and along a wide corridor and then, nodding and bowing, opened one of the doors. I went into an airy room furnished in more austere fashion than my own. A bed stood at one end, but as I hurried toward it a small figure emerged out of the curtained recess and with hands in sleeves bowed before me.

"Allow me to present myself, Honored Lady. I am Haas. I treat your honored husband, the captain. He is ill with the loss of his senses. But if the gods allow, he will recover. It will take many moons."

I stared at the elderly man before me. A black skullcap topped a parchment-colored face; a gray forked beard hung down the front of the black dragon robe he wore. He had an air of such dignity that I checked my first impulse to run to the bed, and putting my hands together, I bowed in return.

"Thank you, Honored Doctor. I am very anxious for my husband but grateful to you for your care of him."

He nodded.

"It is good that you speak Chinese, if not correctly, at least understandably."

"You say that many moons may pass before my husband recovers. Do you mean before he regains consciousness?"

Dr. Haas nodded.

"He may recover his senses before the next moon, but more than one moon will pass before his full strength returns. The injured eye is severely inflamed, and he has a leg wound and suffers from fever."

I bit my lip and said, "May I see him, please, Honored Doctor?"

He stood aside, gesturing toward the bed.

"By all means, though he sleeps and will not wake to know you."

I went toward the recess. A lamp burned beside the narrow bed in which Robert lay. My heart seemed to miss a beat as I leaned over him, seeing the gaunt, colorless face from which the beard had been shaved. Without it he looked younger and somehow defenseless, his mouth revealed more fully, firm yet oddly gentle in the vulnerability of sleep, his profile bonier than ever in the lamplight. A clean bandage was wound around his head and over the injured eye and he wore some sort of cotton gown.

There was a chair by the bed. I was thankful to sit down on it, for I was faint and sick at heart to see Robert lying thus. Robert, so strong and commanding, eaglelike in his swiftness and vigor. I could not bear to see him ill and helpless. Gently I touched his hand, but he did not stir and slept as if nothing would ever wake him again.

When had I come to love him, I asked myself? I had loved Arthur, now I loved Robert. How had that happened in one short year? I knew I loved Robert in a different way from the way I had loved Arthur, who had been gentle and good and kind. I doubted that Robert was any of those things. Yet I was drawn to him as I had never been to Arthur; I had felt a response to his masculinity that I had never experienced before.

A movement by the bed caused me to glance upward. Dr. Haas stood beside me, his hands folded in the sleeves of his robe.

"You grieve for your honored husband, Lady, but do not despair. This sleep which clouds the brain also heals. I promise that all my skills will be devoted to him. Now I suggest that you return to your chamber and rest. It is best that the honored captain should remain in utter quietness. That way the drugs that I shall give him will be the more effective."

"Drugs?" I echoed, standing up in alarm."

"Soothing potions that will help restore him to health."

I moved away to the center of the room, saying, "A message must be sent to Macao, where—where we have come from. Our people will be anxious for us. I do not even know where we are—only that we are at the house of Mr. Yao."

"This estate is known as the Place of Tall Trees," Dr. Haas answered smoothly. "But that will convey nothing to you. It will be best that you speak with the esteemed Mr. Yao himself. He will deal with your problems, I am sure. I will arrange that you visit your honored husband once a day." He bowed. "I bid you good morning, Lady."

I left him, my mind filled with doubts. I hoped that Dr. Haas was as wise and experienced as he seemed. I could only pray that whatever methods were being used would save Robert's life. Meanwhile, I must continue in my roll of the devoted wife so that I could be in daily attendance to him and make sure that no extreme measures were taken.

A week later I was taken to Mr. Yao. To reach him I had to pass through several halls, each one larger and more imposing than the first and all richly furnished with crimson lacquer, fine porcelain, enamel and cloisonné ware, and many paintings on alabaster or silk. It did not take me long to realize that Mr. Yao must be a merchant of great wealth.

Finally I was ushered into yet another handsome room where Mr. Yao sat behind a wide carved desk.

He rose to bow and smile and indicated the small chair opposite him.

"I am honored by the presence of the Number One Wife of Illustrious Captain. I understand you wish to speak with me and it is my pleasure to be at your service. I trust you have fully recovered from your hazardous experiences."

"Thank you, Honored Sir. I am well and rested. My—my esteemed husband has not yet recovered consciousness, but I feel it is more than time that we make contact with the British authorities at either Macao or Hong Kong. An escort will then be sent to take the honored captain and myself back to Macao, where he can be cared for in the hospital there."

I had rehearsed this speech so often in my mind that it came out full spate. When I had finished, I paused breathlessly, my gaze expectant on Mr. Yao's impassive face.

He inclined his head, his black beard resting on his ample chest.

"I understand your impatience, Lady. I deeply regret that I cannot grant your request for the moment."

I stared in astonishment.

"But you *must*. Our families—our friends will think that we are dead. It is most necessary that they should know where we are."

"Their joy will be all the greater when they finally learn the truth," Mr. Yao said in his smooth bland voice. "But until your honored husband recovers his wits no message can be sent."

"But *why?*" I demanded. "I cannot understand the reason for your refusal."

The black eyes, lost in folds of skin, gazed inscrutably at me.

"Content yourself with the fact that your honored husband is being nursed back to health. He is an important man. It is my wish to speak with him when he is recovered."

"*Important?*" I was startled. "Yes, I suppose he is. As the captain of a British ship."

The slanting black eyes seemed to narrow watchfully.

"A ship that carried valuable cargo. You would doubtless know of that?"

"I have no idea what the cargo was. In any case, it was all looted by the pirates."

"Yes, unfortunately that is so. They are—shall we say—independent merchants." Mr. Yao frowned. "But there are possibly other cargoes waiting to be shipped that the captain is aware of."

"I suppose so." I was puzzled by the trend of his remarks. "I know nothing of such things."

Mr. Yao stood up.

"Ah, well, it is not the way of wives to know of their husband's business matters. Though I understand with foreigners, matters are somewhat different. But do not concern yourself, Honored Lady Wife. Return to your apartment, where every attention will be yours. The courtyards and the gardens are at your disposal. You are free to walk in the Deer Park, but, if you please, with a servant in attendance. Good day to you, Honored Lady."

I opened my mouth to protest, to make fresh demands for our release, but the implacable black gaze stayed me and with a murmured, "Good day, Honored Sir," I went out of the room. The servant who had brought me to Mr. Yao was waiting to escort me back to the guest pavilion.

All that day I puzzled over Mr. Yao's words. I was bewildered and unhappy. I could not understand why we should be held as prisoners. For despite the studied politeness with which we were treated, prisoners we were.

Slowly the time passed. I visited Robert every day, but at first there was no change in his condition and he had no awareness of my presence. Yet as the days passed I thought that imperceptibly his color improved, his face looked less emaciated.

I lost track of time. One morning I did some calculations and discovered it was now the beginning of May. I could not believe it. A sense of unreality hung over my entire existence in this strange house that was like a palace. Daily I walked in the courtyards, which were of singular beauty. I had never seen such a profusion of flowering shrubs and flowers, some of which I knew, many which I could neither recognize nor name. I was entranced by the vision of great creamy trumpet flowers on bare branches, which later I was to learn were magnolias. Wisteria I knew, for it had been introduced to England at the beginning of the century. Camellia and hibiscus were familiar to me too, and *Weigela rosea*, which was a shrub grown frequently in Chinese gardens. But many other beautiful and exotic shrubs were strange to me and I could only marvel at the charm and artistry of these Chinese gardens.

Fan-tailed goldfish swam among the lotus- and water-lily-filled pools, and immense golden carp lurked in the shade of the tall blue Japanese iris that mingled with the many lovely primulas. Acacia trees gave shade to sit under and the kumquat tree was smothered with the small white flowers that later would produce juicy fruit.

Often when I walked or sat in the Courtyard of the Second Moon Gate I would hear soft voices and smothered laughter and be aware of unseen eyes watching me, for somewhere near was the Pavilion of the Wives.

Beyond the walls of the courtyards lay the Deer Park, and one day, remembering Mr. Yao's words, I ventured to one of the gates opening into it.

I had no sooner passed through than a tall fierce-looking man appeared from nowhere to confront me.

When I fell back in some alarm he said sternly, "If the lady wishes to walk in park she must have servant with her. Not walk alone in park."

"I—I'm sorry. I came to look, that's all."

"The park is very large. There are deer, other animals roaming at will. It is necessary to have other person with you."

"Thank you. I will remember that."

He looked down at me.

"You wish to walk now? I get boy—he will go with you." And with no more ado he put a whistle to his lips and blew. A moment later a youth in a blue uniform came running up. The first man spoke a few words to him and he nodded and, bowing to me, said, "Lady walk where she wish. I will follow."

A moment later we set off, an odd procession of two, myself walking slowly ahead, followed at a distance by the boy. Once I turned and said, "Will you not walk with me?"

He shook his black head vigorously and said, "It is not permitted. Lady walk alone—me follow."

From where I stood the pagoda could not be seen, for the mass of trees hid it. I turned again and said, "I would like to walk to the pagoda. Is it in this direction?"

"Yes, Lady." He hesitated. "I will lead you to it. You follow now. I go slow for lady."

"Thank you."

We set off again, the slight blue-clad figure a few paces ahead. The trees were dense; pine and cypress and holly interspersed with huge teak trees and a scattering of small oaks. Some ginkgo trees, their fan-shaped leaves of pale green hung about with catkins, moved gracefully in the slight wind; beyond these were the giant woody stems of bamboo and cedar-like evergreens.

Suddenly, the trees opened out to an expanse of water, and from a slight eminence on the far side rose the pagoda, its graceful silvery reflection mirrored in the blue of the lake.

It was seven stories high, tapering to an intricately carved spire. The latticework of each tier was worked in ivory and mother-of-pearl and this gave the entire edifice a strange and rare luminosity. A narrow balcony circled the perimeter of every tier, and above each one rose a roof of pale-green tiles petaled and curved in semblance of a lotus blossom. It shone iridescent in the sunlight, and I thought I had never seen anything more beautiful in my life.

The Chinese boy said softly from behind me, "It is called the Pagoda of the Many Pearls. You like, Lady?"

I gave a sigh of pleasure as I turned to answer him.

"Indeed, I like it more than I can say. Is one permitted to go inside?"

He looked doubtful.

"There is entry, yes, but it is a place of the gods."

"A temple, do you mean?"

He shook his head.

"Not temple for worship but place which Gods of Good Stars visit. Bring much good fortune."

I said slowly, "That is something I could do with. May I go in, please?"

"As you wish, Lady. Entry is over there," and he gestured toward the right. "I wait here for you."

I walked across the sparse grass. At the foot of the pagoda were bushes smothered with feathery white flowers and growing behind them were several enormous golden rain trees. One day in England I should know these as laburnums.

I saw a small latch fixed to a panel of lattice and, lifting it gently, discovered this to be the door. Inside was a circular tiled space. It was dusty; twigs and leaves were scattered across the floor. From the center wound a small delicate wrought-iron staircase.

I could not resist ascending it. Or from the second tier, going up to the third. And then the fourth, the fifth. When I reached the final tier I stepped through an aperture onto the narrow balcony to gaze enchanted at the view before me.

Below me was the blue of the lake and the clearing between the trees. The figure of the Chinese youth, telescoped by distance, gazed anxiously upward, as if for sight of me. Beyond this was the park, or rather, forest, for the trees grew thickly and all but hid the roofs of the pavilions. Slowly I circled the balcony, looking for some sign of habitation, a village or such, but could see nothing but green foliage, truly The Place of Tall Trees. Yet it seemed to me as I gazed that a reflection of light shone over the horizon, as if from the distant sea.

With one finger I traced the pattern of pearl and ivory set on the rim of the balcony. I wondered at the delicacy and skill of the work. But of course the pagoda had been built in honor of the Gods of Good Stars, so that they would visit it and bring good fortune. If only they would shine benignly upon Robert and myself. I was immediately ashamed of my pagan thoughts and wondered what Dr. Howard would think if he knew I had harbored such foolish superstitions.

Yet standing there, I had a curious sense of reassurance, a breath of some happiness still to come, and as I retraced my steps down the narrow stairs, my heart felt lighter. This was another world, different from anything I had known before. A world of different culture and custom; a mysterious world, strange and exotic, colorful and cruel. A world of great beauty and consummate artistry. Even the clothes I wore were different, the robe of soft pink silk, the embroidered slippers on my feet. And the pagoda in which I found myself— the Pagoda of Many Pearls, as it was called—made me believe perhaps other gods ruled here.

I closed the latticed door, knowing I would wish to visit the pagoda again very soon.

The boy waited, bowing and frowning.

"It is beautiful," I told him. "Thank you for allowing me to go inside. What is your name?"

"Lin Sing, Lady. We go now?" he inquired anxiously.

"Yes." I glanced over my shoulder at the pagoda, shining luminously between the trees. The Pearl Pagoda, I thought. That is how I shall think of it.

"Where are the deer?" I called as we walked in single file along a winding path.

"Not here, Lady. In other part, beyond wall. Deer not come near pagoda—in case harm with horn."

"Perhaps you would take me there another day, Lin Sing. I should like to see the deer."

"Yes, Lady. I ask Chang Nien—him head guard."

I was startled.

"Guard?" I echoed. "Is the park guarded then?"

"Yes, Lady. Great master keep guard all around park— guard at all gate. Not want stranger come. Guard have dog also. Keep bad person away."

I remembered the dogs the night we arrived. I had not seen them but had heard the sound of their baying. It seemed that entry to The Place of Tall Trees was not easy. An attempt to escape might be even more difficult.

CHAPTER 12

I SAT WITH Robert every day. Sometimes I visited him twice, sitting with him in the late afternoon, before Wu Shing prepared him for the night. He had still not recovered consciousness and seemed unaware of those about him or of his surroundings.

Then one morning Dr. Haas came into the room when I was with Robert and, after bowing and greeting me, he said, "Good day, Honored Lady. I have come to speak with you."

I stood up in some surprise.

"Certainly. What is it you wish to say?" I glanced quickly toward the bed. "Is it some news of my—my husband's condition? Do you consider that he is making progress?"

He nodded slowly. His forked gray beard hung almost to his waist, a velvet skullcap hid his domed head. Today he wore thick spectacles that hid his narrow black eyes.

"Yes. Honored husband improves. That is to say, his general condition progresses favorably. But"—he paused and looked at me over the rim of his spectacles—"there is a problem we cannot overcome."

"A problem?" I heard my voice sharpen. "Of what problem do you speak, Honored Sir!"

He advanced nearer to the bed and putting out his hand indicated the bandage over Robert's eye.

"It is the eye, Honored Lady Wife. The state of it was beyond repair." Slowly he began to unwind the bandage, While I stood, biting my lip in sudden anxiety. Dr. Haas lifted the bandage away. "I deeply regret—there was nothing more I could do." He stepped back, the strip of linen dangling from his thin hand. "This eye had to be removed lest it endanger the other."

I heard myself gasp, and turned my head away in an involuntary movement. Not in revulsion but because I was grieved to the heart at what I saw. I could not believe it.

I looked across to Dr. Haas, standing still and silent on the other side of the bed. He inclined his head as if to say, "It is so." I forced myself to look back at Robert. At the scarred and hollowed socket where once had been his eye.

I said in a slow, shaking voice, "And the other eye? Is it uninjured?"

Dr. Haas shook his head.

"The vision of the right eye is impaired. I can only hope this is a temporary matter. The inflammation is of sympathetic origin. Do you understand, Honored Lady? The severe and penetrating wound in the left eye was such that a certain amount of infection spread to the right eye. But I trust it will respond to treatment. I removed the injured eye so as to diminish the risk to the good one."

I bit my lip, trying to hold back the questions and doubts that threatened to pour out. What sort of a physician was this elderly man standing before me, that his practice consisted of only one household, albeit a large one. What were his skills, his experience? For all I knew he could be little more than a species of witch doctor and poor Robert had lost his eye in some unnecessary experiment.

I said as quietly and calmly as I could, "Most Honored Doctor, forgive the questions of so ignorant a person as myself, but the treatment of the eye is a very special study. It is not a matter of skill but of experience in a case such as this."

The thin lips above the long beard twisted wryly. He bowed his head and said gently, "My skills, such as they are, Honored Lady, were learned in a good school. I studied for many years at the Branch Hospital of the Medical Mission in Macao under the famous Dr. Parker. Doubtless you have heard of him? He was a highly esteemed American who devoted his life and his skills to the sick people of China, working both at Macao and in Canton. I have treated many such cases as the honored captain's. Unworthy as I am, I may claim an experience commensurate with any other of my profession."

I bent my head and said without looking at him, "I beg you to forgive my presumption, Honored Doctor. But you will understand that I did not expect to find so eminent a personage in this isolated household."

"As to that, Honored Lady, some years ago I was attacked by an illness that threatened my life. It was the illustrious Dr. Parker himself who saved me. But when, after many moons, I recovered, he forbade me to return to the strain of hospital work. My friend Mr. Yao offered me this position as medical adviser to himself and his family. Does that satisfy your curiosity, Lady?"

I felt myself blush at his gently ironic tone. But I was too relieved to be overly self-conscious as I answered, "My heart is made easy, Honored Doctor, to learn that my esteemed husband is in such skilled hands. Pray forgive this ignorant person her unworthy doubts. I have no more to say except to express my grateful thanks to you."

Dr. Haas nodded without speaking and, bending over Robert, began to replace the bandage. As he did so Robert stirred uneasily and murmured a few incoherent words. Dr. Haas paid little attention but went on rewinding the bandage. When he had finished he turned to me and said, "We will keep the eye covered for a few more days. After that a small shield of some sort will be enough. You see how he moves and speaks now? Gradually he will recover consciousness, but his memory may be erratic. He will remember certain things and forget others. Do not worry or question him but leave matters to time and nature."

"When will my honored husband be well enough to travel?" I asked. "I am anxious to send a message to both the British Consul at Macao and to the Central Mission there. Then a reply will come, perhaps even someone in person to fetch us."

Dr. Haas's glance behind the thick spectacles remained impassive on my own yet I had a curious feeling that he had registered surprise at my remark.

"I cannot pronounce on that. All depends upon the progress of the honored captain. One word more. When your honored husband recovers his senses I will tell him what has had to be done. If by some chance, he should wake and speak when you are with him, it will be your duty to reveal the truth. Do not be afraid. Remember, the captain is a brave seafaring man who is not afraid of wounds or even death. He will accept his loss."

I said sighingly, "Yes. I am sure of that. Thank you, Honored Doctor."

"I will take my leave of you now." The small lined face softened. "I think it is perhaps that you too are a brave person, Small Lady Wife. We have a saying in my country which may be of comfort to you. *'To meet ten thousand changing circumstances with an unchanging self.'* The man or woman who can do that has little to fear." He bowed and, turning away, was gone from the room.

I looked down at Robert, at the gaunt face that was little more than a bony mask, for he had lost a great deal of flesh. My heart was heavy with sadness. To lose one eye and have the sight of the other impaired. Would he ever command a clipper ship again? I wondered, and then I thought of Nelson, brave and magnificent with but one eye and one arm.

I touched Robert's thin wrist as if to reassure him. When would he wake? I wondered. It was good to think that the little doctor was so skilled and practiced a man. *"Small Lady Wife"* he had called me. But I was not Robert's wife, nor would I ever be. I had made that claim on impulse, so as to be with him on the final tragic day aboard the *Lotus Wind.* Would he be angry when he discovered my deception, or would he understand? I could only hope it would be the latter.

As it so happened it was not Dr. Haas but myself who was with Robert when he recovered consciousness. I was sitting by his bed, thinking of Sylvia, remembering her sweet ways and her kindness to me. I still had the jade earrings; they were safe in a tiny linen bag I wore around my neck, along with the cameo brooch and the wedding ring that had been my mother's. By now Sylvia must have heard of the shipwreck of the *Lotus Wind* and of our disappearance and she would grieve

for us, as would her parents. I longed to send them a message
of reassurance, but that was impossible. I wondered if she had
received the expected letter from Henry in answer to her own
plea. Dear Sylvia—I would always love her.

Suddenly my drifting thoughts were arrested by a sound
from the bed. *Robert was speaking!* Not the unintelligible
mumblings that lately had issued from his lips but clear and
sensible words.

"Who is there?" he asked, moving his head from side to
side upon the pillow.

I sprang up to lean over him, taking his hand in my own. I
could scarcely speak for joy but said at last in a voice shaking
with relief, "*Robert!* Oh, thank God. You have wakened at
last. It is Megan here—do you not know me?"

He frowned, his right eye puckered to stare up at me.

"Megan? I can't see you properly. This eye—" He put a
hand up to the black silk shield that had been placed over the
empty eye socket. "There's something—I can't—"

I caught his wandering fingers in mine.

"Please don't touch. It is—your eye is covered up. You
were wounded in the battle with the pirates."

He let his hand fall onto the coverlet.

"The pirates? I don't remember."

Recalling Dr. Haas's warning I said hurriedly, "It doesn't
matter. You will remember everything in time. How do you
feel, Robert? Do you wish for something? A drink—or some
food? And Dr. Haas must be fetched for he will wish to see
you."

He shook his head impatiently.

"I want nothing. Only to see. Why can't I see you properly? There is just an outline of someone—that is all. What has
happened to this eye?"

"It is still inflamed; the sight is affected for—for the time
being. But it will be better in time."

He was silent, then he said slowly, "Are we on the *Lotus
Wind?*"

"No. We—we have been given shelter in the house of a
Chinese merchant. You have been well looked after, as I have.
Please don't talk any more. Or worry. I will explain every-

thing when you are stronger. Now you must rest until Dr. Haas comes to see you."

I was still holding one of his hands in mine. I tried to pull it free, but Robert gripped my hand the more tightly.

"How bad is my eye, Megan? This one, I mean." And he touched the patch.

I bit my lip. I did not know what to say, how to tell him the bitter truth. I wished that Dr. Haas were here to break the news to him. I tried again to free my hand as I said, "I told you—the eye was injured through a blow to your head."

"Have I lost the sight of it?"

There was a long silence while we stared at each other, Robert unseeingly, myself with a tear trickling down my cheek. I said slowly and with difficulty, "You have lost the eye itself."

Another silence and then he said quietly, "I see. Minus one eye and with defective vision in the other. I could wish for more cheerful news."

I wiped my tears away with the back of my hand.

"Dr. Haas has every hope that the sight of your right eye will be restored in time. And—and you are *alive*, Robert— what else matters? I thought of Nelson—you could still command a ship."

"Nelson?" He frowned, as if puzzled, then a wavering smile broke across his scarred face. "You are the oddest young woman I ever knew. Nelson. Yes, you are right—there is hope for me."

"I am talking too much and tiring you. *Please* rest. I will tell Wu Shing—he is the servant who has helped nurse you— to fetch Dr. Haas at once."

He closed his one eye.

"Thank you."

Slowly Robert began to recover. Some days he was almost his normal self, though weak and quickly tired; other days he could remember little of what had occurred. Sometimes he spoke at random or answered a question with irritability and often he would speak a few sentences and then fall suddenly asleep. It was bewildering but Dr. Haas assured me that these symptoms were the aftermath of the concussion from which Robert had suffered.

One day something happened that puzzled and distressed me.

I had gone to sit with him but found him still sleeping. Wu Shing retreated to the corridor as I sat quietly down by the bed to wait for Robert to wake and then I noticed he was curiously restless. He moved his head constantly, his face twitched, his lips moved as if he were dreaming, but not happily.

I leaned toward the bed, wondering whether to wake him yet hesitating to do so, and as if aware of my presence he turned his head toward me and without opening his eye murmured something unintelligible.

I said softly, touching the hand lying on the bedcover, "What is it, Robert? Are you awake?"

His one good eye remained closed but he spoke. He said one word which at first I could not catch and then he repeated it clearly.

It was a name.

"*Vanessa,*" he said. And then again, almost imploringly, "*Vanessa?*"

Slowly I straightened up, withdrawing my hand. "*Vanessa.*" The name echoed strangely in my mind and for some unaccountable reason I felt myself shiver.

It was as if a third person was in the room, and on impulse I stood up and instead of remaining with Robert until he woke, I returned to my own apartment. I wondered who Vanessa could be. I wondered to whom this name belonged that Robert should remember her in his dreams. A dream that seemed shadowed and unhappy, if one were to judge by the frown on his face, the restlessness of his demeanor. She was someone from his past, I thought, from the part of Robert's life that I had no knowledge of.

This experience made me realize how little I knew of him, how foolish and useless it was for me to love him. He would never care for me. We had been thrown together in unexpected and dangerous circumstances, but when the adventure was over, we would say goodbye and go our different ways.

I determined that in no way must I let Robert guess my regard for him. I would be more reserved and circumspect in manner.

This resolve was difficult, for a few days later, when I went in to see him, he was wide awake and the first thing he said was "I did not realize until now that I had acquired a wife. Legally, I trust? Or was it a shotgun wedding under duress? I cannot for the life of me remember acquiescing at the ceremony."

I felt my face warm with color, and the more embarrassed because of my own feelings for him, I stammered, "I—I am sorry. I did not know what to do—you were wounded. I thought at first the pirates were going to kill us and then the leader came and questioned me. I told him I was your—your wife so that I could remain with you. They brought us here together, as prisoners."

"As prisoners? Are we prisoners here, then? If so, they treat us kindly enough."

"We are prisoners just the same. Mr. Yao has refused to send word of our safety to Macao until you recovered consciousness. He says you are an important man and there are matters he wishes to discuss with you. What can they be?"

The frown on Robert's thin face deepened.

"I cannot conjecture. But now that I am getting better I suppose he will come and talk with me. You say you have no idea where we are?"

"None. We seem to be in the middle of nowhere. There is a deer park with guards at every gate." I told him of my venture into the park and my discovery of the Pearl Pagoda. "Perhaps when you are stronger, you will see it too. It is so beautiful."

"When I am stronger I shall make plans for us to leave this place," he answered in a harsh-sounding voice. "The sooner your Mr. Yao visits me, the better."

But it was some days before Mr. Yao paid him a visit, for Dr. Haas was still insistent that Robert should in no way be harassed or worried.

To pass the time I thought I would go to see the Pearl

Pagoda again, but before I could arrange this, Wei Liang presented herself to me, saying, "Mistress Lady wishes that I should bring you to her chamber. First, I arrange your dress and your hair, Honored Lady." And despite the fact that I was perfectly clean and tidy, she insisted upon my making a fresh toilette and then, with a pleased smile and bow, she said, "I will lead the way, Lady."

I followed her through the Second Moon Gate and through the courtyard to one of the pavilions set among trees. The hall through which we passed had a marble floor ornamented with mother-of-pearl and precious stones. A second hall displayed magnificent carpets of silk and velvet, and a shining chandelier overhead, ornamented with precious stones. Each apartment was separated from the other by graceful partitions of cypress and sandalwood with designs carved out of the wood so that each room could be seen from the next. As we passed from one room to another the wind bells tinkled above our heads in a sweet and delicate chiming.

The room into which I was finally conducted was on the second floor. On a carved chair at one end of it sat a short stout woman of middle age in an elaborate robe of green satin embroidered in seed pearls and coral. Her black hair was dressed smoothly across her head and was ornamented with jade and gold pins carved in the shapes of flowers and fruit. On either side of her, but at some distance, sat several other Chinese ladies varying in age from early teens to the mid-thirties. Behind them stood a row of children.

Placing the tips of my fingers together I bowed low, and she bowed her head in return and said in Cantonese, "Please to sit down, Honored Lady. I am Madame Yao." She gestured gracefully with elongated nails. "These are other wives of Mr. Yao," and she reeled off a string of names. "Also sons and daughters of Mr. Yao," and a further stream of names, which I could not hope to remember, broke from her. "I have seen you walking in the gardens. I regret that your honored husband has met with a serious accident and I trust that he recovers."

I sat down on the chair that one of the servants brought forward.

"Thank you, Honored Lady. He is much improved. I know he will be as grateful as I am for the generous hospitality that has been extended to us and for the care that the honored doctor has bestowed upon him. I hope that we shall not impose upon the kindness of the honored Mr. Yao too long but may soon return to the city of Macao."

Having performed the ceremony that was expected of me, I sat silent before Madame Yao.

She frowned.

"I do not know the city of Macao. It is a place of foreigners, I understand. My home was in Canton. You have visited Canton?"

"Once, for a few days, Honored Lady," and I described something of the visit to my attentive audience. I answered their many questions and then I went on to tell them something of the work of the Mission. I could see they had never heard of the life of our Lord or the story of the Gospel and they listened in wonderment, as if to some ancient legend.

"It is a strange story you recount to us, and one it is hard to believe is true," Madame Yao said, shaking her head. "But I am aware that foreigners have customs and beliefs very different from our own. You are the first foreign lady who has visited the house of Mr. Yao. Foreign men have come before but no wife of a foreigner."

I was startled by the last sentence. "Foreign men have come before," Madame Yao had just said. What foreign men? I wondered. And when? And how often?

"Were they Englishmen, Honored Lady?"

She shook her head.

"That I do not know. Naturally, I have not seen them. That would be improper. It is something I was told." She added, "I do not think they were holy men, such as you have described to us.'" She changed the subject by asking, "You sit much in the garden and alone. Do you walk in the Deer Park sometimes?"

"I have been once there to visit the Pagoda of the Many Pearls. It is a most beautiful building."

"Yes. It was built to bring good fortune to the house of Mr. Yao and all who dwell therein."

I glanced around the exquisitely furnished room, at the silken robes worn by the ladies of Mr. Yao and more especially the richly elaborate costume worn by Madame Yao, and I could not help saying somewhat ironically, "It certainly seems to have done that."

Madame Yao bowed her head.

"The Gods of Our Ancestors and the Gods of Good Stars have blessed us." She was silent for a few moments, then she said, "It will please me if you honor us with your presence again. You may tell us more of the foreign land far across the sea from the Middle Kingdom, and more of the life of your holy man."

"I thank you, Honored Lady Wife. It would bring me happiness to visit you again." I rose and bowed, first to Madame Yao and then to the other wives in turn and lastly to the alert bright-eyed children who had stood so quietly and so patiently in my presence.

From somewhere unseen Wei Liang appeared and with a final bow to Madame Yao I was led out of the chamber and downstairs and through the several halls and to the courtyard and so back to my apartment.

I was eager to tell Robert of my encounter with Madame Yao, but when I went to visit him next day he said, before I had a chance to speak except in greeting, "I have been thinking —remembering. There was a storm. Was that when"—he paused, frowning, and his mouth twisted as if with pain— "when Te Ling was drowned?"

Hesitantly I answered, "It was the next day—after the storm. She—Te Ling—ran to save George from being swept overboard and—and 'was thrown into the sea herself. She was very brave. I feel—we all feel responsible for her death."

He made no answer but lay silent, staring up at the carved ceiling with unseeing eyes. After a while he said, "You need not. It is I who am responsible. Poor Te Ling. If she had not stowed away so as to be with me on this voyage, she would be alive now."

"She—she loved you." I wanted to ask "Did you love her?" but I dared not.

His broad chest rose and fell on a sigh.

"Perhaps, in her own way. We had become attached to each other. There were times when I was lonely and she was affectionate and honest and—*good*. A man cannot ask for more." He was silent again and then he said on a different note, "If it had not been for the storm we would have escaped being captured by the pirates. The broken mast handicapped us and we could not get away fast enough." He turned a blank unfocused eye upon me. "What happened to the *Lotus Wind?*"

I said slowly and painfully, "The pirates set her alight. She burned. and then sank." My voice trembled. "Oh, Robert—your beautiful ship."

His mouth tightened grimly.

"It is their damnable custom. Such men act upon the belief that dead men tell no tales." He frowned. "I cannot understand how it is *we* are alive."

"I heard one of the pirates speak of you as a 'prize.' That is why they brought you here—as a hostage of some kind."

"But *you*—why are you here with me like this, and no one else?"

"Dr. Howard and his wife and children got away in one of the boats. Some of the crew were with them. I—I fear the rest are dead." I bit my lip and forced myself to go on. "I said I was your—your wife."

"Of course—so you told me. I had forgotten." He turned his head this way and that, as if trying to make out my face. "Well, Megan, I never wanted a wife, but I must admit I'm grateful that you have assumed the role. At least we are company for each other, though I cannot understand why you did not get away with the others. It was Dr. Howard's responsibility to see you into the boat before himself. Did he not attempt to help you?"

"Indeed, yes. He did his best to urge me over the side of the ship but—but I saw you lying there covered in blood—I felt I had to do something to help."

He said slowly, "I remember now. There was a man with a knife coming for us and you—you threw something at him. I

saw him fall over and then I think I fainted." He added in a
puzzled voice, "You saved me, Megan?"

I was silent for a moment.

"I am not sure of that. But—I owed you a life. You saved
me the night of the storm at the Cape. If you had not rescued
me then I should have been drowned—just as poor Te Ling
was."

He was silent then, as if remembering the beautiful Chinese girl who had loved him, and whom he had cared for in
return. To my surprise, he put a hand out toward me, saying,
"So we are quits."

I put my hand in his, feeling a faint tremor pass through
me at the touch of his fingers.

"Yes."

It was strange to sit like that, our hands clasped in each
other's. It made me happy yet it made me sad also, for the
gesture meant little to Robert; it was merely a sign of his
gratitude. When I saw him lay his head wearily on the pillow I
withdrew my hand and said quietly, knowing that this was not
a suitable time in which to recount my visit to Madame Yao,
"We have talked too much. You are tired, Robert. I will leave
you to rest."

The next morning I had a pleasant surprise, for when I
went to visit him it was to find him seated in a chair. He
looked distressingly gaunt and the black patch over the eye
socket accentuated his extreme pallor, but when he turned his
head in my direction, he gave me a grimace that was intended
as a smile and said, "Is that you, Megan? You will see I am well
on the way to recovery, up and dressed, and, I trust, in my
right mind, though I cannot say I am pleased to be garbed like
a Chinaman," and he flicked the stuff of the long robe he
wore.

"You look most impressive," I assured him. "Almost like a
mandarin." The blue satin robe reached to his feet, which
were shod in black velvet slippers, and a darker blue satin
jacket worn over the robe completed the ensemble.

"Thank you, but I have no wish to resemble an Oriental

potentate." He rubbed his chin. "They insist upon shaving me each day—I feel undressed without my beard."

"No man in China is supposed to wear a beard until he is over thirty-five. It is a symbol of wisdom."

"I doubt if I shall qualify for that, whatever my age."

I went to stand beside his chair.

"The important thing is not your appearance but how you feel, Robert."

"I feel less than myself. A travesty of a man, but Dr. Haas informs me that I shall soon recover my strength now that I am no longer bedridden. Let us hope he is correct. Anyway, I am thankful to be up, if only in a chair. I understand from Dr. Haas that Mr. Yao will be coming to visit me shortly. Perhaps after we have talked together I can persuade him to send word to Macao."

"If only you could."

He frowned.

"What sort of a man is he? You told me something of your interview with him and said he was frightening. In what way?"

"I don't know. He was polite enough and yet he was—was hard. Implacable somehow. He seems to think you have some information or knowledge that would be useful to him. Is this so, Robert?"

He shook his head, his mouth tightening.

"I'm sorry. I prefer not to discuss the situation at this stage. It's nothing personal." He added, as if aware of my sense of rebuff, "I am sure you are entirely trustworthy, Megan. But it is better that you know as little as possible of my affairs for you may well be questioned again by Mr. Yao. If there is anything he should be conversant of he will learn it from me, not you."

He spoke so abruptly, with so much of the old harsh Robert in his manner, that I was silenced. Afterward I could not speak as easily and freely as I had come to do and in a short while I took my leave of him.

That afternoon I set out again to the Pearl Pagoda, as if to find comfort within its latticed walls. Yet my walk through the Deer Park was to cause me the greatest anxiety I had yet experienced.

Walking slightly ahead of Lin Sing, as was my habit, and bending now and then to examine more closely the numerous exotic flowers that edged the path, I caught sight, in the distance, of a small speckled fawn moving gracefully under the trees. It was almost completely hidden by the tall grass that grew in this part of the park, camouflaged by its coloring, which exactly reflected the lacy pattern of sunshine as it filtered through the dense foliage. I was enchanted by the sight and followed softly behind the animal, anxious for a closer look. Lin Sing, following my own gaze, tiptoed behind. We had gone thus for about two hundred feet when my foot hit upon some obstacle hidden in the grass, and I tripped, involuntarily crying out as I lost my balance. At the sound, the fawn leaped gracefully into the thick forest, and I found myself entangled in my Chinese robes on the soft ground. I was unhurt and rather exhilarated by the secret chase, and as Lin Sing took my hand to help me up, I looked down to see what had caused my misstep. There, almost completely hidden by a profusion of leafy vines and small purple flowers, was what appeared to be a small tombstone.

I heard an involuntary intake of breath and turned to see Lin Sing recoil, his hand in front of his face as if to ward off a blow.

"Honored Lady," he began, his quivering voice betraying agitation, "we must return at once to the Great Hall."

Perhaps my own dread gave me courage, or the image of the fawn, so wild and yet so imprisoned, strengthened my will, for I spoke with an unaccustumed forcefulness.

"Nonsense," I said as I stooped to brush off the soil and vines that obscured the lettering on the stone, "there is nothing here to harm us."

I knelt once again on the soft earth and strained to make out the inscription, which I realized with a start was in English. A date, 1831, was scratched crudely into the hard stone, and the letters G E O R G E C O L B . . . , the rest hopelessly erased by exposure to the elements.

"Honored Lady, Honored Lady," Lin Sing said, pulling at my arm, "we are not allowed. This is burial place of foreign devils. There will be great punishment."

Turning once again to protest, I closed my lips when I observed the intense fear that had transformed the youthful face of my guide into a mask of terror. I rose then, my mind and heart filled with conflicting thoughts and emotions. Who was this mysterious Englishman lying in a neglected grave somewhere deep inside China? And, if what Lin Sing had said was true and there were other such hidden graves, who were his companions? As I hurried after Lin Sing, anxious to leave this section of the Deer Park behind me, I was struck once again by the chilling realization that the exquisite beauty of our surroundings, like the richly garbed figure of Mr. Yao himself, disguised an interior full of evil and corruption.

As we stood together at the massive gate leading out of the park, I turned once more toward Lin Sing and bowed. I could only hope his fear of punishment would seal his lips. For my part, I decided to say nothing to Robert, for the presence of the tombstone made clear to me that some of the prisoners brought here never left again.

Another week went by and at the end of it Mr. Yao visited Robert. The details of the interview Robert did not reveal, but when I saw him soon afterward, he told me that there was little likelihood of our being rescued as yet.

"We have reached deadlock," he said, frowning. "I cannot agree to Yao's terms of release and like all Orientals he is in no hurry to conclude matters and hopes to wear me down into agreement through attrition."

I opened my mouth to say, "But to what must you agree?" and then I closed it again. I had learned my lesson and knew better than to question Robert a second time concerning Mr. Yao. His secrecy puzzled me but I concluded it must concern some affair to do with the British Navy or with trading matters of which I had no knowledge. And so I said no more, but my heart was heavy with the knowledge I had recently obtained, and I prayed fervently that Robert's stubborn nature would not prove to be our undoing.

CHAPTER 13

I VISITED Madame Yao several times and talked to her and to the other wives about the Mission. The children cheered me with their laughing chatter and on one visit the children sang for me to a soft lute accompaniment played by one of the mothers. In return, I was asked if I would not sing for them.

At first I hesitated, for my heart had little melody in it. Yet the smiling faces were so eager and expectant that I could not refuse, but instead of singing the hymn I had intended, I found myself murmuring the words of an old Welsh ballad.

> " '*Er mwyn y gur a wraeth dy wedd,*
> *Gwna im dru-gar-edd bell ach*
> *Cwnn dy ben gwel oc co draw*
> *Rho i mi'th law wen dir-vion.*
> *Gwaith gn dy fyn-wes berth er thro*
> *Mae all-wedd clo ty ngha-lon.*' "

I saw them staring at me in bewilderment at words and sounds so foreign to their ears, and I smiled and said in Cantonese, "That is the language of my own country. I am from Wales."

Madame Yao shook her head and the other wives followed suit.

"What does it mean?"

"I will translate it for you. It is called *Idle Days in Summertime* and is a love song, though a sad one."

I sang it through again, lingering over the last phrases.

" 'No more the lovers passed their days,
Amid the fields together
Cruel Fate had severed them
And both are brokenhearted.
Had they been wed in summertime
They would not now be parted.' "

My audience seemed to understand, for they nodded and smiled and clapped their hands, and asked for more. But I shook my head and told them I would sing another song another day. Next time it would be a hymn, I decided.

Soon Robert was able to walk, although he still limped from the wound in his leg. Wu Shing produced a stout stick and upon this Robert leaned, and with his other hand on Wu Shing's shoulder, he would maneuver the stairs down to the courtyard where each day he sat.

I usually sat with him for a time and if he wished to take gentle exercise along the paved paths I would substitute for Wu Shing and he would rest a hand on my shoulder or take my arm so that I might guide him. He had difficulty in seeing any object in his path, for the vision of the remaining eye was extremely limited. From what he told me, he had a blurred vision of the world, figures and features were hard to distinguish and he was unable to read or write. He had to take great care when eating lest the bowl tip over or the dish slide from the edge of the table, and he could not manage chopsticks but had to use a porcelain spoon at every meal.

It was sad to see his eyes, those eyes once so keen and hard and of so dark a blue. The empty eye socket was hidden under a black patch, and the other, dimmed and bloodshot, was not properly focused when he looked at me.

We spoke together, and if I learned little of Robert in the process, he learned a great deal about me.

"Talk to me, Megan," he would say, leaning back in his chair. "Tell me some more about that farm of yours in the place with the unpronounceable name," and I would go on to tell him of Hafod Trefeiddan and the great Grwyne Fawr, of my grandfather and my little grandmother and the people I had known and loved. I would tell him of harsh mountain winters and lush valley summers. I spoke of my parents and once we talked of Arthur and the Mission, though I did not tell Robert the tragic circumstances of Arthur's death.

That was the time he leaned forward to touch my clasped hands.

"I am sorry he died and you were left, but it would not have done for you, Megan. You were not meant to be the wife of a clergyman. You are too warm and alive and impulsive. Fierce, too," he added with a slight smile. "Tackling a pirate single-handed."

I shuddered involuntarily.

"I cannot believe I ever did such a thing."

Another time he persuaded me to sing for him. I had told him of my visit to Madame Yao and how the wives had performed for me and I had sung for them in return.

"Sing for me," he urged. "I believe I see you shaking your head. Are you? Please sing something for me. And in Welsh."

So, softly and somewhat diffidently, I murmured a few bars of the song that had been my grandfather's favorite. It was called *"Y Fwyalchen"*—*"The Blackbird."*

Robert sat still and silent until the song was ended.

"Thank you. You have a sweet true voice. Tell me a little of what it means."

"A harpist speaks in praise of the blackbird whose song he loved. He, as a minstrel, has old memories that lend sadness to his own song, but the blackbird's is full of joy. In his song he says," and I sang a few bars again:

> " 'Mae'n dda mod i'c ieuanc' rwy'n gwybod
> Heb arfer fawr drafod y byd,
> Pam peidaist ti ferch, a mhriodi,
> A finnau'n dy garlyn di cy'd!'

which means,

> 'While thou hast no thought of forgetting
> The griefs of a long dreary past,

Thou singest but of joy, naught regretting,
Rejoicing, thou singest to the last!' "

"How strange the Welsh language sounds to me, but it is full of melody."

During these conversations Robert said little about himself. Only once did he answer my hesitant question by saying, "There is little to tell you. My mother died at my birth, my father when I was six. I was brought up by an uncle, my father's only brother."

"That was sad. I hope your uncle was kind to you."

"Yes, in truth he was. He treated me almost as another son." Robert's mouth curled. "Which is more than I can say for my aunt—who bore a grudge against me from the moment I went to live at Hawkestone. My cousin Philip was unfortunately a cripple and delicate in health and she resented the fact of my being a healthy, hulking boy."

"What or where is Hawkestone?" I asked, intrigued by the name.

"It is an estate near Bath. Philip inherited it when my uncle died."

"Were you fond of your cousin?"

"Yes, we were friends. Although I was the younger I took him under my wing, for he feared the many things he could not do and those he could have done his mother would not permit him to try. She spoiled and indulged him to his detriment. But Philip and I had an affection for each other until—"

His voice broke off. He stared straight ahead as if seeing some place or picture beyond my view.

"Until what?" I prompted gently.

He shook his head.

"It is of no consequence. I have had enough of reminiscing for the present."

It had been on the tip of my tongue to ask who Vanessa was—if she was a cousin or part of the Hawkestone household. I had often thought of the name he had murmured in his dream. A name which in some way echoed within me with a warning peal, as if my Celtic blood stirred in premonition. *Vanessa.* I longed to ask "Who was she?" But I could not.

We talked no more that day but a little while later he spoke of being in the Navy and I asked him at what age he had joined.

"I was twenty-four. My uncle died and"—he paused, frowning—"everything changed. I wanted to leave Somerset and so I went into the Navy. It was easy enough to obtain a commission for England was embroiled in the trouble in India and the Navy was needed to ship arms and troops for the battles of Ferozeshah and, later, Sobraon. After seven years I bought myself out."

"Do you ever go back to your old home—to Hawkestone?"

His expression changed. He stood up abruptly, saying, "Never. I have never been back and never shall," and with that he walked stumblingly away, his stick extended before him.

He never spoke again of his family or his boyhood.

He had black moods and during these I avoided him. I understood the frustration caused by his blindness, for having been so strong and active, so much in command, it was understandable that his temper was uncertain. Yet at other times I caught a glimpse of the old Robert. As the day when his hand upon my shoulder tightened its grip and he said, "How pleasantly soft you feel. It is the silken robe you wear. Is it pink— or yellow? I can see only a shadowy form in some light color. You no longer wear one of your prim dark dresses but are robed as a Chinese lady. I am sure it suits you with your straight black hair and dark eyes."

I was thankful that he could not see my blushing cheeks. Because even such an indirect compliment made me diffident, I said stiffly, "We have come to a seat. Will you not take a rest?"

His hand fell from my shoulder as he sat down.

"I can hear water. Are we by the pool?"

"Yes. It is very beautiful. Everywhere there is beauty. The Chinese people have a gift for creating gardens."

He shrugged indifferently.

"Gardens have never interested me. They are too enclosed, too man-made. It is the sea that I love." He added with a sudden vehemence, "God knows if I shall ever command a ship again."

"I am sure you will, one day."

He turned his head to look at me.

"You are trying to comfort me with platitudes. Like a kindly nanny. Or a wife. I keep forgetting you are my self-designated wife. Do you regard me as your husband?"

I said confusedly, "Of course not. I have told you the reason for the pretense."

"And I am grateful for your subterfuge. At least misery has company." He frowned. "If only I could get that devil Yao to agree to send word to Macao without conditions."

A chill came over me at that moment as I remembered the crumbling gravestone I had stumbled upon. Had that Englishman too waited in vain in these beautiful gardens in the hope that a message disclosing his whereabouts would bring about his rescue? Forcing myself to speak calmly, I said tentatively, "You feel you cannot agree to his conditions?"

"I don't wish to. It is blackmail. I wish there were some way to send a message in secret. I wonder if it would be possible—if we could find a servant open to bribery. Except that we have nothing of value with which to bribe anyone."

"No. But perhaps we could offer a reward to be given upon delivery of the message?"

He shook his head.

"I don't know if that would be bait enough. I'll think about it. No use your worrying about it, Megan. It is not your concern."

I was effectively silenced and could do no more than sit staring at the dragonflies that darted in shimmering iridescence above the lotus pool. But Robert's words had set my mind conjecturing and I knew that there was something I had forgotten, something that might hold the key to our escape if only I could think of it.

That night, as I was undressing, the idea came to me. As I unfastened the linen bag around my neck I remembered the jade earrings that Sylvia had given me. They were valuable I knew. Valuable enough perhaps to tempt a servant to deliver a message to the outside world? There was a small village beyond the walls of the Deer Park. I knew that, because when talking with Lin Sing, he had confided to me that his family lived in the "village beyond the gates."

That was it. *Lin Sing*, of course. *He* would have access to the village, for he surely went home at various times. Since our adventure at the "burial place of foreign devils," as he had called it, a conspiracy of silence had bound us together, and of necessity, a mutual trust. If I showed him the earrings and gave him one to take the message and have it sent to Macao, and promised him the second earring when we had received an answer, would he agree to my request, hazardous though it might be for him? I had a feeling that he would.

I could scarcely sleep that night, my mind alive with the idea of escape. I wondered whether I should consult Robert first and then I decided against it on two counts. One was that he did not want to discuss his affairs with me, and the other was that just as he had warned me that knowledge of these matters might prove difficult if I were questioned, so his own awareness of the plan might be of possible embarrassment to him. It should remain a secret for the time being.

The following day I made plans to walk to the Pearl Pagoda.

"Would you mind?" I asked Robert. "I—I feel I need exercise and I think it is too great a distance for you to manage as yet, although I am sure it won't be long before we can go there together."

"Your wifely solicitude does you credit, Megan. But don't worry on my account—I would as soon be alone when the black dog sits upon my shoulder."

I put a hand out toward him.

"Please—Robert—" I began, but he turned away, not seeing my outstretched hand, and sat down by the latticed window.

Lin Sing was waiting to escort me. Soon we were walking under the spreading branches of the cedar trees and along the path that led to the pagoda. Although Lin Sing kept dutifully a pace behind me, he was close enough for us to carry on a conversation.

This morning I asked him about his home, and he told me

of his old grandmother and his parents and his younger brothers and sisters. We reached the clearing where the lake, still and blue, reflected on its waters the silvery curving tiers of the Pearl Pagoda. For a few moments I stood staring up at it in silence, wondering why the pagoda seemed of such significance to me, as if, somehow, it were an important factor in my life.

Leaving Lin Sing squatting on the grass by the water I went through the lattice door and slowly up the winding staircase to the topmost tier. I walked onto the balcony. Everywhere I saw a mass of foliage, like green clouds floating beneath me. Above, a cerulean sky; and far away on the horizon, a shining reflection of light. *The sea.*

As ever my fears and cares fell away, and the strange ambience of the pagoda, at once soothing and benign, descended upon me so that I felt as one in a dream.

For a long time I stood there and then I remembered upon what errand I had come. Carefully I removed the jade earrings from the bag around my neck and concealing them in my hand I went slowly down the stairs. Standing within the shadow of the pagoda I beckoned to Lin Sing, and when he approached more closely, I said, "I have a favor to ask of you, Lin Sing. Before I tell you what it is will you promise me that if you cannot do this thing for me you will never speak of it to anyone else."

He looked at me in puzzlement.

"But what is it you wish me to do, Lady? I shall be honored to assist you in any way I can."

I shook my head.

"Please promise first that you will keep my request a secret between us."

For a moment he hesitated, then he nodded.

"I promise, Lady."

"It is this. Will you take a letter and arrange for it to be sent to Macao? It is a message to our friends there who may be thinking my honored husband and myself are lost to them. If you help us, I will give you this as a reward," and I held out one earring. He stared, first at the earring and then at me, his eyes gleaming at the sight of the jade. "When we receive acknowledgment of the message, you shall have the other one. See?" I showed him the second earring lying in the palm of my hand.

He hesitated, frowning the meanwhile, and then he said slowly, "It is a dangerous thing you ask, Lady. I go to my home only once in a moon. I do not know whom I could trust to do this thing for me."

"The jade is valuable. You would have money with which to help your parents, your brothers. Would not one of them send the message for you?"

He was silent again, staring at the jade in a pensive way. He said thoughtfully, "I have a brother who is a fisherman. Perhaps he knows someone who voyages to Macao. I will ask him."

"But it must be a secret," I said quickly. "Can you trust him?"

"He is my brother. He would not betray me."

"Then take this, Lin Sing," and I put one earring in his hand. "The other will be yours when we hear from or see our own people again. I am very grateful to you, as will be my honored husband. Thank you. We will not speak of this again —it is our secret."

He bowed his head.

"I do not visit my family until the first days of the new moon, Lady, so I ask you to be patient."

"Of course. And thank you again, Lin Sing."

We walked back through the park in silence, Lin Sing no doubt pondering on his errand and myself thinking of Robert and wondering whether after all I should tell him what I had done. But, for the second time, I decided against it.

A week went by. I crossed the days assiduously off my homemade calendar. Would Lin Sing have gone back to his village and his home yet?

Robert was restless, for with returning health his blindness was a frustrating handicap. I knew that Mr. Yao visited him on several occasions and after each confrontation Robert was more short-tempered and frowned more than ever.

One morning I decided to walk to the park and find out if Lin Sing was still there. On impulse I asked Robert if he would care to accompany me.

"Now your leg is so much better it would not be too far to walk to the Pearl Pagoda and—and I could be your guide."

He shrugged.

"There's precious little I shall see of this wonderful edifice. But, yes, I will come. It is something to do and I have had a surfeit of sitting in the courtyard."

When we reached the gate leading from the courtyard, the older guard, who I knew was called Chang Nien, greeted us with a nod and a scowl. I had never seen him smile as yet. Brandishing the stout pole he always carried and staring hard at Robert's black patch and his other unfocused eye, he said sternly, "Where you wish to go? Boy not here today. I get other guide."

"We are only walking as far as the Pagoda of the Many Pearls," I answered. "My husband is handicapped by semi-blindness. I know the way and am to be his guide. May we not go alone, for we cannot run away, as you can see."

He looked first at me and then at Robert, then he shrugged his powerful shoulders.

"No go Deer Park. Go only pagoda. I wait, see you come back."

"Yes. But we shall not hurry. We will rest at the pagoda before returning."

The guard nodded.

"You go now."

Robert had remained silent during this interchange, but as we turned away up the path he said, "Not a very forthcoming character. I couldn't see him properly but he looked a big fellow."

"He is a giant. But sometimes there is a boy here—I told you of him. He is gentle and friendly." I hesitated, wanting to confide in him about Lin Sing but fearing to do so lest I enmesh Robert in my scheme and cause trouble for him.

His hand was on my shoulder, but when he stumbled once or twice I said, "Please take my arm. It will be easier for you."

He slid his hand through my arm and at once we seemed very close. I could feel the warmth of his body against my own and for some reason I felt myself tremble. When he raised his head to sniff the air and say, "There is a smell of pine," my voice was not quite steady as I answered, "Yes. There are pine trees, and cedar here. Can you see them at all?"

"Only a green blur. It is very pleasant under the trees."

"Yes." The sun was high in the heavens now, but the forest was cool and beautiful. "You are not tired with walking?"

"Not at all. I scarcely feel my leg now. Don't fuss, Megan."

"I am sorry."

He pressed his arm against my side.

"I allow for your wifely consideration."

I did not answer him and for a time we walked on in silence. Then, as upon my first visit, we came with surprising suddenness to the clearing. The lake glittered and shone in the sunlight and the pearly reflection of the pagoda danced in its waters.

Robert said, almost wonderingly, "What is this? Water of some kind?"

"Yes. A lake. Can you see the pagoda? Oh, I hope you can."

He screwed up his right eye.

"I see something—very tall and silvery. Is that it?"

"Yes. The carvings are all of ivory and mother-of-pearl and these shine in the sun. It is so beautiful."

He turned his head to smile down at me.

"You are enamored of the place. Do we go inside?"

"If you would like to. But you would not see very much."

"We can rest there, perhaps."

I lifted the latch of the lattice door and guided Robert through. The ground floor was cool and dark and smelled a trifle musty.

"What is there to see here?" Robert asked, staring around.

"Nothing, really. It is dark down here, you see. The higher up you go, the more light, but the staircase would be too difficult for you, I think. It is a spiral one and very narrow."

"I'd like to try. If you took my hand—maybe I could feel my way up to another tier."

"I don't know . . ." I began doubtfully, but he reached for my hand and said, "Come, Megan. Show me the way."

I went first, grasping his big hand firmly in my own. The staircase was an open one, but by holding on to the narrow rail Robert managed to make his way carefully up to the second tier. When I paused, he said, "Now the next."

"We cannot attempt to reach the top," I protested. "And you would not be able to see the view."

"Never mind that. Let's get halfway and then we can rest."

At a snail's pace we ascended as far as the fourth tier and then Robert said, "I think that's as much as I shall attempt. Is there a balcony?"

"Yes. This way," and I led him through one of the arched openings onto the narrow balcony. Robert let go of my hand and leaned against the latticework and stared over the trees.

I stood beside him in silence as, frowning, he tried to make out the view. After a while he said, "It is nothing but a sea of green."

"Yes. From here we look out over the trees. On the other side is the clearing and the lake."

He said impatiently, "It was a waste of time to come. I can't see anything. Perhaps I never shall again." He turned away and groped toward the opening and stumbled through it. I sprang after him, clutching at his arm.

"Be careful! You may fall down the stairway and hurt yourself."

He stopped dead.

"That is all I need. To be told I may tumble and break my neck. There are times when I think it might be a good thing if I did."

"Please don't talk like that. You are so much better. You can walk—you are mobile again. Soon you will regain some of your sight."

He peered down at me, his face bent to mine. His hands came up to hold me by each arm so that I was imprisoned within his grasp.

"I wish I could see you properly, Megan. You are a good little thing. And a brave little thing. I am sorry to sound ungrateful for this life of mine you saved." He said slowly, with a shake of his head, "What made you stay with me that day on the *Lotus Wind*? Was it because you cared something for me?"

"I—I thought you were going to die. I could not leave you so." I bit my lip, aware of Robert's close gaze, wondering if he could see how confused and awkward I felt. And then I lifted my head and spoke with frankness. "If you had, I think I would have wished to die also."

"Instead we are together, in this strange place, as husband and wife. You would make a good wife to any man, Megan, for you are honest and loyal." His mouth twisted. "I have not found loyalty to be a characteristic of your sex."

"You do us an injustice. We are loyal as any man."

He moved a hand to touch my cheek with his finger.

"I think you would be." The finger slid to my chin and he tilted my face to his. "I think you could be a great many things a man might wish for in a woman. Do you realize we have never exchanged a kiss? We will remedy that immediately," and slowly, gently, his mouth came down on mine.

I had never been kissed before. Not like this. Not by a man. Arthur had held my hand once or twice and the day he said goodbye to me he had kissed my cheek in chaste salute.

Now Robert took me in his arms and kissed me warmly and deeply and I felt myself tremble from head to foot, as with an ague. For the first time in my life I experienced the fervor and passion of a man's embrace, and, moreover, that of the man I loved. For weeks I had been in close proximity to Robert. I had seen him all but die; I had hovered over the bed where he lay for so long a time unconscious. I had grieved for him in the loss of his eye, the diminishment of his vigor. We had shared a terrible danger, a forced imprisonment. We had talked together, argued sometimes, confided in each other, myself more especially, and now in the strange and shadowy peace of the Pearl Pagoda we came together. It was little wonder that after the first shiver of awareness I should respond to Robert's kiss. My lips opened under his as a flower to the morning sun. My arms crept about his neck, feeling the rough brown hair between my fingers. Closer and closer was I clasped in his arms, and knew the stirring strength of his hard, lean body against my own.

We sank down onto the tiled floor. If it was hard and cold I was not aware of these things. Only of Robert, of the searching demanding kisses that weakened all resistance. He had unloosed my silken robe and his lips moved caressingly over my bare skin as he murmured my name against my throat. I loved, and I thought that he must love me. But even if this were not true as yet, I could not withstand him. I wanted to give everything of myself and receive in return everything of him. Past, present and future were forgotten in the blinding ecstatic moment that we became lovers.

I do not know how long it was before I returned to my own being. For a long while we lay in each other's arms on the hard, uncomfortable floor without speaking, but at last Robert said gently, "We must go back, Megan. Or the guard will send out a search party."

I guessed by the sound of his voice that he was smiling, but I could not meet his glance. I was still shaken by the intensity of the emotion that I had experienced and I was overwhelmed by self-consciousness. He rose stiffly to his feet and, retaining his grip of my hand, pulled me upright. Tipping my chin up, as he had done before, he turned my face toward him and said quietly, "Do not be shy of me, Megan. I think you are a sweet and wonderful girl. A blind man is not much of a proposition as a husband, but would you consider becoming my wife in actuality, instead of make-believe? We could be married just as soon as ever we are released from this place. Providing we ever are."

I met his half-smiling unfocused glance and I felt my heart lurch with love for him.

"I—I do not know what to say. You once told me you never desired a wife."

"Ah, but that was before one was wished upon me."

I turned my head away.

"Do not tease or I shall think you are not serious."

His voice sobered.

"I have never been more serious in my life. Apart from the question of honor, you would be doing me the greatest of favors. You cheer and comfort me, Megan. You put up with my bad moods and my ill temper. I think—I hope—that you care for me a little, for no woman ever gave herself more generously or more lovingly to any man. Marry me, Megan, and we will try and make a good life together."

I colored at his last words but hesitated before answering him. He had not said he loved me. Had I expected him to? It was enough that he honored me with his proposal.

I said slowly, "Are you sure—Robert?"

"I am very sure. I cannot imagine life without you. We have shared so much together, hardship as well as—happiness."

"Then, I thank you. If it pleases you I will become your wife."

He bent his head and kissed me and I felt the stir of a flame deep inside me. Robert must have felt desire too, for he straightened up abruptly and said, "Come, Megan. We must not linger."

Slowly and carefully we descended the winding stairs. When we reached the ground tier he paused, looking around with a puzzled expression on his face.

"It is odd," he said, "but this place has an unusual atmosphere. Not an unpleasant one—quite the reverse. A sort of benignity. Do you feel it too, Megan?"

I nodded.

"Yes. It is because the Gods of Good Stars lend their goodwill to the pagoda. People who come here are made happy."

He slid his hand through my arm.

"We are happy, Megan. If only because we came together here."

"I hope we shall be happy wherever we are," I answered.

I did not see Robert again that day for he was tired after the excursion to the Pearl Pagoda and slept much of the afternoon. I rested too, but my mind was alert and wakeful with all that had happened to me that day. I was to marry Robert. I could scarcely believe it. We were lovers. A shiver of delight went through me at the remembrance. I had little thought of proprieties or morals. Our lives had been too unconventional, too altered in every way, and what had happened to us was only another part of it.

I slept little that night thinking of Robert. I loved him. I loved him with every part of my being. I could only hope and pray that he would love me a little in return. If he had not been blinded, if we had not been thrown together in such strange and hazardous circumstances, would he have asked me to marry him? I sighed, turning my head restlessly upon the pillow in my doubts. And then I thought, It has happened. If we escape from here, we will be married. And I will do everything I can to make him happy.

I fell asleep toward dawn and was wakened by a tap on the door of my room. Surprised, thinking it was Wei Liang, who would have walked in without knocking, I called, "Come in," and was startled to see a strange manservant standing in the doorway.

"My honored master wishes to speak with you. Please to rise and dress, Lady. I will wait to escort you to my master."

In some trepidation at this early and unexpected summons, I slid out of bed just as Wei Liang came pattering in, muttering imprecations against the servant who had dared to waken me with so little ceremony. With her assistance I was soon washed and dressed and ready to follow the blue-clad figure down the staircase and through the several halls to Mr. Yao's vast and splendid room. As before, he was seated at the carved teak desk, his hands hidden in his sleeves. He did not rise to greet me, but for a long moment after the servant had left the room, closing the door as he did so, Mr. Yao fixed me with an implacable black stare. Then, before I could speak, he said in a coldly harsh voice, "I regret that you have chosen to abuse the hospitality of my house, Lady."

A tremor of fear swept through me at his manner.

"I—I do not understand, Honored Sir."

"I think you understand very well, Lady. If you prefer to pretend ignorance of your dealings with my lower servants I will enlighten you." One incredibly long-nailed hand emerged from the robe and pitched a small object onto the desk. It fell with a thin tinkle and my heart seemed to miss a beat as I saw the flash of green and gold. I knew what it was. Even without a second look I recognized it. The jade earring that I had given to Lin Sing.

I was numbed by the wave of cold terror that swept over me, and as if he was enjoying my alarm, Mr. Yao's wide waxy face broke into a gargoyle smile as he said, "So you have recovered your memory, Lady. This bauble belongs to you, I think. It was recovered from the sly and worthless youth who was foolish enough to be persuaded by your bribery to deceive me. The letter you gave him has been destroyed. There will be no more such communications. It is my desire that you and your husband, who doubtless incited you to this action, will remain here under my roof until I choose that you shall be released."

I was trembling so much that I had to hold on to the edge of the desk to steady myself. I swallowed the lump of fear in my throat and forced myself to speak, though my voice was scarcely more than a thread of sound.

"It is *because* you are keeping us as prisoners here that I have had to resort to these measures. You—you never had any intention of sending a communication to Macao for us. Captain Hawkes knows nothing of my effort to get your servant to help us effect a rescue. I acted of my own will."

Mr. Yao shrugged his immense shoulders.

"It is of no consequence to me which of you plotted this stupidity. Take your bauble and go. And remember, Lady, you are indeed my prisoners until I decide when you shall be free."

"But you can't—it is absolutely wrong. You have no right—" I was babbling incoherently in my fear and anger.

Mr. Yao shook his head.

"It is useless to talk in this way. Be so good as to leave me."

But I could not go without further protest.

"Lin Sing—it is not *his* fault. Please don't punish him," I begged. "He is only young—and poor. I tempted him with the offer of money from this jewelry."

Mr. Yao's narrow black eyes lifted to meet my imploring gaze. He said coldly, "The punishment has already been meted out. A suitable one, in the circumstances," And as I stared at him with growing horror, he added gently, "We have cut off his ear."

CHAPTER 14

I COULD NOT speak for the wave of horror that engulfed me. I could only stare in appalled silence at Mr. Yao, while he gazed back at me, his face blankly expressionless. At last words came in a gasping incoherence.

"You can't—it is impossible. You—you could not be so barbaric. Oh, I cannot believe it."

"I assure you, it is so, Lady. We demand loyalty from our servants. Those who deceive or betray us are punished in ways that will not only teach a lesson to the culprit but serve as a warning to others who might be tempted to disobey their masters."

I turned my head away, unable to meet the bland black stare another second. I felt sickened and at the same time guilty. Now I more fully understood the look of terror I had seen on Lin Sing's face when we stumbled upon the hidden grave, and the meaning of his frightened words: "There will be great punishment." It was my fault this dreadful thing had happened to poor Lin Sing. I was responsible. By showing him the jade earrings and persuading him to take the letter, I had again put him in jeopardy and this time he had received the dreaded punishment.

I said in a muffled voice, "It is so cruel—so inhuman. To cut off his ear." I stopped, swallowing on a spasm of nausea. "I—I must leave you." Bowing my head and without further leave-taking, I hurried from the room.

Outside the room the servant waited to escort me back to my apartment. My knees felt as if they would give under me as I followed him through the splendid rooms filled with their priceless furnishings yet empty of any people but a watchful attendant. The man left me at the door of my apartment and I went in, closing the door behind me, and falling onto the nearest chair, I sat with my head in my hands. All I could think of was poor Lin Sing, young and friendly and kind, and the torture I had unwittingly subjected him to.

I would have to tell Robert what had happened. He would be angry at my deceit, at my taking such action without first consulting him. He would be indignant that the poor Chinese boy should suffer this harsh punishment. But I must tell him, without further delay.

I sprang up and on impulse left the room, and finding a servant in the corridor, I commanded him to take me to the Pavilion of the Men, where Robert resided.

Wu Shing came to the door. Usually smiling and bowing in my presence, today he was solemn-faced and his glance did not meet mine as he inclined his head and said stiffly, "Please to wait, Lady. The honored captain has not as yet completed his dressing."

I wondered at his aloof manner and then a thought struck me. He must have heard of what had happened to Lin Sing and so was no longer friendly toward me. The occurrence would not be kept secret, for Mr. Yao had boasted that inflicting punishment on an erring servant served as a warning to others.

After a short pause Wu Shing returned and, again with averted face, said, "Please, Lady," and gestured for me to go into the next room.

Robert, freshly shaved and dressed in a new robe of dark-red silk, turned, his hands outstretched to welcome me.

"Megan! This is a pleasant surprise. I wasn't expecting such an early visit."

He would have drawn me into his arms, but I said abruptly, "Please, Robert. Don't. I—I have something to tell you. I am afraid you will be angry with me but not more upset than I am myself. The most terrible thing has happened—it is all my fault. I would never have put the boy in such danger if—if I had known how inhumanely he would be punished.

Oh, Robert—" and I broke off, the tears brimming up in my eyes.

He caught hold of my hand and said, "Steady there. What is all this about? What accident has brought you running to me in such distress?"

I took a deep breath to calm myself and slowly, waveringly, I recounted to Robert all that had happened since the first moment I spoke to Lin Sing outside the Pearl Pagoda and placed the earring in his outstretched hand. He listened in frowning silence and I saw the firm jaw tighten as I went on to tell him of my encounter with Mr. Yao and the unfeeling way in which he had told me of Lin Sing's punishment.

When, fighting for restraint, I finished my recital, he said slowly, "It was a foolish thing to do, Megan. Yao rules this place as a despot and he would be a difficult man to outwit. I know something about him."

"Are you angry with me? I would have consulted you, but you—you said the less I knew of your affairs the better and the safer. I thought that would apply to any action that *I* took. It might make things easier if you were not aware of what I planned."

He went on frowning, gazing past me with his unfocused eye.

"Matters are more complicated than that. I should have told you, I suppose. But—" He paused and then shrugged. "It's too late. The damage is done now, and we shall be watched at every point."

"But the worst part is that poor boy," I began brokenly. "Lin Sing. He was—we were—friends. And this awful thing—this cruel infliction—it is *my* fault. I feel so guilty—so responsible." I fought for self-control, but I could not prevent the tears from overflowing, and in my distress, I turned away to hide them.

I felt Robert's hand on my arm. He said gently, "You are crying? Why, Megan, this is the first time I have known you to cry. Through all the dangers and adversities, our imprisonment and uncertain future, I never saw you shed a tear. And now you cry for this poor youth." He put his arms around me and held me so that I wept against his shoulder. "Don't grieve so. I never knew a woman with half your courage and common sense. Do not let go now."

But I could not stop. Now that I had started crying the tears flowed freely for all our past indignities.

Gradually the storm subsided. I lifted my head to murmur an apology, but when I started to do so, Robert kissed me, saying, "My poor girl—my poor Megan. You will feel better now. You made a mistake and someone else paid for it. Accept that fact and stop reproaching yourself. It is the same as when the captain of a ship makes an error of judgment and lives are lost. He cannot sit down in some hazard at sea and repine. He must carry on and do his best."

"You are very bracing, Robert," I said wryly.

"It is my nature, I think. I am not for soft words—or for soft living." He took a handkerchief out of the sleeve of his robe and gently wiped the tearstains on my cheeks. "There, no more tears. You are my valiant-hearted Megan again. Shall we go and sit in the courtyard for a while?"

"If you wish. And—and thank you, Robert."

"For what? You belong to me now and our lives are to be shared."

"Yes. Oh, yes."

He kissed me again, this time with growing fervor, and I felt myself responding to him. Then he put me gently from him and said, "Wu Shing is waiting outside the door. Let us go out to the courtyard where we can talk. There is little privacy here."

The morning passed quietly. Robert seemed content to sit, talking from time to time, and staring at the rich red of the peonies in their raised beds or at the feathery ginkgo tree, with its shivering catkins and fan-shaped leaves, as if he could really see them.

It was a warm morning and we were glad of the shade of the walnut tree under which we sat. I tried to calculate the date and came to the conclusion that it was the third week in May.

The southwest monsoon had set in by now and every day the heat and humidity would increase, but here in the courtyard it was cool and the tinkling waters of the nearby pool made a refreshing sound.

I stole a glance at Robert and thought how much better in health he looked, despite his scarred forehead and the black patch worn over one eye, how handsome he was still, in a hard, clean-cut way. I wished that he would take my hand and hold it in his own. I was too shy to make such a gesture myself. Yet yesterday we had become lovers. We were to be married when we escaped. *If* we escaped. What did Mr. Yao want of us? Of *Robert?* He had proved himself so cruel and harsh a captor that I was now truly afraid of him.

Perhaps Robert caught the trend of my thoughts, for he turned his head and stared vaguely at me.

"I have been thinking," he said. "I shall ask for an audience with Yao. Something will have to be done. We cannot remain trapped here forever."

"Will—will you give him the information he wants?" I asked hesitantly.

He frowned.

"I shall hope to make terms of some kind. Leave it to me, Megan."

"Yes."

After the midday meal, which we shared together in the small room that was used for this purpose since Robert's recovery, we parted, to go to our separate siestas.

I could not sleep for I was thinking of Lin Sing again and wondering where he was and if his sufferings were very great. I would never know, for it was unlikely I should see him again. Mr. Yao would make sure of that.

The afternoon passed. I walked in the courtyard again, but Robert did not come. I returned to my apartment where Wei Liang waited, seemingly as anxious as ever to attend to me. Yet was it my imagination or was her kind little face closed against me, and did her glance slide away from mine when she answered me without smiling? I became convinced that she too had heard of Lin Sing's punishment and knew that I had been in some way involved with him. Now, with all hearts turned against me, would we ever escape to freedom?

And once more my mind turned to the unkempt and forgotten grave I had discovered. Had the Englishman pined away here, a prisoner, year after year, until all hope for his release was gone and old age defeated him? Or had Mr. Yao grown impatient with his guest and hastened his demise?

My thoughts chilled me and I was relieved when Wei Liang left me, though I did not enjoy eating my supper in solitary state. Afterward, I sat by the lattice window stitching at the embroidery that Wei Liang had produced for me a few weeks ago. The design was of an eagle worked on cut silk. Whoever had sketched it had created a bird of splendid authenticity. The powerful wingspread and the proud lift of the head seemed lifelike, and as I bent over it I thought of Robert and how when we had first met he had seemed to me eaglelike in his strength and authority. Now he was maimed, but he was not broken. The stubborn hardness of his character that had once repelled me now commanded my respect and admiration.

I stitched until I could see no more. The servant who had taken away the supper dishes returned to light the lamps. When he had gone I paced the room, lonely and restless, wondering what had become of Robert. During his illness I would not have hesitated to ask one of the servants to escort me to his quarters, but now that he was recovered and we were lovers, I could not do this.

The door opened suddenly and Wei Liang appeared on the threshold.

"Lady, the honored husband requests permission to visit you."

My heartbeat quickened as, turning, I said, "I am happy to welcome him. Please bring him to me."

She turned to murmur something and Robert, his stick held out before him, limped into the room while Wei Liang closed the door behind him.

"I hope I don't call at too late an hour."

"Of course not. It—it cannot be much past ten."

He smiled.

"And a husband is entitled to visit his wife at any hour, don't you agree?"

I did not know what to say to that so I said, "Please sit down. This chair is comfortable I find."

"I would rather stand. I would rather hold you in my arms while I tell you my news."

His arms came about me and he brushed my hair with his lips as I said uncertainly, "Your news? Have you—did you speak with Mr. Yao?"

"Yes. And he has agreed to release us. We are free to leave any time."

I could not believe it. I could not believe the truth of what he was saying. For a moment I closed my eyes, swaying a little within Robert's hold. I opened them to meet Robert's frowning gaze bent on mine.

"He really means it? It is not—not some trick?"

"No—it is true. We are no longer prisoners and can now go from here. It is just a question of finding a boat to take us to Hong Kong. Mr. Yao has promised to arrange a passage for us."

"Can we not send a message at once to our friends to tell them we are safe?"

"We shall be there as soon as any message," he answered. "I doubt if we are more than four or five days out from Hong Kong." His hold on me tightened. "We will be married there, Megan. If you are still of the same mind."

"Oh, Robert." I was in a trance of joy, of relief. "Of course I am of the same mind. But I still cannot believe it. How did you persuade Mr. Yao? How did it all come about?"

"I gave him the information he sought from me." He heard my quick intake of breath and added almost sternly, before I could speak, "No—I would rather you did not ask me what that was. I will tell you at the"—he hesitated—"the appropriate time. Let us get safely away from here first."

"Yes, of course. It shall be as you wish, Robert."

"Thank you." He bent his head and kissed me long and lingeringly and I felt my very being dissolved in love for him. I was so happy, so comforted and relieved that I did not care what the terms of our release were. Soon we would be away from this strange, cruel place and together for always. When, as his kisses became ever more seeking and passionate and he murmured against my throat, "May I stay, Megan? May I remain here with you tonight?" I could only whisper in answer, "I want you to."

We had experienced ecstasy in the Pearl Pagoda, but this night that we shared in my room was something rapturous beyond belief. We lay on the wide bed in the recess, lit only by soft lamplight, and we came together in wild and tempestuous love. Robert's kisses, his hands caressing my breasts and body, roused me to a delight of the senses such as I had never dreamed of, and he in turn was so passionate a lover that we were left at last panting and exhausted in each other's arms.

We slept and we loved and we loved again, and each time was better than the first. In the dawning we smiled at each other and Robert said gently, "You are more than I ever dreamed. More beautiful, more loving, more woman."

I felt my cheeks warm and my eyelids fall.

"I love you."

"I don't deserve such love, but I am grateful for it. I shall cherish you always, Megan. I know that we shall be happy, for there is a flame between us that cannot be put out." He held my fingers to his lips. "Now I am going to leave you so that you may rest. If I stay, there will be no rest for either of us. No, don't move. Just lie there. I wish to God I could see you properly—every single inch of you. But if I cannot do that, I know every part of you, every curve of your lovely body." Drawing his robe about him he bent to kiss me. "Sleep well, Megan. I will wake one of the servants in the corridor to see me back to my room."

He was gone, feeling his way toward the door, closing it gently behind him.

I lay alone on the tumbled bed and I thought that I was Robert's wife in every way now. The formalities to come seemed of little consequence. I closed my eyes in a sweet and heavy lassitude. Only as I fell asleep did I recall that he had never once said he loved me.

Three days later we left The Place of Tall Trees. With as much ceremony as if we had been Mr. Yao's honored guests instead of his unhappy prisoners, we were sent upon our way.

Mr. Yao, murmuring words of felicitations for the journey ahead, bowed and smiled above folded hands. I could not bear to meet that bland, impassive gaze but bowed my head as I spoke some polite phrases of leave-taking.

To Dr. Haas, standing beside Mr. Yao, his grave wise face softened in a smile, I was glad to have an opportunity to express once again my gratitude and to add my sincere wishes for his continuing health and happiness.

I had already taken leave of Wei Liang, and wishing to make some return for her care and attention of me, I bequeathed the cameo brooch to her. She was almost too overcome to accept it, but I pressed it upon her, knowing that its value would be for Wei Liang, as it had been to me, of sentimental rather than material nature.

It was time to go. At the main gate of the courtyard we were placed in separate litters and borne by a party of men along a paved track that circled the perimeter of the Deer Park. It was early morning and a mist lay under the trees. I pushed aside the curtain of the litter, searching for a glimpse of the Pearl Pagoda. I wished that I could have gone once more to visit it.

All I saw now was the topmost tiers of the Pearl Pagoda, shining clear and crystalline in the sunlight above the misty green of the trees. I felt as if my heart, not my mind, held the picture of it, and would hold it there forever.

Soon we had left the park, passing through a great gate set in the high wall. The men jogged at a slow but steady pace along the track running through dense undergrowth. We came to the same narrow creek that I remembered from the night of our arrival many weeks ago. Here we were lifted down in turn and helped into the waiting sampan. There was a rattan awning in the bow and some dusty cushions to sit upon.

Robert looked around at me.

"Well, Megan, we are on our way."

"I still cannot believe it."

He took my hand and held it firmly in his own.

"Nevertheless, it is true. We shall be at Hong Kong in a few days."

"We shall look an odd pair upon arrival," I replied. "We

have only the clothes we stand up in and no luggage whatsoever."

He smiled.

"People will think we are a highborn Chinese couple, until we open our mouths. Are you wearing your yellow robe? It seems to me to be something of that color."

Yes. It is beautiful. I shall want to keep it."

We moored near the bank that night, eating our supper of fish and rice by lamplight. The Chinamen were polite enough to us, though by no means servile, and they congregated at the other end of the boat, leaving us to ourselves.

With the first light of dawn the crew were up and about, serving hot millet and tea to us after we had washed and refreshed ourselves in the river. At midday, when the sun was at its zenith, we moored again under the trees while the men rested and then the boat moved off again downstream.

We came to the mouth of the river in the early evening. The heat of the day had gone and on the smooth pink-tinged sea rode the junk that was to take us to Hong Kong, its brown sails spread wide, as a bird's wing, the ribs showing fanlike against the sky.

The *laodah*, or sailing master, was waiting to greet us and, after politely welcoming us aboard, fell into close conversation with Robert. I was taken below, where small but adequate sleeping quarters had been provided for us. Later, when Robert joined me, a servant brought us a light supper and afterward we went up on deck for some air and sat under the starlit sky watching the sea.

That night I lay in Robert's arms and experienced once again the passion and the piercing delight that had overwhelmed me when we first came together within the walls of the Pearl Pagoda. I loved him so much that I trembled with joy at his touch. Although he had not spoken the words, I felt that he must love me too, for how else could we have been drawn so close to each other and shared such an intensity of emotion?

Yet though we were as one person, with no inhibition or shyness to restrain us, so that I lay naked on the cushioned bed and was ravished by the strength of Robert's hard nakedness, I still felt as if there was a part of him I did not know, as if he gave everything of himself physically but that his innermost heart and soul remained a secret.

The days passed as in a dream; we were between the past and the future, only the present hour existed for us. The weather was hot but not unpleasantly so for a breeze at sea cooled us. On the fourth day we arrived at Hong Kong.

The harbor was crowded with ships of every nation and the blue waters glittered with white and colored sails. A great green mountain, cone shaped, rose behind the harbor, a scattering of white buildings at its foot. The British pilot boat came out to meet us, for Hong Kong was a British possession and had been so since 1842.

From the harbor we were taken by sedan to the British Consulate and there Robert recounted the incredible story of our adventures, and there also I learned from Mr. Farnum, the consul, to my great joy, that Dr. and Mrs. Howard and the children were safe. They had been picked up by a Dutch Indiaman and brought to Hong Kong and then taken to Macao. From there they had sailed for England, where it was hoped Mrs. Howard would recover from the vicissitudes she had undergone.

"Oh, that is wonderful. I am thankful to God that they are safe and well," I said.

"Yes. And they will be equally happy, I am sure, to learn that you and Captain Hawkes are secure also. Mr. Howard was greatly distressed that you should have been left at the mercy of the pirates." Mr. Farnum shook his head. "It is not often we hear of such a satisfactory outcome as yours."

Within the week we were married. A special license was obtained and the British chaplain performed the ceremony at the Legation. Mr. Farnum gave me away and Mrs. Farnum, a lady of much elegance and charm, acted as my matron of honor. There was a delightful wedding breakfast at the consul's villa to which several British residents were invited. Robert and I found ourselves the center of attraction, as much for the events that had befallen us as for the fact we were newlyweds.

This was not an easy time for Robert. He had to learn to adjust anew to life beyond the confines of The Place of Tall Trees. At the pavilion, the handicap of his blindness had been minimized by Wu Shing, who helped him bathe and shave and dress each day. Because our activities had been limited, our walks within the courtyards restricted, he had not found it too difficult to move around. Now a servant of the consul's assisted him in these measures and I was on hand to aid him as unobtrusively as I could.

But he had to acquaint himself with new surroundings, fresh obstacles at every turn. Robert's formidable self-control was stretched to the limit and he sometimes exploded in a temper of frustration. Yet he wanted neither pity nor help and shrugged off all attempts to ease matters for him. Often my heart ached. It was like seeing a wounded lion blundering about its cage.

We were exhausted by the time we set sail for Macao. A Chinese dressmaker had made me several dresses, and Robert had been fitted out in a dark civilian suit to wear until such time as he might find himself back in the uniform of a Merchant Navy Captain. We looked at each other as if we were strangers, until Robert put his arm about me, as we leaned over the rail of the ship waving a last goodbye to our new friends, and said, "Now you are really and truly Mrs. Hawkes. How does it feel?"

I turned my face to smile up at him and say, with a glow of happiness, "It feels as if I had always been married to you. But what of you, the man who told me so firmly he never wished to acquire a wife."

"Ah, well, I have changed my mind." He frowned momentarily. "You have gotten the worst of the bargain, Megan, for I do not know what my future will be. Whether I shall ever be given a command again." He shrugged. "At least I am not a poor man, so we shall not starve."

"I know so little about you, Robert."

"We have all the time in the world to learn everything about each other." He smiled. "Although I feel I could not know you more intimately, Megan."

I seemed always to be returning to Macao from some journey. Now I saw it again with eyes familiar with the curve of pillared white mansions glittering in the sunshine, the old men fishing from the stone walls, the carriages waiting under the shade of the banyan trees, the churches and the convents set among the green, the old fort on the hillside, and, high above everything else, the ruins of St. Paul's, with its long flight of steps and the cross at its summit.

I had come to love the old city, teeming with life—the Portuguese, staid and sober in their fading magnificence; the Chinese, lively and voluble; the British, the Dutch, the French —a mixture of nations that gave color and charm to the little peninsula all but surrounded by the shining blue sea.

Robert had decided that we should go first to the British Consulate and then he would take me to my friends at the Mission whilst a message was sent to Mr. and Mrs. Meade that we were safe and well.

I shall never forget the welcome that awaited us at the Mission: the tears of joy and warm embrace from little Miss Crow; the endless handshaking of Mr. Crow, who was too reserved and austere to give further expression than that of his pleasure at seeing us; Chao Tsan's beaming smile, which stretched from ear to ear; the bowing of the servants; the cries and the laughter and the voices excited with happiness. I was laughing and crying myself, my warm Celtic blood stirred by the display of such emotion.

Robert, as ever, remained somewhat aloof and stood apart with Mr. Crow, answering his many questions and giving yet another account of our adventures. Refreshments were brought, a hot wine was served, amber-brown and aromatic, and tiny puffed cakes similar to doughnuts. Everyone shared in the rejoicing, even strangers who had come to read the tracts in the Mission Room.

In the midst of the general rejoicing, the door opened suddenly and to my delight one of the servants ushered in Mr.

and Mrs. Meade and Sylvia. For one breathless moment we stood staring at one another and then we were hugging and kissing and laughing and crying in turn. Even Mr. Meade gave me an affectionate embrace and a kiss upon my cheek, while Mrs. Meade clasped me to her cushiony bosom as if she would never let me go.

Sylvia, beautiful and gentle as ever, put her arms about me and, pressing her cheek against my own, said, "Oh, Megan—is this really true? It's wonderful, incredible, unbelievable. You are *here*—safe and well. So well. I have never seen you look better. After all you have been through! You know the Howards thought Captain Hawkes was killed and you as good as dead when they left you aboard the *Lotus Wind*? They were desperately upset and poor Dr. Howard constantly blamed himself that he had not forced you into the boat that took them to safety."

"I am sorry to have caused him so much anxiety, but I could not leave Robert—I *could* not. But it is over now, Sylvia dear. We are safe and word has been sent to the Howards from Hong Kong that all is well with us, as we hope it is with them."

"There is a great deal to talk about. You are to come back with us to the villa. Papa and Mama insist upon that. Dear Megan, it is as if a sister has returned to me." She turned her great brown eyes upon me. "And Papa tells me you are *married* to Captain Hawkes. That you were married in Hong Kong. Is that so?"

I felt myself color as I answered hesitantly, "Yes. We—we grew close to each other while we were held as prisoners by a Chinese merchant." I added in a low voice, "I love Robert very dearly."

"Then you are fortunate indeed," Sylvia said in a hard little voice that caused me to glance quickly up at her. What I saw disturbed me. In the first joy of reunion I thought only that she was as beautiful as ever, and, as ever, charmingly dressed—this day in cream muslin with a tiered skirt, and a shallow straw hat upon her golden curls. Now, with dismay, I observed the thinness of her cheeks, the hollowness about her lovely eyes, the tight line of her usually smiling mouth.

"What is it? What is the matter, Sylvia?" I asked sharply. She shook her head.

"Everything in the world. I am engaged to Mr. Henshawe. Yes, you may well look surprised."

"But—but Henry," I said. "Did you not hear from him? Did he not answer your letter?"

"Oh, yes. He wrote very promptly. By return, I would say. He wrote telling me to forget him, for he could offer me nothing, and that I should do better to marry the man my parents had chosen for me."

"I—I am so *sorry*. But—Mr. Henshawe is a good man, I am sure. Can you not—do you not think—" I broke off at the look in Sylvia's eyes.

"Would *you* wish to marry a man for whom you had no feeling—no warmth whatsoever? Do not tell me that is how it is with you and Robert, for I know, from one glance at you, that it is otherwise."

This time I blushed warmly. I thought of the nights we had lain in each other's arms and wondered what it would have been like without the love we shared, and I was silent.

There was no time to say more for suddenly all was bustle and leave-taking. Mr. Meade, in his kind but autocratic way, had made the arrangements for Robert and myself to return to the Villa Cicadela as his guests. Once more there were kisses and embraces, handshakes and bowings, and to a chorus of congratulations and good wishes, we left the Mission.

Robert was as much at home with the Meades as I was and we were both happy to be at the villa, ensconced in a suite of cool, shaded rooms leading onto a wide verandah overlooking the gardens at the rear of the house.

After we had taken a short nap, Robert seemed refreshed and anxious to settle his business affairs. While I dressed he expressed the desire to go downstairs.

"Mr. Meade said there were letters waiting for me at the Company's offices. I want to make arrangements to have them delivered."

"Of course. I will come down presently."

A little dark-eyed Portuguese girl helped me dress and brushed my black hair into shining smoothness. Then I made my way down the wide staircase in search of Sylvia. There was so much we had to say to each other.

Sylvia was not in the drawing room or in the small morning room, and so, assuming she must still be resting, I went back to the drawing room and sat down on the curved sofa in the window. The shutters had been pulled back, making the room pleasantly cool and light.

As I sat there I heard footsteps on the path outside. I rose and moved to the window, thinking it might be Sylvia in the garden, but it was Mr. Meade and Robert.

They walked slowly along the paved path that led past the open window, heads bent, deep in conversation. Mr. Meade was smoking a long cheroot, occasionally waving his hand as if to emphasize some topic, while Robert picked his way with the aid of his stick.

They passed out of sight and I went on standing by the window, admiring the garden—the tall trees, the well-watered flower beds, the sweet-smelling pink and white lantana that grew against the walls.

Mr. Meade and Robert returned, too deeply engrossed to notice me by the window. Mr. Meade was speaking.

I heard him say, "Of course you were taken there in the first place because of the opium. Yao knew there was a supplier. So he held you in hopes of getting to your source."

"Yes," Robert said. "In the end I had to tell him . . ." The sound of his voice faded as he passed along the path and out of sight.

I stood very still, the words I had just heard echoing in my brain. "Of course you were taken there in the first place because of the opium."

What did those words mean? I asked myself, as if presented with some puzzle.

But I knew. I knew immediately. The pieces of the puzzle fell into place and the enigma was solved. Robert had been trading in opium.

I should have known it. Past words and phrases gave hints of it. The cargo of the *Lotus Wind* which had been so eagerly stolen by the pirates. Their leader's remark about Robert being a prize." The way Mr. Yao had questioned me as to Robert's trading interests.

The footsteps drew nearer again. Robert was speaking now, his head turned to Mr. Meade. I caught the words ". . . it was sheer blackmail on the part of that cunning devil, Yao. There was nothing else to do but let him know about the stuff so that we could be free. I realized that . . ." then the sound of his voice was gone again.

I turned, groping blindly for the sofa, where I subsided in trembling collapse.

Now I tried to reassure myself; now I clutched at every straw. It couldn't be true. It wasn't possible. I was jumping to conclusions.

But in my heart I knew it was so. Robert was not only the captain of a clipper ship. He was something more. He was, or had been, a smuggler in the opium trade.

CHAPTER 15

I WANTED TO rush out and confront Robert with the truth that I had learned, but I did not. I went on sitting there in a cold revulsion of spirit until the door opened and Sylvia came into the drawing room.

"Megan—how long have you been here? It was so hot and I was tired and I slept and slept. Did you not have a good rest? You look pale. I am not surprised—you have been through so much." She sat down on the sofa and took my hand in hers. "Why, your hands are like ice. I hope you are not sick."

"No—no, I am perfectly all right. It is just—I suppose, as you say, there is a—a reaction."

"Of course. But it is wonderful to have you here. There is so much I want to tell you, dearest Megan."

I forced myself to sound normal.

"And I want to hear about—about everything. I am grieved for you. I know you loved Henry."

I felt as if it was another person speaking. Somehow I made the right remarks, the correct responses, so that Sylvia, longing for a confidante who would understand, could speak of Henry and the letter she had received from him. Yet even as I listened to her wistful story, some part of my mind was engaged with the fact that Robert was an opium smuggler.

Opium. That vicious drug. The drug that had killed Arthur.

Robert had told me he was not a poor man. Doubtless that was true. I was well aware of the fortunes that were to be made in the opium trade.

At least he had not lied to me, only been evasive in answer to my questions. Would he have told me the truth in time?

"We are to be married in September," Sylvia was saying. "Here in Macao. Will you be my matron of honor, Megan?"

"Thank you. I should be very happy to do so. If it is possible—I do not know Robert's plans. I think he wishes to return to England and obtain further medical advice regarding his injured eye. It may be possible to restore some more sight to it."

She sighed.

"I understand. Poor Captain Hawkes. It was a dreadful thing to have happened. What will he do if he cannot command a ship again? Oh, Megan, I am upsetting you. You look *so* sad and distressed. Please do not worry. Papa has much influence. He will be able to help Robert obtain some other post in the tea trade, if necessary."

Unable to tell her the true cause of my discomfort, I stood up, saying abruptly, "I—I have a headache. It is the heat, I think. And all the excitement of the past few days. Would you mind if I left you and went to lie down again?"

"Of course not. Please don't come down to dinner if you do not feel well. Mama and Papa will understand. Would you like some tea—a *tisane?*"

"No—I will just rest quietly. Thank you, Sylvia." And leaving her gazing anxiously after me, I hurried from the room.

It was true my head was aching and a painful knot of tension throbbed in my brow. I drew the curtain across the window and lay down in the shadowed room. I felt I could not speak to anyone else until I had faced Robert with the truth of what I had heard. After tossing and turning restlessly upon the bed I was about to ring the bell and ask the maid to fetch Captain Hawkes, when, to my surprise, the door opened and he came limping across the threshold of the room.

"Megan, what is this I hear? Are you not well? Sylvia told me you had a migraine."

I sat up, smoothing the skirts of my dress.

"I have a headache, yes. But it is nothing to worry about.

I came up here because I was upset over something I quite accidentally overheard. Something you were speaking of."

He came to stand by the bedside, frowning down at me.

"Something I was speaking of? What was it that it should so concern you?"

I stood up and faced him. Biting my lip, struggling to find the right words, I said slowly, "Just answer me one question, Robert. Have you been trading in opium?"

His expression scarcely altered, save for the deepening frown and a tightening of his hard mouth.

"Yes."

"You—you are an opium smuggler?"

"If you wish to put it that way. I have carried opium cargo in my ship, certainly, and done business with the Chinese Linten Island and up the eastern coast. Does that satisfy your curiosity?"

"It appalls me. I never thought that you—I could not believe what I overheard. You were speaking to Mr. Meade of Mr. Yao. How he had held you—us—because of this cargo." I turned away from him. "Oh, it is horrible, vile. I feel you are *tainted*, as is everyone who deals with the scourge."

"I am sorry you have to be so melodramatic about the matter. I am one of the hundreds—thousands, probably—who traffic in opium. The British government closes its eyes to these facts, even though it is fully aware that the East India Company is as involved as your precious missionaries are."

I swung around on him.

"That is not true. The missions are fighting desperately to have the trade ostracized. They have made representation in the British Parliament; they have protested, roused public opinion against it."

His hard mouth curled.

"Whilst they do that, their ardent followers sail with piles of tracts ready for distribution to the unhappy heathen, knowing that the ships they voyage upon are *opium carriers*. They are as much hypocrites as the East India merchants who take trouble to maintain good relationships with the Chinese authorities while washing their hands of all formal responsibility for illegal trading. It is a question of politics, Megan, and of economics. That is something you know little about."

"It is a question of human lives," I cried. "Of *souls*. Cannot you understand that? It destroys *people*. And solely for money. For the profit to be made. You told me you were not a poor man. Do you mean you have made a fortune yourself out of this sickening traffic?"

"Not a fortune. The venture has been profitable, yes." His voice hardened. "I made a promise to myself some years ago that when I left the sea and returned to England it would be as a rich man. I am only halfway to being that."

"How can you speak in this way? As if you cared nothing for the sorrow you bring to others. Would you have told me the truth, I wonder, if I had not learned of the facts for myself?"

"Possibly. In time. If I felt it was best for you to know."

"Otherwise you would have lived a lie? Using your contaminated wealth to support our lives. When you know it is something that I feel so strongly, so *bitterly* about. I have good cause to know what misery the drug of opium can bring for my—for the man I was once to marry died from it. I was left heartbroken."

He said stiffly, "I am sorry. Very sorry. But I cannot feel personally responsible for—Arthur, was it? We are each one of us masters of our own destinies. For good or evil. It is for us to choose whether we shall be a victim in life or a survivor."

"You are the cruelest, most cynical man I have ever known," I cried.

"And you are the most emotional and impassioned creature I ever encountered."

I said slowly, "I saved your life on the *Lotus Wind*. For what purpose, I wonder?"

"Perhaps because I once saved yours. We were fated to come together."

I put a hand to my throbbing forehead, and at the gesture he said quickly, "I have added to your indisposition. Forgive me. I did not intend to speak so harshly. Don't let us quarrel, Megan. You know the worst about me now. Can you not bring yourself to accept it?" He put a hand on my arm, but I jerked away as if the contact had been that of a leper.

"Don't touch me. I can't bear it. I told you once that I felt I knew little about you. Now I realize I know nothing. *Nothing.* You are as a stranger to me. Leave me alone, please."

His mouth set in a thin line.

"Very well. But first let me tell you why I came to the bedroom to find you. A letter from England was waiting for me here at Macao and it was brought to me whilst I was talking with Mr. Meade. The news it bears is somewhat startling. My cousin Philip is dead. He died suddenly and unexpectedly. Although he has a son, the Hawkestone estate has been willed to me. I have inherited the title. Whether you like it or not, you are now Lady Hawkes." He turned and made his way slowly to the door. Reaching it, he looked back over his shoulder at me. "We leave for England as soon as possible."

The door closed behind him. Shocked and stupefied, I could do nothing but sit with both hands pressed against my aching forehead while I endeavored to comprehend this new thunderbolt.

Hawkestone Park. The great country house in which Robert had been brought up. He had been a boy there, with his cousin Philip. He had vowed he would never return to it. Now he was Sir Robert and I was Lady Hawkes.

I did not want any such title. I did not want to go to England with Robert. I felt as if the love I once felt for him had been destroyed by the knowedge that he had trafficked in the evil trade that had killed Arthur. And he did not appear sorry or ashamed.

I could not bear it. I lay on the bed in the darkened room, hoping and praying that no one would come near me until my chaotic thoughts had returned to some sort of normality.

That night we slept apart from each other in the wide bed. It was as if a sword of enmity lay between us.

The next morning Robert was up and gone to his dressing room before I was properly awake. Mr. Meade's valet had helped him undress the previous evening, for which I was thankful, and now I guessed by the murmur of voices from the next room that the servant was again assisting Robert. I waited until all was silence before ringing for Luisa, the young Portuguese maid, to bring tea and prepare a bath for me.

When finally I came down to breakfast it was to find Mr. and Mrs. Meade and Sylvia seated with Robert discussing his plans to return to England at the first opportunity.

Sylvia sighed and shook her head.

"Now you will not be here for my wedding. Oh, dear. And we are very sad to hear that Robert's cousin has died so unexpectedly." She added, under her breath, "But it is thrilling too. You are Lady Hawkes, Megan. Can you quite believe it?"

"No—I cannot."

She glanced quickly at me.

"Are you recovered from your migraine? You look a little tired and you were so blooming when we first met yesterday. But of course, this news has upset you, as it must have Robert. You are bound not to have slept well."

"I do not think either of us slept well," I answered with perfect truth.

The day passed with much coming and going. Robert went with Mr. Meade to visit the offices of the East India Company and arrange our passages home. Home? England was not my home. I had been but once in that country in my life, and that was when I sailed from the Port of London to China. My home had been in Wales. Now it was to be at Hawkestone Park in Somerset.

Unhappy though I was, I realized that I should have to return with Robert. There was no alternative. As a bride of a few weeks I could not possibly remain in Macao, either with the kindly Meades or at the Mission. The Meades would never understand why I should quarrel with Robert over his involvement in the opium trade to the extent of leaving him. And, of course, I knew in my heart that I should learn to accept the truth of which I had learned. We were married and we should remain in that state. But nothing would ever be the same for me. I knew that too.

Robert was too busy to pay much attention to me that

day or during the days that followed. He had a report to make about the *Lotus Wind* and several committees to attend. Handicapped by his blindness as he was, he sailed to Canton, accompanied by Mr. Meade and the latter's manservant. They were gone for more than a week and during that time I remained at the Villa Cicadela with Sylvia and Mrs. Meade.

Sylvia's fiancé, Mr. Henshawe, was at Canton too, so I did not see him. Only once did Sylvia speak of Henry, and that was to show me the letter he had written to her urging her to forget him. "Put me out of your thoughts and your heart," he wrote. "I can offer you nothing and you deserve the best of everything. I shall be freer in spirit myself if I feel that you will forget me and make a full and happy life for yourself. This is my real farewell to you, Sylvia."

He used no endearments. It was as if he wished to write as kindly but as impersonally as possible. I thought it a brave and good letter and yet I grieved for Sylvia as I saw her tear the letter into tiny pieces and toss it into the smoldering fire of rubbish left by one of the gardeners.

I wondered that she should have accepted Mr. Henshawe, feeling as she did about Henry, but when I touched upon the matter, hinting that perhaps if she waited a while she might meet someone else she would care for, she shook her head and said decidedly, "No. I shall never love anyone but Henry in that way. So one man will be no better or worse than another. Mr. Henshawe will have to do, for I could not face my father's anger all over again."

Before we sailed for England and while Robert was still in Canton, I visited Arthur's grave. I went alone, taking a sheaf of beautiful roses and some hibiscus blooms that I had bought from a stall in the town on my way back from the Mission, where I had been to visit Miss Crow.

The English Cemetery was green and peaceful, shaded by its many trees. I had arranged earlier in the year to have a headstone placed upon the grave and now this had been done. As I placed the flowers in the vase I had brought with me I read the words that Arthur's father had asked me to have engraved upon the stone.

ARTHUR SYDNEY CROSBY
beloved son of William and Ellen Crosby
Born 1819 Died 1852
"Sleep in Peace"

Yes, I thought. Sleep in peace, dear Arthur. I shivered suddenly, turning away from the grave, trying not to think that Robert had been responsible for Arthur's death. That was absurd. And yet, every man embroiled in this cruel traffic was responsible for the death of some victim of the drug.

I gave a last glance at the grave as my heart whispered goodbye. I knew that I should never see it again.

Two days later Robert returned from Canton. He looked exhausted, as if the voyage and the moving about in strange surroundings and the many people he had spoken with had drained him of his last reserves.

Estranged though we were, I had it in me to feel compassion, but when I tried to ease matters for him he turned sharply on me and said, "Stop fussing. I've had enough people leading me about like a tame monkey this past week without my having to endure your ministrations." I made no answer and he went on, frowning, "Do I take it you are over your pious scruples and are willing to accept me once more as a member of the human race?"

"I am reconciled to the damage you have done, if that is what you mean," I answered coldly. "But I shall never think of you as I did, for you are someone quite other."

"I see. It is wifely duty that prompts your concern for me, not love. No matter. Doubtless we shall jog along together in obligatory harness."

"It seems there is no alternative," I said and left him.

We sailed for England the first week in July. It appeared as if every person I had ever known at Macao came to see us off. Not only the kind Meades and Mr. Henshawe, who was now down from Canton, and Miss Crow and Mr. Crow and Chao Tsan and the children I had taught and the servants from the Mission, but even some of the converts I had read with and helped to teach or nurse. With assurances to everyone to write and a promise from Sylvia and Mr. Henshawe that they would visit us at Hawkestone and with tears and kisses and a final embrace, we went aboard the *Red Dragon*, the ship that was taking us to England, to stand waving until the last glittering white church and convent and fortress and mansion faded from sight and all that we could see was a shadow on the shining blue horizon.

I was relieved to find that Robert and I had been put in separate cabins adjoining each other.

"The double cabin is not much larger than these others so I thought it better you should have it to yourself. Space is limited on the *Red Dragon*; it is sister ship to the *Lotus Wind*. Here you will have room in which to retire, if you wish to rest or read or write letters. The cabin steward will assist me in shaving and dressing."

"Thank you." I was grateful to him for his consideration, but I could not speak warmly, as once I would have done.

He stared down at me, his lean face set, the black patch lending him the look of a corsair. Which after all he was.

"Are we to be friends, Megan?" He added slowly, "Will you love me again?"

I turned my head away, though I knew he could not see the expression on my face.

"In time, perhaps. I do not know. You—you are as a stranger to me. I thought of you as someone strong and incorruptible, an honorable man. And—and all the time you were living a lie."

"God save me from such sanctimony. You may spare yourself a sermon for I do not intend to repent."

I swung around on him.

"You are cursed, Robert. As all are who deal in the vile drug. The evil in which you have been embroiled has brought punishment upon you."

He exploded into harsh laughter.

"Because I am blinded, you mean? What rubbish you talk. There are as many saints walking the earth afflicted by calamity as sinners. To be maimed or wounded, to die in war or in peace, is chance, the luck of the game." He turned toward the door. "I will leave you to your meditations, which I am sure are many."

He was gone. My hands were shaking; I was left on edge, taunted by his words, his sweeping condemnation of the tenets by which I lived. I could not feel differently, for I had been brought up in a strong and narrow faith that made no allowance for wavering principles.

It was hard to believe that we had been passionate lovers but a short time ago.

After the stifling heat of Macao it was a relief to be at sea. We cleared Sunda Strait within a week and passing Java Head on the portside set course across the Indian Ocean.

Despite the cooling sea breeze I felt listless and unwell. Sadness at leaving the colorful city I had grown to love and apprehension at the thought of the new life ahead in England with Robert, from whom I was estranged, cast a shadow over me. Then one morning I was overtaken by a fit of nausea that left me wan and shaken.

I lay down again on the bunk, my head swimming unpleasantly. I thought back to the last week, the past month. It was too soon to say as yet. It was only a doubt in my mind, a portent of the future. The possibility that I was pregnant.

I said nothing of this to Robert and we continued in an existence in which while living in close proximity we yet remained a world apart.

The voyage to the Cape was for the most part calm and without incident. The *Red Dragon* was similar in layout to the *Lotus Wind* and when I walked the decks or sat upon the poop I could not help remembering that other journey, outward to China. I had been full of anticipation, excited and happy at the thought of seeing Arthur again and being married to him. Now I was married to Robert.

We came within sight of Africa and soon the coastline steepened and became increasingly rugged. Great cliffs of sandstone and granite towered above us and squalls came swiftly down and the sea roughened. I dreaded that we should encounter a storm similar to the one in which I would have lost my life if Robert had not saved me. But it was now midsummer and we were spared the worst hazards of the wild Cape of Storms, for which I was thankful. My queasiness had increased and more than once I retired to my cabin to retch miserably before lying down.

Robert commented upon this, coming to stand beside the bunk and stare frowningly down at me.

"What is all this, Megan? It is unlike you to be so poor a sailor. You have sailed in rougher seas than this and remained perfectly well."

For a moment I did not answer him, only met his filmed gaze in silence. Then slowly, hesitantly, I said, "Things are different this time. It is not so much sea-sickness as—as another kind of nausea."

"Another kind? What other kind is there?"

I sat up, leaning on my elbow.

"I think I am going to have a child, Robert."

"A *child?*" A look of amazement passed over his frowning face and then his expression softened. "This is splendid news. Are you sure?"

"As sure as I can be—without recourse to a doctor."

The frown was back.

"We have no doctor aboard. That is a problem. But you are well, apart from this sickness, which I understand some-times occurs?"

"I hope so. I have been a little tired but perhaps that is a natural symptom."

"You must rest and take care. Are you happy about this?"

"Yes—I think I am. Are you?"

He smiled unexpectedly, his lean dark face lightening.

"I am delighted. We shall have a son for Hawkestone. You have said very little to me about this change in our affairs, Megan. I hope you have no objections to becoming Lady Hawkes."

"It is something I never imagined in my wildest dreams. I cannot picture what life will be like. A great house—a great estate." I paused, then added slowly, "You once told me you would never go back there. How do *you* feel about it, Robert? Will things be better for you now?"

His mouth set firmly, as if at some inner decision.

"The inheritance is not something I can refuse. Yet frankly, I cannot understand it. The estate came to my cousin Philip, who has died. I would have thought his son would have inherited it. But my uncle willed otherwise. I shall know more when I have seen the attorneys at Bath. They have written only the barest details to me."

He left me and I lay for a while, remembering the look of pleasure on Robert's face when I had told him my news. A son for Hawkestone. Well, I would do my best.

I kept well for the remainder of the voyage home. The sense of nausea diminished except for an occasional spasm, and apart from a thickening waistline and a general slowing up I remained in good health. By the time we reached Plymouth, where we were to disembark, I was nearly five months pregnant. Throughout the time aboard, Robert and I had lived our separate lives, maintaining a surface friendliness but neither of us making any attempt at a closer relationship. It seemed as if the love that had existed between us was gone forever. I was surprised by an aching sense of loss. My heart was gradually turning again to Robert, but he was indifferent.

We were to be taken ashore at Plymouth, leaving the *Red Dragon* to continue its voyage up the Channel to the Port of London. It was September, and as we set off in the hired carriage that was to take us as far as Exeter, where we would put up at a comfortable inn, I remembered that it was today that Sylvia was to be married. I thought of her often as we drove through the golden countryside of Devon. Dear Sylvia, I loved her and I prayed that she would find happiness with Charles Henshawe. When would we meet again? I wondered. I hoped that she would keep her promise to visit us at Hawkestone.

We stayed a second night at Glastonbury and set off for Hawkestone the following day. It was late afternoon when the carriage turned in through a pair of double wrought-iron gates and drove up a long tree-lined avenue. On either side lay a vast parkland where cattle grazed. It was late September and the ground was afire with leaves from the great beech trees, while massive oaks flamed in russet and gold against the clear blue sky.

I sat leaning forward, trying to see everything at once. Then I became aware of Robert stiff and silent beside me. I glanced around and saw him, his head resting against the padded seat, as if he had not the least interest in his surroundings. But I was aware by his very stillness, and the set mouth, of an inner tension. Then I realized that he could not see the approach to his old home. To him it was only a blur of trees and distances.

I said gently, "It is beautiful, Robert."

"I imagine so."

"I wish—" I was about to say, "I wish you could see it all," but I remained silent, and at that moment the carriage emerged into open parkland and the house came into view.

I caught my breath at the first sight of it. It stood on rising ground with few trees around it save for a magnificent silver cedar to the north and one great elm and a tall copper beech to the south. At the rear the trees fell away and I could see a wooded countryside stretching away into infinity. But it was the façade of the house that so impressed me. It was built of rich Bath stone, as I was to learn later, at the turn of the eighteenth century. There were three stories, with rows of long windows facing west into the last of the sun so that the whole house seemed alight with rosy welcome, the warm stone glowing golden in the sunset.

The carriage halted on a sweep of gravel, and almost before the coachman had climbed down, two manservants came hurrying through the double door, one to assist Robert down and then myself, while the other helped the coachman unfasten the luggage.

Robert halted, looking about him, trying to focus his gaze upon the house. And as I waited, ready to guide him to the door, I saw a figure just beyond the threshold. I could distinguish no more than a shadowy presence dressed in black from head to foot. The face was a pale blur; I could not make out if the woman was old or young. But the immobility of the figure, the awareness of a quiet, intent scrutiny, gave me a sense of unease, as if I stared at an apparition or ghost. Then, as Robert took a step forward, feeling with his stick, the figure moved and came out of the doorway and I saw that the silent watcher was a young and beautiful woman, with a small boy following at her heels.

Still she did not speak, but went on staring at Robert, looking first puzzled and then alarmed. She said quickly, "*Robert!* Robert—what is this? What has happened? Have you met with an accident?"

Robert's step faltered. He leaned on his stick, staring in stunned fashion toward the speaker. His brow contracted; his lips moved but no words came. I had taken his arm and now I glanced first at him and then at the woman who had come to greet us.

She was tall and slender, and dressed in filmy black from head to foot, with no ornament save a necklace of jet worn around her throat. The mourning garb, far from detracting from her loveliness, seemed to enhance the pale creamy skin and the soft luster of gray-green eyes. A widow's cap of gauzy black lace scarcely concealed the shining waves of red-gold hair. One arm lay about the shoulder of the boy standing beside her. He was a handsome child with a trace of auburn in his silky fair hair and bright gray eyes that gazed up at his mother.

She said slowly, staring at Robert's scarred face, "I did not know you had been injured in this way. I am sorry." She reached for his hand and held it for a moment in her own and then she turned and said, "Edward, shake hands with your Uncle Robert." The boy did so, saying with grave politeness, "How do you do, sir."

Robert did not answer him. He went on staring as in a trance. I sensed him quiver, felt him take a deep breath, and then he said slowly, and in an almost inaudible voice, "Vanessa! I did not expect to find you here."

PART THREE

HAWKESTONE

CHAPTER 16

VANESSA. The name echoed in memory. Vanessa. I knew that name; I remembered it. It was the name that Robert had called aloud in his delirium. This was Vanessa; this was Philip's widow.

As in a dream I heard her answer Robert, saying, "I stayed—Edward and I stayed on so as to welcome you home, Robert. Your letter to Mr. Jarrold at Bath arrived two weeks ago. He communicated with me immediately. He wrote that you had met with an injury, but I did not know—" She paused a moment, then added brokenly, "We thought at first you were dead."

Robert stood stiffly erect, unmoving, his face expressionless. Now he spoke in a remote-sounding voice.

"No—I am alive. We were saved." He half turned to me. "This is my wife, Megan. We were married in Hong Kong a few months ago."

She took my hand in a soft boneless clasp and brushed a kiss, as light as a butterfly's wing, on my cheek.

"Welcome to Hawkestone, Megan. I hope that we shall be friends."

"Thank you. I—I hope so."

"You must be weary after your long drive. Let us go into the house where you can rest and take some refreshment. Robert, give me your arm. There are only a few steps, as you may remember. Edward, say how do you do to your Aunt Megan and bring her to the drawing room."

She was charming, the perfect hostess. As I shook hands

with Edward, Vanessa led Robert into the house, and we followed after them.

The great hall was spacious and light. There were archways on either side, leading to other rooms. The floor was of handsome tiling; a double staircase with graceful balusters of wrought-iron leaves and flowers curved upward out of sight. On the paneled walls hung gilt-framed portraits in oil. I was impressed and somewhat awed by the evidence of long-established wealth.

The room to which Edward, his small hand clasped in mine, led me was charming, with long windows looking on to a paved terrace, with beyond a stretch of smooth green turf and distant shrubbery. The furniture was of walnut, the chairs and sofas upholstered in green damask silk. At one end of the room stood a concert grand piano of shining rosewood. Vanessa, moving with floating grace, pulled at a bell rope hanging beside the green-painted Adam fireplace.

Turning to me she said, with a hint of apology, "Please forgive my giving orders, for this is your house now, and mine no longer, but just at first, as you are not accustomed to things, perhaps it will be easier." She sat down beside Robert and said gently, "Are you able to see me, Robert?"

"Not well. The sight in this eye is somewhat restricted. It may improve with time." The abrupt, almost harsh tone of voice in which he spoke softened as he added, "I did not write to you about Philip. I knew we should be here as soon as the mail. I am very sorry that he should die like this, so suddenly, Vanessa."

She sighed, clasping delicate hands upon the lap of her black dress. Her eyes were luminous with tears as she answered in a trembling voice, "It was not altogether surprising to me. Nor to Lucien, who has been living here with us. Philip was always delicate, as you know, Robert. It was because of that—it was one of the reasons I—" Her voice broke off and she touched her eyes with a wisp of black lace handkerchief.

Robert's jaw set. He said grimly, "I am sorry. I have upset you."

"No—please. I am over the worst of things." She turned

her head to look at Edward, who had come to stand beside her
to say, "Do not cry, Mama."

She seemed to make an effort, and smiled at him through
her tears.

"No, I must not. See, here is James with the tea things. Be
a good boy and help to look after your aunt and uncle."

"Did you say Lucien was living here?" Robert asked as he
took the plate that Edward brought to him and fumbled for a
cucumber sandwich.

"Yes. He—he was of great help to Philip—with the man-
agement of the estate, I mean."

Robert frowned.

"I was not aware that he understood such matters."

"Oh, yes. He has learned a great deal during the past few
years. It was Philip's wish. He knew that his heart might fail
him at any time and he thought that if—if I was left alone,
Lucien would be of assistance to me." She paused, her wistful
eyes on Robert's face, an expression of sadness on her lovely
upturned face. "Of course, I did not know—I never expected
that—that Philip would will the estate to you."

Robert started.

"*Philip* willed the estate to me? I thought it was my
uncle's doing. Why on earth should he do such a thing? After
all that happened between us—after you and he—" He broke
off and Vanessa, as if realizing his thoughts, turned to glance at
me.

"We are being discourteous to Megan. I am sure she
knows nothing of these matters. Please forgive our rudeness.
But after all this time, Robert and I have a great deal to say to
each other; there are many business affairs to be discussed. But
this can all be done later."

"I understand," I answered. "I have been happy to sit
quietly here and relax over tea. Edward and I have been getting to know each other. He tells me he is five years old. What
a tall handsome boy he is for his age."

"Thank you. And he is a good boy, too." She smiled at
her son. "Well, mostly."

I stood up.

"I wonder if I might be shown to my room. I *am* a little tired, and will rest for a while."

"Of course. I will ring for one of the maids."

Edward sprang up.

"*I* will show Aunt Megan to her room. I know which one it is. It is the big room overlooking the rose garden. The room where you and—Papa—" He stopped, staring at us in confusion.

"Yes, it is the main bedroom," Vanessa answered calmly. "I hope you will be comfortable there. Take Aunt Megan upstairs, Edward, and do not stay chattering to her. Please ring the bell for the maid if there is anything you require, Megan, or if you wish to have your luggage unpacked before you rest."

"Thank you." I hesitated and Vanessa smiled charmingly at me from the low chair in which she sat beside Robert. She was so much the mistress of the house, so calm and assured, that I wondered how she would ever bring herself to relinquish her authority to another person.

After Edward had left me I walked across the wide room to one of the long windows and looked out. Below me was a garden massed with roses of every color and kind. I stood in deep thought. I was not tired but uncomfortable, ostensibly talking to Edward but forced to hear a great deal of what was private conversation between Robert and Vanessa. It was obvious that Robert and Vanessa shared a close relationship from the past. Was it simply as his cousin's wife he had known her? Or had they been friends before her marriage to Philip?

I was puzzled and uncertain. I remembered how Robert had called Vanessa's name when he was ill and deeply unconscious. Why should he have thought of her at such a time? He had never spoken her name before that day or since.

I was surprised and delighted to find letters from Dr. and Mrs. Howard waiting my arrival at Hawkestone. It was a thick package, for Dr. Howard and Mrs. Howard had each written separately, and the children had also inscribed loving missives to me. Looking at Dorothea's large printed capitals and

George's more careful copperplate writing I saw the children clearly in my mind, sturdy George with his dimples and mischievous smile and Dorothea's delicate little face and wistful dark eyes. The letters ended with scrawls of kisses and at the sight of them tears came to my eyes. It was as if their arms came around my neck to hug me in turn, as they had so often done in the past.

Dr. Howard's letter was scholarly and serious, as might be expected, but he wrote with sincerity of his happiness that both Robert and I were safe. "It is truly a miracle, my dear Megan, but miracles do happen when we pray and I have prayed each night and day that you might be found, and God has answered these prayers."

Mrs. Howard wrote even more kindly, sending her fond love and warmest wishes for my future happiness and expressing her joy that it was to such a splendid man as Captain Hawkes that I was married. She added that it was her great wish that we should come to visit her and Dr. Howard at their home in London. After the trials that they too had gone through, their plans were to remain in London for at least a year before returning to China. "If Dr. Howard should decide to go back earlier, I shall not go with him but stay on in England for some time," she wrote. "My health has not been improved by the vicissitudes we endured, as you can imagine. Please write as soon as possible, my dear child, to tell us all is well with you. The children long to see you, as we do."

I was touched by the kindness of my correspondents and promised myself that I would write in answer to them the next day. I would tell them of my coming child and assure them that later, after his birth, we would visit them and hope that they in turn would come to Hawkestone.

That night at dinner I met Lucien Demant. He was Vanessa's stepbrother and of French descent. He was thin and slight, with black hair and melancholy dark eyes, but had a friendly manner that quickly put me at ease.

I was glad of this, for Robert and Vanessa spoke of so many things of which I had no knowledge that I should have again felt conscious of being the "stranger in their midst" if Lucien had not made himself agreeable to me. We found a bond of common interest when I learned that as a very young man he had not only undertaken the grand tour but had ventured beyond Europe to visit both India and China.

"Of course, you must understand I did not live among the Chinese for any length of time, as you have done, Lady Hawkes. But I stayed long enough to be intrigued by so ancient a civilization." The mobile mouth widened in a smile and his warm brown eyes held my own as he said, "I found their courtesy equaled only by that of my own countrymen."

Lady Hawkes. I was still not used to the title, though I should have been by now, and had not Lucien so clearly addressed his remarks to me, I would have thought them meant for someone else.

Vanessa, distracted for a moment from her conversation with Robert as he endeavored to eat some of the roast guinea fowl that the tall young footman had cut up for him, leaned forward to say, "It is no use your talking like a Frenchman, Lucien, for you are almost as English as I am, save for your place of birth. You have lived in this country since you were seven years old and you went to school here."

Lucien shook his head, smiling.

"I am a Frenchman in character and temperament. I shall never be a man such as Robert is. Cool and self-controlled. And silent. I talk too much, to begin with."

"Oh, you are good company, I will say that," Vanessa answered. "You will find much in common with him, Megan, for are not the Welsh a voluble race?" She saw my look of surprise and added gently, "Robert has told me a little about you. How you first met on his ship going out to China. And you shared many dangers, it seems. And then you were married. You must tell me all about it sometime, for it sounds very romantic."

"It was far from being that," Robert said abruptly, breaking into the conversation. "I am sure Megan wishes to forget what she went through, for I certainly do." He pushed his fork to one side of his plate. "I am tired of trying to eat dinner in the manner of a child of six. Would you excuse me if I retire to another room?" At a sign from him, the footman pulled the chair back and, handing Robert his stick, led the way toward the door.

Vanessa stared after him, her beautiful eyes widening in dismay.

"But what did I say? I was only joking. He is so strange and altered, I do not understand him. We had been talking together pleasantly enough."

"He has been through a period of great difficulty and I think, at times, feels very frustrated," I answered.

Vanessa frowned and, rising from her chair, said, "I will go and apologize for seeming to speak foolishly."

I shook my head.

"It would be best to leave him alone. He prefers that."

She stared down at me, the eyes that were more green than gray hardening unexpectedly.

"I have known Robert all my life; we grew up together. I think I may claim to understand him as well as you do."

Lucien leaned across the table.

"Lady Hawkes is right. It is better to leave a man alone when he has such a mood upon him. I am sorry for Robert. To be so handicapped—Robert of all men. He was strong and active beyond most. It is enough to try the patience of a saint and he was never one of those."

"He would not thank you for your sympathy or your pity," I said. I turned to the footman who was proffering a dish and ended the conversation by saying, "Thank you. I will take some of the queen's pudding."

Vanessa shrugged and sat down again. One small foot began to beat a delicate tattoo under the table. She accepted a helping of pudding and then left it untasted. It was obvious that Robert's conduct, or perhaps my comments, had upset her.

When dinner was over I went to sit in the drawing room with Vanessa and Lucien. There was no sign of Robert, but in answer to my question, Humphreys, the butler, told me that he had taken a bottle of brandy to Sir Robert in the library. After a while I made an excuse and retired early to bed.

I lay awake for a long time, my mind restless and ill at

ease. There were tensions in the household that puzzled me. I sensed a proprietary attitude in Vanessa toward Robert and something latent and repressed in Robert's attitude to her, which I could not fully understand. Daunted by her beauty and assurance, in some way I feared Vanessa. I wondered if Robert had once been in love with her.

In the morning I woke alone in a strange bed in a strange room. For a moment I could not recollect where I was and gazed up in bewilderment at the striped blue-and-cream bed hangings, the tall mahogany posts, the matching blue-and-cream silk curtains at the long windows. Everything was in most charming taste, the turquoise-and-cream carpet, a curved chair in buttoned rose velvet, a low stool of the same material beneath the graceful mahogany dressing table with its Regency mirror and gleaming silver candleholders. There were other pieces; a sofa table by the bed, a round oak table with a bowl of roses upon its shining surface. Pictures and mirrors and books; nothing dark or heavy or obtrusive. An entirely feminine room, the room that Vanessa and Philip had shared.

The door of the dressing room opened and Robert stood on the threshold.

"Good morning. I tried not to disturb you last night, you were sleeping so soundly. How do you feel?"

"Lazy and a little disoriented. I have wakened in so many different places lately. How are you, Robert? You came late to bed, I think."

"I dozed over a glass of brandy. Well, we are home now, Megan. There will be no more different rooms in which to waken. Do you think you will like it here at Hawkestone?"

"How could I do otherwise? From the little I have seen it appears to be a beautiful house, as are its surroundings. It is very large," I added.

He frowned.

"Yes. And there will be much to do. It is the devil that I can neither read nor write. There will be so many papers and letters to be gone through. I cannot leave it to Lucien any longer. Perrin, the estate steward, will help me, but from what I remember he is a practical rather than a paper man."

"Could—could I not help you, Robert? Perhaps I might read your letters to you? Or write them?"

He shook his head.

"Thank you. I don't doubt your capabilities, but you know nothing of the running of a country estate. Nor of a country house, for that matter. It is a world in itself. Of course, Vanessa will be of help to you while she is here. She can explain things, give you advice, just as Lucien will be of use to me. I shall want to ride around the farms, and someone will have to go with me." His mouth twisted. "In case I should fall off the horse."

"I would have gone with you." I looked down at my form, bulky beneath the bedclothes. "But—but it would not be sensible to do at present."

"No." He smiled unexpectedly. "You have more important work to do. To cherish our son and bring him safely into the world."

"You are sure it will be a boy."

"I hope that, naturally. I should be pleased to have a son like Edward. He is a fine boy. But if it is otherwise I shall not object." He gave me a hard unseeing stare. "We must see to it that we have a boy the next time."

I did not answer but looked away from him. I did not wish to feel I must produce a son to rival Vanessa's.

When I came downstairs, after taking a breakfast of tea and toast in bed, for I had little appetite first thing in the morning, it was to find Robert and Vanessa already gone out.

"Miss Vanessa drove the master in the pony carriage, my lady, seeing as he can't ride horseback, and Mr. Demant was riding alongside so as to explain matters to the master," Humphreys told me. "I was to tell you they would be back in good time for luncheon."

"Thank you." I was at a loss what to say or what to do. Humphreys waited, head bowed politely, as if for some instructions. I said quickly, "It is such a beautiful morning, I—I will take a walk in the grounds."

"Certainly, my lady. The trees are at their best now with the autumn colors. Is there anything else, my lady?"

"Not—not for the moment, thank you, Humphreys."

"This way then, my lady. I will open the side door for you, it leads onto the terraces."

I walked slowly out into the warm September sunshine. Everything glittered and shone. A heavy dew still silvered the grass; spiders' webs traced lacy patterns on the roses climbing against the golden stone. Beyond the flagged terrace, steps led to a wide lawn, and beyond that the drop of a ha-ha and then the park, extending in sunlit vistas as far as the eye could see. It was beautiful and my heart and senses were touched by such splendor.

But I had never felt more lonely or alone in my life.

A small voice said from behind me, "Good morning, Aunt Megan."

It was Edward. He came forward and, in the most courteous manner possible, gravely shook my hand, saying politely, "I trust you slept well?"

I managed to conceal a smile at such old-fashioned demeanor and answered gravely, "Yes, thank you, Edward. I hope that you did too."

"Oh, yes, I always do. But I heard Mama saying to Uncle Robert when he wanted to go upstairs to tell you they were going for a drive that it was best not to disturb you."

"Did you not wish to go with them?"

He shook his head. I thought again what a handsome child he was, with his silky fair hair and regular features and bright gray eyes fringed by long brown lashes.

"I could not, for Deborah, she is my nursemaid, is teaching me to read. Soon I shall have a governess. But I am free to play now." He gazed up at me. "Would you like to see my pony, Rory?"

"Very much indeed."

He took my hand in his own small one and said, "We must go this way." He led me to the end of the terrace and down a flight of shallow steps to the graveled path that led around the side of the house to an archway set in a high wall of faded pink brick. We passed under this into a stable yard with stalls on either side and a glimpse of a harness room through an open doorway where a man sat polishing a saddle.

A boy was sweeping wisps of straw from the cobbles, and at our entry he glanced up and, touching his forelock, said, "Mornin', m'lady—Master Edward."

"Good morning, Tom. We have come to see Rory."

"Aye. He be over there, waitin' for you, Master Edward. Reckon he's lookin' forrard to you takin' him for a ride this morning, same as usual."

Rory was a Shetland pony, reddish-brown in color and of rotund build. He had a shaggy mane and very dark bright eyes, and he nuzzled Edward eagerly as he searched for his accustomed tidbit.

"Oh, dear, I should have remembered to bring him a carrot or an apple, as I always do in the afternoon. He will be so disappointed."

The stableboy came up to us.

"Beggin' your pardon, m'lady. 'Ere's a bit o' carrot for ee, Master Edward, to give the pony. He allus looks for it, don't ee?"

"Thank you, Tom. Here, Rory," and Edward held out the piece of carefully sliced carrot to the pony, who took it with zestful greed.

When the pony had finished the treat and been patted by Edward and myself, we left the stables, for Edward decided to forego his ride in favor of a walk by my side. We walked along the path that appeared to circle the wall. Some way along, a green-painted wooden door was set in the brick, and Edward said, "The kitchen garden is here. We can go in if you will lift the latch—I cannot reach it."

I lifted the latch as directed and stepped through the opening into an immense kitchen garden enclosed on all sides by the brick wall. All manner of vegetables were growing in beds, with celery banked high and cauliflowers and Brussels sprouts and cabbages in profusion. Net cages protected soft fruit bushes from marauding birds, though the currants and raspberries and strawberries were through bearing now. There were pear and plum trees and nectarines trained against the warm south wall. It was a warm and peaceful place, and when we came within view of a wooden seat sheltered by a late-flowering honeysuckle, I suggested to Edward that we should sit down for a few moments.

He perched beside me, his short legs swinging above the ground. This morning he wore a sailor suit and above the white collar his pink cheeks shone. He had already endeared himself to me. The quaintness of his manners, his air of old-fashioned courtesy, caused me an inward smile, but I thought him the dearest little boy and hoped wistfully that I might have a son not unlike him.

"When we leave here will I be able to take Rory with me?" Edward asked suddenly.

I was startled.

"When you leave? Yes, I am sure you will. But—but is it arranged that you are to leave, and where do you go to?"

He frowned, staring down at the ground.

"I do not know. But Mama said now that you and Uncle Robert had come to live at Hawkestone we would have to leave. I do not want to go away." He looked around at me, his gray eyes anxious. "Do you not want us here, Aunt Megan?"

I felt a pang of contrition. As if it were my fault that Edward looked so sad at the thought of his departure from Hawkestone. I said quickly, "I do not wish you to go away unless you have to. But it is not for me to say. Hawkestone belongs to your Uncle Robert now. It is something he will arrange with your mama, no doubt."

"I hope we do not have to live with my grandmama, for she is so cross and fierce that she frightens me. And her house is very small and there is no park in which to ride Rory." He frowned. "There are stables, but not many for Grandmama keeps only one horse."

"Where does your grandmama live?"

"I do not know, but it is not far from here, because we drive there in quite a short time. She is Mama's mama and is very, *very* old. She is bent over and her face is thin and all wrinkled. She looks like a witch," he added.

I felt the conversation was moving onto dangerous ground so I stood up and said, "Perhaps we should be going back to the house. It will soon be time for luncheon."

As we walked slowly along the path I thought of what

Edward had said concerning his mother's departure. It was wrong of me to feel that I did not want Vanessa to remain at Hawkestone. She was lately widowed and perhaps was more sad at heart than she cared to reveal. It must also be a bitter disappointment to her that the estate should come to Robert and not to herself as Philip's widow and Edward's mother. This turn of events seemed to me cruel and unfair, yet she showed no trace of resentment and had welcomed Robert and myself to Hawkestone with every grace. Why then did I not like and admire her as I should? Was I envious of her? Envious of her extreme beauty, her poise and charm, and envious, above all, that she might mean more to Robert than he would acknowledge.

That morning set the pattern for the days that were to follow. At Robert's insistence I rose late, having breakfasted in bed. By the time I came downstairs it was to find him driven out by either Lucien or Mr. Perrin, the steward. Sometimes he went on horseback and almost invariably Vanessa accompanied him. If she did not, she was there to greet me, gracious and beautiful, in one of the black dresses that were so becoming to her and which, for all their somberness, never looked like mourning.

I was unused to the hierarchy of an immense country house and was at a loss to know which servant dealt with this or that matter. I gave few orders for I did not know what to say when queries arose. Vanessa, with gentle apology, would take over the situation, explaining to me afterward what should have been done. But often she would say, "Do not trouble yourself about it, Megan. You will learn in time. Well, as much as you need to know. Mrs. Rowley, the housekeeper, is in charge of the household and Humphreys deals with everything else."

"Thank you." But I went on feeling inadequate and very much aware of my shortcomings as mistress of Hawkestone.

Because Vanessa was in a period of mourning we had few outside visitors and entertained only members of the family or close friends. Once again I felt a disadvantage, for those whom I met were curious concerning Robert's unknown wife, and when they asked about my previous life and background, they reacted with scarcely concealed surprise or puzzled amusement. It was clear that Robert's friends, and these it seemed were Vanessa's also, could not understand how he had come to marry the unknown granddaughter of a Welsh sheep farmer who had gone to work in a mission at Macao. I began to wonder myself, and it did not help to recall that it was I, in the first place, who had assumed the role, albeit falsely, of Robert's wife. In circumstances other than the strange ones in which we had found ourselves I doubted if he would have considered marrying me. As the days passed and I grew more awkward and cumbersome in my pregnancy, my self-confidence dwindled and I became more unsure of myself than ever.

Madame Ormonde was invited on several occasions to dinner. She was Lucien's mother and Vanessa's stepmother, for Vanessa's own mother had died in childbirth when Vanessa was but three years old. A few years later her father had married Estelle Demant, who had come as a young widow with her son to England, an émigré from the French Revolution. She was now an alarming old lady in her late seventies, with glittering black eyes and hair of unlikely reddish hue. She spoke English in a harsh broken accent and had a disconcerting habit of talking to herself in muttered asides, so that one overheard thoughts better not expressed. As after my own introduction to her, when I heard her quietly murmur, "Is it possible dis little pairson is Robairt's wife? So black of hair and so much *enceinte*. What will Vanessa do now I wonder?"

I wondered that too, for the weeks were passing to Christmas and no more had been said of Vanessa's leaving Hawkestone. Lucien went to and fro from Springhill, his mother's house, which was situated a few miles beyond the boundaries of the park. But always he returned, to be Robert's companion and assist him in matters concerning the estate, and still Vanessa deferred charmingly to me and remained, in fact, if not in name, the chatelaine of the great house.

One morning Robert suggested I should drive out with him. I had been taken several times around the estate so that I was familiar with the immediate countryside and had visited Madame Ormonde in the small dark house with pointed Gothic windows and ivy-covered walls, which seemed so in keeping with its fiercely eccentric owner. To drive alone with Robert was a rare experience and I welcomed it.

It was a cold but dry day in early December. The leaves were long gone from the trees, but the Great Park looked as beautiful as ever, with the bare branches of elm and silver birch outlined against a pale-blue sky. To the west, where the city of Bath lay, the horizon was softened by blue shadows. From time to time as we drove along, Jenkins, the groom, would turn his head to say, "We are coming to Orchard Farm now, sir," or "Thomson's cottage is on the side of the road here, sir," and Robert would give me a short history of the place or the tenants, to which I listened with interest.

I had thought the morning's drive was for Robert and me to enjoy each other's company, but I soon learned it was not. Its purpose was to break the news of his decision. For decision it was. There was no question of consultation. He did not wish to send Vanessa away.

"Well?" he demanded with a hint of impatience.

I swallowed and said in a stiff-sounding voice, "Hawkestone belongs to you, to do with as you wish. I—I must be in agreement with whatever you say."

"It will be best for you too, Megan. Our child is to be born next month. If Vanessa is with us, seeing after things, it cannot be of other than help to you, for you will not be as active as usual for a while."

"I suppose not."

"It is settled then. I will tell her when we get back to the house. She will be glad, for I know she dreads the thought of living at Springhill with Madame Ormonde. She has told me so, many times."

I didn't doubt it. I forced myself to feel sorry for Vanessa; I tried to put myself in her place. Would I not have done the same as she? Hoped that the cousin of my late husband would take pity on me and allow my son and myself to remain in the beautiful house that had previously been my own home?

It was only natural. And so I would do my best to be friends with Vanessa and hope that, in turn, she would feel the same way about me.

CHAPTER 17

THE WINTER DAYS closed in on us. I grew slower and heavier in movement, and on account of my condition and Vanessa's period of mourning, Christmas was a quiet time, with only Madame Ormonde, her companion, Miss Tindall, Lucien and a distant cousin of Vanessa's as guests. I thought back to the year before, when I had been at the Mission and we had celebrated Christmas together; the Howards and Mr. and Miss Crow, the servants, the Chinese children and some of the converts. And how New Year had been a festival of noise and light and color. I thought that this was a lonely household for a small boy like Edward, who had few playmates of his own age.

Earlier on, Vanessa had come with charming grace to thank me for agreeing to share Hawkestone with her and Edward.

"I am to have the apartment in the west wing. There are rooms above for the servants and there are back stairs, so we shall be quite separate and you and Robert will be left undisturbed." She gave me a glance from under her narrow eyelids. "I am sure that is what you both wish."

For some reason I felt unreal with Vanessa, as if either she or I were not the person each appeared to be. I do not know who was to blame. Whether I was more stupid than I thought myself or Vanessa less pleasing than her outward aspect. I only knew that I was uneasy with her and constrained in her presence.

The days passed slowly through January. Vanessa put

aside her black dresses and emerged in shades of rich violet and mauve and soft lavender, in which she looked even more beautiful.

Our daughter was born to us on the twenty-sixth of January. She hurried into the world as eagerly and as happily as she was to go through life. Within a few hours of the first pains she had arrived, and though, for Robert's sake, I had wished for a son, one glance at the tiny puckered face in my arms convinced me that I could not love any child more. She was small and neat, with huge eyes in a heart-shaped face and a feathering of light-brown hair on her head.

She was named Imogen. The meaning of the name was "beloved child" and that is what she was to us both. If Robert was disappointed to have a daughter in place of a son, he showed no evidence of this. Only Vanessa commiserated with me, saying, as she brought the gift of a silver bracelet for Imogen and a book of Mr. Wordsworth's poems for me, "What a pity you have a daughter first time. Robert so wanted a son. But perhaps you will be more fortunate later."

By the end of February I was up and about again. I nursed Imogen myself and so my social activities were limited, although we went to Bath on more than one occasion, either to visit friends of Robert's or to make purchases at the elegant shops in Milsom Street.

"You need some new dresses," Robert announced one day. "Go with Vanessa. She will take you to the—right places; she has excellent taste."

"Thank you," I said with an irony in my voice that caused Robert to look around at me.

"I am not disputing your good taste, Megan, but you have not had the opportunities in the past to indulge in fashion, and Vanessa can advise you regarding the right things for the right occasion."

"Does it matter so much? We do not lead a very social life, do we?" I did not add "And you cannot see what I am wearing."

"Our social life has been restricted for various reasons. You were pregnant, Vanessa in mourning. My own activities are limited. But things may not always be like this. I am proposing that we shall go to London next month. You wish to visit your friends the Howards and I am going to see some man in Wigmore Street who is a specialist in eye injuries. Vanessa has heard of him from a friend and she thinks there is every hope that he might be able to do something for this eye."

Vanessa. Always Vanessa. What Vanessa said and thought and did.

I fought the sense of irritation that rose within me and said as calmly as I could, "Yes. I am sure that is a wise thing to do. You will remember Dr. Haas said that there was every likelihood that some of the sight of that eye could be restored."

Robert shrugged.

"Dr. Haas! I shall have more faith in Dr. Simpson's opinion than that of the old Chinese man."

"He was good to us."

The hard expression softened momentarily.

"Yes, he was. I did not mean to disparage him. It was a strange experience we went through together, Megan. Do you ever think about it?"

"Sometimes."

"So do I." I felt him glance at me, though I knew he could not see the look on my face. "I remember the Pearl Pagoda. Do you realize, Megan, that Imogen could have been born from that first—the first time we came together?"

I blushed.

"I do not think that is so. It—it must have been later."

"Do you still hate me for what I did? The opium trading, I mean."

"No. But I do not find it easy to understand why you should have become entangled in such traffic. It could not have been solely for money." I gestured at the handsome room in which we stood, the library, with its paneled walls lined with books, and the painted ceiling, the massive mahogany desk and chairs, the great globe of the world on its brass stand. "You had all this—this had been your home."

He said harshly, "It belonged to my uncle and then to Philip. I never expected to inherit it."

"What was he like—Philip? You said he was delicate—a cripple. He does not sound the sort of man someone like Vanessa would marry. She is so—so very beautiful, she could have chosen anyone."

"She chose Philip. That is he in that portrait over there. He had rheumatic fever as a child; it left him crippled and affected his heart."

I walked slowly over to the portrait he had indicated. It was an oil painting and showed a young man, tall and slight and with stooping shoulders, as if his frail body had not the strength with which to bear the height of his frame. He had fair hair worn rather long and hollowed blue eyes. There was an expression of sweetness in the melancholy face that touched and drew me to him.

"He looks gentle and good," I observed.

"He was both those things."

"Edward resembles him, except that he is sturdy and strong."

"He has Philip's disposition."

"And—were you friends, although you are so different a person?"

"Yes. I think I told you before—I fought Philip's battles for him. He—looked to me—leaned on me."

I felt myself frowning.

"Then what was the quarrel that sent you away from Hawkestone?"

"I do not wish to discuss it here and now. If you will excuse me, I will leave you. I have much to do elsewhere."

He left me so abruptly that I was left staring after him in mingled puzzlement and dismay. I looked back to the grave, delicate face of Robert's cousin and thought that I should never understand any member of this family.

The only one I grew close to was Edward. He was both loving and protective toward Imogen and would sit for hours beside her cradle, gently rocking it with one small hand while Imogen gurgled and smiled at him. He regarded her as something between a doll and a playmate, though of course she was much too young to take any part in his games. But he would toss a ball up and down before her or dangle an ivory ring on a silver chain above the cradle and her eyes would move to watch it. I wondered that an active little boy should be so content to spend so much time with an infant such as Imogen and then it dawned on me that Edward had been lonely for a long time, for one day he said to me, "Imogen is not my sister, is she?"

"No, she is a sort of second cousin. *Your* father was Uncle Robert's cousin and so you are members of the same family."

He nodded.

"It is nice to be a family. And it is *almost* like having a sister. I am glad you have come to live here, Aunt Megan. It is much nicer now, for there is always someone to talk to or play with." He frowned. "Papa would read to me, but he was not well, you see, and often I was told I must not disturb him."

I could not forbear to say, "And your mama? Did she read to you too?"

He shook his head.

"Mama was too busy. She had to go out a lot, and she told me it was because of Papa's being ill and that I must stay with Deborah." He looked up at me. "I am to have a governess when I am six. Will Imogen have her too?"

"Not for a long time. When will you be six, Edward?"

"I am not sure. My birthday is in the summer, but I cannot remember the date."

I smiled at him.

"We will have a birthday party in the garden. Would you like that?"

"Oh, very much. Who will come to it?"

"Why, everyone. And all the children you know and who are your friends."

His small face fell.

"I do not think I know many other children. Only Sydney and Amelia and Bertie. They are my *real* cousins and they come and visit us sometimes from Bath with Uncle Stephen and Aunt Louise, my father's sister."

"Perhaps they will come and visit at the time of your birthday, and then you will see them again."

He clapped his hands, dancing up and down.

"Oh, yes. I will tell Mama and she will arrange it."

It was decided that we should go to London early in June. Robert did not wish to stay with Dr. and Mrs. Howard and so arrangements were made for us to go to a quiet hotel in St. James's.

"You will be able to visit them as often as you wish," he told me, "and they are welcome to come to the hotel for luncheon or dinner, but spare me days and nights under the roof of missionaries, if you please."

"I am very fond of the Howard family, and I look forward to seeing them again."

"Certainly. Why should you not? But I am not particularly interested."

I said no more. Because of the coming visit to London I had postponed the shopping expedition with Vanessa to Bath. I thought I should prefer to choose my new ensembles myself, or at most, under the guidance of some helpful saleslady in a London store. I did not want my dresses and bonnets and mantles selected for me by Vanessa.

Imogen was to be left in Deborah's care for the four weeks we would be away. I was reluctant to say goodbye to her, but to take her to London would do her little good and I felt that I should accompany Robert, especially as he had made an appointment with the surgeon in Wigmore Street. So somewhat sadly I kissed my little daughter goodbye, and after hugging Edward, I said goodbye to Vanessa and Lucien and stepped into the carriage. We were to travel to London by train and the carriage would take us as far as the railway station at Bath.

Lucien was now living at Hawkestone. After retreating to his mother's home at Springhill for a few weeks, he had, at Robert's urging, returned to take up residence at Hawkestone.

"I cannot do without you, Lucien, and that is the truth. I am too handicapped to do the work of the estate alone, and it is no use leaving it all to Perrin, good fellow though he is. Vanessa knows as much as you do about the running of Hawkestone, but I cannot go riding and driving about the place all the time with her. It will not do."

Vanessa had smiled her slow, languorous smile at him.

"I have no objection, Robert."

He did not see the smile nor did his face soften at the caressing tone of her voice. He answered abruptly, "Thank you, but you have enough to do tutoring Megan in the ways of managing the house."

To tell the truth Vanessa wasted little time upon this and I learned little. What Vanessa did not decide, Mrs. Rowley, the housekeeper, did and I was seldom consulted. Mrs. Rowley was a tall austere woman always handsomely dressed in black bombazine. I admit I was somewhat in awe of her and was not confident enough to overrule any of her suggestions. Not that I wished to. They were always practical and admirable, but I felt very much lady of the house in name only and not in fact.

I knew that Vanessa was displeased to be left behind at Hawkestone, but there was nothing else she could do, for Robert had taken it for granted that she would return his kindness to her by taking on that responsibility.

So we drove away on a fine sunny morning in June, accompanied by Pearce, Robert's valet, who was of great assistance to him, and Hetty, my young personal maid.

I had never been to London in my life and the first few days had all the excitement of seeing a great and fashionable city. I was astounded at the traffic, at the carriages and carts and cabs that thronged the busy streets. I had never seen such handsome shops or such a collection of rare and beautiful merchandise on display. The hotel in St. James's was quietly luxurious, with every comfort to hand, and from there we drove along The Mall, past Buckingham Palace, which I was thrilled to see, and through Hyde Park, with its great trees and well-dressed people strolling by or riding in the Row.

Our first appointment was with Dr. Simpson, the Wigmore Street surgeon. While he gave Robert a thorough examination I waited in the small but elegantly furnished reception room, hoping and praying that he would have good news for Robert concerning his remaining eye.

He came out speak to me while Robert finished dressing.

"I am sorry, Lady Hawkes, but for the present nothing can be done for your husband. It is a question of time. The nerve of the injured eye may repair itself and I should prefer to leave matters until we see what progress is made. Later, if there is no improvement, I can attempt an operation, but this is dangerous. If it fails, Sir Robert might lose the sight in his remaining eye. He would be wholly blind." He heard my slight gasp and gave me a reassuring smile. "I have had to prepare you for the worst that can happen, but believe me, I have every hope that nature herself will do her good and customary work and heal the damage that has been done."

"Thank you," I answered somewhat unsteadily. "Does my husband know this?"

"Certainly. He is not a man whom one could or would attempt to deceive. The fact is, he is eager to undergo the operation, but I am of the opinion that we should leave matters as they are for at least a year. Ah, here is your husband now. Sir Robert, I have put the facts to your wife and think, unless I am mistaken, she is content to leave the decision in my hands."

"I am indeed, Dr. Simpson."

Robert nodded, frowning.

"I appear to be outvoted." He put out his hand. "I am extremely grateful to you, sir, and will endeavor to possess my soul in patience."

"Come and see me again in six months. That is, unless there is any change, which I rather doubt. Goodbye, Sir Robert—Lady Hawkes," and after a firm handshake and a bow, we were ushered out to the waiting carriage by an attentive manservant.

"So we are as we were," Robert said. "I could have wished he was ready to operate. Let it be kill or cure, I say."

"Don't speak in that way," I protested. "You have every chance of recovering your eyesight if you will be content to wait and see how things go."

"My dear Megan, I have waited a year. More than a

year." He shrugged. "Well, there is nothing more to be done so I must grin and bear it." He turned to me. "Do you mind if we return to the hotel now? Dr. Simpson's examination and the lights in my eye seem to have given me a headache. I should prefer not to drive any farther."

"Of course. You must rest."

I could see that Robert was in some distress, so I left him in the darkened bedroom and retired to the adjoining sitting room where I wrote letters to Sylvia and to Miss Crow.

We dined quietly that night and next day Robert was recovered and insisted that I should go shopping.

"I should like to go to my club—I hope to contact a friend of mine there. Your maid can accompany you and, Megan"—he put his hand out to seek mine—"take this and do not stint yourself. I wish you to buy anything you wish. Within reason," he added with a slight smile.

"This" was a draft for two hundred pounds. I stared at it in amazement.

"I cannot," I gasped, but he lifted his hand to silence me.

"Open an account at any store you please. And don't look like that, Megan. We shall be entertaining while we are in London and it is your duty, as well as your pleasure, to look as charming as possible. I may not be able to see you, but I can picture you in my mind, and when you have bought up half the store you may display your purchases and describe each one to me."

"You—you are very generous, Robert. Thank you."

Hetty, who was young and pretty, with sparkling dark eyes and rose-pink cheeks, drove with me in the hired carriage to a recently opened store that had a reputation for quality. There I put myself under the guidance of a gray-haired vendeuse whose appearance was almost as elegant as the show of fine dresses and mantles placed before me.

Hetty, standing discreetly in the background, stared bemused, and when I tried on various ensembles, she nodded and beamed with as much delight as if she were buying something for herself. I could see it was only with great firmness that she restrained herself from applauding.

Feeling recklessly extravagant, I bought three dresses in all. One was of shell-pink satin draped with matching ninon, displaying a somewhat décolleté shoulder line that at first dismayed me, but which, with the saleslady's encouragement, I reluctantly accepted. It must be admitted I had never seen myself in anything half so becoming, for the soft pink set off my dark hair and eyes and the dropped shoulder line revealed the creamy smoothness of neck and arms. One day dress was of kingfisher-blue silk with four tiers and a fichu bodice, and the other was a biscuit-colored muslin ornamented with vertical stripes of dark red and fastening to the throat with small red buttons. In addition I bought a fine white cashmere cloak lined with pink silk to match my evening dress and trimmed with golden-brown fringe.

I bought two new bonnets, one of straw, poke-shaped and trimmed with a band and bow of cream satin ribbon, and one set off the face, with a trimming of roses to one side and tied under the chin with ribbon in an old-rose shade.

I bought slippers and gloves and a pair of silk mittens and a new nightdress and matching silk peignoir in palest blue edged with swansdown. Lastly I bought a handsome new shawl of paisley pattern on a rose-colored ground. And then, because I had known what it was to have little money and few pretty things, I bought a shawl for Hetty. It was of plaid design in a rich green that set off her fresh coloring to perfection. She was so delighted that her eyes suffused with tears and for a moment she could not speak.

At last she stammered, "Oh, my lady—it be too good. I never expected to have anything half so beautiful. I dunno how to properly say thank you, ma'am, but I be ever so grateful."

"Then say nothing, Hetty. It is a present to you for your next birthday, if you wish. You can tell the other servants so."

Robert was at the hotel waiting for me when I returned.

"Oh, Robert, I have bought some delightful dresses. I have never possessed so many beautiful things in my life. Thank you for your generosity."

"I am happy for you. And tomorrow you must wear one

of your new dresses, for my old friend Commander Gordon is coming here with his wife to have dinner with us. And then you will wish to visit Dr. and Mrs. Howard, so you had better make arrangements to do so."

"You will come too, Robert?" I inquired anxiously.

He hesitated.

"If I must. And of course, you shall invite them here."

"Thank you. I should like to do that."

Commander Gordon was a big, burly man, a few years older than Robert. It was obvious that he and Robert were old friends and they had much to talk about. Mrs. Gordon was tall and fair and elegantly dressed, so I was glad that I was able to wear the pink silk dress and do Robert credit. We found topics in common, for she had visited Macao and also Hong Kong. She had four children and was delighted to hear that we had a daughter.

"You must miss her. Your first parting. But when you return you will find even a few weeks have made a difference and she will have grown." She added in a low voice, with her head turned away from Robert, "It is a tragedy that your husband should have lost his sight. William told me how it happened and all I can say for comfort to you, my dear, is that he and you were lucky to escape with your lives, for the piracy of the China Seas is a byword. I have personally known people who have been captured and were never seen again."

"Yes, we are both thankful. And we have hope that Robert's eyesight may improve in time or by operation," and I went on to tell her something of what Dr. Simpson had said.

"You must both come and dine with us," Mrs. Gordon said as she and her husband bade us good night. "Would a week today be convenient?"

I waited for Robert to answer and he said with more warmth than I had seen him display for some time, "Yes, I am sure it is. Thank you, Elizabeth."

When they had gone we made our way slowly up to the second floor, where our suite was situated. There was a dressing room for Robert's use, but tonight he followed me into the main bedroom.

"I will not disturb Pearce," he said. "If I could trouble you to unfasten these buttons and take out the studs and cuff-links from my shirt, I should be grateful."

"Of course." I put out my hand to ease off the satin-lined evening coat and laid it on the chaise longue at the foot of the bed.

Robert, tall, surprisingly handsome despite the black eye shield and scarred forehead, said, "I wish I could see you in your new dress. Elizabeth Gordon told me how charming you looked. Her words were 'What beautiful eyes your wife has.' I think I told you that myself once, Megan."

My fingers trembled as I unbuttoned the embroidered waistcoat.

"Yes." I laid the waistcoat on the chaise longue beside the jacket and began to unfasten the cuff links in his frilled shirt. As I did so Robert reached his hands out and rested them lightly at either side of my waist.

"You feel very small and slender." He smiled slightly. "A little while ago you told me you looked like a cottage loaf."

I tried to smile in answer, but I was trembling inside with a strange and unaccustomed emotion.

"I think I am back to normal."

"I'm glad to hear that." He lifted my hand from his sleeve and held it to his lips, while his other arm tightened about me. "Megan, it's been too long a time," and with slow deliberation he bent his head and kissed me.

At his touch, at the feel of his lips on mine, I felt something explode within me. As if some barrier that had held me firm and strong had been dynamited to the four winds. Past antagonisms, reproaches, censure, disintegrated and were no more. I was as much in love with Robert as I had ever been.

We kissed with a passion as intense as before. We swayed in each other's arms and only when Robert murmured, "Let me help you out of this," did I remember that I was still wearing the delicate new pink dress. With shaking fingers I slid out of its silken folds and unfastened the crinoline while Robert finished his own undressing. As I sank down onto the bed, he turned the gas lamp low and came to lie down beside me and folding me once more in his arms began to kiss me with a deep and searching hunger that roused my own desire.

I was happy again, so very happy to love and be loved by Robert. I would forget his past and think only of the future. We were married now, united in the closest and most meaningful way possible, and no differences must remain between us. And one day he would say the words I longed to hear but which he still had never spoken, "I love you, Megan."

CHAPTER 18

THE WEEKS we spent in London were as a second honeymoon, recalling the times we had been together at The Place of Tall Trees and on the Chinese junk sailing to Hong Kong. We made love and found a new delight in each other, and when I looked in the mirror I saw that a bloom of happiness lent me an air almost of beauty. My dark hair shone, my eyes looked larger and more luminous, my skin glowed. I marveled and wished with all my heart that Robert could see how transformed I was by his love.

The sense of joy and well-being was added to by the reunion with Dr. and Mrs. Howard, not to mention George and Dorothea. It was arranged that I should go to their home for luncheon and Robert would come and fetch me later in the day and so renew his acquaintance with the Howards.

"My dear Megan, this is one of the happiest and most satisfying days of my life," Dr. Howard told me as he embraced me with unexpected warmth. "To think that you are alive and well and safely married to Captain Hawkes. I cannot describe the distress I suffered that you should be left behind on the *Lotus Wind* that dreadful day." He shook his head. "It was through no intention of mine."

"Oh, no, indeed, Dr. Howard. I felt very guilty that I had not obeyed your command to disembark with you all, but at the time I could do no other."

"It was God's will that you should save the man who has since become your husband."

Mrs. Howard, smiling and tearful at one and the same

time, embraced me with loving warmth and congratulated me upon my marriage.

Though it is dreadful that your poor husband has lost his sight. Is he able to see at all?"

"A little. Everything is a blur, but he is so independent that he has learned remarkably quickly to find his way about. I do not know how."

"And you are Lady Hawkes now. It is hard to realize. Little Megan. I shall never forget when you first came to us at the Mission. You were so sad." She broke off. "I should not have said that. You will not wish to remember those days."

"I shall always remember Arthur," I said gently. I changed the subject by adding, "Do not let us talk about me but tell me how you are yourself, dear Mrs. Howard. Have you quite recovered from what must have been a terrible ordeal in the open boat?"

"It was indescribable. The heat was blistering and we had little water and there was the constant dread of more pirates coming down upon us. But this past year in England has restored me and I am better in health than I have been for some time."

I could see that she had put on some weight and her face was less pale and wan than it was formerly.

"I am glad. Will you return to Macao?"

She shook her head.

"Not for a while. Dr. Howard may go back at the end of the summer. I am to remain in England with the children. We have rented a house in Basingstoke, near my sister, and the children will go to school there." She turned her head as the sitting-room door opened. "Ah, here they are. We did not dare to let them see you before we had an opportunity to first talk together. They will give you no peace, Megan, for they have never stopped speaking of you."

George and Dorothea surrounded me, kissing and hugging me and chattering in high, excited voices until Dr. Howard said, "Children, children, one at a time, if you please. What is it you wish to say, George? And Dorothea, you shall speak in a moment."

But it was wonderful. So much happiness and joy and the

children had grown beyond recognition—George, tall for his age, and little Dorothea, big-eyed as a lemur, with sticklike arms clutching at my waist. We were breathless by the time we sat down to luncheon, and I was relieved that Robert had elected not to be present at his first reunion, but to arrive later, when we had calmed down.

Robert arrived in time for tea and he and Dr. Howard were soon in deep conversation. From what I overheard, they were recalling once again the terrible time after the pirates had taken over the *Lotus Wind*.

Before we left Dr. and Mrs. Howard it was arranged that they should come to dinner at the hotel one evening and also that I would take the children and Mrs. Howard for a drive another afternoon and they would return to take tea at the hotel.

"Now are you happy?" Robert asked as we drove away from Tavistock Square. "Has everything been arranged as you wish?"

He was smiling so I knew that his sardonic tone of voice was not meant unkindly.

"I am very happy. But not merely on account of seeing the Howards again."

He put his hand over mine.

"I am happy too, Megan. Or as much as I shall ever be."

With that I had to be content.

The days passed quickly in various social affairs. Robert seemingly had more friends living in and about London than in the vicinity of Hawkestone. We went one evening to the theater to see Charles Kean, son of the famous Edmund Kean and husband of Ellen Tree, who was now playing with her in a series of famous revivals at the Princess's Theatre. I was enthraled. I had never been to a theater of any kind in my life and I was grateful to Robert for taking me, knowing that he could see nothing of the performance but must be satisfied merely listening to the spoken words.

It was time to return to Hawkestone and I could not be sorry, for my little Imogen was waiting there for me and I longed to see her again and hold her in my arms.

I could hardly pause to greet Vanessa, who came forward to welcome us, but hurried over to Deborah, who was standing in the background holding Imogen. As I took her from her nurse, Imogen stared at me out of eyes that were of so dark a blue and so like Robert's had once been that they brought tears to my own. Then two chubby arms were outstretched toward me and she smiled, as if she recognized me at first sight.

Edward came to stand beside me and as I kissed Imogen's silky brown hair I reached down with one hand to touch his cheek and said, "It is nice to see you again, Edward darling. Have you been taking good care of Imogen for me?"

"Oh, yes, Aunt Megan. Look, she has another tooth. She has four now—I counted them."

"So she has. She is growing fast. Soon she will be sitting up."

"She is sitting up now, m'lady," Deborah interposed. "As straight and proper as you could wish to see, in her high chair or in her bassinet."

"I cannot believe that four weeks have made so great a difference."

Vanessa, who had been talking animatedly with Robert, drifted toward me.

"Is the baby worship over now?" Her gray-green eyes surveyed me closely. "I do not need to ask if you have enjoyed your visit to London for you look remarkably well. That is a new dress, is it not?"

"Yes—I did some shopping while I was in town."

"I do not blame you. The London shops are very tempting." She smiled, but the smile did not quite reach her eyes, which observed me in a curiously assessing way. Although she had noted it, she did not say if she approved the kingfisher-blue dress I was wearing. She herself was in a gown of mousseline de sole in a delicate lilac shade, which set off her creamy skin and red-gold hair to perfection. On her head she wore a trifle of lace in lieu of the widow's cap. She had never looked more beautiful and I knew that the small improvement in my own looks was nothing by comparison with Vanessa's loveliness.

I thought that we should soon settle down into the pattern of life at Hawkestone as before, but something happened that changed all this.

We had been back less than a week when one evening, as we sat in the drawing room after dinner, Vanessa went to the piano, saying over her shoulder to Robert, "You look tired. Shall I play something for you—you used to enjoy my music."

Robert indeed looked tired. Since he had returned he had been out every day on the estate. The steam boiler, which powered both the sawmill and the mortar mill, had broken down and there had been difficulty in finding someone to do the necessary repairs.

Now, without lifting his head from the back of the chair upon which it rested, he said, "Please do. It will be pleasant to hear some music."

With a graceful swirl of silken skirts, Vanessa sat down at the keyboard of the Broadwood concert grand. Her thin fingers picked out a few slow notes and then she played Schumann's Symphony No. 4. She played well and expressively, and as the music continued I saw Robert's face soften and relax.

When at last she finished and sat back with delicate hands folded on her lap, Robert said, "Thank you, Vanessa. You play even better than I remember."

"I have practiced a lot." She sighed wistfully. "Philip wished so often that I should play for him." She glanced across at me. "Do you play the piano, Megan?"

"Hardly at all, I'm afraid."

To my surprise Robert said, "Like most Welsh people, Megan sings. Most charmingly, too. Sing for us now, Megan."

I hesitated.

"Do you think— Perhaps Vanessa would not—"

Robert shook his head firmly.

"She would enjoy to hear you. And I certainly would. You used to sing the one about the blackbird for me at—at Yao's. Sing it for us now." He added, smiling, "And mind it is in Welsh."

Somewhat reluctantly I went to the piano stool, which Vanessa had vacated, and sitting down on it picked out the first few notes and then, slowly, I began to sing. At first my voice was uncertain and quavering, for I was very aware of Vanessa's amused expression as she went to sit beside Robert. And then with the sweet words, which I had sung not only for Robert, but very often to my grandparents, my voice grew stronger and I forgot Vanessa's critical presence and lost myself in the music.

I sang it through to the end—"*A finnau'n dy garlyn di cy'd!*"

When I had finished there was a moment's silence before Robert said, "Thank you, Megan. That is one of my favorite songs."

"But did you understand a *word* of it?" Vanessa inquired. "It is a most primitive language. You have quite a pretty voice," she added perfunctorily.

"Megan has sung it for me in English as well as in Welsh, so I understand the story it tells," Robert answered. "She sang often for me when we were together at The Place of Tall Trees. We had few recreations and there was little to do."

Vanessa's eyes narrowed.

"You seldom speak to me of your adventures, Robert. I would like so much to hear of your experiences."

Robert shook his head.

"I prefer to forget about them. As does Megan, I am sure. Though I can tell you this: it was Megan who saved my life. I should not be here now if it were not for her courage."

"Is that why you married her?"

The words fell so sharply through the quiet room that for a moment no one spoke. Then Robert said carelessly, "It may be one reason. What do you think, Megan?"

"It is possible."

"You do not consider there are other grounds for our union?"

At the suggestion in his voice I felt the color come up into my cheeks. I was aware of Vanessa's glance at me, as in some confusion, I answered, "Perhaps there are."

Robert's ironical mouth twisted as if at an inward amusement, but he said no more and shortly afterward Lucien, who had been to Springhill to dine with his mother, entered the room and the topic was forgotten in general discussion.

I spent most of the following morning writing a long letter to Sylvia. She and Mr. Henshawe planned to visit England in the autumn and I was anxious to extend a warm invitation to them both to come and stay at Hawkestone for a few weeks. I should be happy indeed to return some of the kindness and hospitality I had received from Sylvia and her parents and I said as much in my letter.

When it was done and I had put it on the hall table, ready for posting, I went out onto the sunlit terrace and down the steps onto the lawn, thinking to walk a little way before luncheon. Time often hung heavily on my hands and I had conceived the idea of asking if I might teach Edward his first lessons, instead of the governess who was to be engaged after his sixth birthday in July. I knew I should enjoy it and I hoped Edward might too, for we were the best of friends. I was wondering how to approach Vanessa on this subject when, to my surprise, I heard her call my name and, turning, saw her coming up behind me.

She advanced, an enchanting figure in a dress of striped lavender voile with a flat-crowned straw hat upon her head.

"May I join you in your stroll?" she asked with charming diffidence.

She so seldom sought my company and we scarcely ever spoke together unless in the presence of other people that I could hardly hide my wonderment.

"Of course. I—I was hoping to have a talk with you."

It was Vanessa's turn to look surprised.

"Really? What about?"

"I was thinking—wondering about Edward. I understand he is to start lessons soon with a visiting governess. You may not know, but I have taught children and I should so love to teach Edward. Just the first simple lessons—reading and writing and his arithmetic tables. Would you agree to this?"

She stared at me for a moment.

"I have no objection. But is it not rather an undertaking?"

"No. I am used to working with children and Edward is so lively and intelligent it will be a pleasure. As well as something to do," I added somewhat wryly.

"You find it dull living in the country?"

I shook my head.

"Not at all. I am used to living in the country, but Hawkestone is such a complete world in itself." For some reason we had walked by the side of the house in the direction of the estate yard, and looking around at the joiner's shop and the blacksmith's shop and wagon shed and paint store, I gestured almost helplessly. "This functions without any help from me. I do not fully understand it, though I would like to." I hesitated. "You are of assistance to Robert, as is Lucien. But I feel idle and useless. That is why I should like to teach Edward. It is the one thing I am capable of doing."

Vanessa shrugged.

"Then by all means do so. It would take a lifetime for you to comprehend the running of such an estate as Hawkestone. It is all but self-sufficient, as you can see. Everything required for daily existence is undertaken or produced by the estate. The farms supply the food, the woods the game, the river the fish. Behind you is the sawmill and the outer yard with the tumbrel and donkey cart. Do you know how many men are employed here?"

I shook my head.

"Twenty-four—and nine indoor servants."

I glanced at her, filled with astonishment that anyone so lovely and delicately feminine should be so versed in these practical matters.

"You know a great deal about it."

"I should. I have been in or about Hawkestone all my life."

We had come through the outer yard and stable yard and now were at the block of buildings set between the yard and the house. Vanessa paused at an open doorway and with a wave of her hand said, "See—here is the laundry. To the right of it is the bakehouse."

I looked in and saw a great box mangle with two maids

standing beside it. As the handle was turned, a box heavy with stones trundled backward and forward over the revolving wooden rollers so that the clothes beneath them were pressed smooth. Above, stretched drying racks, warmed from a small stove set beneath them, while, at the same time, flatirons and goffering irons for crimping starched collars were heating on an iron shelf above the stove.

"It is all extremely efficient. Was it always so?" I asked, after a final glimpse into the bakehouse, where a fire of fagots burned under the scuffle ovens and crusty brown loaves were being slid in and out on peels.

"Yes, indeed. In my father-in-law's time the estate was run like a vast machine. He was an exacting man, and Philip's mother was equally so. It distressed them both that Philip suffered such poor health and in consequence never applied himself to running Hawkestone in the way he might have done."

We turned and walked slowly back toward the gardens.

"You were of great help to him—and Lucien too."

She shrugged.

"We did what we could. Now it is Robert's turn. He too is handicapped, but if he recovers the sight of his eye it will make all the difference to him."

"Yes. And there is every hope of that."

I felt her sideways glance upon me.

"Have you not wondered why the estate should have been willed to him by Philip and not to me in trust for Edward?"

"Yes—it—it has puzzled me at times. Perhaps your husband felt it would be too big a responsibility for you, as a woman?"

She gave a small, sharp laugh.

"Considering that I undertook that, with Lucien's help, I admit, almost since the day I married Philip, I am certain it was not for such a reason. No, it was to atone to Robert that Philip left Hawkestone to him."

I stared at her.

"*Atone*? Had—had Philip injured him in some way then?"

"Yes. But surely Robert has told you something of all this—surely you must know about us?"

The sunlight seemed to dim and I felt a creeping chill come over me.

"Us? You mean yourself and—and Philip?"

We halted as if by common consent upon the stretch of lawn below the terrace. Now Vanessa turned to face me directly. She said in a gentle, almost kindly voice, "I mean Robert and myself. We were betrothed to each other."

I felt as if the breath had drained from my body. I could not speak, only stare at Vanessa's lovely face in blank bewilderment.

She said quickly, "I am sorry. This has come as a shock to you. Robert should have told you." She added slowly, "Of course, the engagement was not publicly announced, but everyone who knew us supposed that we should marry."

I managed to find breath to say in a quivering voice. "But you married Philip instead. Why?"

"It is a long story. Shall we sit down here while I tell you what happened?" She gestured to a nearby wrought-iron seat and I sank down onto it with shaking limbs.

For a moment there was a silence between us and then Vanessa said quietly, "Robert and I had known each other since childhood and as we grew older we fell in love. He wished to marry me but his prospects were uncertain. My father would not agree to our engagement so we made a secret promise between ourselves that we would marry. Then my father died, leaving only sufficient money to keep my stepmother in her home. She did not want me and was forever urging me to make a good marriage. This I could have done more than once but I wanted only Robert. He had joined the Royal Navy when Philip's father died and was hoping for a captaincy, which would enable us to marry. But when Philip inherited Hawkestone, he was distraught and overwhelmed in settling the affairs of the estate. He, like Robert, had always loved me and now he begged me to marry him. He told me he thought he had only a limited time to live. I was sorry for him and Robert was away at sea. And so, foolishly, I gave in to

Philip's pleading and agreed to marry him. We were married quietly here in the chapel at Hawkestone."

I said on a deep breath, "And Robert. What did Robert do?"

"He never returned to Hawkestone." She sighed. "He wrote a bitter, cruel letter to me. He could not forgive me—or Philip. He left the Royal Navy, and with the money he had been saving for us, he bought a ship of his own and went into the tea trade." She frowned. "I do not know why—he might as well have stayed on in the Navy."'

"Perhaps he thought he would make more money that way," I said, for the odious trade he had been engaged in was quite a bit more lucrative than tea.

She turned her head to look at me in surprise.

"Why should he want that? He was no longer planning to be married."

"No," I said. But he had married. He had married me. Though I could not think for what reason, if he was still in love with Vanessa. Was he?

As if she read my thoughts Vanessa said softly, "For a long while Robert thought harshly of me I know, but that he has forgiven me is shown by his inviting Edward and myself to share his home. Philip hoped he might do this when he left Hawkestone to Robert, in an attempt to recompense him for the unhappiness he caused."

"Can possessions do that?" I inquired with a trace of bitterness.

She shook her head.

"It was not the sole reason. Philip told me he expected to die while he was still a young man. He knew that I had married him out of pity, and that though I was fond of him, I did not love him in the way I had loved Robert. By leaving Hawkestone to Robert he hoped to bring us together, for he knew that if he left the estate to me, Robert would never ask me to marry him, but by leaving Hawkestone to Robert, we might in time come together again and share the estate with our children. Of course," she added quickly, "Philip did not know that Robert would marry someone else."

"No. It must have been a—a surprise to you," I said in a faint-sounding voice.

"Indeed it was. But if you and Robert are happy, that is all that matters."

"Yes." I felt too disturbed to sit beside Vanessa for another moment. I did not want to hear any further confidences, unhappy or otherwise. I wanted to be alone to think over what she had told me.

I stood up abruptly.

"Thank you for—for being so frank. I think I will go in now—it will soon be time for luncheon."

"Yes, I will come with you."

We walked over the grass in silence. Although the sun was still shining, the warmth and brightness of the day seemed to have gone and I was aware only of a cold shadow fallen across my life. On the terrace we parted and I made my way slowly upstairs to my room.

Now I knew why Robert had never once said that he loved me. Why he had said, "I am happy—*as much as I shall ever be.*" Because he still loved Vanessa. Was it true what Vanessa had implied? That if Robert had not married me, he would have married his cousin's widow?

He had never loved me. I knew that now. He had married me for three reasons. For convention, because we had been thrown together at The Place of Tall Trees and we had become lovers. For convenience, because he was handicapped and needed a wife and an heir, which, incidentally, I had not given him. And lastly, because I had, on a mad impulse, called myself his wife and put the idea into his head.

In his delirium he had called Vanessa's name, proving that she had remained in his thoughts. He had loved her so much that she had all but destroyed him by marrying Philip. Robert must have guessed that Vanessa had married Philip only out of pity and for his inheritance, the great estate of Hawkestone, which she had known, and perhaps desired, all her life. But he had gone off not only into the tea trade but into opium smuggling in an attempt to amass a fortune, as so many others had done. To prove what, I wondered? To prove to Vanessa that he too could become a rich man, and that she would have done better to wait for him?

Now, by a trick of fate, he had inherited Hawkestone and everything that went with it. Including Vanessa.

I paced the room in a turmoil of thought. What was I to do? Make the most of second best, because I loved Robert? But how could I do that with Vanessa's lovely presence ever before me? How could Robert, for that matter? Yet he must want her at Hawkestone, for he had invited her to make her home with us.

I felt like someone in a trap, as if enmeshed in a snare of unhappiness from which I could not escape. What, I wondered, with something akin to desperation, was to be the end of it all?

Somehow I summoned up enough resolution to present a front of calmness when, at last, I went down to luncheon. Robert was there, as was Lucien, both having been out all morning. Thankfully, Vanessa did not put in an appearance, for usually at midday she ate with Edward in her own apartment, though very often in the evening she joined us, at Robert's request, for dinner.

I struggled through mouthfuls of food that felt as ashes in my mouth. Afterward, with a murmured excuse, I stole away from the house and through the sunlit gardens into the park. I scarcely knew in which direction I was going, only that I wanted an activity of body that would dull my restless mind. The grazing cattle turned their heads to stare at me as I made my way through their midst. I walked on, unseeing, leaving the park and taking a winding path that led through a heavy growth of rhododendron and laurel. Suddenly, the path dipped and I found myself slipping and sliding down a steep incline. The trees were so thick they met overhead and then, before I realized, I was at the foot of a dell. All around rose green slopes dense with trees and shrubs. Birch and pine stood tall and straight above clumps of stiff dark holly; willow and alder drooped with feathery grace above a pool of mirrorlike blue water. A stillness lay over everything. Not even the chirrup of a bird broke the silence.

I sank down onto a fallen log and for a moment closed my eyes in an exhaustion of mind and body.

Gradually the peace of the little dell stole over me. I opened my eyes and gazed around and as I did so I felt a start of recognition, as if I had visited this quiet and secluded place before. But I knew I had not. Why then was there something familiar about the green world that enclosed me, the expanse of shining water? Suddenly I realized that although it was smaller and more enclosed, the topography of the dell resembled that of the Pearl Pagoda. The same tall trees, the same sense of an oasis of quiet, a pool instead of a lake. Now I observed that on the far side of the pool, the land extended back into a small clearing or plateau before the steep sides of the dell rose again in a mass of trees and shrubs. Here perhaps could have stood the Pearl Pagoda.

Time passed and I sat as one in a trance, my thoughts numbed, aware only of the deep unhappiness encompassing me. Then, as the reflection of light from the summer world above and beyond the dell began to fade, I realized I must return to the house.

Rising stiffly from the log, I began the steep ascent, holding on to the overhanging branch of a tree to steady myself, pulling at some trailing root to keep from falling back into the hollow below. More than once I stumbled to my knees but at last I reached level ground. Here I found the winding path by which I had come and soon I was in the Great Park. A man on horseback was riding toward me and I saw that it was Lucien. He raised his hat and, dismounting, said, "Why, Megan, *here* you are. Robert has been anxious for you. Surely you have not walked from the village?" He broke off, his quick glance scanning me from top to toe. "Your dress is torn—did you fall?"

Glancing down at my skirt I saw that the side of it had been ripped by the brambles and the lace edging of one sleeve was hanging loose. My hands were grimy, my shoes covered with dust. At Lucien's further glance I put my hands up and felt leaves and twigs caught in my tangled hair.

"I—I walked down—well, fell rather—into a sort of hollow. There is a pool at the bottom. It was steep and—and very overgrown. I did not realize I was so untidy."

Lucien smiled, his dark eyes kind, his wide mouth gentle. "We call it the dell. Robert, Philip and myself used to play there as boys, but no one ever goes to it now." He put a hand out toward me. "Let me help you up onto Starlight. You look as if you had walked far enough."

I hesitated and then, thankfully, I put my hand in his. He held my hand thus for a moment and then placed his other hand gently on top of mine, imprisoning it between his own. Then his eyes sought mine and he uttered the words "Dear Megan," and then, as if recalled to his senses, he lifted me quickly onto the mare's back, where I perched somewhat precariously sideways in the saddle.

My thoughts so much in turmoil by the events of the day, I chose to pretend nothing had happened until I had a chance to better sort out my feelings.

"I am afraid I am taking you out of your way. Were you not returning to Springhill?" I asked, as Lucien led the horse slowly back in the direction from which he had come.

"There is no hurry. I am to stay with Mama for the weekend—she demands my company from time to time." He slanted a humorously wry glance at me. "Especially when Miss Tindall is absent. She has gone on her annual visit to her brother in Bristol. I expect she is glad to be relieved of her duties for a while. Like all old ladies, my mother can be very exacting."

We reached the drive and Lucien lifted me down with no trace of his former intimacy.

"You had better find Robert and assure him you are safely returned or he will begin to think you have been carried off by the gypsies."

I managed a smile, feeling grateful to Lucien for his kindness and half behaving I had imagined the entire encounter.

Yes, I will do that. Please give my best remembrances to Madame Ormonde. And thank you for bringing me back."

He bowed his graceful dark head.

"My pleasure."

I walked into the house by the side door. There was no sign of anyone. Robert would be dressing for dinner, Vanessa and Edward in their apartment. I stumbled wearily up the stairs and along the wide corridor to my room. A pier glass was facing me as I walked in and I stared in consternation at the reflection that presented itself. With my torn dress and disarranged hair and dust-smeared face I looked indeed like one of the gypsies Lucien had referred to.

I put my hand on the bell rope to ring for Hetty, when the connecting door between the bedroom and dressing room opened and Robert appeared on the threshold.

"Megan—is that you? I thought I heard someone moving in here. Where on earth have you been? It is past six o'clock. I was beginning to feel anxious, for you left no word where you had gone to." He moved across the room to stand beside me, set-mouthed and frowning.

"I—I have been walking in the park."

"All afternoon?"

"I sat down for a while and rested."

He put a hand on my arm.

"What is the matter? You sound—strange."

At his touch I shivered and involuntarily I moved away. He came after me.

"Something has upset you. I can tell from your voice. What is it? Did something or someone alarm you?"

I swung around to face him. The words were out before I could check myself. I said quickly, stammeringly, "Why did you not tell me about Vanessa? That—that she—that you— that you were once in love with each other and planned to marry."

The frowning line between his brows deepened, his mouth thinned to a hard line.

"Who told you of this?"

"Vanessa herself. She thought I must know, that you would have spoken of it." My voice wavered and I paused to take a deep breath to steady myself. Then I said slowly and with difficulty, "She is still in love with you. Are you in love with her, Robert? Is that why you asked her to make her home here—at Hawkestone?"

He said grimly, "If I were, that would be the last thing I should wish to do. Surely you can see that? You are my *wife*,

Megan, the mother of my child. There is no question of being in love with Vanessa."

"But you are not in love with me, Robert. I know that now. I think I always knew. I hoped—I dreamt for a little while that perhaps you might be. But I believe, whether you know it or not, that in your heart you have never stopped loving Vanessa."

He said harshly, "I stopped loving her when she married Philip."

I shook my head, feeling unutterably sad.

"You told yourself that because it is what you wanted to believe. Do you know that when you were ill and unconscious at Mr. Yao's, you called her name out loud? She was in your thoughts even then. I wondered whom she might be."

"People talk all manner of nonsense in a delirium."

"Perhaps." I looked at him although I was aware he could not see the expression on my face. "What are we to do, Robert? Vanessa thinks that Philip left Hawkestone to you because, when you inherited, in time you might marry her. Do you think that is true?"

He was silent, as if considering. Then he shrugged.

"I suppose it is possible. Philip was a romantic. And if he had a guilty conscience that he had persuaded Vanessa to marry him out of pity, it is the sort of quixotic gesture he might make. But what sort of man did he think I should be to accept Vanessa as a gift with the estate. I tell you, Megan, it is over and done with. There can never be anything between myself and Vanessa. I wish to God I had never asked her to stay on here, but I was sorry for her—and for the boy. And she and Lucien have been of help to me."

At the mention of Lucien, I heard again the soft voice uttering my name and felt the pressure on my fingers as his hand held mine. What, I wondered, was Lucien's role in all this?

Robert ran a hand through his hair as if suddenly the situation was beyond him.

"Promise that you will put this foolish nonsense out of

your head. We have the future to think of, Megan. Not the past."

If only he had put his arms about me just then; if only he had held me close and kissed me and said, "You are the only one, Megan. I love you." I could have forgotten and forgiven anything. All that Vanessa was and had been would have ceased to matter to me. I would have been sure of Robert's love.

There was a long silence in which he waited frowningly. Then, shrugging, as he had done, I said quietly, "It will not be easy but I will try to do as you ask. Now, if you will leave me, Robert, I will bathe and dress. Otherwise we shall be late for dinner."

He hesitated. I saw his hand go out to me, but I moved away and after a pause he turned toward the dressing room, saying stiffly, "As you wish."

The door clicked behind him. The moment in which we might have drawn close to each other for the rest of our lives had come and gone. From now on I knew that there would be an unseen but impassable barrier between us.

CHAPTER 19

DURING THE WEEKS that followed, Robert and I were remote from each other. I held aloof from him and he did not approach me. This isolation would have been more marked if it were not for the fact that Lucien, never repeating what I now believed to be a product of my own fantasy, took it upon himself to offer me companionship on my long walks through the park. And also, a series of visitors now descended upon Hawkestone. First came the Howard family, arriving two days before Edward's birthday, which was on the twentieth of July. It was the happiest of occasions save for the shadow of melancholy that lay over me because of my growing sense of estrangement from Robert. But the other participants seemed to enjoy themselves to the fullest, which was some consolation.

Edward was particularly happy for he was surrounded by children of his own age. From being a lonely little boy he had now several playmates, for as well as George and Dorothea, with whom he was at once on friendly terms, his cousins from Bath arrived too on a visit. Five children scampered about the garden, five children played upon the swings and the seesaw, five joyous voices were raised in fun and laughter, and it must be admitted, on one or two rare occasions, in tears, for even the best of friends may have their differences.

On the day of his birthday, which was warm and sunny, a table was spread beneath the great copper beech and a feast was laid out for the party. Several other children had been invited, including the vicar's four children and two from another house in the vicinity. Vanessa was joint hostess, graceful and smiling, in a dress of palest-pink sprigged silk, which set off her rich coloring marvelously. Lucien had arranged for a Punch-and-Judy show to be performed after tea and birthday cake.

Imogen was too young to enjoy the show, as was small Bertie, who was but a few months older. I kept them beside me, especially when Punch became a trifle too vociferous and began to thump Judy and Toby in traditional style. Imogen hid her face against my shoulder while Bertie gazed reproachfully up at me.

"He has hurt the poor lady," he whispered.

"It is only a game, darling. See? Toby is wagging his tail."

They were not to be consoled and we had to take a stroll to the swings as a diversion.

Just as the children got on well together, so did Edward's aunt and uncle with Dr. and Mrs. Howard, and it gave me pleasure to see Uncle Stephen, as I called him, strolling upon the terrace with Dr. Howard, while Aunt Louise seemed to find a great deal in common with Mrs. Howard.

It was a sad day when the cousins took their departure. Edward, George and Dorothea raced the length of the drive, as far as the West Lodge, to wave a last goodbye to the carriage.

The Howard family was to leave after the weekend, so the following day it was arranged to take a picnic lunch to a nearby beauty spot. Vanessa chose not to come with us, but Robert and Lucien were in attendance, both on horseback, for Robert now rode regularly, though always with Lucien or one of the grooms.

When we returned in the late afternoon it was to find Vanessa entertaining a visitor on the lawn. She smiled and waved, beckoning for us to join her.

Robert, who could see none of this, said, "Is someone there? Who is it?"

"It is Harry Summers," Lucien answered shortly. "What the deuce is he doing here? Vanessa said nothing to me of his coming."

"Perhaps he arrived unexpectedly," Robert answered indifferently. We were almost up to them and I saw that the man, who had risen to his feet and was awaiting our arrival, was tall and heavily built with dark hair and complexion. Introductions were made all around and fresh tea was ordered for us, while the children were taken indoors by Deborah.

Robert seemed to know Mr. Summers and they spoke on matters of mutual interest, farming and stock and timber, but Lucien was unexpectedly quiet and sat frowning and silent on the fringe of the group. When at last Mr. Summers took his leave, Vanessa walked to the drive with him and watched him ride away with a smile and wave of her hand as if saying goodbye to an old and dear friend.

Lucien turned to Robert and I heard him say, "I suppose Summers thinks he is in the running again now that Vanessa is—"

He broke off and Robert, glancing at him with a cryptic smile, said, "Now that Vanessa is out of mourning you mean?"

Lucien looked embarrassed, as if he had been less than circumspect.

"Well, it is natural enough. She is young still and beautiful."

Robert said slowly, "Is she as beautiful as ever—or has she changed at all? I cannot see her clearly."

Lucien seemed to sigh.

"She is *more* beautiful. No man could see her and not love her."

Before Robert could answer they had moved out of earshot and I was left wondering at the implication of Lucien's words, aware of a faint hope that Lucien might be right and Vanessa would marry again and leave Hawkestone.

On the morning the Howard family was to leave us, Dr. Howard sought me out in private and to my great surprise said, "Not only do I wish to thank you for your hospitality and kindness to us, but I wish to add to that my own personal thanks to you for Robert's most generous gift to the Mission. I feel sure you are in part responsible, Megan, for you know well how dear its welfare is to my heart."

I could only stare at him in puzzlement.

"Robert's gift? He has said nothing of this to me. Do you mean he has given some money to the Mission?"

Dr. Howard nodded, his black brows creased in a frown.

"A very generous donation. I cannot tell you what a help it will be to us in our work and expansion. But perhaps I should not have spoken of this. Perhaps your husband kept it a secret because he did not wish to have you embarrassed by my expressions of gratitude. Forgive me, Megan. All the same I feel in my heart that it is *your* love and dedication to the Mission that has prompted Robert to make this munificent gift." He pressed my hand between his own two. "I will say no more."

I hid my bewilderment as best I could. Knowing Robert's criticism of missionaries and his lack of sympathy for their activities I could not understand how he had come to make such a gesture to Dr. Howard. As he had been so careful to say nothing to me of the gift, I felt I must respect the secret. But I was puzzled and touched, too, by such evidence of kinder feelings.

After Dr. and Mrs. Howard and the children had gone, the house seemed very quiet. Imogen and, more particularly, Edward looked lost without their recent playfellows. To occupy Edward I suggested that we begin our lessons together, and so each morning for an hour or more I taught him the rudiments of his letters and first numerals. During this time Imogen was usually in her bassinet in the garden, with Deborah sitting beside her, busy sewing or crocheting.

Edward was an apt pupil and I enjoyed teaching him. At the beginning Vanessa descended upon us once or twice, full of admiration for my scholarship and Edward's studiousness.

"But of course, your father was a teacher, was he not?" she said upon one occasion. "This must come naturally to you."

"Perhaps it does."

"Well, *I* could not attempt it. I should not know where to begin." And with a light kiss upon Edward's golden head, she was gone.

The next guests to arrive were Sylvia and her husband. I was longing to see her again and anxious to return in every way possible the kindness I had received from her and her parents, but Edward was disappointed to hear that there were no children coming.

Sylvia arrived on September 14, the day the allied armies landed in the Crimea, a time of portent for everyone. We flung our arms about each other, oblivious of Robert and Charles, who were shaking hands and exchanging polite greetings.

"Dearest Sylvia—how wonderful to see you again."

"My darling Megan, how sweet you look. You have not changed one scrap and you are a mother now."

"Yes. You will see Imogen later. Oh, Sylvia, I cannot tell you how happy I am to be with you again."

"Nor I you."

Arms about each other, we went into the house, where she paused to exclaim, saying, "I had no idea Hawkestone was such a magnificent house. And the drive up through the park was beautiful. Such lovely trees and views."

"I am glad that you like it. Now I must speak to Charles and ask him to forgive my impoliteness."

Charles Henshawe was the same tall distinguished-looking man I remembered, but, if anything, his gray eyes were more melancholy than ever, which vaguely disturbed me. I had imagined that married to Sylvia he would have shed his cloak of sadness and improved in spirit and manner, but this was not so. We shook hands and he smiled warmly enough at me and then I left him to Robert's care and went upstairs with Sylvia.

In the guest room, carefully prepared and filled with welcoming flowers from the garden, I studied her more closely. As she removed her bonnet from her golden curls I thought she was still the most beautiful girl I had ever known. More beautiful than Vanessa even, for although Vanessa was tall and elegant, with perfect features and superb coloring, her loveliness, in my eyes, was marred by one small defect. Her eyes, more green than gray, had narrow lids and this sometimes lent her a harsh, almost staring look. That fraction of an inch of eyelid, which, to my mind, lent glamour and an air of languor, Sylvia possessed, and Vanessa, for all her beauty, lacked. Sylvia's golden-brown eyes were soft and deep beneath the heavy white lids and drew one to her with sweet beguilement. The shadow of wistfulness did not detract from her charm; indeed, it may have added to her sweetness.

She expressed a wish to see Imogen immediately and so I took her to the nursery on the next floor where Imogen, seated in a high chair, had already started upon her midday meal. She paused, silver spoon in hand, to stare with wondering blue eyes at Sylvia. She was not a shy child and loved company, and when Sylvia smiled and spoke to her, she chattered and gurgled in return, banging her spoon upon the ledge of the chair as if in welcome.

"Oh, she is a darling. And so lively. I would love to hold her, but perhaps I should not when she is eating." She bent to kiss the petal-soft cheek and smooth back the mouse-brown hair, whispering, "You are the dearest little girl."

The month of Sylvia's visit was one of Indian summer weather. One golden day followed another and with the turning of the leaves the Great Park blazed with color, and at night a huge silvery moon rose above the roof of Hawkestone, lighting the terrace and the sleeping garden with its bright beams.

It was a month of entertainments, too. There were tea parties on the lawn and picnics by the river. There were dinner parties, with the long table laid with snowy damask and set with shining silver and sparkling glass. All manner of people whom I had never met before were invited, and Robert renewed his friendship with various residents of the county. Now that her period of mourning was over, Vanessa was usually present at these parties, and Lucien too. Even Madame Ormonde graced them on more than one occasion.

Sylvia was curious regarding Vanessa.

"It is very good of Robert to have invited her to share his home. You do not mind, Megan? But she is so beautiful I suppose she will marry again. Mr. Summers seems very attentive to her."

"Yes." I hesitated, longing on the one hand to confide in

Sylvia and yet on the other hand feeling that Robert's association with Vanessa was better not discussed, even with Sylvia.

"Was Vanessa very devoted to her husband?" Sylvia
asked. We were walking in the gallery, hung with family portraits and furnished with some rare and beautiful pieces. Sylvia
was interested in the house and I had already taken her on a
tour of the main bedrooms, including what was called the
State Bedroom, which boasted a particularly fine carved and
gilded tester bed, hung with gold damask, and a beautiful eigh-
teenth-century Chinese wallpaper.

"I think *he* was very devoted to her."

Sylvia shrugged slim shoulders.

"I see. It was one of those marriages. I sensed she was far
from heartbroken by his loss. Was Philip at all like Robert, his
cousin?"

"Not at all. There is a portrait of him in the library downstairs. Robert said he was both gentle and good. Edward takes
after his father, I think, though he is stronger and more robust,
for Philip had very delicate health."

Sylvia paused to admire a long case clock in a fine tortoiseshell lacquer case, then moved slowly on, and after a moment she said, "If I could have a daughter like Imogen or a son
like Edward I should not feel my marriage was wasted. I am
hoping so much that I may be pregnant."

I turned swiftly to her.

"Do you think you are? Is it possible? Oh, Sylvia—"

For a moment we embraced and then she said, pulling
free, "It is too early yet to be sure. But I pray that it may be
so." She sighed. "I am not happy, as you are, Megan. I do not
love Charles and I fear I cannot. Not—not in the way that
would make everything so much easier for us both." She hesitated, looking down the gallery to the west window at the far
end. "Do you understand what I am trying to say?"

I bit my lip, remembering the word "*wasted*" that she had
used a moment ago.

"I think so. But it—it is not so important, is it? That you
should love Charles in—in that way. He is a fine man, a good
man. And he loves you so deeply, Sylvia. Perhaps in time . . ."

My voice trailed off, for I felt I was treading on uncertain ground.

"It is impossible. I can only submit—I can never respond, for there is no feeling of love. It is as simple as that." She moved away abruptly and walked on, passing the black japanned bureau cabinet and the Samuel Scott painting of the *Thames at Westminster* and the Louis XV black lacquer encoignure without seeing them.

I followed after her and we came to a halt by the west window, overlooking the terrace and the steps to the lawn. I slid my hand through her arm and said without looking at her, "I hope that you may have a child soon, Sylvia."

"Thank you. I thought I should want a son, but since I have seen Imogen I feel there is something especially dear about a little daughter. Did Robert mind that your first child was not a boy?"

"He has shown no sign of it. He dearly loves Imogen. I hope there will be an heir for him later."

"*You* are happy, Megan. I am glad. You love Robert very much I think."

"Yes." That was true. I loved him with all my heart; I wished only that he could love me as much in return. Yet, remembering what Sylvia had told me just now, I was grateful that even if Robert might still dream of Vanessa, at least there was an attraction between us, albeit a physical one. If that was not a kind of loving, what was it?

That night I came down early to dinner for I wished to inspect the flower arrangement for the table. Although Vanessa had imperceptibly retained the reins of Hawkestone in her hands I was gradually undertaking some decisions. Lately, Mrs. Rowley had consulted me upon some query or other and Humphreys deferred to me occasionally. For tonight's party I had undertaken to arrange dahlias and autumn leaves and I now wished to see that they had been placed correctly.

Everything was as it should be and I was taking a last look at the gleaming table when a sound behind me caused me to turn around. To my surprise I saw Robert come slowly into the room. He could not see me standing by the table and crossed to the fireplace, feeling his way with his stick until he came to the marble mantelpiece. A log fire burned in the grate and for a moment he leaned with hand outstretched toward its warmth. Then I heard him sigh and saw him put an arm along the mantelshelf to lean his head against it.

Something in his attitude, the gesture of weariness, touched my heart and I moved from the table and said gently,

"Why, Robert, you are down early tonight, as I am."

He straightened abruptly at the sound of my voice.

"Yes. I thought I would like a glass of sherry. Will you join me?"

"I'd like to. Let me pour it for you." I crossed to the console table and lifting the cut-glass decanter poured out two glasses.

As I placed one between his fingers he said, "I cannot see your dress. Is it red?"

"It is a deep shade of old rose. A new dress that I chose in Bath with Sylvia."

"You have enjoyed her visit, haven't you? So have I. I have grown attached to Charles and we have had some good talks together. He knows Canton and Macao and the Pearl River almost as well as I do."

"Do you miss it very much, Robert? The sea, I mean, and all the life you had?"

"Let us say that if I could choose, it is the old life I should prefer."

"And yet you have so much. Many would envy you Hawkestone."

"I expect so." His filmed eye regarded me over the rim of the glass. "And you, Megan? Do you wish you were back at the Mission?"

I shook my head.

"I cannot say that I do, although I loved Macao and all the kind Chinese people I knew there." I hesitated and then said on an impulse, "Robert—Dr. Howard told me of your generous gift to the Mission. He was so grateful. You did not speak of it to me, but I would like to say thank you too. It was kind and—and unexpected."

His mouth twisted in the old sardonic way.

"Call it conscience money. You told me once I was cursed, do you remember? Perhaps I am trying to placate the Fates." He could not see the expression on my face, but he must have been aware of my movement of protest. He said quickly, "I am sorry. I should not speak so lightly. I gave the money to Dr. Howard in an attempt to make amends for the past. It was made illegally and I realized it would be wrong to keep it. So I gave two-thirds of the money to the Mission, because its supporters work *against* the opium traffic. The other third has been donated to the School for the Blind."

I stared at him in amazement.

"But it—it is so unlike you."

He shrugged.

"This is what happens to a man when he marries a missionary. She reforms him. He does things entirely out of character."

"You will not be serious even now. But I think you have done a good deed, Robert. And a good deed brings a blessing."

"There, you see, you are just like Dr. Howard. Ready to go down on your knees and thank the Almighty on the slightest pretext. I was afraid Dr. Howard was going to do so on the rug of the library. I was very relieved that he didn't. I should have felt foolish."

"Oh, Robert." I scarcely knew whether to laugh or cry. "But why did you not tell me?"

He put down the glass and reached for my hand.

"We were at variance. It was difficult to talk to you. But I did it to please you, Megan. Because you were unhappy over the things I had done and I knew how much you cared for the Mission."

He seemed about to draw me to him when some awareness that we were not alone caused me to turn my head. The dining room was not yet fully lit; only the candle sconces on either side of the fireplace and two massive candelabra on the side table gave light until the silver candlesticks on the table itself should be lit for dinner. In the shadowy doorway between the half-light of the dining room and the lamplight from the hall the figure of Vanessa stood watching us, just as on the first day of arrival at Hawkestone she had watched us.

A frisson of fear touched my nerves. I felt again a sense of dread, as if the quiet figure menaced me in some fashion. How absurd. I checked my irrational thoughts and, stepping back from Robert, turned to greet Vanessa, even as she stepped into the room, smiling and saying, "I believe I heard the first of the carriages arrive. How charming you look, Megan. That rose color becomes you."

"Thank you." I wanted to say, "You look beautiful," but I could not, although it was true. Vanessa was wearing a gown of deep dark violet. A gleam of diamonds at her throat and her astonishing red-gold hair were the only notes of color against the somber silk, yet she seemed to radiate vitality and light.

Robert broke the moment of tension.

"We had better make ready to receive our guests, Megan," and gestured for me to walk ahead of him into the hall.

The first person to arrive was Mr. Summers. Tonight as we shook hands he gave me a closer scrutiny. Although he was in his early forties he was still a bachelor. He was good-looking, with hard, dark eyes and a high color. He had a full, sensual mouth, which detracted from his looks, and a rather loud voice, but his manner was cordial and friendly. I was not certain whether I liked him or not, but Vanessa greeted him with a charming warmth.

It was a most successful dinner party. I had recovered from the momentary sensation of alarm that I had felt and was in cheerful spirits because of Robert. My heart was softened toward him and this showed in my voice and manner and seemed to evoke a similar response from him. It was as if our meeting earlier in the evening had brought us together again. If sometimes Vanessa turned a frowning glance in my direction I did not allow it to disturb me.

That night Robert came to my room and we were passionate lovers as before. My fears and doubts were put at rest and I forgot about Vanessa.

At the end of October Sylvia and her husband left us to go to London, where they were to stay with Sylvia's sister.

"When I know for certain I will write to you," she whispered as we said goodbye to each other. "Beatrice has an excellent physician who has seen her safely through all her confinements. I shall ask her to make an appointment for me with him."

"I pray that your wish will be granted. Take care of yourself, dear Sylvia."

"Yes. We shall see each other again before long. If matters are as I hope, I shall not return to Macao with Charles. I would wish for my child to be born here in England."

After they had gone the house was quiet again. Edward and I settled down to our lessons, and with the hunting season now begun, Vanessa rode out every week or so, invariably in the company of Harry Summers.

They made a striking pair; he so dark and determined-looking, seated on one of his massive hunters, and Vanessa graceful and lovely in black habit and tall hat, the snowy stock crisp beneath her chin, her green eyes sparkling at the prospect of the chase.

"What a pity you do not hunt," she said to me, with no trace whatsoever of regret in her voice. "It is such an exciting sport. But you ride, don't you?"

"Yes, I ride." I thought of Dylan, the Welsh cob upon whose sturdy back I had ridden along the mountain paths and down the valley tracks. Now I had Betsy, the pretty little mare that Robert had bought me soon after Imogen's birth. I rode her often but only within the vicinity of Hawkestone.

Lucien was standing by and he said kindly, "Why do you not join us, Megan? I would see that you came to no harm."

I shook my head.

"Thank you, but—I do not care to hunt."

Vanessa's green eyes widened in astonishment. It was as if I had said, "I do not care to breathe or eat or live." She shrugged in dismissal of my foolishness.

"Then there is no more to be said," and with a nod to the groom, she was assisted into the saddle of her mount and, waving her crop, set off down the drive, followed after a moment's hesitation by Lucien.

It was a bright, frosty day. I was tempted to have Betsy saddled and take one of my decorous rides into the country-side, but with so many people out hunting I felt my own inadequacy and so I decided instead to walk to the dell.

It had become a favorite retreat, and very often I walked across the Great Park and along the wooded path, to stumble down the steep incline to the pool, where I would sit alone with my thoughts for a while.

Today it was utterly still. I heard no sound other than the gentle rustle of a falling leaf. A mist wreathed in ghostly vapor between the trees; a solitary robin came to perch near me and for a moment broke the silence with a few notes of its sweetly plaintive song.

It was too cold to sit for long on my favorite log and the idea came to me that it would be pleasant to build a small summerhouse or shelter on the level stretch of ground at the far side of the pool. It would provide a useful refuge from winter weather or unexpected summer shower. One might picnic here or read or paint. I should like to paint the pool and the reflection of the trees upon its smooth surface.

I had tried more than once to walk around the pool, but the thickets of trailing bramble and ferny undergrowth pre-vented me. Much of this would have to be cleared, I decided, as I planned what could be done. Some railed steps would be built into what was a veritable cliff leading from the wood at the top. There would be a wooden seat in place of the log upon which I sat and perhaps a stone lion or some such thing to stand guard beside the pool, just as was done in Chinese gardens. I had a yearning to create something of a Chinese effect in this quiet place. If Robert would allow me to do so.

Robert, upon being approached, frowned and said, "The dell? I had forgotten about it. We used to play there as boys— it was a good hiding place. But what can you make of it? Wouldn't it be better to build something in the garden here?"

I shook my head.

"The garden is already laid out to perfection. I should like to create something different. It is a natural beauty spot, but it is so overgrown and difficult of access. If we could free the path to it—and build steps down the slope. The pool needs clearing too, but it is not stagnant. I think it is fed by a spring for the water is almost transparent."

Robert gave me one of his rare smiles.

"I can see you have thought a great deal about it. Do as you wish. One of the carpenters can build you a shelter and a couple of the gardeners will soon clear the undergrowth."

"Oh, thank you, Robert. It will be such an interest for me and when it is done the children will enjoy playing there I am sure."

With the weather being open and dry, two men were put to clearing the paths and building a flight of steps down to the pool right away. The pool was dredged and the rushes and reeds and water plantain were cut back. The sallows and osiers were thinned or dug up so that there would be room for some ornamental shrubs. Once a way was made to circle the pool, I was able to walk to the small plateau where I intended the summerhouse should be built. This would be done last of all for I wanted to plan the design of it myself.

One afternoon I had been down to the dell to see how the work was progressing. Dusk had set in early, for the days were short now, and the gardener and the boy who was his assistant were already packing up their tools in readiness to leave.

"Can't do no more today, m'lady," old Sam Pritchett informed me.

"You have done splendidly."

He pursed his lips.

"Weather is agin us. Reckon rain be on the way and there'll be no workin' here tomorrow."

"There will be other days."

"Aye. And worst of it be over now, m'lady. 'Tis proper tidy from what it were."

"Yes, I scarcely recognize it. In the spring we will plant flowering shrubs. It will be beautiful."

He glanced around somewhat skeptically, for with the newly dug earth and open space where the bramble thickets had spread their tentacles, the dell looked denuded and bare.

"If you say so, m'lady."

I smiled, for I was so sure of how it would look, of the picture I carried in my mind.

"You will see."

I left them to finish their task and made my way back along the now leveled and widened path that led to the Great Park. I crossed this and came to the ha-ha and so onto the lawn, and then I halted abruptly.

A man and a woman were standing in the shelter of the copper beech under which we so often sat. The woman wore a cloak but the hood was thrown back and I caught a gleam of red-gold curls. *Vanessa.* The man had his back to me—he was tall and hatless so that I could see his black head. They were in close conversation and for a moment I thought the man must be Harry Summers. Then Vanessa tossed her head, as if in argument, and walked away, and as the man went after her I saw that he was Lucien.

Neither of them had seen me for I was shrouded by the dusky light and I too wore a dark cloak. I remained immobile, waiting for them to move onto the terrace and so into the house.

Lights from the house shone onto the terrace, illuminating the two figures as if they were on a stage set. I saw their frowning faces, the quick gestures of argument or denial. I saw Vanessa put out a hand to touch Lucien's cheek. He seized the hand in his own and, bending his head to kiss it, reached for her other hand and pressed his lips to this, holding both clasped against his breast.

I was startled by the intimacy of the scene. They were like lovers. I was shocked too, thinking of them as stepbrother and stepsister. But of course, there was no blood tie. It was permissible for Lucien to be in love with Vanessa, and that, from the scene I had just witnessed, he must surely be.

A shaft of light fell across the terrace from the opening of the casement door to the morning room. It faded as the door closed behind Vanessa and Lucien. I was left staring into the darkness, wondering uneasily what such a revelation could mean.

CHAPTER 20

THE SCENE BETWEEN Vanessa and Lucien remained etched in my mind for a long while. I found myself watching her, and, more particularly, Lucien. I saw by his expression, the intensity of his dark gaze upon her at times, that it was true. He loved Vanessa. I felt certain she was very attached to him, but I felt she was not in love with Lucien. It was Robert she loved. She had as good as told me so.

Early in December a letter arrived from Sylvia.

"I know you will be as happy as I am, dear Megan," she wrote, "to learn that my prayer has been granted and I am to bear a child in the spring. I need hardly tell you that Charles is elated by the news and has agreed to let me remain here with Beatrice when he returns to Macao after Christmas. I have written to tell mother the wonderful news and it would not surprise me if she decided to come back to England as soon as possible, but of course, she cannot be here now until after my confinement." She went on to tell me other news and ended her letter by saying, "Write and let me know when you are to visit London with Robert and we shall surely meet. I had such a happy visit with you both at Hawkestone."

I was happy beyond words to hear Sylvia's news and as I folded up her letter I said a prayer of thankfulness and asked God to take care of her.

Christmas came and went in a flurry of excitement. It was Imogen's first Christmas and the sight of the tree, decorated in the way that had become the fashion through the young queen, filled her with delight. She was almost a year old and was now walking. A trifle unsteadily it must be admitted, and with many an unexpected tumble, but holding Edward's hand, she would stagger about the room and around the great tree, chattering to herself and speaking the few words she was able to pronounce.

Edward was wonderful with her. He would crouch at one end of the rug, holding out his arms and calling, "Imogen— come to me. I'm here. Come to Eddy," and she would stumble toward him, her little arms outstretched. They loved each other dearly and I marveled that someone as cool and sophisticated as Vanessa should possess so affectionate and warm-hearted a son. Was it his father's temperament Edward had inherited or had Philip left a gentler influence on the child through example?

There was to be a New Year's Eve ball at Hawkestone. The suggestion had come from Vanessa.

"It is so long since we had anything like that. Do say yes, Robert. Megan will love it. I am sure she loves balls as much as I do." She gave me a perfunctory glance. "Don't you?"

I had never been to a ball in my life but I did not say so. I shook my head while Robert frowned thoughtfully and then, as Vanessa put her hand on his arm to say softly, "*Please*, Robert," he nodded.

"All right. But please do not bother me with the arrangements for it."

"You shall not hear a whisper of our plans. Except for a list of the guests, which I will read to you, and you shall say if you are agreeable to it."

She was completely in charge of the affair. Not that I or anyone else could have organized the ball as well as Vanessa. She chose the list of guests, which, having been presented to Robert, was approved, and the invitations were sent out. The food, the flowers, the musicians who were to come and play for the dancing, were determined by her. It was not for me to resent her assumption of authority for I could not have planned it half as well, having no conception of what to do, and scarcely knowing the guest who had been invited, save a few friends and neighbors in the locality.

Vanessa paid me lip service from time to time, saying airily, "We shall have to have as many plants from the hothouse as possible. I have told Jameson to have them in readiness. Don't you agree?" or "There will be fifty of us to sit down to supper. There must be no heavy dishes. Oyster soup first and cold pheasant and chaudfroid of chicken and Mrs. Fuller will cook a Westmoreland ham—it is always popular with gentlemen. Charlotte russe and tangerine chartreuse are agreeable desserts. What do you think?"

I had few suggestions to make and felt both inadequate and ineffectual. Vanessa was so suited to the running of a great house; she knew every facet of entertaining. I could only nod and say, "It sounds splendid."

New Year's Eve was a cold, frosty night with a sprinkling of snow, fortunately light enough not to impede the horses. The whole house was ablaze with light, the great chandeliers glittering and shining, the oil lamps filled and glowing from every corner and shelf. Huge fires burned in the dog grates with footmen in constant attendance to see that they did not burn low for lack of fresh logs. There were flowers everywhere, the hothouse plants that Vanessa had decreed: camellia and chrysanthemum, azalea and amaryllis, delicate primula and jewel-bright gloxinia. The dining-room table was particularly beautiful with Christmas roses in white china bowls set among trailing sprays of ivy and maidenhair and with tall wax candles in shining silver holders.

Vanessa herself had never looked more lovely. She was wearing a new dress of white satin embroidered with a myriad of tiny iridescent glass beads that caught and held the light as she moved. White lace mittens and a garland of white roses holding back the red-gold curls completed a picture as glitteringly beautiful as Hans Andersen's Snow Queen.

I had not bought a dress for the occasion as the one of old rose was new that season and I had worn it very little. It looked well enough, with my dark hair and hazel eyes, but no woman present could compete with Vanessa.

She was the center of attraction. From the first moment, when, standing beside Robert and myself, she welcomed the guests, who were her friends as much or more than Robert's or mine, she drew and held everyone's attention. Her would-be partners hovered about her, Harry Summers well in evidence, Lucien a slim shadow at her side; other men, other husbands, all eager to pay court to the most beautiful woman in the room.

Perhaps it was wrong of me but I was comforted to think that Robert could not see her as clearly as the others could, that he would not be another moth to the flame. And yet, paradoxically, I longed for him to be able to see her and yet choose me. As if he would, I thought sadly. Not one of them would. It seemed to me as if every man in the room was in love with her that night.

But it was Robert whom Vanessa wanted. She turned to him as the first of the fiddles began to tune up.

"Will you start off the dancing with me, Robert? Lucien will take Megan."

He shook his head.

"You know very well I cannot dance with anyone."

"That is nonsense. You see well enough so as not to bump into people. And I will guide you." She touched his hand gently. "Please, Robert. It is so long since I danced. Not—not since Philip—" She broke off on a wistful note.

Robert hesitated; then as the musicians burst into full sound, he shrugged.

"Very well. But if I tread upon your toes or tear your dress, I will not be held responsible."

She smiled brilliantly and perhaps Robert saw something of her smile, of the dazzling figure before him, for his face softened as he took her hand in his and was led to the center of the floor.

For a moment they circled alone, the tall man in the dark evening dress suit, the black patch across one eye, and the lovely woman in the glittering white dress that shone and sparkled with every swaying movement.

Lucien bent his dark head to me and said somberly, "May I have the pleasure, Megan?" and we too moved onto the floor, followed in turn by the other dancers.

It was an evening to remember. Vanessa's triumph was fully justified, for she had planned it from the start, and I could not be envious of her success. Robert and I danced twice together, a mazurka and a slow waltz, and he danced with Vanessa a second time. But she was too besieged by other partners to have dances to spare, and Robert, despite her assurances, felt uncertain in his steps and so did not dance with anyone else.

Some time after supper I was dancing with Lucien when, as we passed the open doorway where Robert stood smoking a cheroot and talking to an elderly man, I saw Harry Summers approach him. Something about his glowering expression, the high color of his dark cheeks arrested my attention. He bowed stiffly to Robert and said something to him while Robert, with a look of surprise, nodded and held out his hand to shake that of Mr. Summers'. Then, turning on his heel, with head erect, the latter strode away.

Lucien had viewed the little scene as I had and now he said, "What was amiss with Summers? He looks in a thoroughly bad temper. Not that he is particularly equable at the best of times."

"Perhaps he had bad news of some kind—he was obviously taking his leave of Robert."

"Perhaps so."

Shortly before midnight a rousing Sir Roger de Coverley was played in which everyone joined with zest. Then there was the joining of hands and the singing of "Auld Lang Syne" until the very roof of Hawkestone seemed to vibrate with the sound of our voices.

An entourage of footmen and maids appeared with trays of piping-hot soup to warm the guests before they braved a drive home through the frosty night. The last goodbye was said, the last wish of "Happy New Year" spoken by the final guest and the great doors of Hawkestone closed upon the winter scene. The ball was over.

Vanessa flung herself down upon one of the settees and rested her bright head against the cushioned velvet.

"I am exhausted. But it went well—do you not think so,

Robert? It was like the old days. Do you remember the wonderful parties Philip's parents gave when we were young? When I married Philip I hoped we should do the same, but he had little inclination for entertaining." She sighed. "He never felt well enough."

"Poor Philip," Robert said.

"Poor me, too," Vanessa answered. "It was sometimes very dull, you know. Perhaps things will be different now we are all together at Hawkestone."

Robert did not answer, and Lucien, leaning over the back of the settee to gaze down at Vanessa, said, "Harry Summers left in the deuce of a huff. What upset him? Do you know?"

Vanessa shrugged.

"I am afraid he was angry because I refused his proposal of marriage."

There was a pause in which no one spoke. Then Robert said coolly, "You refused him? I thought you were going to change his bachelor ways for him. He has been an attentive suitor these past months."

"I realized there would be too many things to change in Harry. Including his fondness for wine and predilection for the gaming tables."

"Poor devil." Robert shook his head. "You did wrong to encourage him, Vanessa, if you could not love him."

"I did not encourage him—well, perhaps a little. He was always at my side in the most persistent fashion, and he can be good company when he is in an agreeable mood. As for loving him or anyone else—that is not possible, for I have only ever loved one man." Her voice softened to a caress. "You should know that, Robert."

"I know that you loved your husband or you would surely not have married him," Robert said harshly. "We have had enough of this discussion of matrimony. It is more than time to say good night. Are you ready to go up, Megan? Good night, Vanessa. Good night, Lucien," and with an abrupt nod of his head he turned toward the door, leaving me to take my farewell of Lucien and Vanessa.

Robert seemed full of a suppressed anger, but whether it

was at Vanessa or at himself I did not know. I was not angry so much as upset by Vanessa's manner toward Robert. And depressed, too.

Harry Summers' attentions to her had given me the hope that she might marry him and leave us alone, but she had spoken just now as if she had no intention of marrying again or of every going away from Hawkestone. The thought of her constant presence in the house cast a shadow over me, and as Hetty, who had been dozing by the bedroom fire, sprang into wakefulness to help me take off the rose dress and crinoline, I was so deep in thought that she said kindly, "You'm tired out, m'lady. An' no wonder. Dancin' round for hours. But I expects you enjoyed every minute of it all."

I looked at her round little face and sleepy dark eyes and was filled with compunction that she should stay up so late to help me prepare for bed.

"Yes, it was a wonderful evening. And thank you for being here, Hetty. You are a great help. Especially when you brush my hair so nicely." I caught her glance in the mirror and we smiled at each other as she drew the silver-backed brush gently through my long black locks. It seemed to me that someone as young and pretty as Hetty should be dancing until the small hours, not sober married people like Robert and myself.

For some weeks after the ball the weather was too wet and cold for much progress to be made at the dell. But as February mud and rain gave way to the winds of March, the ground dried sufficiently for work to go on again, and the foundation of what was to be the summerhouse was laid.

I say what was to be the summerhouse, for as time went on I changed my mind as to the design of it. I found myself wanting to build something more ambitious than a mere summerhouse. I wanted it to be an artistic creation, pleasing to the eye and of unusual design. I wanted to build a replica of the Pearl Pagoda.

Of course I could not. That would be impossible. But gradually, with the efforts of Isaac Jennings, the carpenter, and myself, a small but graceful form of pagoda came into being. It was of three tiers, with a curving Oriental-style roof set on six slender pillars. Each tier was enclosed with fine latticework interspersed with arched openings, each successive tier being repeated in smaller fashion, and the pointed roof of the third tier was surmounted by a copper spire and ball. The ground had been slightly raised to set it above the level of the water on either side and here shrubs and trees were to be planted.

It was not the Pearl Pagoda, although that is the name I intended it to be known by; there was no mother-of-pearl ornamentation or silvery stone or marble, but it was charming in its own fashion and of distinctly Chinese origin.

Isaac stood back, scratching his head in wonderment at his own skill.

"Never seen nothin' like it, m'lady. Be like somethin' in a book or paintin'. When you fust told me what you had in mind I admit I was beat. And then you drew that picture for me and all the time you was explainin' how we was to go about it and now look. It's a marvel."

"It is thanks to you, and your assistant, John, that the building has turned out so successfully. I only showed you what I wanted. I am grateful to you both."

He shook his head.

"Pity as Sir Robert won't be able to see it fully, now 'tis finished. Reckon he's seen many such a thing as this on his travels."

"I am sure he has."

Robert, of course, was brought to see the finished product, but as Isaac had said, he could only make out the curving outline of the roof topped by its graceful spire and was not able to see the detail or the way the land around the pagoda had been leveled for the planting of evergreens and flowering shrubs.

"If you are pleased with it, Megan, I am pleased," he said. He turned to Lucien, who had brought Robert down to the dell. "What do you think of it?"

"I am full of admiration. It is both so unusual and charming. I shall come and paint it when your woodland garden is complete."

Vanessa walked to see it the same week, accompanied by

Edward, who ran about in high delight, exploring every facet, clambering up the minute staircase of wrought iron, coming out at each tier in turn to call and wave to us.

"Be careful, Edward," I called warningly. Fortunately his small head only came level with the top of each encircling balcony so there was no danger he would fall over.

Vanessa glanced carelessly upward.

"He will be all right." She glanced around. "It is certainly quaint and charming in its own way." Her eyes narrowed. "What made you build something like this?"

I said slowly, "The dell reminds me of a place I knew in China—where we were prisoners. There was this beautiful pagoda. I could not begin to describe it. I felt happy there. We were—" I broke off, aware of Vanessa's frowning gaze, of whom I was speaking to.

"But I thought you had a terrible time—that you were captured by pirates and Robert was wounded."

"That was on the *Lotus Wind*. We were taken as prisoners to the house of a Chinese merchant, but he did not treat us unkindly, although he—he could be very cruel." And I shivered at the memory of Mr. Yao.

She stared incredulously at me.

"How could you be happy then? I don't understand."

"I don't understand myself. It—it was a serene and peaceful place, that is all." I turned away. "I wonder where Edward is. Had we better call him?"

At the sound of his name Edward appeared from behind the pavilion.

"I like it here. It is a good place in which to play hide-and-seek. Shall we bring Imogen tomorrow?"

"Yes, we might do that. Later on we can picnic here. Would you like that?"

He jumped up and down.

"It would be fun. Let's come soon."

A few days later I had a delightful surprise. I was in the nursery reading with Edward when Grace, one of the parlormaids, came to the room to say, "A gentleman has called to see you, m'lady. He is waiting in the library to speak with you."

"Who is it, Grace? Did he not give his name or a card? Are you sure it is for me and not Sir Robert?"

"Oh, no, m'lady. 'Twas you he asked for immediate like. He told me his name, but it was too outlandish for me to remember. He is a foreign gentleman—from—from China, m'lady."

I stared.

"From *China.*" I stood up quickly. "I will come at once. Edward dear, put your book away. I think our lesson must be over for this morning. Run and tell Deborah and then you may go out and play in the garden."

I hurried down the wide staircase. The library door stood slightly ajar. I pushed it open and then halted in astonishment.

It was Chao Tsan who stood waiting for me. An unfamiliar Chao Tsan, with his queue cut off, clad in a dark suit set off by a white shirt and stiff white collar. He bowed before me, his hands clasped against his chest.

"Most Honored Lady Megan, may I offer you my esteemed greetings."

I bowed my own head, folding my hands in the familiar gesture of politeness.

"Thank you. You are a welcome guest to this house, Chao Tsan."

"I am grateful to you for your gracious hospitality. I trust I find you in good health. As also Sir Robert, your honored husband."

"We are both well as we hope that you are."

"Thank you. I too am well." He smiled suddenly, his round face beaming with pleasure, and he was once more the old familiar Chao Tsan, despite his European dress.

I said spontaneously, "I'm so glad to see you again, Chao Tsan."

"And I am happy beyond words to see you, most Honored Lady Megan. And to thank you from my heart, as I hope to thank the Honored Sir Robert, for your generous gift to the Mission. It was Dr. Howard's wish that I should come in person to do this. As it was that I should bring you a humble present in return."

"A present? How very kind of you." I gestured toward a

chair. "Please sit down, Chao Tsan. My husband is out, but he will join us later. I am sure he will wish you to stay at Hawkestone for a few days. Are you able to do that?"

He bowed his head.

"Thank you, Honored Lady Megan. I had intended to find lodgings at some inn."

"No, we cannot allow that. You must stay here with us. But tell me, before I ask you about the present you have brought for us, how is it you are no longer wearing Chinese dress?"

"That is for when I am in China. Now I come to England, I wear English clothes. He smiled widely. "It is as you say, 'When in Rome—' "

"I understand. Are you to be in England long?"

"Six months—perhaps longer. I am to work at the Mission in Bermondsey, Honored Lady Megan."

"You will enjoy being in London and seeing something of its historical grandeur."

He hesitated, then said, "The gift that I have brought for you—it is outside on the hired carriage in which I came. May I ask you, Honored Lady Megan, to come and inspect it?"

"Yes, indeed, I am longing to see what it can be."

I stood up and led the way out to the front drive, where a horse drooped between the shafts of a carriage standing in the shade of the trees. On the roof of the carriage was strapped an unwieldy bundle of sacking. Chao Tsan spoke to the driver and between them the package was carefully lifted down onto the gravel. It was large and untidy in shape and was tied firmly with strong cord.

Tsan stood back, dusting his hands, and said diffidently, "Perhaps this is not a suitable place in which to unfasten it. There will be much straw. I think a stable or shed would be better, Honored Lady Megan."

"Of course. One of the footmen can take it around to the stables. Tell the driver to carry your luggage into the house, Chao Tsan, and let him go."

In a few moments the carriage had been dismissed and Alfred, the second footman, had carried the package to the stable yard, where he proceeded to cut the cords and untie the wrapping.

"Thank you, Alfred. That will do splendidly. You may go," I told him, for I wanted to view my somewhat curious-seeming present with only Chao Tsan as witness.

Alfred's tall back disappeared around the corner of the stables and as Tsan bent down to open the last piece of covering I saw that the gift was a collection of rare shrubs and plants.

"Oh! Oh, Tsan, you could not have brought me anything I should treasure more. You have brought them all the way from Macao? I can't believe it. What will Robert say? He will be so pleased for me. He knows I am making a garden of my own—I have built a sort of pagoda. I will show it to you later." I bent over the thin branches, the moss-enwrapped roots. "This is labeled *Weigela rosea*. And *Lonicera fragrantissima* and forsythia. And what are these little plants? Oh, meconopsis and some *Dianthus chinensis*. And this evergreen, what is it? *Cupressus funebris*—a weeping cypress. I hope it grows and flourishes." I straightened up. "Who packed them so wonderfully well and labeled them with Latin names? Not you—Tsan?"

He shook his head, smiling.

"A good friend of Dr. Howard's who is an ardent botanist and horticulturist. Some of these plants have already been established in English gardens, but we know it is not easy for people to obtain them through nurserymen and so he sent to you and the Honored Sir Robert this unworthy gift for the illustrious house of Hawkestone. I came direct from Plymouth, where I disembarked, for I was anxious that the plants should be delivered immediately to you."

I sent for one of the gardeners and told him to water the shrubs and plants and put them in a sheltered place in readiness for planting the following day.

Tsan and I had much to talk of. He had news of Miss Crow and her brother; two new recruits had come out from England and would be doing some of Tsan's work; Dr. Howard had gone to Amoy, but later Tsan himself expected to work there and Dr. Howard would go back to Macao.

"He is anxious to travel inland again, as he did two years ago," Tsan informed me. "He wishes to form more inland missions." He shook his head. "It will not be easy."

Robert appeared in time for luncheon and was amazed to see Chao Tsan. Yet, oddly, I could see he was pleased to talk with him and hear news of Macao and Canton. They discussed the growing exasperation between the British and Chinese governments. China was now exporting to Britain tea and silk to the value of 13 millions or more, while the sale of opium had risen to 6 millions and was a constant source of anixety to the Chinese government. As they talked I breathed a prayer of thankfulness that Robert was no longer involved in the vile trade.

Vanessa and Lucien dined with us that night and Lucien found points of interest to discuss with Chao Tsan, having traveled to China in his youth. Vanessa was gracious enough, though her curiosity was obvious, and when she heard that Chao Tsan and I had worked much together and that he had taught me Chinese, she lifted an amused eyebrow as she said, "Really? Do say something to us in the language, Megan. Is it as outlandish as your native Welsh tongue?"

I answered calmly in Chinese,

She stared blankly at me.

"What does that mean?"

I translated the phrase into English.

"Language is the amber in which a thousand precious and subtle thoughts have been safely embedded and preserved."

Vanessa shrugged and did not answer.

The next day was ideal for planting the new shrubs, for although it was in the main a fine day in early May, a soft sprinkle of rain fell intermittently.

"I don't think we shall get wet," I assured Chao Tsan. "We can shelter in the pagoda if it rains when we are there, but I would like to supervise the planting. Take this cloak of

Robert's. It will cover you in case of a shower and I will take mine."

Edward insisted upon accompanying us, as his lessons had been put aside. He was greatly taken with Chao Tsan, who, like all Chinese, was particularly agreeable to children, and the fact that Edward had met and played with George and Dorothea Howard formed an instant bond between him and Tsan.

I saw the look of surprised pleasure on Tsan's round face at his first glimpse of the pagoda.

"It is beautiful, Honored Lady Megan. Of great excellence." He bowed his head. "I take it as an honor to my country that you should build here such a replica of one of our own traditional buildings."

"I am glad you like it, Tsan. You know what your countrymen believe—that a pagoda brings a benign influence to the house or city within the vicinity in which it stands."

"That is so." He smiled. "Even as a Christian I would not despise such a belief. To create anything in a virtuous spirit brings good fortune because it attracts right and proper vibrations. Equally, thoughts, actions, deeds performed in baseness, will end in disaster because these attract bad or evil motions." He bowed his head again. "We are of the same mind I think, Honored Lady."

"Yes." I smiled at him. "These plantings should burgeon for they will be executed in the happiness of friendship."

Edward stared up at me with round eyes.

"What a funny way of talking," he said. "It sounds like a book."

"We will talk no more," I assured him. "Now, Edward, here is a trowel for you to use and you shall help me while Perkins will dig some nice deep holes for the bigger shrubs. Tsan, I will give you this small fork for you must help too or the plants will not flourish as they should, for you are responsible for bringing them here."

The four of us spent a happy morning. It was warm in the dell and fortunately we had no more rain than a refreshing shower. The sun came out, beaming rays of gold through the green of the overhanging trees. From somewhere in the park above us a cuckoo called, clear and sweet and repetitive, an intrinsic part of the summer day.

I had suggested to Robert that some of the shrubs be planted in the main garden, but he had shaken his head, his lean face softened by a smile.

"No. Keep them for your own garden. You have built your Chinese pagoda; now have the shrubs and plants from China itself around you there."

Chao Tsan stayed with us for four days and then he left for London. We said goodbye, bowing with folded hands in formal politeness.

"Perhaps one day you will return to Macao on a visit, Honored Lady Megan. I shall live in that hope."

"Perhaps. Who knows?" I thought of Sylvia, returning with her child to Macao to join her husband. Perhaps someday we might go out to visit her. I thought how much I should love to see that strange and magical country once more. "We shall see you in London, Chao Tsan, for we shall be visiting the city when Sir Robert undergoes further examination of his eye."

"I trust that the outcome will be favorable to the Honored Sir Robert." He bowed again and, turning, went down the few steps to the carriage in which he was to be taken to the railway station at Bath.

The plantings settled in successfully and it was not long before they made fresh growth. As the summer days lengthened I spent more and more time at the dell, sometimes with the children, often alone, rarely with Robert. I had taken up sketching again and I delighted in making fresh aspects of the trees or the pool or the Pearl Pagoda. One afternoon when I arrived it was to find Lucien seated at an easel painting a watercolor of the scene.

"You have caught me. It was to be a surprise for you. You had better not look."

"May I not? I should like to so much," and at his nod and shrug of resignation I stepped forward to look over his shoulder at the painting.

"But it is *beautiful*," I exclaimed in surprise. "So—so accomplished. I had no idea you were an artist of such skill, Lucien."

He shrugged again.

"It is my one talent. I thought once of going to Paris, of painting professionally. But I did not."

I stared at the painting, the light and shadow of the trees caught so delicately, the graceful curving lines of the pagoda with its muted reflection in the blue waters of the pool. I could not understand why it was so perfect, why something in its execution touched the heart so that it seemed as if it were a poem on paper.

I said slowly, "You *are* a professional, Lucien. You have a great talent. I can see. You should not waste your time here— just helping about the estate. You should be in Paris now. Why don't you go? It is not too late to begin to paint as you should."

He shook his head.

"No, I could not go away from Hawkestone."

"But Robert would not mind. He cannot see your work, but if I told him he would understand. He has never asked you to stay, has he?"

"No. It is nothing to do with Robert. It is—I could not leave Vanessa."

I stared at him in silence, the words of protest dying on my lips.

"Is it—Vanessa who wants you to stay on here?"

Again he shook his head.

"It is I who cannot bring myself to leave her. We have always been so close. Even when she was married to Philip, it made little difference. We have been together all our lives— brought up together."

"You cannot always live in her shadow," I began, and then stopped.

"But that is what I shall continue to do. I would not wish it otherwise." He smiled a curious twisted smile and continued in a voice tinged with melancholy. "Vanessa is a witch who has cast a spell over me. I would do anything in the world for her."

For a moment we were both silent as we looked at the

graceful lines of Lucien's painting. And then he said, in quite a different voice, as if he had decided to banish whatever heavy thoughts had been on his heart, "But let us talk of you. Vanessa is my stepsister and I have known her all my life. But you, my dear Megan, I am only now beginning to know." And with a sweep of his arm he indicated the clear blue surface of the pool and the gentle curves of the pagoda. "You are more than beautiful, Megan," he said. "You create beauty wherever you go."

His eyes sought mine and the intensity of their expression made me lower my own.

"And Robert," he continued, "has neither the eyes nor the heart to recognize it."

Then he rose suddenly and in one swift motion had drawn me into his arms. For a fleeting moment I was so overcome with emotion that I remained motionless in his embrace. And then I struck out at him with both firsts, pushing him backward with the fierceness born of my outraged feelings.

"How can you!" I managed to exclaim when I had broken free of his encircling arms. "How dare you!"

We stood now, some two feet apart, and as I fought to gain control of myself, I watched Lucien's face twist once more into that strange, ironic smile and slowly and solemnly, as if pronouncing a doom upon us both, he said, "Robert loves Vanessa."

I could stand no more. Gathering my skirts around me, I turned my back on Lucien and, slipping and sliding in my haste, ran as fast as I could along the garden path back to Hawkestone.

I heard Lucien several steps behind, calling my name, imploring me to wait, begging me to listen. But I had heard more than I had ever wished to hear and scurried along as quickly as my heeled slippers and the terrain would allow.

When I entered the house I passed quickly through the main hallway and was about to mount the first step of the staircase when the sound of lowered voices gave me pause. I glanced into the drawing room and there, standing face to face in the light from the casement window, were Robert and

Vanessa. I could not hear what they were saying, but as I watched, as one mesmerized or frozen in a bad dream, Robert lifted his hand and gently ran his fingers over the fine features of her face. I watched transfixed as Robert's strong fingers moved lightly over her eyes and nose, lingered over her lips, and passed down over her chin, and then his hand dropped to his side. I turned slowly and tiptoed up the stairs, overcome by an inexpressible and profound sadness.

I knew then I had made the dell my sanctuary and built the Pearl Pagoda because for some reason Vanessa's presence in the house frightened me.

Was that too strong a word? Perhaps I meant over-shadowed. No, it had something to do with fear. I was not happy in the house, beautiful though it was. The atmosphere chilled me and it was only when I was in the garden or the grounds or the Great Park that I felt truly at ease. The day I discovered the dell I found again a sense of reassurance, because it had reminded me of the Pagoda of the Many Pearls, which had breathed peace and serenity. And so I had built my little replica, as if in so doing I would ward off some shadow of danger I could not account for.

But danger had followed me even there. I shuddered at the recollection of my encounter with Lucien, even more so at his revelation, which I knew in my soul to be true.

But I resolved to say nothing. I could not, for my heart-ache was compounded by a different kind of knowledge. I had just found out I was once again pregnant.

CHAPTER 21

I WAITED until Dr. Jessop had confirmed my suspicions before breaking the news to Robert.

"We shall have a son this time," I assured him. "I promise you."

I had decided to settle for whatever portion of love Robert had reserved for me, for after all, I had no other choice. And perhaps, I told myself, as the days went by, our son would win some love for his mother.

I do not know why I felt so certain that it was a boy I carried under my heart, but with every week that passed, the conviction grew and I pondereed dreamily on possible names and wondered if he would be brown-haired and blue-eyed like Robert or dark like myself. Despite everything that had occurred, I was happy through the golden days of high summer, spending much time in the dell, sewing and reading while seated on my wooden bench beside the pool, glancing up to see the pagoda, so pretty and so graceful amidst the blossoming shrubs that Chao Tsan had brought as a gift to me, feeling still the peace of this quiet spot falling on me like a benediction.

To add to my happiness a letter came from Sylvia to say that she had been safely delivered of a baby daughter who was to be named Harriet Rose. Her mother was already on her way back to England where the house in Belgrave Square would be reopened and Sylvia and her mother would live there for some months, until it was decided when Sylvia should return to Macao. I knew she did not wish to do this, but poor Charles must miss her very much and there was little likelihood that at the moment he could contemplate leaving the

East India Company at Canton to live in England, as Sylvia wished to do.

As I pondered on these things something happened that brought me, for the first time, into open conflict with Vanessa, and my world was shattered.

It began the night I discovered Hetty had been crying. She was dressing my hair before dinner one evening and as I glanced into the mirror I saw not the reflection of myself but the pale disk of Hetty's face with its shadowed eyes and tear-stained cheeks.

I turned on the stool to look at her and say gently, "What is the matter, Hetty? Are you not feeling well?"

She gaped at me, her soft mouth half open, fresh tears welling up into her dark eyes.

"Oh—'tis nothing, m'lady. Just—just a bit of an 'eadache."

"Are you sure?" I put my hand to her arm. "You have been crying. Are you unhappy about something?"

Her face worked, she could not speak, only double her fist against her mouth in a pathetic attempt to retain her self-control. Then, the tears coursing down her cheeks, she whispered, "I'm in trouble, m'lady." She turned her head away. "Terrible trouble."

There was a silence and then I said quietly, "Perhaps I can help you, Hetty. Tell me of your trouble."

She swallowed, letting her hand fall to her side.

" 'Tis that I'm with child an'—an' there be no chance that he—the father of the bairn—will marry me."

I caught my breath.

"Oh, Hetty. Poor Hetty. Do you mean he is married already?"

She nodded dumbly.

"And do you wish to tell me who the man is?"

" 'Twouldn't do no good, m'lady. He can't marry me and that's that."

"He will have to help you in some way. If only with money."

"Aye—mebbe. But you see, m'lady, I won't be able to stay here. I'll have to be leavin'." She wiped the tears away with the back of her hand. "Dunno what'll happen to me—with no reference nor nothin'."

"You won't have to leave," I said firmly. "*I* shall not dismiss you. You have done wrong, Hetty. You know that without my telling you. You have acted wrongly and foolishly, but words and reproaches will not put matters right. We must think what is to be done for the best. Have you told your mother as yet?"

She shook her head, biting her lip.

"No, m'lady. But—but time is comin' when I'll have to—afore I begin to show."

"And will she help you? Keep the baby so that you may continue at work?"

Again she shook her head.

"I can't say as to that, m'lady. But she's a good mother to me—to us all."

"And your father, what will he say?"

"He be dead these past four years, m'lady."

That made it easier perhaps. A mother might not be so stern as a father. On the other hand, money would be less plentiful. It would be more necessary than ever that Hetty should remain at work if her mother was a widow.

I said slowly, "I will think what is to be done for the best. But having told me so much, I must ask that you tell me the name of the man involved, Hetty. He has equal if not more responsibility in this matter."

She stared at me for a minute and then said in a low voice, " 'Tis George McDow—he be one of the gamekeepers."

I frowned, trying to link the name with the man. Suddenly I remembered. It had been one day in the woods last autumn when I was walking with Robert, guiding him along the path. He had paused to speak to a tall well-built man—something concerning the pheasant coverts. It was the first time I had seen him and I remembered he was called George McDow.

"We will try to find a solution, Hetty," I said reassuringly. "Try not to get upset and do not speak of this to anyone else."

"Oh, *no*, m'lady. And *thank* you, m'lady."

I was distressed for Hetty—she was but eighteen and a sweet, good girl. I thought of George McDow, whom I recollected as a man in his early forties. Not unhandsome, with sherry-brown eyes in a brown-skinned face. A man with an air of knowing what he was about. Too old and experienced for Hetty.

I considered the problem for a long time and then I decided the best thing to do was to tell Robert. If it was advisable for anyone to speak to George McDow that person would have to be Robert.

When I had finished recounting the story to him he frowned and said, "McDow? What a damn nuisance—he is one of my best keepers. Are you sure the girl hasn't been involved with anyone else and is putting it onto George?"

"I am quite certain that is not the case. Hetty is an honest girl—and innocent, I am sure, until this happened. I blame McDow. He is a married man with a family and twice her age."

Robert went on frowning.

"You are probably right. I believe he is not always on the best of terms with his wife—she is something of a nag."

"Perhaps she has cause to be."

Robert shrugged.

"What do you want me to do? Get McDow to admit the paternity of the child and see his wages are docked for Hetty's maintenance?"

"I suppose that is all one can do as he is not free to marry her." I shook my head. "Poor child. She is so young to have this—this responsibility on her shoulders. It is vital that she retains her position here for the time being and then returns to us after the baby is born. She hopes the grandmother will care for the child. She is a widow."

"Hetty should have thought of all this before she went romping off with McDow," Robert said a trifle grimly.

"It is something that could happen to any one of us. You know that, Robert, as well as I."

He turned and gave me a rueful smile.

"Yes, that is true. All right—I will speak with McDow as soon as possible."

Two days passed. Robert did not say if he had seen George McDow and I did not question him, for I knew he would arrange matters in his own way. Hetty was subdued, her dark eyes seeming to question me, but I made no further reference to the situation.

The following morning I went to the library to speak to Robert, but as I opened the door, to my surprise I heard Vanessa's voice saying, "She will have to go. There is no question about it." At my entry she turned and I saw her frown and then shrug as she said, "You have arrived at the right moment. We are discussing your maid and the predicament she has gotten herself into."

I glanced quickly at Robert, but he shook his head imperceptibly as if to discount Vanessa's words.

"I was not aware that such a matter concerned you, Vanessa," I answered quietly.

"Of course it concerns me. George McDow came here as a gamekeeper when Philip's father was alive. I have had dealings with him on many occasions. Now he comes to tell me that Robert wants him to acknowledge the paternity of this girl's child. It is of great embarrassment to him and his wife and in the circumstances he wishes to give his notice. That is absurd. He is one of the most capable men on the estate. It is better that the girl should be dismissed."

"But that is not fair. Hetty is very young. I—I feel she has been injured by someone who is older and experienced enough to know better. She is my personal maid—I do not wish her to leave."

Vanessa glanced toward Robert.

"It is for you to persuade Megan to view the situation sensibly. Obviously I cannot. She has so little knowledge of running a large household and dealing with the problems that arise with staff that she does not understand these matters."

Robert's mouth set in a thin line.

"I told you that I did not think Megan would be amenable to Hetty's being dismissed. She feels a certain responsibility for her and it is not for me to interfere."

"You mean you do not object to George McDow's departure after his being at Hawkestone for so many years?"

"I do not approve of it. He is a very useful man."

Sensing an opportunity, Vanessa said in a more placatory tone of voice, "Yes, he certainly is, and was of great assistance to Philip in the years when—when Philip was not so able to take care of matters himself."

Robert's set mouth relaxed at the mention of Philip, but he said nothing.

Vanessa continued, saying, "I have as good as promised McDow that you would reconsider the situation and send the girl away. With some compensation, of course, and an assurance from him that he will pay toward the child's keep. Then he would not have to leave. He does not want to—it is only that Mrs. McDow is being difficult in refusing to remain on here if Hetty is still working in the house."

Robert listened, frowning, and then slowly he nodded his head.

"I think perhaps you are right, Vanessa. A man's morals do not necessarily affect his capacities at work and McDow is an excellent gamekeeper. It is true as you say that our family owes him some loyalty, and if Hetty will be taken care of . . ."

I felt my face redden as I understood that Robert was undermining my authority in favor of Vanessa. For a moment I could not believe it, and then I said, "Perhaps Vanessa feels she should make all the decisions in this house."

Vanessa's narrow eyes hardened as I spoke, her red lips thinned.

Then Robert took a step forward.

"Please do not speak to Vanessa in that way, Megan. She had done what she thinks best for the entire household."

Vanessa gave me one glance from slitted green eyes, then her expression changed; it was as if a mask fell over her face.

"Dear Megan," she said, taking my hand in hers, "forgive me if I have distressed you. I only wished to save us all from further unpleasantness."

Before I had a chance to reply, she left us, the door closing quietly behind her. For a moment Robert and I stared at each other, and I was about to angrily protest what I took to be despicable and insulting treatment when I saw Robert frown suddenly and press his hand against his good eye.

"What is the matter? Is your eye painful?"

"Not so much painful as—as blurred. I could scarcely see Vanessa. Or you, for that matter."

"Has it just come like this? I thought you could see reasonably well with that eye, but not pick out detail."

"It has grown worse the past week or so. I did not say anything thinking it was some temporary matter." His mouth set in a hard line. "Surely to God I am not to lose the sight of both eyes."

I flung myself at him, all thoughts of Vanessa dismissed in a flood of new anxiety.

"Oh, *no*, Robert. No. It is some—some small defect. But we must make arrangements for you to see Dr. Simpson again as soon as possible. You cannot leave the matter."

"No, that would not be wise. I will write to him. Or you may write for me, if you will. But let me get this matter of McDow settled first."

I pushed him gently into a nearby chair.

"No, Robert. We will write to Dr. Simpson first so the letter will be ready to be taken in the letter bag when the mailman calls. You can attend to McDow later and I will speak to Hetty." My hand rested on his shoulder as I bent to kiss him on the cheek. Whatever Robert's feelings for Vanessa, I was still his wife.

I could see that Robert was now much handicapped by the defective vision in his one good eye, and though I tried hard not to show it, my fears for his eyesight grew. I wrote to Sylvia telling her that we should be in London at the hotel in St. James's, where we had stayed before, and that I would send a message to her after we had visited Dr. Simpson.

The morning of Robert's interview with the specialist we were both on tenterhooks, Robert showing it by no more than set lips and frowning brows, myself by chattering a little more than usual, as if in an effort to keep a cheerful aspect. It was a relief to descend from the carriage at the house in Wigmore

Street and find ourselves facing the outcome, for better or for worse.

I sat in the waiting room, my hands clasped in prayer, and at last Dr. Simpson came out to me, his thin face softened by a hint of a smile.

"The situation has changed somewhat, Lady Hawkes," he informed me. "I have discussed it with your husband and he has accepted my advice that an operation is necessary now upon the defective eye. If matters are left, the result may be total blindness. If the operation is successful, not only will this new trouble be cleared up, but there is a possibility that with the release of pressure upon the optic nerve his eyesight might be considerably improved." He heard my gasp of relief, for he added slowly, "I must warn you, Lady Hawkes, as I have warned Sir Robert—it is a gamble either way. The condition of the eye will deteriorate if left. The operation may save it, but equally, it may prove of little effect."

I bit my lip.

"I understand. We must be guided by you. When—when did you expect to operate?"

He glanced at the silver-framed calendar on the table.

"Let me see—it is September the tenth today. I think in three weeks' time I should be free to perform the operation. Usually this is done at the patient's home, but in view of the circumstances and the fact that I shall wish to have a constant check of the situation, I suggest that Sir Robert stay here in London at the small annex next door to my house. Here, from time to time, patients from a distance or from overseas are accommodated. It is a convenient arrangement, and Sir Robert is perfectly agreeable to it."

"Yes. Yes, of course." I felt disappointed that Robert would not be at Hawkestone, under my care, but I realized that if the operation had any difficulties, it would be better that he should be under daily supervision of the surgeon who was to perform it.

Robert, who had been dressing with the help of an attendant, now joined us and various details were settled before we said goodbye to Dr. Simpson and returned to the hotel.

The next night we dined with Sylvia and Mrs. Meade at the latter's London home. Mrs. Meade was as warm and welcoming as ever, and full of sympathetic concern for Robert, which he bore with aloof patience. But Mrs. Meade did not commiserate with him for too long for she was all eagerness to tell us of her granddaughter, Harriet Rose, and to show us the wonder of the new baby. I truly rejoiced to see the tiny golden-haired child sleeping in her befrilled bassinet, and to know that Sylvia had achieved her heart's desire. I had never seen Sylvia more radiant or more shiningly happy and I thought that in the joy of her little daughter she would forget Henry and, in time, draw nearer to Charles, who was so devoted to her.

The following night Mrs. Meade and Sylvia and also Sylvia's sister Beatrice and her husband, Geoffrey, dined with us at the hotel, for we were to return to Hawkestone the next day. It was quite a merry party and I think helped to distract Robert, who had been frowningly introspective the past week or so. As Sylvia and I said goodbye to each other we made mutual promises that she should visit us at Hawkestone again, in company with her mother and baby Harriet, before she returned to Macao.

Vanessa put in an appearance within an hour of our return to Hawkestone.

"I have been so anxious. What is the news, Robert?" And when he told her something of the arrangements ahead she smiled reassuringly. "I am sure this operation will be completely successful. It may make all the difference to you, Robert. Just think—if the sight of your poor eye is restored."

"It is a great deal to hope for," Robert answered briefly. "But thank you for your concern, Vanessa."

"You know I will do anything I can to help—while you are incapacitated, I mean." She gave me a quick sideways glance. "Megan herself will be handicapped as time goes on." She hesitated, her narrow eyes considering. "When is the child due, Megan?"

"Sometime in mid-February, I believe."

"Another winter baby. Let us hope, for everyone's sake, it
will be a boy this time."

I smiled, almost to myself.

"I have a conviction it will be."

She looked away from me, her lips thinning.

"You are fortunate to have precognition of the event."

"It is my dearest wish. And Robert's."

She said no more and after a few moments went quietly
away.

A few days passed. Robert immersed himself in the affairs
of the estate, consulting first with Mr. Perrin, the steward, and
then with Lucien, who acted so often as his go-between, being
quick and active. The month of September was a particularly
beautiful one, with still golden days. I walked often to the dell
to sit in the shelter of the Pearl Pagoda.

One afternoon I was thinking of going there again when,
to my surprise, Vanessa met me upon the terrace and said,
"What a beautiful day. I am going for a ride through the
Great Park. Why don't you come with me, Megan? It would
do you good."

For some reason I hesitated.

"I—I have not ridden much lately."

She flicked her crop against her full-skirted riding habit,
her green eyes mesmeric upon my own.

"It will not harm you. Betsy is such a gentle creature; she
will be perfectly happy to walk quietly along the rides, and
the fresh air and exercise will do you good."

Still I hesitated, aware of an inner reluctance that I could
not account for. Yet I should welcome Vanessa's gesture of
friendship, and the day was perfect, the blue sky and crisp air
inviting. Suddenly the idea of riding quietly among the golden-
leaved trees of the park was irresistible. And it was better to
go in someone else's company.

"If you do not mind waiting for me while I change I shall
be happy to come with you, Vanessa," I said.

"Of course. Do not hurry yourself. There is plenty of
time."

The skirt of my riding dress was somewhat tight, as I

had feared it might be, but the long jacket fortunately concealed my curves.

I was glad I had agreed to Vanessa's suggestion. The Great Park spread for miles, encircling Hawkestone, and there were rides cut between the trees, unencumbered by cattle.

If Vanessa had desired my company, it must have been for my own well-being rather than as a conversationalist, for she spoke little to me. For the most part she rode a short way ahead. I did not mind. I was more than happy to look about me, to see the glowing colors of the trees, the tawny stubbled fields, the blue-shadowed distances. In a few weeks' time the leaves would be gone, the great oaks and the tall beeches stripped, and the color would fade from the landscape and be seen only in the winter skies.

We appeared to be circling the Great Park for we rode on and on without ever coming to the boundary wall. After crossing open land again with a vista of distant hills, we came to a thickly planted copse and here Vanessa reined in her horse and turned to say, "We will go this way. I do not wish to tire you and it is a shortcut back to the grounds and the house."

I checked Betsy, staring somewhat dubiously at the dense growth of trees ahead.

"But is there a ride cut through?"

"There is a narrow track and the ride is only for a short distance, then we come to the open park, nearer to the house." She smiled reassuringly. "I will lead the way."

While I still hesitated, reining Betsy in, Vanessa rode forward and in a moment was hidden from sight by the enclosing trees. There was no alternative but to follow her and yet I was aware of a deep reluctance to do so. Betsy, tossing her head impatiently, decided the matter for me and I urged her forward into the copse and along the narrow pathway.

The trees enclosed us immediately. I was surprised how dark it seemed in the wood after the mellow sunshine of the park. The track meandered this way and that but was well defined and Betsy had no difficulty in following it. A little way along Vanessa was waiting for me. She waved her riding crop and moved forward again, calling loudly, "Follow me, Megan."

As I obeyed her I wondered at my own fearfulness. The wood was dark certainly, and the trees overgrown on either side of the track, but Betsy picked her way with dainty care. Yet I felt apprehensive, as if some unknown hazard lay ahead of me. It was foolish because Vanessa was riding ahead, and if there were some pitfall or obstacle, she would be the first one to encounter it.

Vanessa was out of sight again. When I rounded the next bend it was to find her dismounted and standing by Perseus, fumbling with the saddle.

I halted Betsy, and Vanessa turned to say, frowning, "This girth is slack. I am just going to tighten it. Don't wait for me, Megan. I shall be but a moment, and if you walk your horse slowly, I will soon catch up."

I glanced uncertainly about me.

"I will wait for you. You know the way better than I."

She gave me an impatient glance.

"You have only to ride on and you will be out of the wood in a few moments."

She made me feel foolish. With a shrug, I gave Betsy her head and she set off slowly along the track. I glanced back over my shoulder and saw Vanessa still tugging at the saddle girth, then the path curved and she was out of sight again.

It was quiet in the little wood. Quiet and dark. I listened for the sound of birdsong, a late robin or the friendly twitter of a hedge sparrow. I looked over my shoulder, hoping to see tall Perseus trotting up behind, but there was no sign of him or his rider. The best thing was to go steadily on and so reach the end of the wood where I would wait for Vanessa.

A thicket of bramble threw spiky arms across the pathway. Betsy sidestepped to avoid the tangle of briers, and as she did so, there was a sudden startling eruption, as from the underwood itself. Something immense and black leaped into midair before us and a raucous cry rent the air. I could not have said what it was—whether animal or human. I had an impression of wavering black wings, like a gigantic bat, of a staring black face or mask, the rest was a blur of terror as I fought helplessly to hold Betsy in check. It was impossible.

The trembling little mare was more terrified even than I. She reared, fighting for the bit, and I had to hold on tight to remain in the saddle. The next moment she bounded forward and dashed at headlong pace along the track, blundering this way and that with every turn. I hung on desperately, feeling if we could but reach the end of the wood I could let her go across the park and gradually calm her to a halt.

I saw the glimmer of light—the open space of the park—ahead.

And then it happened.

I was so intent on steadying Betsy and retaining my seat that I was not aware of the overhanging branch of the tree ahead. I never saw it. But I felt it. It was as if someone stretched out a long arm and swept me clean out of the saddle. One moment I was on Betsy, the next I was in midair. A terrible jarring of bone and body shot through me as I rolled senseless upon the ground. Then I was lost in dark oblivion.

CHAPTER 22

I WOKE FROM a delirium of pain and anguish. I was lying in the four-poster bed at Hawkestone but had no remembrance of how I had arrived there. Faces bent over me, as through a cloud, Dr. Jessop, Robert, Mrs. Crosbie, the midwife. Another face, unfamiliar, pale hair and light eyes. Where was Hetty? For hours—days perhaps?—I lay in a darkened world while those about me fought for the life of my child.

It was in vain. The child was stillborn and I was left empty and exhausted, my only emotion one of utter weariness.

I slept and woke, woke and slept. One day I opened my eyes to find Robert leaning over me. His hand came out to clasp mine. He said gently, "Megan, my poor little girl, are you feeling better? We have all been anxious for you."

"Yes, I am better."

He kissed me and sat back in the chair, my hand still held in his.

"You have had a bad time of it, but Dr. Jessop says you are over the worst. You will begin to pick up from now on."

"Yes." I swallowed on the lump in my throat. "We—we lost our son, Robert. It was a boy, wasn't it?"

He nodded gravely.

"Yes. I am sorry, Megan. Sorry for you and all that you have been through."

The tears coursed slowly down my cheeks, but Robert could not see them.

"If only I had not gone riding—with Vanessa. It would not have happened—the—the accident."

His grip on my hand tightened.

"You must not reproach yourself. Or Vanessa. She is very upset. She has called constantly to see you, but you were never conscious."

I turned my head away.

"I do not wish to see anyone but you. Not yet." I closed my eyes against the thought of visitors, of people. Of Vanessa. I did not want to think about Vanessa. If I did so I would remember and I feared to do that.

After a pause Robert went quietly away and I fell into uneasy sleep. When I woke again, someone was moving softly about the room, putting things in drawers, tidying up.

I called feebly, "Hetty? Is that you, Hetty?"

A woman, tall and thin, with graying fair hair, came to stand beside the bed.

"No, my lady. Hetty has gone. I have been engaged in her place. My name is Grace."

"Grace?" I remembered the pale eyes, the primly pursed mouth.

"Yes, m'lady. Lady Vanessa engaged me."

"I see."

"Is there anything you'm be needing, m'lady? A drink of something?"

"Not for the moment. Thank you, Grace."

"M'lady." She padded silently away and I was left longing for Hetty and thinking that I did not feel at ease with Grace.

Vanessa came to see me, quiet and subdued, fresh flowers in her hands, a look of gentle contrition on her face.

"How are you, Megan, my dear? You have undergone a great ordeal and we have all been very anxious for you."

"I am better," I answered, as I answered to everyone.

She shook her head.

"To lose your son. It is grievous. Poor Robert is heart-broken. And I feel somehow responsible. If only I had not suggested that we ride that day, Megan. Can you forgive me? For I cannot forgive myself."

"Please do not concern yourself," I began stiffly. I did not want her condolences. "It—it was just an unhappy accident.

Something frightened Betsy and she shied out." My voice rose excitedly as the picture formed in my mind once more. "It was the—the man. He jumped out of the bushes. He wore a long black cloak and a tall hat. He shouted and waved his arms and frightened Betsy. She shied and—and—" I could not go on but sank back tremblingly upon the pillows.

Vanessa laid a cool hand against my forehead.

"My dear, you are still feverish. You must keep quiet and rest. There was no man. No one at all. The park and grounds were thoroughly searched after you kept calling out aloud in your delirium of some figure you imagined you saw. It was a trick of the light. A bird, perhaps an owl, flew up suddenly from under your feet and startled Betsy into shying."

I said tiredly, "He wore a black cloak—he waved his arms like wings."

Vanessa shook her head.

"This fantasy will fade from your mind as you grow stronger. Try not to dwell upon it. I will leave you to rest, my dear."

When she had left me I lay back thinking, But it was not a fantasy—it happened. And yet I felt uncertain, as if Vanessa had half succeeded in making me think it was all imagination.

Robert put his head around the door.

"You have had a visitor. That will have cheered you."

"Yes."

He came nearer to the bed, and I reached out to clutch his arm. I said quickly, fervently, "Robert, you believe that I saw a—a man in a black cloak. He—he waved his arms like wings."

"I think you saw something, yes. Something that startled Betsy, who is so gentle and quiet."

I heard myself sigh.

"If only we could find a trace of something. But I am told you have searched all around the thicket."

"Yes. Of course I could not help, but I was up there with Jenkins and with Barlow, the coachman, and they looked everywhere within the vicinity. But what could they find? The grass and undergrowth had been trampled down, that was all."

"We must try to forget about it," I said mournfully.

"That would be wise." He bent to brush a kiss on my forehead. "Rest now. You sound a little tired."

For a month I remained in my room, sad and remote from the outside world, devoid of feeling save for the heaviness of heartache and loss. It was the worst time of my life, worse than after Arthur died, or when Robert and I were captured by the pirates and we had feared for our very lives. The short days of November went by, and then one morning after Grace had helped me dress, I crossed to the window to look down at the garden. A few late roses still bloomed, frosted and brown, the bushes almost leafless and no other color left elsewhere. As I stared listlessly at the view I heard voices and leaning forward saw Robert walking along the center path between the rose beds. He was not alone. On one side of him was Imogen and on the other walked Edward. Imogen held his hand in her own and kept looking up at her father, laughing and chattering in her usual lively fashion. They came to the end of the path and Robert halted, glancing uncertainly this way and that. Imogen said something, tugging gently at his hand as if to guide him, and as they turned to the right, which led toward the stables and outbuildings, Edward reached for his other hand and between them they led Robert slowly out of sight.

The scene moved me in a way I could not describe. For the first time I seemed to emerge from the frozen introspection of my own grief to feel sympathy for someone else. I was touched by Imogen's care for her father. She was not two years old and yet I saw something loving and oddly protective in her smile and gesture. Edward, too. And something else registered with me for the first time since my illness. I had forgotten the increasing handicap of Robert's blindness. I had forgotten that by now he should have undergone the operation that might restore his eyesight in the good eye. How could I have been so selfish and self-absorbed? I felt ashamed that I had had so little thought for Robert or for anyone else, and I resolved from now on I would make more effort to consider other people.

When Robert returned at midday I was lying on the sofa beside the drawing-room fire. Ernest, the tall young footman, had carried me downstairs and Grace had made me comfortable with rugs and cushions. The effort of it all left me weak and trembling, but by the time Robert put in an appearance I was restored and able to give him a smiling welcome.

He was extremely pleased to see me downstairs and the children rushed to hug and kiss me, Imogen's embrace being especially warm and affectionate.

"Oh, Mama, Mama," she said over and over again, and she burrowed into the narrow space between my knees and the edge of the sofa.

Robert pulled up a chair beside me and Edward leaned against the arm.

"I did not expect this happy surprise," Robert said. He shook his head. "We have all missed you. Will you stay down for luncheon with us today?"

"Yes. Ernest can bring the sofa table over and I can have a tray of something." I smiled at him. "I intend to come downstairs every day from now on."

"Well, hasten slowly, as the saying is. But it does my heart good to see you so much recovered."

I reached for his hand.

"I have been selfish, thinking of no one but myself. I had forgotten that you should have gone for the eye operation long before now. You must have it done soon, Robert, or the eye may be damaged permanently."

"I could not have left you, Megan, so naturally matters were postponed. A month or two cannot make that much difference. I hope to have the operation performed sometime after Christmas."

"Yes, it must be arranged as soon as possible."

Two days later, as I sat in a path of sunlight by the morning-room window, busy at my embroidery, Robert came in at the casement door. He looked serious and preoccupied, and without preamble he came over to my chair and said, "Have you seen anything like this before?"

I stared down at the piece of cloth in his hand, torn and black and dusty. Slowly I took it from him, and as I did so, I saw that there was a strip of ragged crimson silk attached to it, a lining to the black cloth.

"It is the cloak!" I cried excitedly. "It is a piece from the cloak the—the man wore. I saw the flash of crimson when he—he waved his arms. Where did you find it, Robert? You said there was nothing there when you searched."

"I sent the gardener's boy—Billy Prior—into the midst of the thicket. He is small and his clothes ragged and patched at the best of times. I promised him a new jacket and breeches if the clothes he was wearing were much torn. So he wriggled his way into the thicket with zest and was successful in finding this piece of cloth entangled on a bramble branch." His face hardened. "This cloak belonged to Lucien. He wore it every year at Halloween to amuse the children. It was a poor joke he played on you, Megan."

He crumpled the cloth in his hand and turned and walked out of the room.

I was astounded at this piece of news. What could it mean? Why would Lucien try to harm me? My mind went back to that afternoon near the Pearl Pagoda when he had embraced me. I knew he did not love me, even if he had come to me out of loneliness. Would he then have tried to revenge himself upon me for rejecting him? If indeed, as I well believed, he was in love with Vanessa, why would he attempt to hurt, possibly even kill me, thus removing the last obstacle to a marriage between Vanessa and Robert.

I shook my head, trying to clear my mind and focus my thoughts. None of it made any sense.

It was a few days later that, after dinner, Robert rang for James and asked him to tell Lady Vanessa that he would like her to see us in the drawing room. I was surprised but made no comment and in a short while Vanessa was shown into the room.

"Good evening, Megan. Good evening, Robert."

Robert inclined his head stiffly.

"Good evening, Vanessa. Please sit down."

She did so with a rustle of silk skirts. She gazed ex-

pectantly at Robert, but he turned away and paced the length
of the room before returning to stand in front of her.

"This is not easy to say, Vanessa. I scarcely know where
to begin, for the fact is—" He paused, and then after a long
silence, he said firmly, "Two years ago, Vanessa, I returned to
Hawkestone to find you were here waiting to greet me. It
was a great surprise to you to learn that I was married."

"Yes," Vanessa answered almost incoherently, "yes, it was
a shock."

"I did not know what to do for the best. I felt I could not
ask you to leave Hawkestone and in the end I decided to invite
you to make your home with us."

"It was very good of you, Robert. Edward and I will
always be grateful."

He turned a frowning glance on her.

"You have shown your gratitude in a strange fashion.
Playing a malicious joke on Megan so that she all but lost her
life."

"Surely that is an exaggeration."

Robert shook his head.

"No. I have spoken to Lucien and learned the truth, that
there was a deliberate attempt to frighten Megan's little mare."

I sat in stunned silence. They had plotted it between
them. But why?

And then the words Lucien had uttered that afternoon at
the Pearl Pagoda returned to me. He had said Vanessa was a
witch and he would do anything in the world for her. Suddenly Lucien's strange actions of the past all became clear. Yes,
indeed, Lucien loved Vanessa, loved her enough to sacrifice his
own happiness—and that of anyone else—in order to help her
gain her objective.

Robert bit his lip, as if considering his next words.

"I do not know what I expected of you and Megan living
under the same roof. Perhaps some sort of sisterly cooperation,
a friendship of sorts, but I see now you had nothing to give
Megan. You resented her presence here as my wife. You did all
you could to make things difficult for her." He paused. "In

view of these facts, Vanessa, I must ask you to leave Hawkestone and make a home elsewhere."

She sprang up in one swift movement.

"Robert, how can you say such things about me? They
are not true. Megan has run worrying to you with this tale and
that and prejudiced you against me."

"No, Vanessa. I have thought and observed for myself.
This house has been full of disharmony instead of affection
and friendship and trust. I am sorry, very sorry, but there is no
alternative. I say again, I must ask you to leave Hawkestone
within the next few weeks."

Vanessa all but wrung her hands.

"But where shall I go at such short notice?"

"You can stay with your stepmother until you find a suitable establishment. There will be no financial worries. I will
make a settlement on you."

Vanessa expressed no gratitude, but turned a look of almost venomous hatred on me.

"This is your doing. Pretending always to be so quiet and
good, but you are not as meek and mild as you look."

"That's enough, Vanessa," Robert interrupted harshly.

"You have humiliated me, Robert."

"I have not intended to. I am the one at fault. I should
never have invited you to stay in the first place. It was not a
feasible plan."

"Then there is no more to be said."

She turned, slim and erect, very lovely in the dress of
soft grosgrain taffeta despite the unaccustomed pallor, the lines
of tension in her face.

Robert crossed to the bell rope.

"I will ring for James to escort you back to your apartment."

"Thank you."

In a few minutes she was gone. I put my hand out and
caught hold of Robert's.

"Oh, Robert, you are trembling."

He put his arm about me.

"Come, the worst is over. These things have to be said.

We could not leave malice, deceit and envy to fester in our lives. Now we can live as we would wish to live, Megan."

"Yes." I was aware only of relief.

A few days later I heard the sound of a carriage and to my surprise recognized Madame Ormonde's rather shabby conveyance. Jenkins ushered her into the morning room and I could see immediately that she was distressed.

"Do sit down by the fire. How are you, Madame Ormonde?"

"I am very upset this morning. Have you heard the news? No, I can tell that you have not. Lucien and Vanessa have gone to France. They went on the packet from Weymouth yesterday evening."

"To France?" I echoed. "That is rather surprising news."

"It is upsetting news, for I do not know why they have gone there. Or rather I suspect that Lucien has gone with the idea of reclaiming some part of the estate that was confiscated during the troubles. Things are settling down a little in France, but I think he is optimistic, for at best the property was little more than a farm in Normandy and a few rented cottages. Oh, it has upset me, to go so suddenly and unexpectedly.

Vanessa has sent a message to you," Madame related, as if as an afterthought. "She asks if you will keep Edward at Hawkestone until she can send for him to be with them."

At that moment Robert came in and the whole story had to be repeated.

At last, comforted and sustained by some warming cherry brandy, Madame Ormonde took her leave and Robert escorted her to her carriage.

"It is a surprising action," Robert said when he returned to the morning room, "but I can understand Lucien wanting to get away from his mother, although that sounds unkind. But he could not live at Springhill with her and do nothing, and he has little means of his own. Perhaps there will be a favorable outcome from his application in France."

Edward came into the morning room just before luncheon. He was accompanied by Mr. Forbes, his tutor, who had been engaged during my confinement. Edward was very upset to hear that his mother had gone to France, but we cheered him with the prospect of the adventure of traveling to France to join her later.

We settled down to a quiet household without Vanessa and Lucien. A curious sense of peace seemed to pervade the house. The winter sunlight seemed more serene, the bare trees tranquil in their austerity. It was as if a cloud had been lifted from Hawkestone.

Christmas was a quiet time. Mr. Forbes was an orphan and happy to spend his vacation with us. We had also invited Uncle Stephen and Aunt Louise from Bath with their three children, so Edward and Imogen were going to have quite a cheerful party. Madame Ormonde came to stay for a few days over the holiday. She had received several letters from Vanessa from which she quoted.

" 'Things seem to be working out very favorably, for Lucien has made contact with a relative of his, Etienne, Count de Briseville. He is an extremely rich man, for although much of his wealth had been confiscated by the authorities, he was fortunate enough later on to receive considerable recompense, so now we have gone to live in his house outside Paris.' "

"I am glad," I said, "that things are turning out fortunately. You see, dear Madame Ormonde, it has all been for the best."

She shook her head doubtfully.

"Well, we must hope so. Etienne, who is elderly, was always a kind and generous man. I am sure he will do what he can for Lucien."

When Christmas was over, arrangements were made for Robert to have the operation on his eye. Robert would not permit me to go and stay in London while the operation was being carried out.

"It would be a worry for me to think of you alone in London, and you are not strong enough yet to take a lot of strain and worry."

And so it was arranged that Sylvia, together with Harriet

Rose and Mrs. Meade, should come and stay at Hawkestone with me while Robert was in London.

"You will not have a chance to be depressed," Robert remarked.

"I would rather be with you," I said, "but certainly to have Sylvia here will be a great consolation."

Our guests arrived a few days before Robert was due in London. Pearce, his valet, was to attend him, and although I knew Robert was going to be in the best of hands, the moment of his departure was a tearful one.

Sylvia and Mrs. Meade did their best to cheer me up, and Harriet Rose received a great deal of our attention. She was a dainty, pretty baby, with a fluff of golden hair and roseleaf skin. Her eyes were not as dark as Sylvia's and I had a feeling they would eventually be gray, like her father's.

"She is *beautiful*," I told Sylvia, as I held Harriet in my arms. "Charles will simply adore her."

Sylvia smiled.

"He is wildly impatient to see her. He is missing us a great deal, but I expect to return to Macao in February."

"I am glad. You must not be too long apart."

She smiled wryly.

"No, especially as I should like a brother or sister for Harriet. Don't look so startled, Megan. It is not that I yearn for Charles; it is that I wish for children and one cannot have those without a husband."

Her expression changed. She leaned forward to kiss me.

"Oh, Megan, I know how you, too, must so long for a child. More so, perhaps, than even I, having lost one so recently. My heart grieves for you. But let us not talk of sad things. Here is Imogen just longing to hold Harriet, but that would be rather dangerous. Come, Imogen, and sit by me and hold Harriet's rattle."

The days seemed to pass slowly and anxiously. Every day a note from Pearce arrived reporting progress. "The master had a good night." "Last night we were a little restless." "Dr. Simpson is very pleased with the master's progress." Though they were stiff, stilted letters, written for Robert, I carried them around like so many love letters and read them over and over again.

Edward asked wistfully when his mother would arrange for him to go to France to be with her.

"I am sure it will be soon, Edward dear," I said, ruffling his silky fair hair.

"It is not that I wish to leave here, Aunt Megan, but of course I want to be with Mama."

"Of course you do, and do not forget you will be coming to spend long holidays with us at Hawkestone. Oh, dear, Imogen will miss you so much."

One day Sylvia suggested that we walk to the Pearl Pagoda to pass the time. It was a cold winter day, but the walk to the dell was very pleasant, and as we approached it, I saw above the bare trees the curving tiers of the pagoda, its delicate latticework outlined against the blue sky.

"I remember when you first wrote and told me that you were going to build the Pearl Pagoda and make a little world of your own in the dell."

"Chao Tsan brought me many rare and beautiful plants from China when he visited us. Wasn't it kind of him?"

We turned to walk home, for the wind had grown a little raw. We climbed the steps from the dell and walked through the woods to the park.

Sylvia said, "There's a carriage. It looks like Robert's curricle."

I turned to look. I could not believe my eyes. Robert, with the assistance of Pearce, was alighting from the curricle. He came directly and quickly toward me, which astonished me, for he had always had a hesitancy in his step. It was as he drew near that I saw what had happened. His eye gazed at me, a deep, dark blue. I saw Robert as he had been before. The tears came coursing down my cheeks.

"You can see."

"The operation has been a complete success."

"Oh, thank God. How do you feel?"

He had both my hands in his.

"I feel splendid. I feel as though I am myself again. Dr.

Simpson says my eye will be good as new. It healed quicker than we had expected and I couldn't wait to get back to you and see the look of surprise on your face."

Sylvia came forward.

"This is wonderful news, Robert. We are so happy for you."

"Thank you, Sylvia. You have been a good friend to us both at all times. We shall not forget."

Sylvia smiled and blushed.

"Oh, Robert."

We turned to go into the house. Robert looked tired and I took his arm as we walked up the steps.

"Come along and sit by the drawing-room fire and I will order tea."

He stretched out his long legs and sighed with happiness.

"Oh, it's wonderful to be home, and with every day that goes by I shall feel stronger."

James had no sooner brought the tray of tea, buttered toast and sandwiches than Mrs. Rowley came into the room.

"Excuse me, sir, I do not wish to interrupt you, but this letter came only a few moments ago."

"Thank you, Mrs. Rowley. "I cannot believe I can read again," Robert said as he slit open the envelope. He was silent for a few moments, then he passed the letter over to me, saying, "Well, this is rather startling news indeed."

I glanced through the letter. It was from Vanessa and was brief. It said:

"I am now married to the Count de Briseville and I shall be making my home at Compiègne. Would you be kind enough to break the news to Edward and tell him that he will soon be here in France with us. Etienne is a most kind and generous man and he looks forward to meeting Edward."

There were a few more scrawled words.

I handed the letter back to Robert.

"We did not expect this. I suppose it is a good thing."

"Undoubtedly," Robert said. "She is settled for life and will have a big establishment to run."

"And Lucien?" I asked.

"He is to make his home with them. Did you not read that?"

"Poor Madame Ormonde. This is another upset for her."

"I do not suppose she will be very bothered."

The door opened and Edward came in with a little rush and then paused. Imogen brushed past him and rushed to her father's knee, gazing up into his face with long and joyous pleasure.

"Oh, Papa, Papa, Papa, you can see, you can see me now."

Robert gave her a hug and a kiss.

"Yes, I can see you as you are now, Imogen, instead of through a blur, and I see the dearest little girl with beautiful brown eyes looking at me."

Imogen was not pretty. Her eyes were too big in her small face and her mouth too wide, but she had the happiest of expressions.

"Edward, come and sit down and have tea with us," I said. "I think your uncle has news for you."

Edward looked inquiringly at Robert, who held a hand out to him to draw him nearer to his chair.

"Edward, we have had a letter from your mother. I expect this will surprise you as much as it has done us, but she has married again."

Edward stared at Robert in surprise. He was seven now. Even at five he had been mature, and now he regarded Robert with a strangely solemn look.

"Married? Whom has she married?"

"She has married a cousin of Lucien's, Count de Briseville. I believe he is a good, kind man, though elderly. Your mother hopes to send for you at the earliest opportunity to come live with them in France."

Edward glanced from Robert to me and back to Robert.

"I shall be leaving here," he said uncertainly.

"Well, yes, your home is with your mother."

Edward said no more, but looked very thoughtful as we partook our tea. I could see that he was happy but uncertain, and I felt sorry for him.

The next evening at dinner Robert informed me he had written to Vanessa.

"I went over to Springhill and broke the news to Madame Ormonde. She is not too pleased about the affair. I think she feels that Vanessa will usurp Lucien in Etienne's interest."

The weeks passed slowly. Robert regained his strength after the operation and soon he was riding about the estate with a confidence and command that I had not seen for a long time and I thanked God for the miracle that had been performed.

Edward came to me more than once to inquire wistfully if I thought his mother would be sending for him soon. I would pat his shoulder and say as reassuringly as I could that I was sure she would send for him as soon as possible, but no doubt there were things to settle and arrange in her new home first. Vanessa had written one or two scrawled notes to him, full of exclamation marks and endearments, but with little news.

Sylvia was returning to Macao within a week or two and Robert and I were invited to spend a few days with her and Mrs. Meade at the latter's home in London so that we should see something of one another before she sailed.

"You look so much better, Megan," Sylvia said. "That drawn, peaky look has gone. Now you must rest and grow robust and perhaps soon you will have another baby to look forward to."

"Oh, I hope so indeed."

I was sad to say goodbye to Sylvia, but I knew her place was with Charles and she seemed happy to be going back to Macao.

Robert and I enjoyed the days in London very much. Robert was able to get about and see everything and insisted on buying me some new dresses that he could choose himself, and altogether there seemed much to see and do before we returned to the quiet routine of Hawkestone.

The night we drove back was wild and wintry. Flurries of snow drifted past the carriage windows and the coachman slowed the horses to a walking pace more than once.

We were thankful to find a warm welcome and bright fires in every room and a joyous reception from the children, who danced about us and could not stop chattering.

We had scarcely eaten dinner when Humphreys came into the room and, approaching Robert, said, "This message has just come for you, m'lord. It is urgent I understand."

Robert somewhat impatiently ripped open the envelope and then gave an involuntary gasp as he read the contents.

"What is it?" I asked anxiously.

He handed the letter over to me.

"I know no more than you will when you have read it. It is Madame Ormonde. She wishes, demands rather, that I should come over immediately to Springhill for she has had bad news from France."

"I will come with you," I said.

"There is no need. I would rather you stayed at home, Megan."

I shook my head firmly

"No, Robert, we will go together. If Madame Ormonde is upset I can perhaps be of more comfort to her than you."

Once again the carriage was brought out with fresh horses in the traces and, wrapping ourselves up as warmly as we could with fur cloaks and a fur rug, we set off through the dark night.

The drive up to Springhill was little more than a rough track. The carriage rocked and swayed slowly up the winding length.

There was little light from the house to welcome us, but at our approach one of Madame Ormonde's ancient servants held open the door. We were taken immediately into the drawing room. It was some time since I had been to Springhill, and it seemed strangely neglected and shabby. The rugs worn and thin, the lights few and not bright. Madame Ormonde crouched like a wizened monkey on the settee by the low fire.

"Oh, thank God, you have come," she croaked, without getting up. "I could not write the news."

"When news is this?" Robert demanded somewhat impatiently.

Madame Ormonde stared up at him, her dark eyes glittering in her wrinkled face.

"Vanessa is dead," she said.

Robert stared incredulously.

"*Dead!* What are you saying?"

"The letter came from Lucien this evening. It seems there was an accident. Some brigands or highwaymen or such like who had been roaming the country, following various people whom they thought might carry money with them, rode after the Count de Briseville's carriage. The coachman whipped up the horses, but at a turning on a hill the coach came to grief and Vanessa was thrown out and was killed immediately, her head having hit a rock."

"Oh, God," Robert said, "what a thing to have happen."

I was shocked to the core of my being. Vanessa dead. That beautiful, vibrant creature. Surely she should have been immortal. I could not weep for her for I had never loved her, but she had been so challenging and alive that her death in some way diminished me. Yet if I, who had never had any real feeling for Vanessa, felt like this, what of Robert, who had once loved her so dearly. He must be heartbroken. I took a step toward him.

"Robert, I am so sorry. Poor Vanessa."

He frowned down at me.

"I must leave for France immediately to attend the funeral. Edward will come with me."

"*Edward.* Oh, poor, darling little boy. How will we break the news to him?"

"I will tell him," Robert said grimly. He looked toward Madame Ormonde. "Come, Madame, we will take you back to Hawkestone with us. You must not stay here alone.

She stared at him in bewilderment.

"Will Lucien come?"

"It is doubtful. Megan, ring for Madame Ormonde's maid and see that a case is packed for her."

Robert left early the next morning, Edward at his side, pale-faced in his black suit, his eyes puffy from weeping. When they had gone the house seemed very quiet. Madame Ormonde stayed in bed for several days, as the shock of Vanessa's death seemed to have made her quite ill, but I suspected it was not Vanessa she grieved for but was worried about Lucien and what he would do.

A few days later Robert returned with Edward, the latter strangely quiet and composed. Imogen ran to hug him.

"Oh, Edward. Come see baby rabbit."

With Edward thus distracted and Imogen's hand firmly clasped in his, they set off along the garden path.

Robert was quieter than usual. He seemed to have withdrawn into himself. One morning I was going to the stables with sugar for Betsy when I saw Robert standing and staring up at the wall above the mounting block. I crossed over to him and saw the initials "V.O." engraved on the stonework. I could make no comment and turned and walked toward Betsy's stall. Robert came after me.

"What is it, Megan?"

I said unsteadily, "You are grieving for Vanessa."

He shook his head and said a little sadly, "No, I am reproaching myself. If I had not sent her away, she would be alive now."

"Don't think like that, Robert. *Please* don't think like that. I know how much you loved her."

He gave a sharp exclamation, a dismissing gesture of the hand.

"What I felt once for Vanessa is water beneath the bridge. Gone like my youth."

He leaned forward and gathered me closely in his arms and, laying his cheek against my own, said in a controlled but deeply emotional voice, "You mean everything in the world to me, Megan. When they brought you back on the improvised stretcher after Betsy had thrown you and I saw you lying there so still and white and cold, something broke within me. I remember thinking, 'If Megan is dead my life is over.' I held you in my arms. I tried to bring you back to life. I wanted to tear the heart out of my own body and place it in your still breast. I wanted to give my blood to warm you. But there was nothing I could do. Dr. Jessop sent me away. I cannot describe the awful sense of fear and aloneness that came over me as I sat through the night waiting, listening."

I said tremblingly, "Oh, Robert, I didn't know. I didn't realize you cared so much."

"Of course, because I never told you how much I loved you. I took everything for granted—your warmth and sweetness, the sound of your laughter, which always lifted my heart, your voice lilting in some Welsh song." He shook his head, frowning. "How could I have been so stupid, so self-centered? My only excuse is that we came together under strange circumstances. It was inevitable, lonely and isolated as we were at The Place of Tall Trees, that we should turn to each other as we did. You were no longer a girl, but a woman and ready for marriage; and I, who had vowed to remain a bachelor for the rest of my life, needed a wife. I did not think you were in love with me, although I knew there was a strong physical attraction between us. That was important, but I still felt that it would be a marriage of mutual convenience. Then we came back to Hawkestone to find Vanessa waiting for us. We did not get a chance to come together as we might have done, but I love you, my darling, and I shall love you to the day I die."

I could not believe I was hearing all the words I had longed to hear from Robert, and all I could do was lean into his embrace and return his fervent kiss. Luckily the stable yard was deserted, for it was the men's dinnertime, but I did not think Robert, in his present mood, would have cared if half the staff had been watching.

We were happy, and with every year that passed, our happiness, like our deepening love, grew and encompassed the lives of our friends and family.

I eventually had two sons, which delighted Robert, and then a second daughter.

Edward and George Howard remained friends all their lives, and George often visited us. Mrs. Howard died while still quite young, and Dr. Howard remained in China, where he died in his mid-eighties, revered and esteemed by his many Chinese colleagues.

Dorothea, delicate and appealing, married a wealthy ship-owner from Bristol and had two children, and she too remained part of our lives.

Imogen and Edward remained the dearest of friends. I had half hoped they would marry each other, but Edward chose one of Sylvia's three beautiful daughters, and after some time, for she was in no hurry, Imogen fell in love with a wealthy landowner, who in turn doted on her. Their home was near Devizes, so they were never far from us and mutual visits were frequent.

Much later on we visited Macao and stayed with Sylvia and Charles and their family. It was good to see old friends again, including Miss Crow and her brother and Chao Tsan. Dr. Howard was not there, for he was working at an inland mission. This was after the Trade of Peace with China had been signed in 1860. Everything seemed the same and yet there were changes. The fast, beautiful clipper ships were no longer being built for the tea trade, for steam had taken over. Robert was regretful.

"We shall never see it as it was," he said as we stood looking out over the shining expanse of the great Pearl River with its ceaseless flow of traffic. "We had the best of it, Megan."

"We think so. Perhaps others think the new ways are best."

"Perhaps, but to me those were wonderful days."

I gazed inland toward the brown hills and I thought of the mighty land that ran between them. The Middle Kingdom proud and secret. I thought of the Pearl Pagoda delicate and beautiful, hidden among its trees, and for a moment I longed to see it again. I heard myself sigh.

"Terrible and wonderful," I answered. I slid my arm through Robert's and turned to smile at him. "But mostly—wonderful."